"A chilling ghost tale... a suspenseful trip into a nightmare house that is all too terrifyingly real. With an eeriness like quicksand, it grabs you, holds you, sucks you in. *The Chanting* brings you face-to-face with horror at its subtle best."

—Lisa Cantrell
Bram Stoker Award-winner
and author of *Torments*

"Deftly interweaving a believable setting with occult tension, a tender romance, and a mother's greatest nightmare, Beverly T. Haaf's *The Chanting* triumphs as a humane horror novel in which evil unexpectedly pays the price of love."

—Carole Nelson Douglas
author of *Probe* and *Counterprobe*

"A chilling tale of a woman and child haunted by a great evil... and love lost and love found. Beverly Haaf tells a story of horror, romance, and suspense in the spine-tingling tradition of Mary Higgins Clark."

—Linda Cajio
author of *Nights in White Satin*

"A spooky old house, a crazy old woman, ghostly children at twilight and a chill on every page. A change-of-pace horror tale that will hold you in thrall. Beverly T. Haaf—a scary new voice in the haunted house of horror.... Atmospheric, chilling and thought-provoking, *The Chanting* is a whole new experience in modern horror."

—Joseph A. Citro
author of *The Unseen*

ATTENTION: SCHOOLS AND CORPORATIONS

POPULAR LIBRARY books are available at quantity discounts with bulk purchase for educational, business, or sales promotional use. For information, please write to SPECIAL SALES DEPARTMENT, POPULAR LIBRARY, 666 FIFTH AVENUE, NEW YORK, N.Y. 10103

**ARE THERE POPULAR LIBRARY BOOKS
YOU WANT BUT CANNOT FIND IN YOUR LOCAL STORES?**

You can get any POPULAR LIBRARY title in print. Simply send title and retail price, plus 50¢ per order and 50¢ per copy to cover mailing and handling costs for each book desired. New York State and California residents add applicable sales tax. Enclose check or money order only, no cash please, to POPULAR LIBRARY, P.O. BOX 690, NEW YORK, N.Y. 10019

The Chanting

BEVERLY T. HAAF

POPULAR LIBRARY

An Imprint of Warner Books, Inc.

A Time Warner Company

POPULAR LIBRARY EDITION

Copyright © 1991 by Beverly T. Haaf
All rights reserved.

Popular Library® and the fanciful P design are registered trademarks
of Warner Books, Inc.

Cover design by Anthony Russo
Cover illustration by Eric Anderson

Popular Library books are published by
Warner Books, Inc.
666 Fifth Avenue
New York, N.Y. 10103

A Time Warner Company

Printed in the United States of America

First Printing: January, 1991

10 9 8 7 6 5 4 3 2 1

Memories of summer evenings:
The voices of two mothers, each calling
three children in safely for the night.

The echoes linger yet....

1

The sounds of the baby crying pulled Janet from a deep, dreamless sleep. The crying, thin and fretful, sharpened, weaving its way in and out of her dawning consciousness, pricking, needling, drawing the blood of awareness. Lonely... it sounded almost as if little Becky felt lonely. Struggling to sit up, Janet untangled herself from the bed covers, mindful of not jostling her husband Clay, who was annoyed if she disturbed his rest.

Slipping her slim legs over the edge of the bed, she reached for her robe. Her fingers closed upon soft, plush fabric. How strange, she thought. It felt like her fleece wrap instead of the thin cotton she wore in this southern heat. Puzzled, she withdrew her hand, then caught her breath as the room suddenly seemed to shift around her. She gripped the edge of the mattress and the sense of motion ceased. Becky wailed on. It was an odd cry, the cadence strangely rhythmic, the child's voice sounding huskier than usual. Janet got to her feet. Not bothering to hunt for her slippers although the floor seemed oddly cold, she hurried toward the door.

There was no door.

Bewildered, she strained to pierce the dimness.

Enough moonlight filtered into the room so that she felt

she should be able to see, yet nothing looked familiar. She realized she had somehow gotten turned around so that she faced a flat, featureless wall. Off to the side, instead of one window, there appeared to be two. She tried to blink away her double vision. Her eyes found the black shape of the door opening, the door left wide as always so that Becky's slightest sound would be audible. Relieved, she hurried toward it.

Her head and toes struck painfully against something solid and unyielding. She stumbled back, gasping, almost losing her balance. Clearing her head, she realized the door was shut. Her heart started to thump, and she stared at the dark rectangle, as tall and narrow as an upended coffin. It bore no resemblance to the ivory-colored panel she had painted herself. The surface looked more like varnished wood, the dark color having deceived her into thinking it yawned open to the corridor outside.

For a moment, alarmed confusion held her motionless, then she hurriedly pushed her way into the corridor. Blackness, thick and womblike, enveloped her like a cloak. Confusion deepening, she wasn't sure which way to turn. The teddy-bear night lamp in Becky's room that should have showed the way must have burned out. But she knew the way, she told herself, trying to fight off unreasoning panic. She knew the way well. Yet as she moved along, the corridor seemed alien: the baby's cries echoed as if several children were crying at once. Had her hearing been affected when she bumped into the door? Now that she was almost at the nursery, Becky's cries sounded more distant than when she had first awakened. Janet reached urgently toward the doorway of the child's room.

Becky's room was gone!

Frantic, Janet ran her hands over hard, cold plaster. Panic scattered her thoughts. The door was walled up, sealed over, trapping Becky inside! Her seeking hands found a ridge that should not be there. Wood, waist high, flattened like a chair rail. Pulse pounding, she suddenly realized she was lost. Lost—unable to find her way around in her own house. Her heartbeats seemed to clog her throat. How had she gotten so mixed up? What was happening to her? Her breath came in stricken gasps as she searched for the light switch. The switch wasn't there.

She suddenly felt too terrified to take another step. She had no idea where the stairs lay. One step in the wrong direction and she might tumble down the entire long flight. Sweat trickled coldly along her ribs. She longed to call for Clay, but even in her terror, she held her tongue. He would be furious if she awakened him for such a foolish reason— getting lost in their own house.

And then, ever so faintly on the dark air there came a suggestion of smoke: a mere wisp of an odor, more secret than the smile of a poisoner. It was gone in an instant, yet its hint was enough to jolt her into action.

"Becky!" she screamed, blindly beginning to run, thinking of nothing except reaching her child. "Becky!"

Light exploded with eye-searing brightness.

"Janet?" a voice called. "Is that you?"

Janet came to an abrupt, disbelieving stop as she recognized the voice of her sister. What was Fran doing in Alabama?

"Janet?" Fran called anxiously. "Are you all right?"

Stunned, Janet watched as her sister hurried forward, her thickly quilted robe flapping like dark birds about her sturdy, athletic legs.

"I heard someone bumping around," Fran said. "Was it you, Jan? What happened?"

As if in a fog, Janet lifted a hand to touch her bruised forehead. "I walked into the door," she said slowly, finding it difficult to speak. "Somehow, I—I was all turned around." She put her hands over her ears. "Things sounded . . . strange, all distorted." She remembered thinking she smelled smoke, only there was no smoke. "I got up because the baby. . ."

Her voice trailed off, leaving nothing except an awkward, painful silence.

"The baby," she said, knowing as she repeated the word that something was wrong, terribly wrong.

"Oh, honey." Fran's face constricted. "Honey, you've been dreaming."

"But I heard..." Dazed, Janet looked around. She saw the painted plaster and the neat stencils of seashells above the wainscotting, blue shells against white; press a shell to your ear and hear the lonely cry of the lost child, lost forever. Her hazel eyes widened as she recognized the walls of the restored pre-Revolutionary house in Princeton, New Jersey, where Fran lived with her husband Warren.

Suddenly everything became achingly clear. Janet had come to stay with Fran the previous day, and it was the middle of October, not summertime. Clay had not been sleeping beside her. She was staying alone in Fran's guest room because she and Clay were getting a divorce. And she couldn't have gotten up in response to Becky's cry because Becky had been dead for five months. More months than the child had lived. That small white casket, closed forever, that sweet face, sealed for all eternity in the smothering darkness. It all came back to her, the awful truth sinking in, crushing her like a leaden weight.

"It wasn't Becky I heard," she said in a dull monotone, as if reciting a lesson she must learn. "It was somebody else's baby."

"You were dreaming," Fran repeated softly. "Nobody living nearby has a baby. No one anywhere on this block."

Ignoring her sister's words, Janet ran a shaking hand through her dark, feathery curls. "It wasn't Becky I heard crying, because she didn't cry that night. If she had, I could have helped her. I was always alert to her slightest sound."

"I know, honey. I know." Fran slipped an arm about the smaller woman. "Let's go down to the kitchen. It's your first night here and you're getting adjusted. No wonder you felt all turned around when you awoke. I'll make hot cocoa and we can talk."

Shaking her head, Janet moved free of Fran's touch. She drew a breath. "I'm all right." Although still disoriented, she pulled herself together enough to manage her normal tone. "Really, I am all right. I'll stop by the bathroom and then go back to bed."

She was aware of Fran's worried eyes following as she stepped into the bathroom. "Take a couple of aspirins," came the call. Janet hesitated, then drew a paper cup from the dispenser, ran water, and swallowed two aspirins. As she stepped out, she saw Fran watching, still in her role of big sister.

"I'm fine now, honest," Janet insisted, forcing a smile. She hoped the commotion hadn't awakened her brother-in-law. But even if it had, she supposed Warren would never react with the kind of anger Clay would have shown. Poor Clay, always protecting himself from injustices, most of them imagined. Despite all that had happened, she could only pity him.

Back in the guest room, Janet looked at the moonlit rectangles of the dormer windows and wondered how she could have deluded herself into thinking she was still in the Alabama house. Shivering from cold, yet reluctant to return to bed, she folded her arms across her small breasts, remembering their fullness when they had been swollen with milk. Drawn to the window seat, she peered out.

The three-quarter moon was screened by a gauze of clouds that transformed the sky into a pale, inverted bowl of colorless light. The moonlit scene was black, white, and gray. As cold and impersonal as a stopped frame from an old, forgotten film. The geometric angles of houses were partly obscured by dark brooding shapes that by daylight were magnificent trees: grand oaks, tall drooping hemlocks, pines, and maples.

Her gaze moved to the Queen Anne–style house which had property that touched Fran's back yard at one corner. From the rear, the structure was partly hidden by the thickly tangled branches of a copper beech, but Janet remembered how it looked from the street. Her thoughts drifted back to the previous spring, when she and Clay had visited Fran before leaving for the South.

Taking a walk around the block, they had seen a FOR SALE

sign in front of the Queen Anne. Painted yellow, it had tall, pointed gables, decorative shingles, and a turret. A welcoming atmosphere had seemed to beckon to them. Standing with Becky cuddled in her arms, Janet had suddenly thought how wonderful it would be if she and Clay could change their minds about moving so far away, and instead, live right there in Princeton. She remembered how—

Her thoughts broke off abruptly as she once again heard an infant's cry. The sound was thin and incredibly pure, as though it were floating in a nearby opened window. She strained her eyes as if expecting the sound to become visible, glistening like a silver thread in the moonlight, inviting her to trace it back to its source. As mysteriously as it had begun, the cry ceased. It was as if it had never been.

A shudder vibrated through Janet's slender frame. Frances said none of the neighbors had a baby. Even if she were mistaken, would anyone keep windows open on such a cold night? Her own were certainly closed. She touched the icy slickness of a pane with trembling fingers; behind it was a storm window.

How could the sound have reached her?

2

The sparkling sunshine that teased Janet's eyes open in the morning failed to dispel the shadows of her restless sleep. *Becky.* She remembered how she had awakened in the night, thinking that Becky was still alive and crying for her. Troubled, she stared around the sunny bedroom, mentally retracing her mistaken steps of the night before. She saw where she had gone wrong: the direction which would have led to the hallway in the Alabama house led only to a blank wall here.

It occurred to her that she might have been sleepwalking. Even though she had never had a sleepwalking experience in the past, it offered a perfect explanation. Then, frowning, she remembered having heard the crying again, strange and rhythmic, after she returned to her room. She certainly had been wide awake then—hadn't she?

She reached for her clothes. Everything about the episode was disturbing. She no longer wanted to think about it and she hoped her sister wouldn't want to talk about it either.

Downstairs in the kitchen, she found Fran putting bacon into a microwave, which, when not in use, was concealed by a ruffled curtain. Fran, a nostalgia buff, had gone to great lengths in preserving the quaint kitchen. The old refrigerator, with its white porcelainized coils piled on top like a hairdo, and a stork-legged sink, sat in proud display, while the dishwasher and big double-door refrigerator were inconveniently stashed in the pantry. A charming conceit, Janet thought, but perhaps not as false as what she was doing; pretending to live in the present while her heart remained in the past, holding a phantom child pressed to her breast.

"Morning." Fran tapped the controls that started the bacon cooking. Her cheery briskness announced in sisterly shorthand that no reference would be made to the night unless Janet initiated the subject.

Relieved, Janet took a seat at the oak table. "Has Warren already left for classes?"

"About fifteen minutes ago." Having waited to share her breakfast with Janet, Fran broke eggs into buttered custard cups. "Scrambled okay?"

"Perfect."

Warren, who had authored what was considered the definitive book on the subject of medieval musical instruments, taught at the university. Janet remembered that Clay had considered Warren's special area of study ludicrous.

"Medieval instruments?" he had guffawed. At the time,

8 / BEVERLY T. HAAF

he himself had been a computer programmer at a small state college. "What kind of clown would sign up for one of his classes?"

"Court jesters," Janet had responded, smiling to keep it light. Keep it light... keep it light. That had been the watchword for any hope of peaceful coexistence with Clay.

Fran had just finished pouring juice and coffee when the oven timer buzzed. She transferred the bacon and eggs to a platter and took a seat across from Janet. "Dig in," she ordered. "As soon as I saw you at the train station yesterday, I thought to myself: That girl is as thin as a scarecrow! Tomorrow I'll fix your eggs along with good old Philadelphia-style scrapple. Bet you haven't had that in an age." She wagged a finger. "I'll put some meat on your bones."

Janet wrinkled her nose. "Bossy as ever, aren't you? You sound like the witch from the gingerbread cottage, inviting me in like Hansel and Gretel to fatten me up."

At thirty-three, Frances, the older by nine years, was built on a Junoesque scale, with corn-yellow hair, powder-blue eyes, and a wholesome, outgoing smile that brought out her deep-cut dimples. Janet's own appearance was dramatically different, her figure petite, her expression reserved, her hazel eyes, with their thick fringe of dark lashes, tilted exotically. The ancestry of the sisters was English and Norwegian, but their father had joked that Janet's looks proved a Gypsy once swung on a branch of the family tree.

"I'm glad I don't have to dash off this morning," said Fran, who was owner-manager of The Magic Spoon, a tearoom at a small shopping center just outside of Princeton. "There's something we have to discuss." The eyes she fixed on Janet were serious. "It would be too soon to ask this except I have a special reason. Have you given any thought as to what you'll do now that you're on your own?"

Janet couldn't help sighing. Here it was, she thought: Advice Time. Fran had married a widower, and after helping guide his four teenage children into adulthood, she had channeled her considerable energies into making the Spoon a relaxed, yet stylish luncheon refuge for young suburban matrons. But now, with a dependable staff, it was obvious she had regained time for her favorite mission—telling others what to do. Actually, a lot of her ideas were good. It was just that she tended to come on awfully strong.

Guardedly, Janet admitted, "Yes, I've thought about a job. I suppose my best bet will be secretarial work."

Fran grimaced. "Said with the joyous anticipation of jabbing a stick into your eye. What about your journalism? Any ambition to take it up again?"

Janet remembered her once-cherished enthusiasm to transform the world through the power of the press. She had pinned a slogan on her bulletin board that read, "Look out world!" She was the one who should have been looking out. At nineteen she had dropped from college to see Clay through his schooling and remained loyal as he abandoned one job after another in his sour struggle to find a niche where he felt his genius would be recognized and jealous colleagues would no longer conspire against him.

"The reason I brought this up," continued Fran, "is because the community adult school needs a newsletter editor. The person from last year bailed out without notice and they're in a bind. Classes are starting next week, so if there's a chance you're interested, you should apply before they grab someone else. Not that I'm trying to push. Maybe what you need most is a chance to rest, but then again, a distraction might be better." She handed over a brochure. "The job wouldn't pay much, but it's a way to update your work experience and meet new people."

Janet had certainly heard worse suggestions. She saw that the classes were to be held at the high school. "What would they want?" she asked thoughtfully. "The word *editor* can mean different things."

"We can find sample newsletters to show what's been done in the past." Fran poured more coffee for them both. "The mall where the Magic Spoon is located has a great newsletter. The editor, Ida Aaron, is a friend of mine. I'm sure she'd be glad to give you helpful tips. If you want the job, that is. As I said, I don't mean to push."

Such restraint, thought Janet, amused. It didn't take second sight to know Fran was concerned about her rattling around the house all day with nothing to think about except the loss of the baby and the divorce. The episode during the night had no doubt intensified her concern. And, no wonder! To have dreamed so vividly that she heard a baby crying, waking to think she was still back in Alabama, and then trying to act on it . . .

Fran pulled her purse from the counter and took out an appointment book. "Even if you're not interested in the newsletter, I think you'd enjoy meeting Ida. How about if we plan lunch together next Monday?"

"That sounds fine." Janet realized she had already made up her mind to apply for the newsletter position. When Fran and Warren had invited her into their home for an indefinite stay, it had been as a family member. But she had no intention of sponging. She wanted no settlement from Clay even had he been willing, so she had to find some type of employment. As Fran had pointed out, the newsletter would be a way to get her feet wet.

Finished with her breakfast, Janet glanced out the window in time to see a Siamese cat streak by, followed by a dark-haired little girl who looked about eight years old. The child's jacket was open, revealing a lace-trimmed pink taffeta dress. "Is that the way children around here dress for school—so fancy?" Janet asked.

Fran looked. "That's Gina. She doesn't attend school because she's handicapped and has a special tutor. It's probably the housekeeper's day off and the poor child had to get herself ready this morning." Fran's voice reflected disapproval. "She's a foster child of the Stocktons, the couple throwing the get-together we're taking you to tomorrow night."

"That solar energy thing?"

"Yes." Fran hesitated, and then, as if unable to hold back her feelings, she added, "Tommy and Veronica Stockton are wealthy, and given to crazes. The latest one is energy conservation. They've invited a speaker to the party in the hope of firing up the rest of the block on the subject. Gina is a craze from a few years back. She's an orphan, a survivor from an earthquake disaster in Italy. I don't know what strings Tommy pulled to get her." Fran shook her head. "When it's hot tubs, racquetball, and sun power, who cares if you pick up a trend then drop it a month later? But no one should be allowed to do that with a child."

"You mean they don't treat her properly?"

Fran stood and slung her jacket about her shoulders. "As far as material things are concerned, Gina lives like a princess. But Tommy is away a lot on business and Veronica has her social obligations, so the child is usually left in the care of a housekeeper. She has problems relating to other kids, but who gives a damn? Not Tommy or Veronica. She's a fad they've grown tired of."

After Fran left the house, Janet went to the window hoping for another look at Gina, but the child was no longer in sight. Sighing, she sat down again and leafed through the school brochure more thoroughly. Most of the instructors were professionals in their fields of expertise. She wondered if the editor's job would be solely to oversee the mechanics of the publication, or if it would also entail writing copy. She remembered interview assignments as a student. It would be scary to do interviews after so many years, but it would be interesting as well.

She carted the breakfast things to the dishwasher, then tucked a house key into the pocket of her jeans and went outside.

The autumn sunshine was thin despite its deceptive brightness, but she rejected the impulse to go back and borrow a heavier jacket from Fran's closet. Let the temperature drop, let the wind blow—she could take it. She had learned strength and independence the hard way and had no intention of slipping backward. After the deaths of their parents, Fran had watched over her during high school with such smothering protectiveness that she had entered college ripe for a rebellion she hadn't been equipped to handle. But that was all water over the dam. Both sisters had changed.

Although Fran was still Big Sister in capital letters, the discussion about the job showed she was trying to offer suggestions rather than take total command in her old way.

Ignoring the chill fingers of wind tugging at her dark curls, Janet looked up and down Quince Street. The section, a long-established residential area of the famed university town, had homes that were quaint, historic, or interesting, but nothing truly imposing. She wondered which direction would take her past the Stockton house. She decided to go left. The landscaping of the fifth house looked professional enough for the wealthy Stocktons, although its modestly pillared, Federal-style facade had none of the ultra-modern panache she had been led to expect. Fran certainly had been critical of the couple. She wondered what she would think for herself when meeting them Saturday.

At the corner she turned and skirted a property that held a swimming pool with dead leaves clotting in rain water on its black plastic cover. The view running through the back yards of the houses on the other side of the block was interrupted halfway down by a privet hedge that extended from a latticed rear porch. Janet felt the cold seeping into her bones and was about to turn back when she caught a swirling glimpse of pink. Squinting against the watery sunlight, she recognized Gina weaving through the privet, playing hide-and-seek with the cat.

As she watched, a hunch-shouldered woman emerged from the latticed porch, hurrying despite the stiff, arthritic movements of her age-thickened body.

Seen at a distance, the profile of the woman's face was like a nutcracker, the prow of her nose and jutting chin threatening to meet. She was dressed from head to toe in black, and a black shawl was knotted over her hair babushka style. The perfect witch for a real gingerbread cottage, thought Janet, shivering.

The woman clapped her hands sharply, startling the cat into streaking off. Equally startled, Gina looked up, and the woman made urgent gestures, clearly signaling her to leave. As if performing a well-practiced role, the child hesitated only briefly before slipping through an opening in the hedge. The greenery seemed to close around her as neatly as if she had been swallowed.

3

Gina obviously wasn't afraid of what must be the neighborhood crone. If anything, it was the old woman herself who acted fearful. Maybe she disliked cats. Or even children. The woman waited an anxious moment before painfully retracing her steps back into the house.

Janet waited, too, wondering if Gina would return. A cloud moved over the sun and the wind gusted sharply. Feeling the sting of grit, Janet noticed a child's sandbox near the closed swimming pool. A toy truck, abandoned and rusting, lay half buried in the sand and beside it lay a red shovel and the broken arm of a plastic doll.

There was no further sign of Gina, and Janet suddenly wondered why in the world she was dawdling, standing around nearly freezing to death. It was time to return to her room and unpack.

A half-hour later she had emptied her two suitcases and organized the closet and bureau drawers. She had gotten rid of her heaviest clothing before moving to Alabama and now that she was back North, she would need a warm coat. That evening, she and Fran were going shopping; she decided to make a list of what to buy.

Pad and pencil in hand, she tucked herself into the cozy window seat only to find her attention drifting out through the glass. The sun had come out again, and the back yards were spread below like a series of little parks. She was annoyed to find herself remembering the broken, abandoned toys in the sandbox, and she thought about Gina. The child's handicap didn't seem to be physical. Perhaps she suffered from a learning disability. Was she now studying with the tutor Fran had mentioned, or was she home alone? Janet imagined her sitting silently in an immaculate but sterile living room, her pink taffeta skirt crisp around her knees, dressed and waiting for a party that never happened.

With a sigh, Janet resolutely applied her thoughts to her clothing list, wishing the melancholy image of a lonely child had not stolen into her mind.

She printed the words, *Winter Coat*, then let the pencil rest idle, her eyes again traveling to the window. There was no way to tell from inside how forbidding the air could be. From her elevated view she admired beds of russet and wine chrysanthemums, a wrought-iron bench and an old-fashioned grape arbor. She looked on to the yards of the houses which faced the street on the far side of the block, her gaze lifting to the copper beech. The trunk of the tree soared above a thicket of pines, the smooth gray limbs stretching skyward in a magnificent tangle that seemed created for the capering of elves and other woodland sprites.

Smiling, Janet leaned forward, thinking that as autumn leaves drifted free, she would have an increasingly better view of the house that had interested her in the spring. With a start, she focused on the back porch which peeked suddenly through the branches, showing latticework as stark and white as bare bones. During her walk, she hadn't been aware that the porch was attached to the yellow Queen Anne house, but now she could see that it was. And that's where the black-garbed woman lived.

How wrong, she thought, disquieted. She remembered how lovely the garden of that house had been in the spring, so inviting, as if created to welcome little children. None of her business of course, but how wrong it seemed that a person living there would chase a child away.

4

That evening, after having decided upon a coat, Janet was standing in Epstein's department store dressing room, wearing the jacket of a wool suit she had also decided to purchase. Hoping to make an extra outfit, she had tried on a plaid wool skirt she thought would coordinate with the heathery fawn of the suit. It had been too big and Fran had gone to find another in a smaller size. When Fran finally returned, she was carrying several garments.

"Sorry I was so long," she apologized, "but I looked around to see if there was anything else you should try while we were at it."

Janet frowned. "I told you that a second skirt for this suit is all my budget can handle."

"I know, but still..." As Fran leaned to place the clothing on a chair, her shadow, bowed and dark, loomed against the compartment wall. Janet was reminded of the old woman she had seen during her morning walk.

"Tell me something," she said as Fran handed her a plaid skirt, "that property that corners at your back yard—who's the elderly woman who lives in the yellow house?"

"You must mean Rose. Dressed like a mourner, right?"

"She was wearing all black, yes." Janet pulled on the skirt and zipped it. "Oh, I do like this plaid, but look—" She slipped her fingers easily inside the waist band. "Too big."

Fran wrinkled her nose. "Skinny thing—I was afraid of that. I brought along another, but the colors aren't quite the same."

Janet's thoughts returned to the old woman as she slipped

off the skirt. "Anyway, I saw this woman, Rose, outside this morning. She seemed sort of odd."

"Odd?" Fran dimpled. "Tactful description. The poor thing spends hours wandering about her yard muttering to herself. Watching her can be spooky. Not that I know much about her. The family hasn't been here long—the house only sold last month."

Surprised, Janet remembered the appeal the house had held for her. "I figured such an attractive place would be snapped up right away. Why ever would it stand empty for so long?"

"Who knows, but it did. Take off that skirt and that jacket too." Fran turned to the clothing she had brought in. "I want you to try on something different."

"You didn't bring another suit, did you? I've already decided on this one."

"No, and I don't want to hear anything more about your budget. If you like this, it's an early Christmas present, and I insist. Here, have a look. Ta-da!" Fran held up a dress, a draped chiffon in a soft apricot shade. "I figured you could wear it tomorrow night."

Janet liked it at once, but her expression remained dubious. "I hadn't planned on buying anything so dressy. Isn't my beige silk okay? Besides, you said that tomorrow evening was just a neighborhood get-together."

"I neglected to explain that for the Stocktons, a 'get-together' means a cocktail party." Fran handed over the dress. "Try it. Your beige silk is over four years old and you owe yourself a treat. And for goodness sake, in a livelier color than beige!"

The dress had a high-necked bodice and semitransparent sleeves that seemed especially designed to flatter thin arms. Janet found that its soft color brightened her complexion and brought out an emerald sparkle in her eyes, making her look more as she had before the events of the past summer.

"Big sister still knows best?" Fran demanded, her tone knowing.

"This time, yes," admitted Janet. Fran did so enjoy

being right. Janet pivoted before the mirror, viewing her reflection from different angles, aware of how the full skirt moved sensuously against her legs. "Yes," she repeated, smiling at her sister. "I like it."

The next morning, helping with Saturday chores, Janet went to sweep Fran's front walk. It was a beautiful autumn morning, crisp and invigorating, without the cold of the previous day. She wondered if Gina was out playing around the neighborhood. The prospect of being in the child's home that evening and meeting her foster parents both intrigued and pained her. How could people fortunate enough to have a child fail to appreciate the fact? She hoped that Fran had exaggerated the couple's failings.

With the sweeping finished, Janet was breaking off the last of summer's marigolds for a bouquet when she saw Rose coming up the other side of the street, looking confused and exhausted. In her dark, foreign-looking garb, she seemed out of place, as though her figure had been superimposed upon the scene by clever camera work. Oblivious to her surroundings, the old woman shuffled from the sidewalk and into the street. Halfway across, she stopped, and agitatedly cast her gaze from side to side. It was clear that she was lost.

There was no traffic and Janet hesitated, waiting for her to start moving again. When this failed to happen, she took matters in hand and went to her.

Up close, she marveled that she had imagined anything sinister about the old woman. She could see that she had once been handsome, but now was wrinkled and toothless with sunken lips and cheeks that distorted what had been fine bone structure. Her expressionless eyes were colorless, filmed with the milky gray of age. The grizzled hair that poked from the folds of the babushka was clean, as were the black skirt and blouse and belted sweater.

"It's a fine day, isn't it?" Janet said companionably, undeterred by the woman's empty stare. She touched her arm in the hope of guiding her toward the pavement. "The entire weekend is supposed to be nice before it turns cold again."

Rose cocked her head in a birdlike way. "Hot," she mumbled vaguely, looking past Janet's shoulder. "So hot. Everything burning hot."

Janet wondered if this was some sort of reverse comment about the weather. Rose's accent was unidentifiable and her missing teeth caused a lisp which further distorted her words.

"All gone, all gone." There had been a bright, if empty, note in Rose's voice at first, but it changed, becoming fearful. "All gone!" Her eyes darted anxiously, then briefly focused on Janet. "They were with us," she said, as if imparting an urgent message, "then they were all gone."

Despite the wrinkles and stooped shoulders of the figure before her, Janet felt she confronted a bewildered child. Making an instinctive gesture to comfort as well as distract, she offered one of the marigolds. "Here, take one of these. Look, a bright orange one."

Becoming calm, Rose accepted the flower and held it to her breast. "All gone, all gone," she lamented mournfully, gazing once more into space.

Taking her arm and saying she would see her home, Janet led her safely to the sidewalk. Rose trudged along willingly. They were halfway to the yellow house when a black Oldsmobile purred to a stop against the opposite curb. The driver's door opened and a smartly dressed woman in her late fifties emerged. Her coloring was exotic—her complexion olive toned, her hair a glossy black. As she hurried toward them, Janet observed the cut and fit of her suit, thinking that the woman's outfit would make her own new clothes seem common in comparison. The pearl and ruby jewelry looked genuine and the upswept style of the woman's hair emphasized a face of classic beauty that transcended age.

"Oh, Rose," the woman cried in relief as she reached them, touching the older woman's arm. "Oh, Rose . . ." Looking at Janet, she nervously moistened her lips, showing a hesitant, uneasy reserve that seemed out of keeping with her sophisticated appearance. "Thank you for extending kindness to my sister. I am sorry you have been troubled." Her voice was soft and the phrasing of her words had a stilted, unfamiliar cadence although the actual pronunciation held no accent.

"She's been no trouble," Janet assured. "I was just seeing her home."

The woman's eyes were like golden-brown cabochons—cat's eyes, tiger eyes. They widened, as if in alarm. "How did you know where she lives?"

"Because we're on the other side of the block. I'm staying with my sister Fran Elwin. My name is Janet Fairweather."

"Oh, the Elwins—yes, I understand." The woman was flustered. "I am Muriel Renner. My husband and I"—she gestured toward a figure that was only a shadow in the closed car—"were grocery shopping when Rose became separated from us."

While listening, Janet had been covertly comparing the two women. Making allowance for the ravages of age, she could now see a certain similarity between the bone structure of Rose's face and that of her much younger sister. Remembering how the old woman had repeated the words *all gone*, Janet said, "I think Rose tried to explain about being lost. She must have been hunting for you."

"And I have been driving up and down, hunting for her," Muriel answered, faint exasperation in her tone. She observed the marigold which Rose held like a small sunburst against the dark sweater. "I see you have given her a flower. It is a surprise she accepted it. She allows few people to approach her." Softening a trifle, Muriel allowed herself a brief smile, then reverted to formality. "Thank you again." She took her sister's arm. "We will be leaving now."

The woman led Rose to the car, helped her into the back, then closed the door with a firm deliberation, as if making sure that the old woman understood she was not to get out again until told. As Muriel took her place at the wheel, Janet caught only a glimpse of the male figure in the front passenger seat before the door closed again.

The big car drove off soundlessly, its sparkling windows and glossy black finish reflecting the light like mirrors. Janet watched until it turned the corner, then she walked back to Fran's house.

"I just met two of your neighbors," she announced as she returned the broom to the kitchen, where Warren was helping Fran wash windows.

"Who, the Gilroys next door?" asked Warren.

"No, Muriel and Rose from behind you." Janet placed the bouquet on the table. "It's funny how I just asked about them last night."

Fran asked, "Did you also meet Dr. Renner?"

"Oh?" Janet digested this information. "Muriel's husband is a doctor?"

"Yes, Dr. Herman Renner. He's a retired child psychologist."

"I didn't meet him—he stayed in the car. The fact that he's a doctor explains Muriel's elegant clothes. Not that she wouldn't be beautiful anyway."

"Isn't she gorgeous! If I could look like that when I reach her age!"

Warren, a big-boned, darkly bearded man, observed his wife's jeans and bandanna-wrapped hair with a wink. "Then right now, you would have to look as glamorous as she must have looked at thirty-three."

"Oh, shut up," Fran admonished good-naturedly. "Instead of making wisecracks, why don't you go into the dining room with the stepladder and get things ready for me to do the windows there."

After Warren left, Janet asked, "Does Muriel have an accent, or what? I couldn't figure it out. And what an unlikely pair of sisters." She couldn't help grinning. "Not that we know what folks say about us."

"Twirp! Who knows indeed? They're from Argentina. Muriel is unquestionably a Spanish aristocrat, but Rose looks like a peasant bag lady." Going to the sink, Fran ran fresh water into the scrub bucket. "Two weeks ago, we threw a party to welcome the Renners to the neighborhood.

I don't know what they did with Rose, but she didn't come. Hired a sitter maybe. Muriel's awfully reserved and seemed nervous. She clung to her husband's side all evening and barely said a word. Old Herman is more outgoing, only in a condescending way. Not actually offensive, understand, but it's clear he considers himself a cut above the common herd."

"Renner?" The name had just struck Janet. "I'd expect a Spanish-sounding name from Argentina."

"He's originally from good old Freud-land, Austria—I told you he was a psychologist, didn't I? To escape the Second World War, he fled to South America, where he met Muriel. They've been married for almost forty years. As young as she still looks, she must have been only in her teens. They moved to this country because of his health." Rolling her eyes, she added, "His heart specialist is in Manhattan, so don't ask me why he bought a house in Princeton."

"Manhattan is only an hour away," reasoned Janet. "A lot closer than Argentina. Or Austria."

"Well, I suppose that's true enough," Fran agreed with a laugh. "He struck me as a scholar, so being near the university might be the draw. Still, it doesn't seem practical."

Janet's brief glimpse of the figure in the car had told her nothing about the doctor's appearance. Curious, she asked, "Will the Renners be at the party tonight?"

"Probably not. Here, let me get you a vase for those flowers." Rummaging in a cupboard, Fran said over her shoulder, "I think Dr. Renner made a special effort to attend that first neighborhood gathering. Even then, he had to leave early. You can tell he's not well just by looking at him."

Janet was disappointed. The image of Rose and Muriel stood vividly in her mind and she felt an odd eagerness to meet the doctor. But regardless of how he looked, she already was convinced that the Renners were all wrong for the yellow house. The place had impressed her as needing someone young, people with a growing family.

Not ready to relinquish the subject, she said, "Rose looks so much older than Muriel. It was hard to find any resemblance at first. It's as if Rose has led a terribly hard life, while Muriel has been a pampered pet. Sort of a country mouse-city mouse difference."

Backing out of the cupboard, Fran handed Janet a squat, earthenware jug. "From the way Muriel dresses, Dr. Renner is the one who does the pampering. He looks a lot older than she does too, although that might be because of his illness. Still, I think European men like to marry younger women and then show them off like ornaments. Those flowers would look nice right here on the kitchen table, wouldn't they? They match the colors in the floor."

"Might even spark it up a bit," said Janet, looking critically at the fifty-year-old linoleum, a drab tan, orange, and green block pattern that Fran had preserved with a clear plastic finish. In her opinion, the only thing in its favor was that it matched the outdated sink.

Warren's call came from the other room. "If you want my help, Frances my love, get a move on. The stepladder is ready and waiting."

"Yes master," called Fran, gathering up her cleaning supplies.

Alone, Janet arranged the flowers, her thoughts returning to the occupants of the yellow house.

5

As the day progressed, the weather turned brisk again. By evening, Janet was more than grateful for the warmth of her new coat as she walked with Fran and Warren to the Stockton's party. She was between them, and the manner in which Fran had wordlessly jockeyed her into that position both amused and annoyed her. It was clear that Fran felt little sister needed the protection of their larger, more bulky bodies.

Black-bearded Warren was a sturdy man with a barrel chest and broad shoulders. Years back, when Fran had begun dating him, Janet had felt instant approval simply because of his size. At that time Fran had just broken up with a fellow so frail and scrawny she could have worn him as a lapel pin, and Warren's burliness brought her full figure into comfortable feminine proportion. Later, when Janet had gotten to know him better, she learned he also balanced out Fran in other ways, tempering her tendency to steamroller people "for their own good," and serving as a quiet, appreciative foil for her lively enthusiasm. The serenity of their home was due as much to his sure stability as to Fran's more voluble warmth and caring.

Warren nodded his shaggy head as he related incidents from a day of judging tryouts for a fraternity musical. What with the troubles in her marriage, it was actually Janet's first evening out since Becky's death and she suspected he was trying to make sure she felt at ease.

"Here we are," he said, interrupting himself as he steered them toward the Stockton's Federal-style house. A mercury lamp theatrically spotlighted the columned facade, showing the eye-catching changes that had been made since Janet had seen the house the previous day. On the left of the wide stoop sat a shock of Indian corn, and next to it were three candlelit jack-o'-lanterns on a bench. The blue-painted front door was decorated with a straw wreath wound with gold ribbons and more Indian corn.

The jack-o'-lanterns welcomed Janet with flickering eyes and leering, gap-toothed mouths. An errant breeze wafted the smell of scorched pumpkin across her nostrils, reminding her of Halloween nights long past: cider-crisp darkness, sweaty costumes, and tightly clutched candy bags. She remembered shrill giggles smothered by painted masks and frantic dashes past vacant lots. Had that shadow been a ghost? Did you hear a growling from behind that tree?

"I bet Gina helped carve the pumpkins," she speculated with a reminiscent smile as Warren reached toward the doorbell. "That's always so much fun for kids."

"Maybe," Fran answered doubtfully. "They're done awfully well. I don't know who would have taken the time to supervise."

The door was opened by a thin, red-haired man. "Fran and Warren! Good to see you!"

"Arthur—hello!" Fran greeted the man who closed the door behind them and reached to take their coats. So this is where Gina lives, Janet thought, seeing the open doorways of lighted rooms on either side of the deep foyer.

"Our host and hostess are busy, so I've appointed myself doorman," Arthur announced, shaking hands with Warren as he waited for the women to shrug free of their outer garments.

Fran introduced him to Janet. "Glad to meet you," he said warmly. "I'm putting the coats upstairs. Here comes Veronica."

Janet had no more time to look around the formal, high-ceilinged entry before Veronica was upon them, a striking woman with upswept, champagne-colored hair, heavily mascaraed blue-gray eyes, and a broad, out-thrust jaw that no amount of artful shading could minimize.

"Fran's little sister!" she rhapsodized, pressing both of Janet's hands in cool, be-ringed fingers. Snaring them with fragrant clouds of perfume, she moved the trio into the adjoining living room, where taped Mozart played background for a crowd talking and laughing companionably as a waiter ferried refreshments among them.

The walls, draperies, carpeting, and most of the upholstered pieces in the room were shades of white, the starkness dramatized by splashes of brilliant color. A vivid Scandinavian tapestry hung over the white marble fireplace in which flames danced brightly, and a sea-blue sectional couch in a conversation area was flanked by tall crystal vases holding tropical blossoms. There was no hint that a child inhabited the house.

Pausing just long enough to allow Janet to absorb the impact of the decor, Veronica asked, "Now, you're from Alabama, aren't you dear?" The swinging diamonds in her ears matched the clip on the padded shoulder of her turquoise satin dress.

"I only lived there a few months," Janet explained, aware of Fran hovering protectively at her elbow. She trusted that Fran hadn't revealed the tragic details behind her move.

"I'm a southerner too," Veronica confided with a glistening smile and Janet realized the woman hadn't listened to her reply. Her voice now exhibited a slight drawl that had been absent before. "My Tommy is also from the South. We're Virginia Stocktons, not the-founder-of-Princeton Stocktons like everyone always assumes."

Feeling she was expected to say something, Janet ventured, "I know there is a Stockton Street in town."

"Oh, so you're aware of local history?" asked Tommy Stockton, coming up to peer over his wife's shoulder. He was wearing a three-piece gray suit with a sapphire stud in his gray silk tie. "You'll want to meet Kirby Orchard—he's around here someplace."

Veronica introduced Janet to her tall, glossy-handsome husband. His hair was a flaxen shade similar to Veronica's, and his manly jaw was even wider. Janet thought they looked like a pugnacious Ken and Barbie.

He flagged the waiter, and as his guests selected drinks, he expounded: "Stockton Street was named for a Quaker from Long Island, who gets the credit for founding the town of Princeton back in the 1700s. The old Quaker meetinghouse that Stockton built still stands. But, as Veronica has possibly mentioned, we're the Virginia Stocktons."

"Oh, Tommy, I *just* explained," giggled Veronica coyly.

"We'll circulate on our own," Warren offered pleasantly as Tommy parted from his wife, excusing himself to meet new arrivals.

"Why, bless me, but no!" corrected Veronica, laying a hand on Janet's arm. Her southern drawl was thickening like corn-starch gravy over a flame. "You and your lovely spouse can circulate—you already know everyone! But there's someone our little visitor must meet."

Swept across the room, Janet found herself brought to a stop before a plump Friar Tuck of a man somewhere in his sixties. His thick glasses covered pale, friendly eyes and his bald head was neatly circled by a fringe of graying hair. He had been deeply engaged in conversation with the younger man beside him, but upon Veronica's arrival, they turned toward her with polite and expectant attention.

"Kirby," said Veronica, "this sweet little gal here has been just dying to meet you! She's Janet Fairweather, Fran Elwin's little sister from Alabama. Janet, this is Kirby Orchard. And—" She turned to the younger man, who appeared to be around thirty. "Janet, you must also meet our guest of honor for the evening, Ben Yates."

"A pleasure indeed," Ben said, echoing Kirby's greeting. He had pleasant, irregular features and crisp-looking brown hair.

He was about to say more, but Veronica hooked him by the elbow. "Come along, Ben, dear. Sorry to drag you away, but so many are eager to meet you. A chore, I know, but so necessary to help your talk tonight serve its best purpose." Her drawl had mysteriously fled.

"Well," said Kirby, the expression on his jowly face pleasant as he and Janet found themselves alone. "Such an intriguing introduction from Veronica. Why have you been so eager to meet an old duffer like me?"

"I don't exactly know," she answered honestly, her smile erasing any possible sting. Recovering from the force of Veronica's presence, she mentally backtracked to the conversation in which she had first heard Kirby's name. "Actually, Tommy Stockton suggested we meet. He didn't explain why, but it might be in connection with Princeton history. Does that ring a bell?"

"Exactly the right note," answered Kirby with a cheerful

nod, puffing his waistcoated chest and considerable paunch with unconscious pride. "I'm a cinema arts instructor by profession, but local history is a hobby. You have questions about the town?"

Janet laughed. "That was a misunderstanding. But tell me about your film classes. I adore the work from the thirties and forties."

Kirby beamed. "As do I!" He launched into an elaboration which was interrupted when Fran breezed by, checking, Janet was sure, to make sure little sister wasn't languishing in a corner. Fran introduced her to a silver-haired couple, their neighbors, the Gilroys, then moved on. Janet lost sight of Kirby as the Gilroys took her to meet others.

She soon began to feel tired. Her curiosity about Gina had made her anticipate the evening, but with the child nowhere in sight, her energies started to flag. Dropping out of the conversational stream, she found herself remembering the previous autumn, when she had proudly donned her first maternity dress. Remembering her bright hopes for the future, she was dismayed to feel the sting of tears. Lord—one drink and she was getting maudlin.

The traffic had started to drift in the direction of the dining room and she allowed it to carry her along. The smell of food made her realize she was hungry. The vague thought crossed her mind that judging from the delicious aromas, the banquet table promised to be a lot less artificial than the hostess. She couldn't help wondering if Veronica was always so "on."

In the dining room, a long, white-clothed table was spread with a tempting array of dishes. Janet had just picked up a plate and moved into line when she heard a masculine voice near her ear. "Beat me to it. I was about to find you and ask if I could bring you anything."

She turned to look up at Ben Yates. "It's just as well you didn't," she responded, warming to the twinkle in his gray eyes. Something about his manner encouraged her to tease. "It's quite a feast. I wouldn't have wanted to miss a thing."

He grinned. "For you, I would have been willing to make

a million trips." Taking a plate, he stepped into line beside her.

"Promises, promises," she bantered, liking him, her weariness supplanted by a feeling of gladness that he had joined her. "Say, what *is* that dish over there? Curry, but with slices of what—papaya?"

Shrugging, he spooned some onto his plate. "Don't know, but I'm game for adventure."

"I can tell," she said, wanting to know more about him. "That's quite a tan you have considering it's October."

He chuckled. "I've just returned from three weeks in Arizona. It was a business trip, but as good as a vacation for me. I was studying new designs out there for using solar energy and wind."

"Is that what you'll be talking about tonight—things you learned on your trip?"

"To an extent, yes," he said as they filed on down the table, "but I'll let you in on a secret. We've gathered here tonight in the name of status—shall we install a few solar panels, put in a glass room with lots of thermal mass? What we want to know is, what's the latest in conspicuous consumption?"

"Sounds as if you're a cynic."

His laugh was good-natured. "Not really, but I guess I am sounding that way. Our hostess manages to set a certain *tone*, if you know what I mean."

Janet looked heavenward. "I do indeed."

With unspoken agreement they were hunting for places to sit together when Veronica rushed up. "Oh, Ben, good! You've already filled your plate. Could you bring it along to the library?" She turned to Janet. "Oh, I'm just so sorry to be taking this dear man away from you again, but there's literature I want to distribute after his talk, and I *must* have his approval first."

With little choice except to go, Ben flung a look over his shoulder. "Later," he mouthed to Janet as Veronica led him off.

For a moment, Janet felt very alone. Then, seeing Warren seating himself on a cream-colored settee, she joined him.

"All this white," he sighed, uncomfortably balancing his plate on his knees, looking like a grizzly at a tea party. He placed his punch cup carefully on the snowy carpet by his feet. "Makes me feel I should bring along plastic to spread before I dare lift a fork."

Janet found it relaxing to be with someone she knew after making small talk with so many strangers. She watched as a tan cat padded up and nosed Warren's drink. It was the Siamese she had seen with Gina. Pleased, she thought that if it was the little girl's pet, her life must not be as empty as Fran had made it sound. She imagined Gina snug in her bed, confident that her foster mother would save her special treats from the party. Yes, that's surely the kind of mother Veronica really was.

With the arrival of fruit and chocolate-rich French pastries, the crowd was directed to take dessert into the living room, where Ben would give his talk. Fran, like a brood hen, wanted Janet close under her wing, but she and Warren had seats in the front and Janet preferred a place farther back. She settled upon a spot where she could stand, leaning against the end wall of the living room, the foyer just behind her. Ben was really quite nice-looking, she thought as she watched him take his place in the front of the room. It was good that she had come to the party, she decided. Getting out, associating with people—yes, it was good for her. She waited expectantly as Veronica introduced Ben to the gathering.

He spoke well, his pleasant tenor carrying clearly. Although it was evident that he believed energy conservation was of vital importance, there was nothing of the fanatic in his approach. Most attractive too, Janet thought, in his casual loden-green corduroy sports coat. She wasn't sure whether he was an architect or a builder. Fran could be counted on for the answer. Listening to him speak, she judged that he was a person who could take things seriously without taking himself too seriously as well. A comfortable kind of trait.

Caught up in her thoughts, Janet only gradually became aware of the smoke drifting from the fireplace. Certainly, Tommy should be jumping to fix the draft or something, but no one moved. Actually, the smoke wasn't visible. There was only an increasingly evil smoldering—more repulsive than anything she had ever smelled from a fireplace before. She surveyed the crowd, seeing the broad shoulders of men in their suits and dinner jackets and the women in their low-backed party dresses all leaning toward Ben in rapt attention. Surely, the others were as disturbed by the smoke as she, so how could they sit as if oblivious to a reek that was worsening by the second?

It suddenly occurred to her that the smell probably wasn't from the fireplace at all. It must be from the jack-o'-lanterns outside. Instead of guttering themselves lifeless, the candles had started to consume their hosts. Yes, what else could the sickening stink be? That charred, nauseating odor, so thick on the air that she could barely breathe—burning pumpkins. It was the only explanation. And she alone had detected it because she was the closest to the front door.

Unnoticed by the others, she slipped into the foyer. Hidden from the view of the living room, she peered through the glass door panel, thinking that if flames jumped to the dry corn shocks, there was no telling what else would go up. The Halloween display was too far to the side of the porch for her to see, but at least there was no flickering reflection of flames. Relieved, she quietly eased the door open, confident she could easily take care of the matter by throwing a little dirt into the smoldering pumpkins, smothering the fire before harm was done.

She stepped onto the porch and stopped dead. Clearly illuminated by the spotlight, the three jack-o'-lanterns grinned placidly from the bench, the candles within them safely extinguished to blackness. Baffled, she stared. If not burning pumpkins, then what? She sniffed, unable to detect even a hint of the smell. The source of the burning—it had to be inside after all. Only then, why had no one else seemed aware of it?

She was still standing in perplexity when she heard the thin, distant wail of an infant. Attention captured, she tilted her head, realizing that there *was* a baby in the neighborhood. Through some trick of the chill night air, the sound echoed, making a chorus of lost, lonely cries. Memories of Becky leaped into Janet's mind. Biting her lip, she waited tensely for the crying to cease. *Go to your baby, mother*, she begged silently, tears springing to her eyes. *Go to your baby while you can*. Blessedly, the sounds faded. Shivering, arms hugged about herself, Janet waited another moment, then eased back inside the foyer.

It wasn't until the door was closed behind her that she realized that the foyer was free of the smoky odor. Unbelievably, that dreadful smoldering, that stench, was now totally gone. Only the mingled scents of the party—the food and drink, cigarettes and perfumes—filled the air.

6

Janet leaned back against the door, grateful that she couldn't be seen from the living room, where Ben was continuing his talk.

What had happened to the smoky smell? Her thoughts whirled in confusion. It seemed impossible that the dreadful odor could have dissipated so completely. Had she imagined it? No one else in the living room had noticed it. Unless she was having some kind of olfactory hallucination... The thought frightened her, and she dismissed it with a shake of her head. She must calm down.

Suddenly, she felt a hard, nervous spasm in the pit of her

stomach and knew she was on the verge of being sick. After not having much of an appetite for months, she realized she had gone wild, bingeing on a bizarre combination of unaccustomed foods. She could hardly expect anything but trouble. That Indian dish—delicious, but with what kinds of spices and herbs?

A cheering thought momentarily overrode her discomfort: perhaps the phantom smells had been due to an allergic reaction. Yes, why not? She had heard of things just as odd. Her stomach squirmed again and she hastened toward the steps.

At the head of the staircase a light to the right guided her toward the bathroom. *Carpeted!* she thought in dismay as she rushed in and shoved the door shut behind her. Without a doubt, she was going to upchuck all over Veronica's downy-soft rug before reaching her desired destination.

But once on her knees, she felt the pull of imminent sickness blessedly lessen. She rested her arms weakly on a puffed and padded toilet seat and gazed bleary-eyed down at the rug, which thankfully had been spared. It was a shade Veronica's designer probably called pale raspberry, but a grateful Janet was thinking it was more the color of Pepto-Bismol. Soothing, quieting Pepto-Bismol.

When she finally rose to her feet and stared at her reflection in the mirror over the sink, she saw that her complexion was pale and the hazel color of her eyes washed out, almost bleached, giving her that zombie look she'd had during those first weeks after Becky's death.

Becky, dead. The words seemed to toll in her mind like a mournful iron bell. She stared hopelessly into the mirror, wondering if the time would ever come when sorrow would cease to catch her unaware; when she could hear a baby cry without her first instinctive thought being that it was her child. The crying she had heard earlier—if only by some miracle it could have been her own dear baby. If only she could rewrite history and go rushing to her, reaching her in time, saving her...

She felt in no condition to return to the party. Maybe it

had been too soon to get out and try to socialize after all, especially among so many strangers. It had been too much of a strain. She decided to wait upstairs until after Ben's talk. Once the crowd started milling around again, she would find Fran and say she was calling it a night.

Stepping into the hall, she looked across the landing of the open staircase to a lamplit room where coats were piled across a bed. As she headed toward it, she moved past the stairs and heard the blurred, distant murmur of Ben's voice from below. To her right was a deep, bay-windowed alcove that overlooked the Stockton back yard. What was probably a sunny hideaway by daylight was now murky, the mullioned panes admitting a ghostlike, cobwebby glow that spread over a small upholstered bench sitting in the bay.

Skirting the bench, she was startled by a movement in the shadows. She caught her breath, her heart leaping into her throat.

"*Gina*," she gasped, recognizing the child even as her body still reacted with trembling alarm. She clutched an arm of the bench and stifled a relieved laugh.

The little girl, dressed in a long nightgown, had apparently been looking out the window until Janet had disturbed her. Her face showed indistinctly in the poor light, her dark eyes soft smudges of blackness in the moth-white triangle of her small face.

Realizing that Gina had probably been as startled as she, Janet sank to the bench so she wouldn't continue to tower over her.

"Gina," she said softly, glad for an opportunity to talk with the child. "I'm sorry if I scared you." When Gina offered no response, Janet continued in a soothing tone, "Actually, I guess we scared each other, didn't we? Say, I bet you're wondering how I knew your name." She realized that Veronica might speak of her neighbors primarily by first names. "You know Mrs. Elwin—Fran Elwin? She's my sister, and I'm staying with her, right down the block. Just five houses away."

Gina continued to stare at her mutely. Her dark eyes, lost

in the shadows, gave no clue as to what she might be thinking. With a sense of defeat, Janet realized that further attempts to draw her out were probably hopeless. Children were told not to talk to strangers. How were they to judge which situations were exceptions? The little girl had been minding her own business in her own house and then some strange lady popped from nowhere and started quizzing her. No wonder she held her tongue.

"I'm sorry, Gina," Janet said softly, feeling a surprising depth of regret at being unable to establish contact. "Maybe we'll see each other again—some time when your mommy is with you. Then you'll know it's okay."

Reluctantly, she started to arise from the bench. The view from the window caught her eye. The moonlit panorama showed a perspective far different from that of her own window, yet the dramatic silhouette of a particularly massive tree must be the copper beech in the Renner yard. The house, the beech tree . . . The scene was beautiful, yet at the same time, oddly disquieting.

She felt Gina's fingers touch her arm.

Startled, she stared blankly at the child, then heard the small voice.

The sound was so thin and disembodied that Janet wasn't positive that Gina had spoken at all. She felt the small fingers close upon the fabric of her sleeve, pulling with a strange urgency.

"Yes, Gina?" she said. "Yes?" Janet found herself sinking to her knees, putting herself on eye level with the child, whose face now seemed to swim in the misty half-darkness.

"Yes, Gina? What did you want to say?"

Gina spoke in that same eerie fashion, and this time the words traveled clearly: *"I heard your baby."*

Janet gasped, feeling as if a blade of ice had been drawn along her spine. She knew she could not have heard correctly.

"I heard your baby," the child repeated. Lifting her hand to Janet's face, she looked deeply into her eyes. Those gentle fingertips, moving in a warm, smooth caress against

the frozen marble of Janet's cheek were the only reality in a world gone suddenly mad.

"*I heard it on another night, and again tonight,*" came that small, disembodied message. "*I heard your baby crying.*"

7

On Monday at lunch time, Janet sat with Fran and Fran's friend, Ida Aaron, in a booth at the Magic Spoon. The walls of the restaurant were decorated with antique wooden kitchen implements, a collection of iron weather vanes, and stencils of Pennsylvania Dutch hex signs. One of the signs, composed of a stylized three-branched blossom, reminded Janet of clover. Hex signs were supposed to be a farmer's protection against demons—don't let lightning strike my barn, keep my cows giving sweet milk. Years ago, she had carried a clover leaf tucked in her wallet, one that had four leaves not three. Maybe all types of clover brought good luck. She wondered what had happened to the one she had carried. She had lost it, that was for sure.

Fran's voice intruded into her reverie. "Now we'll get the benefit of an expert's opinion." They were having coffee, and Fran had just pushed previous issues of the adult school newsletter across the table to Ida.

Janet nodded and tried to arrange her face into an expectant expression, but nothing could shake the sense of detachment that had held her for the past thirty-six hours. Over and over in the back of her mind, those haunting words echoed: *I heard your baby. I heard your baby crying.*

She had been stunned at the sound of Gina's small voice, so ghostly in the otherworldly mood of the Stocktons' moonlit hall. So Gina had heard the baby too; yet what had told the child to link it with her? She wished she had retained the presence of mind to ask, but in her shock, she had simply fled to the coat room. By the time she was more composed, Gina had left the hallway. How could the little girl have known a crying infant could represent only one thing to her—Becky, dear lost little Becky? She felt as if Gina had magically seen straight into her grieving heart as easily as if she were transparent.

The voice of Ida Aaron broke into her contemplation and she realized she had been nodding automatically, pretending to listen without hearing a word as Ida talked.

"So, you see, Janet," Ida was pronouncing in conclusion, poking a competent finger at the newsletter copies, "you've got no worries. First you concentrate on interviews with new instructors, then fill in with quotes from old instructors and students. Piece of cake."

Janet forced herself to get in tune. Enthusiasm manufactured while you wait, place your orders now. "Ida, the way you've analyzed these old issues is terrific. Thanks to you, I'll have heaps more confidence at my interview this afternoon."

After Ida left, Fran chortled. "I'm glad you and Ida hit it off, but wait till you hear what I've been holding back! When I picked up these newsletters, the director said no one else had applied, so the job is yours. Classes start tonight. You're to check in with the office at seven o'clock and go straight to work."

"*Tonight?*"

"That's right." Fran's tone was smug. "The interview is no longer necessary. The new editor, my dear, is you."

"But, you let Ida think—"

Fran shrugged. "I wouldn't want her to get the idea you won the position only because I ran interference."

For a moment, Janet forgot everything except how swiftly she was being plunged into the job. What a stunner—leave it to Fran. "When you said I'd get my feet wet, I figured I'd have a chance to test the water first."

Fran dismissed her concerns with an airy wave. "Writing interviews and scraps of chitchat is no problem. It's exactly what you did so well for the high school newspaper. And don't I remember straight A's from those journalism classes?"

"Only one year of them."

"You've gotten dumber since then?" Fran opened her purse and drew out her car keys. "Have a little confidence in yourself, kid. I certainly do."

Warren had dropped Janet off at the Magic Spoon on his way to a seminar, and now Fran was extending her lunch hour to return her home. In the car, after briefly discussing Ida, Fran turned the conversation to the topic Janet least wished to discuss, the Stockton party.

"How did you like Kirby Orchard? He's a love, but when inspired, his wit can be wicked. Once he did a routine about a couple who had been picked up by a spaceship. He handled it as if he were reading from a *National Enquirer* article, but we soon realized he was parodying how Veronica and Tommy would report such an experience. So funny, only I can't remember exactly what he said. Except that it was deliciously mean."

Unable to resist, Janet mimicked Veronica's sugary drawl, extrapolating, "We're not the Martian Stocktons, we're the Venusian ones."

Fran exploded into laughter. "Yes, yes, exactly! You've got their number." Turning the car from the highway to the winding road which would eventually lead to her block, she said more soberly, "Actually, Veronica can be all right if you catch her without Tommy. Then she stops acting as if she's auditioning for a part in a play."

Regretting her crack about the Stocktons because it just encouraged Fran to continue discussing the evening, Janet once again relived those devastating moments with Gina. Her inner ear still seemed to reverberate with that eerie message: *I heard your baby crying.*

A flash of understanding suddenly illuminated her mind. Swallowing a gasp, she didn't see how she could have been so incredibly stupid. She wanted to laugh aloud at her idiocy. How could she have thought there was something supernatural in Gina's words when the truth was so obvious? Fran must have discussed Becky's death and Gina had simply overheard.

Janet realized there had been no need to introduce herself to the child. Alert to the new face in the neighborhood, Gina had known perfectly well who she was. She had probably heard Fran say something to Veronica like, "My sister is coming to visit with me a while. She recently lost her baby." *Lost*. That was the word people always used. "The baby had seemed so healthy. Such a terrible thing." So on the night of the party, when Gina heard a baby crying from some nearby house, she had made what seemed a logical connection. Perhaps the child didn't realize the word *lost* was a euphemism for "death." She remembered Gina's small, upturned face, a pale triangle in the moonlight. Perhaps she had believed her information would help locate the missing infant. Janet was touched by the thought.

For a moment she felt warmed, but then she started wondering just what else Fran had revealed about her to her friends. Although she found it too painful to discuss Becky's death with anyone except Fran, she didn't mind if others knew about it. Her marriage breakup was different. It was no one's business unless she chose to reveal it herself. She had assumed Fran would realize this, but there was no assurance. It made her uncomfortable to think she might be meeting strangers who chewed over her marital woes.

Clearing her throat, she ventured, "Fran, I want to know something. I'm not going to be mad, or anything—I mean, I'll understand, but have you said much to people about why Clay and I split?"

Fran took her eyes from the street, which was nuggeted along the curbs with the bright fool's gold of poplar leaves. "I couldn't say much—you've never seen fit to share any details."

Janet flushed. "I suppose that's true."

"Suppose?" Fran's voice rose and it was obvious a nerve had been struck. "Look, all along I thought you were the most blissfully contented hausfrau in the Western hemisphere. I had misgivings about Clay. I felt he was jealous of any relationship you had outside of him, which included me. But I hadn't a clue your marriage was in trouble until you wrote and said you were getting a divorce. It was clear that you didn't want big sister to mix in. I guess you had too much of me calling the shots when you were young."

Janet was surprised at her sister's insight. Had Fran allowed her to gradually test her wings as she grew up, she doubted she would have flown off so wildly at her first taste of freedom. But she also knew that her sister had always been motivated by the best intentions.

"I'm sorry, Fran," she said, reaching across the seat. "I must have hurt you. When I was a kid, I told you everything."

Fran's voice softened and went husky with emotion. "Yeah, well, I learned a lot from watching Warren's kids grow up. Things I wished I had known with you." Her natural buoyancy asserted itself. "But back to your original question. I didn't speculate about your troubles to anyone. Remember, you called to let us know about Becky's death when Warren and I were on vacation abroad. And, by the time we reached home, your letter informing us of the divorce was waiting. I decided to keep my lip buttoned and let you decide how much you wanted people to know. All I've said is that you're staying with us while you work over some personal decisions."

"Wait a minute," said Janet as Fran pulled the car into her driveway. "Okay, nobody on this block knows my marriage broke up, but they know about Becky, right?"

"Not from me, they don't. You and Clay only visited once with Becky and never met our friends. I'm sure there have been times when I've mentioned you, but there's been no reason for anyone to really remember."

"But when Becky died . . . I mean, when a person's baby dies, people remember that!"

"Yes, they would have—had I said anything." Fran switched off the engine. "As I just explained, as soon as Warren and I came home, we started planning your visit, so

I kept mum." Worried, she studied Janet's face. "What's the trouble, Jan? Would it be easier had I told people about Becky? Knowing how you are, I had assumed—"

Janet shook her head. "That's not it. It's just that somehow, the word must have gotten around. How else would Gina have known about it?"

"What's she have to do with this?"

"When I went upstairs at the Stockton party, Gina was in the upstairs hall. That baby was crying again and this time, Gina heard it." Janet couldn't suppress a tone of self-justification. "You see, there really is a baby somewhere in the neighborhood."

"The one you heard crying that first night?"

"Well, it has to be, doesn't it? And Gina had to have learned I lost a baby because why else would she have thought it was mine?"

"What makes you think she believes that?" Fran's voice was oddly flat. "How would you come to that conclusion?"

"Because Gina said so, of course." Janet was irritated by Fran's quizzing. "When I found her at the window at the head of the stairs, she apparently had just heard the sounds of the baby. She looked directly at me and said, 'I heard your baby. I heard your baby crying.'"

Even as Janet repeated the words in their new, harmless context, they retained the power to make a chill run down her spine. She shrugged off the feeling. "I don't know why you're so defensive about this, Fran. I told you it was all right if people knew."

Fran's expression, which had been unreadable, began to break up, her lips trembling, tears appearing in her eyes. "Oh, Janet," she breathed softly. "Oh, Jan . . ."

"What is it now?" Janet had been annoyed with her sister's obtuseness and was even more annoyed by this new and decidedly odd behavior. "What in the world is wrong with you?"

"It's not me, Jan, it's . . ." She reached for Janet's hand. "What you're telling me Gina said about your baby couldn't have happened, Jan. None of it. Remember I told you she was an earthquake victim? She's the only survivor of her family, and the experience caused a terrible shock. She's perfectly healthy except that she's lost the power of speech. That's her handicap, Janet. She never could have told you anything about hearing a baby. Gina can't talk. She couldn't have told you a thing."

8

That evening, Janet called a taxi for transportation to the high school. Fran had wanted to drive her, but she would have none of it, or rather, she would have nothing to do with Fran.

When Fran had dropped her bombshell about Gina's supposed inability to speak, Janet had flatly refused to accept it.

"All right," she had argued, "maybe Gina wasn't talking in the conventional sense—it was more of a whisper. But I understood her perfectly."

"And said she had heard your baby? Oh, Janet." Fran's wholesome face had reflected dismayed concern. "Even if by some miracle she did manage to speak, it would be Italian, not English."

"Oh, is she rumored to be deaf as well?" Janet had demanded with uncharacteristic sarcasm. "If she's been in this country any time at all, she's picked up some English. Certainly enough to say a few simple words."

Once inside the house, Fran had insisted on phoning the Magic Spoon to explain she wouldn't be returning that afternoon.

"This is ridiculous," Janet snapped when Fran hung up.

Fran's lips were drawn in a thin line. "Maybe, but I can't

go back to work and leave you. You should see yourself. You're as pale as a ghost."

"Can you blame me? It isn't exactly pleasant to discover my only sister thinks I'm a lunatic."

"That's not true. But you've been under a terrible strain. It's understandable if your nerves act up in funny ways."

Sure, nerves, Janet thought sourly. Nervous breakdown was more what Fran really meant. The conversation was pointless and Janet ended up seeking refuge in her room. Thank goodness there had been no occasion to mention the burning smell. She could just see big sister frantically dialing the hotline for Fruitcakes Anonymous. Or maybe she would have gotten the bright idea that hearing voices had been an allergic reaction as well. Janet made a sound of disgust. Whether Gina's words made sense or not was no longer the question. The child had spoken, she had heard her, and Fran could like it or lump it.

Warren wasn't home from his seminar by dinner time, so Janet took a snack to her room rather than face Fran alone over the dining table. When her taxi arrived she merely called a brusque, "I'm leaving," over her shoulder as she went out the door. As she rode off, she supposed Fran was watching from the living room window, but she refused to look back.

Arriving at the high school, she gaped at the ivy-covered stonework and leaded windows of the Gothic stone building.

"This looks like one of the university buildings," she observed aloud as she got out and paid the driver.

"It's the school you wanted, miss."

She took only a moment more to stare, then headed toward the entrance with purposeful steps. She entered the school office, still too stirred up over her disagreement with Fran to feel the butterflies she might have expected otherwise. The meeting with the director went smoothly, leaving her encouraged about the job ahead. As annoying as Fran could be, Janet knew she owed her a lot—not that she intended to admit it until after she had cooled down.

Having decided that her first newsletter issue would

center around impressions of the first class night, she followed directions to the auditorium, where a brief orientation meeting for students and instructors was scheduled. It was an impressive room with long, velvet-draped windows, an ornate balcony, and a stage that would credit any professional theater.

"Princeton High is like no other high school you can think of, right?" asked a plump, balding man who had stepped into the room just ahead of her and turned to catch her look of awe.

"Neither outside nor in," she agreed, still staring. "My school looked like a brick box, and our auditorium was also our cafeteria and gym." She shifted her gaze to the man and recognized him as Kirby Orchard. "Hi! I'm Janet Fairweather—we met at the Stocktons' party."

"I remember—I'd never forget such a pretty face," he asserted with a friendly smile. "You're a relative of the Elwins."

"Fran's sister." She accepted a seat beside him, and in answer to his question about her purpose, explained about doing the newsletter.

"Then you won't be wanting to spend time with me. I'm not one of the new fellows you'll be seeking to interview—I'm an old-timer." He pointed out his class description in the brochure.

She frowned. "I figured you would be teaching about films, but what's this?" Aloud, she read: *"Old House Genealogy. How to go about researching the history of your home."*

He nodded, rubbing a hand over his balding head. "That's an offshoot of my interest in local history. Wonderful houses in the Princeton area. House genealogy satisfies that urge to root through the past in the same way as family genealogy, but without the risks." Seeing her frown at the word *risk*, his tone became mischievous. "To learn that your roof once sheltered a rumrunner is fascinating stuff, my dear, but to learn that great-grandma supplemented her egg money with tête-à-têtes with the hired man is hard for some to take."

Janet laughed, liking him. "Well, I hope to eventually settle somewhere near my sister. If I ever find an older house to buy, I'll take your course and have fun learning how to ferret out its skeletons."

"Fun it is. You'll learn that some houses even have intriguing patterns. I helped the Umsteads, the former owners of your sister's house, study its background. We learned that in its long history, all the owners have been middle-aged or elderly people."

Janet looked thoughtful. "That's probably because it's fairly small. Fran and Warren could never have been comfortable there when his four children were with them. There are only two small bedrooms and one bath."

"It would then make an ideal first home for a young couple, wouldn't it? But that's never happened."

Janet narrowed her eyes. "Are you hinting that something besides practicality is afoot?"

He shoved his glasses up his snub nose. "More things in heaven and earth, Horatio? Odd as it sounds, it seems that invisible factors must attract certain types of people to certain homes—not always, but in enough cases to add an extra thrill to my research."

"It sounds as if you're talking about haunted houses."

With a wink, he lowered his voice to an ominous note. "Maybe I am. But I can't list that in an adult school brochure now, can I?"

The room had been filling as they talked and the appearance of the school director forestalled further conversation. After a welcoming speech, last-minute scheduling changes were announced and the group was dismissed for their classes. Kirby saluted in parting and trundled off.

Janet accompanied the director back to the office, asked a few more questions about the newsletter, then borrowed a typewriter to record her impressions for her first editorial. When she had finished, she studied the list of new instructors and was pleased to discover that Ben Yates was teaching a course on conserving home energy. At the break between the two hours of classes, Janet, starved from her skimpy supper, went to the cafeteria. The bad news was that only coffee and ginger cookies were being served. The good news was that Ben Yates was seated alone at one of the tables.

Coffee in hand, she approached him. She had remembered him well: tanned and fit, with a vigorous outdoorsy appearance. The bright cafeteria lights disclosed touches of chestnut red in his dark, wavy hair. He was dressed in jeans and a crew-neck sweater.

Recognizing her at once, his face broke into a pleased smile. "Janet!" he said, standing. "Glad to see you!"

Pleased by his warm reception, she took the chair he offered. Explaining about the newsletter, she said, "Have to warn you—since you're one of the new instructors, I'll be calling for an interview."

He raised a brow. "Why can't we do it tonight?"

She shook her head. "Maybe a Lois Lane could breeze through like lightning, but I'm new on the job. I'll need more time than just these few minutes."

"I didn't mean during the break. I was talking about after classes."

When she hesitated, he explained, "I missed my dinner, so when I'm through here, I planned to go out for something more substantial than coffee and cookies. I'd enjoy your company."

"Oh, my," she sighed, "you're rattling the bars of the right cage. In another hour I'll be ready to kill for a hamburger."

His grin made the irregular lines of his face look almost handsome. "You've got a date if you don't mind walking uptown."

"Sounds fine with me."

"Great. I know a perfect place near Nassau Street. Look, here comes a crew to drag me back into class and pick my brains about wood stoves." He glanced at his watch. "I'll meet you by the front entrance at nine-fifteen."

By the time Janet met Ben, she had phoned Fran to say she would be late. Her only explanation was that she had run into someone she knew, and she hung up before Fran could ask questions.

Outside, it was surprisingly warm for an October evening and Janet was glad she had worn a jacket instead of her new coat. As they started on their way, Ben told her he was renting an apartment uptown. "After we eat," he said, "we'll get my car and I'll drive you home."

Dreamily, she inhaled the rich autumn fragrances of drying leaves and wood smoke as if they were perfume, her mind free for the moment of all thoughts of the past. "Maybe I'll still be in the mood for a walk. I don't think uptown is all that far from my sister's house."

"Is it near the Stocktons' place?"

"On the same block."

He seemed pleased. "Then let's play things by ear. After such a late supper, I'll probably want another stroll myself."

When they reached Nassau Street, which was fairly deserted on a Monday night, he began pointing out landmarks along the way, saying that Scott Fitzgerald, who had been a student at the university, had made mention of several locations in his writings.

In the restaurant, over hamburgers, french fries, and coffee, Janet questioned him for her article, learning he was thirty-one and a New Jersey native. His courses in several state colleges had eventually added up to his degree in physical science, and his present job was with a construction firm that specialized in energy-conserving architecture.

"And, as of six years ago, I'm single," he added meaningfully.

She pretended to study her notes. "Did I ask that?"

"No. But having told you gives me the right to ask the question back." He looked at her left hand. "I don't see a ring."

She didn't know how she felt about the conversation becoming more personal, but after a moment of silent debate, she answered, "There was one, but that's all over now except for signing the final papers."

"Then it's all happened a lot more recently than mine."

"Not so recently in a sense," she explained, finding herself responding honestly and in more detail than she had planned, although not about Becky—she couldn't talk about that. "The marriage was a mistake from the start. It was the kind of situation where we were both at fault." She was thinking that Clay had never deceived her. She had wanted to see someone other than the actual man and maybe her idealistic blindness had been unfair to them both.

"A lot of times, the fault is simply being too young," mused Ben, combing his fingers through his hair. The red-brown waves had a crisp look, but Janet suspected they would feel soft. His tone was reflective. "I had known my girl all through high school and our wedding was the week after graduation. We should have waited. Two years into college, we both knew we wanted different things out of life. Still, we tried to make a go of it. Thank God, at least we didn't start a family in the hope it would be a cure."

Color leaped into Janet's cheeks. A family. Becky. And there had been no cure, only additional pain. Hiding her flush, she turned to put her notes into her purse. When she dared look up again, her voice held forced brightness. "If we're going to walk, we'd better get started. I don't want my sister to worry."

Outside, they found the waning moonlight filtering through a haze of clouds. Although the sky glowed, only a pale reflection was cast downward, painting halos around the street lamps and playing tricks with the shadows.

Ben tucked his hand into the crook of her arm as they crossed the first street and she made no protest when he left it there as they continued on. She told herself she could hardly feel it through her jacket and that if she had worn her heavy winter coat, she probably wouldn't even know it was there.

They fell into a mutual silence, the only sound that of their feet crunching through the leaves. Janet was thinking that in one way, Ben's willingness to exchange confidences had been satisfying, yet in another, it disquieted her. Perhaps what was most troubling was her willingness to respond in kind. He was a person she felt she could become attracted to very easily, but was she ready to even think of a new relationship?

When reaching Fran's block, he turned one street too soon.

"We live one more down," she corrected. "On Quince Street."

"That's just the other side of this block, right?"

"Yes."

"Then we'll go around the long way." She could tell he was smiling. "I like the idea of prolonging the evening."

When they resumed walking, he slipped his hand down along her sleeve and found her hand. His fingers laced with hers in a manner that was companionable rather than threatening. After a second she allowed herself to relax, enjoying his warm, firm touch, appreciating the way he modified his long stride to keep in step with her.

They were almost past the yellow Queen Anne before she realized it. Her steps lagged.

The house was set farther from the street than its companions, allowing room for a half-circle drive in front, where the Renner's black Oldsmobile sat like a dark animal, hunched and waiting. Alongside the house, another driveway allowed access to the rear. The downstairs was in darkness, but an upstairs light wafted like a mist through gauze draperies in the turret room.

"Janet?" Ben questioned, but she was lost in thought, remembering that spring afternoon when she had stood with Clay before the house, Becky clasped snugly in her arms.

Back then, the windows had been curtainless, but instead of lending the empty structure a look of abandonment, the unadorned spaces had offered an eager, expectant air, as if in welcoming anticipation of whoever might move in. Lured by an unspoken fascination, she and Clay had been drawn down the driveway and into the back garden. A wonderful sensation of peace had flowed over her that long-ago afternoon. Standing with tulips, daffodils and azaleas at her feet, time seemed to cease. She remembered thinking, *This is perfect. Perfect*. Hugging Becky close, the crown of her downy head soft and sweet against her breast, she had wished with all her heart that she and Clay could buy the yellow house.

Instead, they had moved far away to a location where all their hopes had ended in disaster, and other people now called the yellow house their home.

Ben spoke her name again. Coming back into herself, Janet shook her head and started to move on. But then, abruptly, she paused again.

"Listen," she said quietly. "Did you hear that?"

"Hear what? No. Oh . . ."

"You heard it?"

"No. But I thought I saw something. A squirrel maybe. Only squirrels aren't out at night, are they? Anyway, there was some small animal moving through the shrubs along the drive. A rustling in the bushes—that's what you must have heard."

She shook her head. "No, it wasn't anything like that. There. There it is again. Listen."

Her body stiffened as the sounds of a child's whimpering clearly reached her ears. The soft cries of distress seemed to come from behind the house.

Ignoring Ben's sharp whisper for her to stop, Janet hurried down the darkened driveway.

9

Scarcely aware of Ben at her heels, Janet moved along the drive, past the house and into the garden. There, the spreading branches of the beech cast deep shadows over the leafy, damp grass. Other sources of light were cut off by the privet and evergreens bordering the property, leaving the entire area in relative darkness. The smell of leaf mold lay heavy in the moist air. Suddenly uncertain, she paused, turning her head from side to side, listening.

"Janet!" Ben whispered urgently, catching up with her. "What are we doing? We're in somebody's back yard!"

She didn't answer.

"Janet!" Ben whispered again.

"Shhh!" she hissed, silencing him. Once again, the whimpering reached her ears. It seemed quite near. She turned toward the sound, then caught her breath in surprise.

There in the far corner of the garden, flanked by a growth of dark bushes, was the child, a little boy who looked about four years old.

Janet blinked, hardly able to believe the way he was dressed for an October night, naked except for a pair of white, drawstring drawers. And he looked unhealthy, his body painfully thin, his belly bloated. Apparently unaware of being observed, he continued to weep softly. He was angled so that she couldn't see his face. A certain awkwardness of his stance convinced her he had injured one of his legs.

"Come on, let's go," Ben said, his tone low, but imperative. "We can't go prowling around somebody's property without good reason." His voice, hushed as it was, was enough to start a dog in the next yard yipping. A dog with a louder, baying bark joined in. Ben grabbed Janet's arm. "Let's clear out, and now!"

"But, Ben, that child—" Her eyes returned to the little boy. He was gone. Remembering the ease with which Gina had disappeared through the hedge, she pulled free and was about to cross the yard when lights in the second floor of the house went on, laying bright, rectangular slabs across the grass.

"Now we've done it!" Ben snatched Janet's arm again, and this time she went willingly as he hauled her toward the row of pines which ran along one side of the Renner property.

Feeling through the branches, he muttered in relief at

finding there was no fence. He turned against the trees, clasped Janet to his chest, and plowed his way backward, his arms and broad back protecting her from the stabbing pine needles. Gasping, they emerged safely on the other side. Still in the circle of Ben's embrace, Janet was quiet a moment, catching her breath. Then, becoming aware of the warm, male strength of his body against hers, she tried to move away.

He resisted for a second, whispering into her ear, "Does it go into the newsletter that I'm also quick, resourceful, and brave?"

"A regular knight in shining armor," she whispered back and was relieved when his grip relaxed. It had been a long time since she had stood enfolded in a man's arms and it unnerved her. The moonlight was brighter on that side of the trees and she hoped he couldn't see that she was flustered. She moved to peer back through the branches. As she watched, the lights in the Renner house went off.

"Guess they figured there was no cause for alarm after all," Ben said, looking over her shoulder. "What were you chasing in there?"

Janet turned with surprise. "Didn't you see that little boy?"

"I didn't see anyone."

"Well, he was there, only he must have slipped through the hedge to the adjoining yard. The way he was crying, I'm sure he was in some kind of trouble. I think his leg was injured. We shouldn't leave until we learn what's going on."

"You mean he went through where those dogs are?"

"Yes."

"Then he belongs over there. Listen—the dogs have almost stopped. If a stranger trespassed, they would be raising more of a ruckus, not less."

Although Janet saw the logic of Ben's reasoning, she wasn't ready to abandon her argument. "That still doesn't explain why a child would be out so late, hurt and crying. And he was dressed only in some kind of underwear!"

Hearing her distress, Ben slipped a comforting arm about her. "He probably went outside for some adventure and got scared. I remember getting scared my first night out in a back-yard tent. Little kids are like that." He gave her a reassuring squeeze. "Hear how those dogs have calmed down? The boy is probably back safe in his room by now. Let's get you home. Where's your sister's place?"

"We're already in her back yard." Distracted by the pressure of his arm, she pointed, using the movement to draw away from him. "It's that house there." Still distracted, she gave one last reluctant glance over her shoulder, then directed Ben across the garden and around to the front entrance to Fran's house.

"So, you're Janet's mystery man!" Fran exclaimed upon seeing Ben at her door. Shaking her blond head, she stepped back so they could come inside. "Here's my little sister, new in town, but saying she had run into a friend." Fran's laugh showed her frustration. "I couldn't figure it out."

Janet smiled as Fran pretended dismay when Ben said he couldn't stay for coffee. She knew darned well her nosy sister couldn't wait for him to leave so she could learn everything that had happened at the adult school.

"You must come back another time," Fran told him at the door. Then she asked, "By the way, did you two come through the back yard? I was in the kitchen and I thought I heard voices."

"We cut through the block," Ben answered. "Janet thought there might have been a child in one of the yards—hurt or something. She heard crying sounds. But I guess it was nothing to worry about."

At his words, Fran flashed Janet a quick, anxious glance, then told Ben, "I'll walk you to the gate." She edged him out the door before Janet could react.

With a sinking heart, Janet knew Fran had misread the situation, linking the crying child with the episode of the crying baby. Now, she was taking Ben out to quiz him, never stopping to realize she'd end up convincing him the woman he had walked home was a mental case.

Standing frozen at the door, she watched their progress down the walk. Her worst fears were realized when Ben abruptly veered off and vacated the property at a fast clip.

"Thanks a bundle, Sis," she said bitterly as Fran came back inside. Vivid in her mind was Ben's touch, that brief moment in his arms when it had seemed he hadn't wanted to let her go. To be held, comforted, protected—to be *wanted*. She hadn't realized how much she had missed that part of life. Now it was over between them before it had begun.

"Oh, Janet ..." Fran's tone of apology changed to defensiveness. "All right, yes, I told Ben about the other night—about you thinking you heard the sounds of crying then too. But I also told him about your own baby and I know he understood."

"Lovely." Turning, she walked stiffly into the living room. "It's a good thing I already completed our newsletter interview. After your private chat, Mr. Benjamin Yates will be keeping his distance."

"Jan, he's not that kind of man, I'm sure of it." Catching up, Fran tried to take Janet's hand. "Come on, let's sit down and talk."

Janet pulled away. "Talk about what, my wild imagination? The fact that you think I belong in a looney bin?"

The sisters were still squabbling when the doorbell interrupted. Janet, who remained in the living room as Fran answered, heard her exclaim Ben's name, then say, "A cat? Ben, why are you carrying that cat?" Hardly daring to believe that he had returned, Janet hurried to the hall and saw him standing with Gina's tan cat in his arms.

Seeing her, he grinned broadly. "Mystery solved! While I was talking with your sister, I caught sight of this cat on the prowl. Remember when I spied movement in the bushes at that other house? All of a sudden, I remembered my mother's Siamese cat. Everyone always said it made sounds like a crying baby. I put that together with something your sister said, and well—"

As if in response to Ben's words, the animal, wanting to get down, uttered a surprisingly human-sounding miaou of complaint. Understanding at last, Fran cried, "Oh, Janet! All along, what you mistook for a baby, was only the Stocktons' cat, Pagoda." Her express was relieved, but contrite. "Honey, I owe you such an apology. To think our fussing was caused by a cat!"

Taking the cat from Ben, she placed it on the stoop. The creature immediately tried to dash back inside the house. "No more of your sneaky cat tricks," Fran ordered with a laugh, turning the animal around. "You're a naughty girl, Pagoda—go home!" She stamped her foot. With a wail that did indeed sound infantlike, the cat darted off. Fran looked gratefully at Ben. "I don't know how to thank you. Things are so simple once they're straightened out. Would you believe that my sister and I were actually having words over this?"

"Glad I could help," Ben said, looking pleased with himself.

This time when he left, it was Janet who saw him to the gate, where he promised with a smile, "I'll call you." With his promise warming her heart to a surprising degree, she went back inside, where Fran apologized again. "Janet, I'm so sorry. To think I doubted you without ever considering another possible explanation. I'm ashamed of myself. Will you forgive me?"

The warm glow Janet had felt with Ben faded. So, everything was explained, was it? She swallowed painfully. She knew she and Gina hadn't mistaken a mewing cat for a crying child. Besides, how could Fran so blithely forget the discussion of whether or not Gina could speak? But why stir things up? She hated arguing, and if Fran was willing to believe the presence of the cat explained everything, so be it—for now, at least.

10

It rained all day Tuesday, a chilly, nasty drizzle that washed all autumn coloration from the scenery. Wearing a heavy sweater against a damp cold that persisted despite the central heating, Janet sat hunched over Warren's typewriter, endlessly reworking her "first night" piece, marveling that she had initially felt satisfied with such a miserable effort. She did two new teacher interviews over the telephone and wrote up rough drafts, but could make no progress with the notes gathered from her interview with Ben. His smile and the remembered warmth of his fingers entwined with hers kept getting in the way of the words she tried to place on paper.

That evening, Warren answered the telephone and told her that "a pal from the adult school" was on the line.

Heart skipping a beat, Janet hurried to the phone. The caller was Kirby Orchard, offering her a ride to the school on his next class night, that following Monday. Since his home was just down the street, it would be easy enough to pick her up. She told him his offer couldn't have been better timed. Monday evening was when she was to deliver her first newsletter for the director's approval.

She was disappointed, however, that the caller hadn't been Ben. Maybe he'd had second thoughts. A woman who had lost a child and who was in the process of a divorce might seem a bit much, even for a casual friendship. After all, he was a man in business, and an extremely attractive one. No doubt he had plenty of demands on his time—ones that didn't come equipped with possible complications.

Wednesday was another dreary, rainy day, but then at

noon, Ben called from a booth somewhere in western Pennsylvania where he was on a job. The connection was so filled with static that he said goodbye before his three minutes were up, but not before promising to call again when he reached home that weekend.

With lifted spirits, Janet finished lunch, then noticed that the rain was slackening. The prospect of returning to the still-unfinished newsletter suddenly seemed a lot more dismal than the weather. After checking the stew simmering in the Crock-Pot, she borrowed an umbrella and a pair of Fran's old boots and went out the back door. She told herself that the fresh air would inspire her creative energies.

Outside, the air smelled pleasantly earthy and the rain had become a foggy mist. She poked around in the remnants of Fran's vegetable garden, discovering a few small but perfect tomatoes. Leaving the umbrella staked by the tomatoes as a reminder to take them in, she meandered farther until finding herself by the pines where she and Ben had emerged Monday night.

Peering through the long-needled branches, she looked into the garden of the yellow house, remembering the little boy she had seen. She also remembered that the yard had been in darkness until the upstairs house lights had cast their rectangles across the lawn. How could she have seen the child so clearly?

She established where he had been standing—a secluded corner where hemlocks formed a background for a planting of azaleas. The foliage of the low shrubs was presently a dull burgundy, but she remembered that in springtime, the spot had been alive with shades of pink.

When she had asked Warren about the children living in the neighborhood, he had said Gina was the only youngster except for several teenagers. If he was right, then the little boy must be a visitor—and a poor relation at that, judging from his malnourished appearance.

Her mind was still occupied with thoughts of the boy when the door to the latticed porch opened.

Rose emerged, garbed in her customary funeral black.

Stiffly, she made her halting way down the steps and across a brick path to the wet, leaf-littered grass. Her expression was harried, and her shrunken lips moved as though she were muttering to herself.

With helpless sympathy, Janet watched through the bushes as the woman embarked on a slow circling of the yard, wringing her hands as she trudged. Like the grim shadow on a sundial, she doggedly shuffled through the carpet of wet leaves on the slight incline, laboriously tracing and then retracing her path. Janet realized that the poor soul was undoubtedly senile, but her repetitive actions made it look more as if she had been placed under an evil spell.

Janet was just about to withdraw from the scene when Rose's foot slipped and she went down on one knee. Janet held her breath and waited. Apparently uninjured, Rose attempted to rise to her feet, but her efforts were futile.

Realizing that the woman's arthritic knees were probably too weak to enable her to get up without assistance, Janet pushed through the pines, although the needles stabbed and the rain-laden branches released showers. Feeling as if she'd been wrestling wet porcupines, she burst through to the other side and paused to shake water from her hair. Despite the commotion of her arrival, Rose, intent on her own struggles, took no notice.

Janet went to her and knelt. Employing the same matter-of-fact tone she had used that previous Saturday on the street, she said, "These leaves are slippery, aren't they? Here, just sit down and rest a moment while I have a look at you."

Rose didn't protest as she was examined for possible sprains. Janet found no undue swelling. "Does anything hurt?" she asked, gently rotating the woman's black-stockinged ankles.

Instead of answering directly, Rose replied with the sensible complaint, "Wet—ground wet."

"Yes, and I imagine you feel soaked." Deciding there was no harm done, Janet reached for her hand. "Here, let me help you get up." Rose stared at Janet, then darted an anxious glance left and then right, as if fearing a reprimand from some invisible source. Looking at Janet again, she timidly extended her gnarled, blue-veined hands, the gesture as trusting as that of a child.

Touched by her defenselessness, Janet carefully lifted the woman to her feet. She felt far more frail than the bulky swaddling of her clothing had led her to expect.

"Are you all right now?" she asked. "If anything hurts, we should get help before you try to walk."

"Fine. Fine, everything fine," Rose asserted in a sing-song, holding on to Janet as she stepped in the direction of the latticed porch.

"Let's go around to the front," Janet said. "The back porch has too many steep steps."

"Sister," Rose said.

"You want to see your sister? Let's see if she's inside. We can ring the doorbell."

"Sister," Rose repeated.

"We'll find her," Janet assured, hoping that Muriel was indeed at home.

Rounding the side of the house, Janet was relieved to see the black Oldsmobile sitting in the front drive. Carefully, she assisted Rose up the wide, shallow steps to the porch.

Muriel answered the bell and recognized Janet at once.

"Oh, no! Was my sister out in the street again? Please, come in." Taking Rose's arm, she beckoned Janet into a spacious entry hall that contained a polished mahogany staircase. The hall, with its heavily paneled walls, was saved from utter darkness by the light coming from a wide, undraped window on the second-floor landing.

After hearing of the mishap, Muriel put Rose into a chair next to a telephone table and knelt to check for injuries much as Janet had already done. The nape of her neck showed not a wisp of upswept dark hair out of place. Diamond rings winked with the motion of her slim fingers.

"She seems fine," she said to Janet as she stood, "but the fall has no doubt shaken her." Her hands fluttered. "Miss Fairweather, I cannot thank you enough." Janet noticed she seemed more at ease on her home turf than she had that day on the street. "My husband and I were dressing to go to the store. It might have been another ten minutes before I discovered that Rose needed help." Shaking her head, she gave Rose a meaningful glance as she added firmly, "Rest assured that my sister will be well protected while we are away."

Rose uttered a choked cry. "Please, don't turn the key!" Her voice cracked with fright. "I will be good. Don't turn the key to my room."

"Hush!" Without raising her soft voice, Muriel's hissing admonishment was nevertheless sharp. "You know you cannot be trusted." Remembering her visitor, she flushed. "Forgive us, Miss Fairweather. There are times when my sister forgets her promises, and must be locked in. It is always for the shortest possible time and is not a punishment. Please understand."

"Yes, of course." Janet saw that Rose had resumed wringing her hands. It was obvious that she had a horror of being confined. Abruptly, Janet offered, "Mrs. Renner, if it would help, I'll stay with your sister while you're gone."

Muriel's gold-brown eyes looked hopeful, then she shook her head. "The imposition is too great."

"No, my afternoon is entirely free." Janet suspected her offer was based more on a desire to avoid the newsletter than any noble impulse, but staying to help suddenly seemed of vital importance.

Expression indecisive, Muriel frowned in the direction of her sister. As if presenting an answer to the dilemma, Rose pointed at Janet, asserting, "She gave me a flower." She revealed a sly, toothless grin. "A flower, but not a rose."

Janet was delighted by this pun, but the weary smile flitting across Muriel's face indicated that the jest was well-worn. "She does like you, that is true," she murmured to Janet, still undecided. "She has saved the flower you gave her—" Muriel broke off as sounds came from beyond the arch leading to the dining room. "That is Dr. Renner!" she whispered, standing stiffly at attention, as if expecting a member of royalty.

The overcast light falling through the upstairs window

gave the scene the murky, faded tones of an old photograph as an elderly man moved into the entry, his walk rapid and shuffling, like that of a wind-up toy. When he stopped and shakily grasped the back of Rose's chair for support, Janet half expected his feet to keep churning ineffectively even though he no longer moved forward.

In his late seventies, he wore a black suit that fitted his shoulders well, but his shirt collar gaped about his stringy neck. His white hair was wispy, and his skin, which had an unhealthy pallor, was stretched tightly over his gaunt features. He reminded Janet of pictures she had seen of an ancient Egyptian Pharaoh.

"This is our neighbor, Miss Fairweather," explained Muriel as Janet stepped up to greet him. "Twice now, she has extended kindness toward our Rose."

The doctor inclined his head to peer at Janet through the top of his round, frameless trifocals. "Ah, yes," he murmured. "I saw you from the car." His voice was stronger and more steady than Janet would have supposed. Releasing the chair, he reached to take her hand. She noticed that his fingernails, curved and yellowed, extended beyond his fingertips. He bowed over her hand in the Continental fashion. "I am Dr. Herman Renner."

Janet responded with her own name, thinking that the doctor's dry, leathery palm was like the skin of a lizard. Withdrawing, she said, "I believe you've already met my sister and brother-in-law—Fran and Warren Elwin?"

"So I have." Nodding, he again grasped the back of the chair. "At the welcoming party. A charming gathering of charming people."

"Miss Fairweather has offered to stay with Rose while we go out to get your medicine," said Muriel. "It is so kind of her." A certain wistful note suggested that while she would like to accept the proposition, she was resigned to her husband's immediate veto. Instead, he seemed to give the matter thought.

"Indeed?" he asked, lifting his brow.

Muriel explained about Rose's fall. "Although she doesn't

appear to have been injured, it seems unwise to take her out. But confining her is so upsetting, and since Miss Fairweather has offered..." Allowing her words to trail away, Muriel awaited her husband's decision.

He eyed Janet closely. "It would be no inconvenience?"

She shook her head. "As I explained to Mrs. Renner, I have the afternoon free. While you're out, maybe you'll want to run some other errands as well."

"Ah, this is extremely neighborly." His smile showed elongated, discolored teeth. "My wife and I appreciate this a good deal."

"Well, Miss Fairweather," breathed Muriel softly, surprise at her husband's approval evident, "let me show you around."

"Please, call me Janet," Janet asked, not wanting to explain that her name was really "Mrs." Fairweather, a correction which might lead to questions about the whereabouts of Mr. Fairweather and additional explanations.

After a hesitation, Muriel acquiesced. "Of course—Janet." The informality seemed to make her feel ill at ease.

She led the way through the dining room and into a study. A television screen showed a game show in progress, but the Cole Porter song in the air was from an FM stereo radio.

"Rose is usually most content sitting right here," Muriel said, indicating a rocking chair. "She likes the pictures on television—the program doesn't matter. She rocks for hours, watching pictures and listening to her music. We keep the television sound off unless there is a program we wish to watch."

Muriel glanced around as if hunting for something. "She also has a little battery radio that she sometimes likes to hold. I do not see it now, but she will know where to find it. It is tuned to the same station as the stereo." Muriel gave Janet a look that pleaded for understanding. "Rose's mind has become slow and simple, but she can be reasoned with. She will be satisfied to sit with her music, I am certain."

"We'll be fine," Janet assured, accompanying the woman back to the entry hall where Dr. Renner had pulled winter coats from the closet. Muriel helped him with his black alpaca, then slipped into a peach-colored cashmere that softened the austerity of her dark, classic beauty.

Pausing at the door to pull on white kid gloves, Muriel's face knit as she tried to think of anything else Janet should know. "If Rose wishes to go upstairs, insist on the rear stairs by the kitchen. A stair lift has been installed there for Dr. Renner's convenience. Rose dislikes the device, but after today's fall, it might be best for her to avoid climbing steps."

The couple left, Muriel leading her husband down from the porch and into the car. She took her place behind the wheel, giving Janet one last anxious look before shutting her door. As the big car eased away, Janet glimpsed the white-gloved hand lifting in brief farewell, fluttering like a trapped moth against the window's tinted glass.

11

Janet turned from the door and saw Rose edging furtively toward the dining room. Puzzled, she watched silently as the woman disappeared around the archway. After a moment, the black-swathed head reappeared, neck stretched like a turtle's. When Rose saw that she was observed, she grinned and ducked back. Janet realized that the old woman was playing a game. She could imagine Muriel being embarrassed and scolding the woman for such antics. It seemed best not to encourage the situation.

Rose peeked around several more times, but when Janet did nothing except stand and watch, she gave up and proceeded into the study. Janet followed. By the time she arrived, Rose was settling herself in her rocker.

A medley from *Oklahoma* poured from the stereo. Rose

began rocking. Taking a seat on the couch, Janet lifted a copy of the *Wall Street Journal* from the coffee table. She leafed through it, skimming an article on energy conservation that made her think of Ben.

Laying the paper aside, she studied the room. Except for a collection of old oil paintings and a rosewood secretary with glass-fronted bookshelves, the furnishings were nondescript. One painting was of killed game—a rabbit and a pheasant hanging over a table that held a bowl of fruit and a half-written letter. The others were landscapes, all in elaborate gilt frames.

She looked at Rose. Rocking busily, the old woman's attention was fixed on a soundless rerun of *My Favorite Martian*. The program gave way to advertisements. A rubberfaced waitress blotted spilled coffee and a pretty blonde put aside scuba gear long enough to serve her beaming family some canned soup. Rose rocked steadily, her attention on the silent screen never wavering. The rhythm of her chair didn't change as *Oklahoma*'s rousing overture slid into the lyrical "Oh, What a Beautiful Morning."

Janet got up to examine the paintings. One landscape included Gypsy dancers, but close up, the illusion of costumed figures was reduced to blobs and swirls. Hung beside it was a painting of a similar scene, only with that one, the closer Janet moved, the more fine details she saw. She wished she had a magnifying glass. The faces of the tiny figures even appeared to have eyelashes.

Moving on to look at the books, Janet saw that the volumes had tooled-leather jackets. But, instead of titles and authors being printed on their spines, there were numbers. A narrow, clothbound journal lay on a shelf. Janet figured the journal recorded the book titles, but when she tried to check, she discovered that the glass doors were locked.

Disappointed, she found her attention drifting back to the detailed painting. The expressions on the tiny faces were so perfect it was uncanny. It would be easy to believe the artist was a sorcerer who miniaturized his victims and trapped them forever. At least they looked happy, frozen behind the varnish with smiles on their faces, dancing for all eternity on shoes that would never wear thin.

She turned from the painting and saw there was no smile on Rose's face. "My music," she complained, gesturing as if cupping an object in her hands. "Upstairs. My music."

"Your battery radio?" asked Janet, remembering what Muriel had told her.

"My music," Rose repeated, her toothless lisp adding emphasis to a newly stubborn tone. She got up and Janet saw she was headed toward the main staircase.

"If your radio is upstairs, your sister said you must use the stair lift." Janet went after her and took her arm. "Show me the lift," she coaxed, trying to sound especially enthusiastic because Muriel had warned that Rose might be reluctant. "Is it like an elevator? I'd like to see it, but I don't know where to look."

Rose acted as if she wanted to refuse, but then, jaw set, she led Janet through the dining room and into the kitchen. Begrudgingly, she pointed out the steep staircase. Along one side of the ascent, a chair and footrest contraption were bolted to a metal track.

"Isn't this nice!" Janet raved. "So much easier than climbing steps. So very nice—it must be fun!"

In the face of such exaggerated approval, Rose folded her arms and glared. "Nice. You go."

The unexpectedness of the woman's sarcasm took Janet by surprise. "Do you hate it so much? All right. I'll get your radio, but I'll walk up, okay? Where will I find it?"

"Room, always my room."

"I don't know where that is," Janet explained patiently. "You'll have to tell me."

Rose's wrinkled face showed confusion at the prospect of giving directions. Then, her eyes glinted ingeniously. "By my flower."

Janet guessed Rose might mean the saved marigold. "Okay. You wait here and I'll try to find your radio." She started up, glad for an excuse to see more of the Renner house.

The stairway opened upon a dark, narrow hall that had two closed doors. Trying the doors in turn, Janet found first a den, then a bedroom that had been converted to storage. The hall ran to the landing at the head of the main staircase and the large window that she remembered viewing from the downstairs entry. The clouds had parted and beams of sunshine now struck through the glass. Reaching the bright area, she saw that more rooms led off from a long railed gallery which ran around the opening of the staircase.

The first room proved to be yet another storage area. Starting down the length of the railed passage, Janet wondered if she would ever come upon the sleeping quarters.

After going only a few steps, she paused to glance back over her shoulder. She wasn't sure what had caught her attention. It could have been either a sound or a glimpse of motion—she wasn't sure which. Perhaps a bird outside had brushed across the big window. She squinted against the light. Nothing was at the window now.

She turned and moved a few more steps, then stopped again, starting to feel uneasy. Was someone behind her? Her flesh prickled even though reason told her that if anyone was there, it had to be Rose.

Gripping the rail, she edged cautiously back to the dark hall, which was empty, then retraced her steps to the rear staircase. She peered down the steep, open well and emitted a sigh of relief; she had been steeled for the old woman's leaping out with a mad screech, black rags flying.

Shaking her head over her lurid imagination, she returned to the railed passage and followed it to a room at the front corner of the house.

"Bingo!" she murmured victoriously, spotting the small radio on a night table next to the single bed. Also on the table was a vase holding the wilting marigold. The wall behind it was brightly decorated with magazine cutouts of kittens and puppies. Janet was about to step inside for the radio when she realized that the turret room was just across the way. She decided to take a quick look.

She found herself on the threshold of the master bedroom. Here at last was the serene, welcoming atmosphere that seemed most fitting to the house.

The turret was a romantic hideaway, with sheer draperies, hanging plants, and a cream-white satin chaise. In the main portion of the room, a beautifully colored oil painting of a peacock, posed in a mythical Eden, hung above the white satin bed. The picture glowed with the richness of a museum piece. The lustrous draperies around the bed and the windows were patterned with fruited vines in the mellow tones of the painting. Across the blue-green carpet, a partly opened door led to a bath. Another door opened to the den she had seen at the head of the back stairs. With doors on either side, the den efficiently connected the master bedroom to the rear of the house.

After one last admiring look, Janet returned to Rose's room. Radio in hand, she stepped back into the corridor. It was then that she saw—definitely *saw* something move.

There! In the corner near the second storage room—just to the left of the big window. Something was there. But as she stared breathlessly into the sun-drenched spot, she saw nothing but the meeting of two plain walls.

She blinked in confusion. Had she left the storage-room door ajar, only to have it closed just now by some draft? But no, the movement hadn't been by the door. It had been in the corner.

Her pulse jumped. There, again! Only this time, the motion had come from the right of the window, as if something had momentarily darted out from the narrow corridor, then back again.

Another movement. *Closer*. Along the railed passage! The very instant Janet whipped her head around to see, it was gone. But something had definitely been there. But what could dart by so quickly, then disappear without a trace? At that moment she became aware of a faint rustling sound, like silk brushing against a screen. The hairs on her arms lifted. The sound was as soft as a breath, but with a different rhythm than breathing. Like a chilly, unworldly draft whispering along the corridor.

A sweaty, crawling sensation tingled along her nerves. Breathlessly she waited, ears stretched, eyes smarting from strain. She heard a car going by outside on the street. An ordinary, mundane purr of an engine, totally unrelated to the eerie sounds heard only a moment before. But what *had* she heard? Or seen for that matter? Surely there was nothing odd in the hall. Except, perhaps, her own peekaboo imagination, playing a game that Rose might enjoy...

Rose. Oh, my! Better get down to her at once.

Not admitting a certain relief that the quickest way downstairs meant avoiding the railed corridor, Janet hurried into the master bedroom and on through the den to the back hall. Not glancing back toward the gallery, she swiftly made her way down the steps.

Bursting into the kitchen, she found Rose at the table, a finger in her mouth. Eyes round and startled, the old woman's face was a portrait of guilt. A sugar bowl sat before her, spilled sugar all around. She snatched her wet finger from her mouth and tried to hide it. Then, cunningly, she took the offensive.

"Too long, too long," she scolded, as if Janet was to be blamed for whatever happened during her absence. "My music. I want my music."

More than a bit out of breath, Janet sank into a chair, relaxing now that she was downstairs again. The kitchen, with its white-painted cupboards, red formica counter tops, and contentedly humming refrigerator offered a soothing, practical atmosphere. Any fanciful moods in this room would be confined to an extra bay leaf in the stew or frosting twirls on a cake.

"My music," Rose repeated petulantly.

Still catching her breath, Janet pushed the radio across the table.

Rose poked the "on" switch with a finger. Grains of sugar still clung to the arthritis-swollen joint. She smiled blissfully as the strains of "Everything's Up to Date in Kansas City" filled the air.

12

It wasn't until after Janet accompanied Rose back to the study that she figured out what had unnerved her upstairs. The window showed that a brisk wind had sprung up, and as she watched, a lusty gust swirled handfuls of orange and blood-red leaves as high as the trees from which they had come. She remembered her thoughts about a bird flying across the upstairs window and suddenly, the answer appeared: what had seemed to be phantom movements in the corridor had been shadows cast by leaves blowing across the outside of the sunlit glass. A shadow here, a shadow there—gone before she could focus upon them. The sounds had been caused by leaves as well. Dry, windblown leaves rustling and fluttering against window screens in the gallery.

So, with all this explained, she reasoned she should go upstairs and prove her theory right; except that after she returned to the stairs and stood with a foot on the first step, she couldn't make herself do it.

She told herself that she shouldn't leave Rose alone again. Rose, with her two radios and a rerun of the *Rockford Files*. Rose, who didn't care that the radio station was broadcasting what must be a stuck tape because all the tunes from *Oklahoma* were playing a second time. Rose, who seemed absolutely, totally, one hundred percent content. Yet when left alone before, she had made a sugary mess of the kitchen table, hadn't she? Who knew what she might get into next?

But as Janet returned to the study she admitted to herself that her real reason for not going back upstairs was because, in retrospect, the atmosphere in the upper gallery seemed, well . . . *eerie*. Okay, so the sights and sounds she'd noticed had been caused by blowing leaves, but regardless, hadn't something been out of kilter up there? Hadn't there been an aura that was unwholesome? Then, mocking herself for being foolish, she listed what the aura of an old house—any old house—was really composed of: stale air, musty carpets, and beams riddled with wood rot silently decaying behind flaking plaster. Uncozy images indeed, but nothing more.

Despite this reasoning, uneasy doubt still itched at the back of her mind when the Renners returned, Dr. Renner coming in as Muriel paused behind him to shoo away the Stocktons' Siamese cat, which apparently mistook any opened door in the neighborhood as an invitation.

"Has Rose been a problem?" was Muriel's first anxious question when finally inside.

"She's in the study with her music," Janet answered. "She's been fine."

"I will let her know we are home." Muriel went directly to the study without putting down the bag she carried or slipping out of her coat. She returned a moment later, looking more relaxed.

"She seems quite content," she told her husband, placing the bag on the telephone table. She helped him off with his coat and hung it, then hung her own. To Janet, she said, "We were able to visit several different stores for things we needed and to take a little time. We appreciate your kindness."

"Yes, it was a help that you were here," Dr. Renner added as he shuffled mechanically toward the coat closet.

"I'm glad I could do it." Janet took her jacket from the hall chair and put it on, saying to Muriel, "Rose refused to use the stair lift, so I went upstairs to get the radio for her." With deliberate ambiguity, still scratching away at the thought that there might be something odd about the upstairs of the house, she tagged on, "She seemed afraid," thinking that if Muriel had ever noticed anything odd herself, the comment would provide an opening.

"Yes," Muriel agreed, missing the cue entirely, "she does dislike the lift."

So that was that, concluded Janet, amused at her disappointment. Imagine, hungering for tales of ghouls in the attic. She became aware of Dr. Renner's attention. He stood before the opened closet, hands stilled in the job of folding his silk neck scarf. Head tilted so he could see her properly through his trifocals, he studied her with fixed intensity. It was as if he were waiting for something untold to happen, something unpleasant; as if he were watching a dangling spider about to drop upon her head. Uncomfortable, she focused back on Muriel, who had continued to speak.

"For the past week," mused Muriel, "Rose has been restless in a way I have never seen before. Things are so . . . so difficult for her."

That evening at supper, Janet told Fran and Warren about being at the Renner house. Buttering a biscuit, she said, "I felt like a baby-sitter, like a teenager again." She was exaggerating, but still, she did feel more her usual self. It was good, she realized, to be caught up in this new interest.

"What's the inside of the place like now?" Fran asked. "If I remember correctly, the living room is huge."

"I never saw it," Janet answered, thinking it must have been behind the paneled door to the left of the entry. "We sat in the other side of the house. Except for a bookcase and some paintings that looked like valuable antiques, the decorations are nothing special—except for the master bedroom, that is. When I went upstairs to get something for Rose, I peeked in. Spectacular!"

Warren, who was ladling himself more stew, interrupted, his black-bearded face questioning: "Anybody want more of this while I'm at it?"

"I do." Fran passed him her bowl. "What was so special about the bedroom?"

Janet described it in glowing terms. "You know, only two of the bedrooms are in use. It's a big house for three people." She thought of Kirby Orchard's contention that similar types were drawn to certain houses. "Did older folks live there before?"

Fran shook her head. "The Fiorellos, who were there

before the Renners, were a young family. They had five kids, but one son was crippled with a muscular disease. He died not too long before they moved away."

Janet winced at the pain of their loss. "Still," she said, "it does seem like a house for a young family, doesn't it?" So much for Kirby's theory.

Warren asked Fran, "Wasn't there another couple with a grown-up bunch of kids in that house when we first came here? What were their names? Seems like they suffered some kind of tragedy too."

Fran opened a packet of Sweet'N Low and poured it into her coffee. "Several tragedies—a real run of bad luck. I met the woman—Mitchum, Mary Ann Mitchum. Her divorced sister had been killed in an accident and they took in her daughter. The niece lived with them a year or so, then she drowned on a school picnic. Very sad."

That night in bed, Janet kept remembering the neighborhood sorrows Fran and Warren had spoken of. Sternly, she told herself that dwelling on the misfortunes of strangers served no good purpose. Just as dwelling on the loss of Becky served no good purpose. She adjusted her pillow for what seemed like the hundredth time and lay staring into the darkness, trying to turn her mind to more innocuous thoughts.

The Renner master bedroom was certainly attractive. It put the appearance of that railed gallery to shame. Why, that had been as bare as old bones. Bones, rattling old bones—what spooky analogies! But then, the gallery *had* been spooky. Funny what imagination could do. It annoyed her to recall her lack of courage about going upstairs a second time. Her thoughts drifted. She turned over, wondering if she should rewrite the interviews she had finished that evening. Whatever, she had plenty of time before facing the director. She still hadn't written the interview with Ben. *Ben*. He said he would call before the weekend. But the weekend was still two days away.

Sighing, she rolled over again and at last felt herself starting to relax, sinking down, knowing she was slipping into a dream even as she felt her consciousness surrendering . . .

In her dream, the taxi stopped and she got out. The driver, who appeared to be Dr. Renner, called her attention to the fine architecture of the school. She felt it would be rude to tell him it looked like a plain concrete block, not nearly as nice as her own school had been. Inside, Muriel sat behind the director's desk. She told Janet that she was to work in the nursery instead of the office.

The nursery, which was lighted by a row of jack-o'-lanterns, was filled with the cribs of sleeping children. A door at the far end stood open to reveal the Renner back garden and the copper beech.

The person who had been caring for the class until Janet's arrival was Gina. She wore a nun's habit and kept a vow of silence because it had enabled her to use a special sign language that was most effective with the children.

The children may start crying, Gina told Janet, her hands moving in their special way.

Alone now, Janet was alarmed as the infants and small children in the cribs did begin to cry. The cries became shrill and panic-stricken. Nothing Janet did calmed them and she frantically prayed for their mothers to come. She knew something terrible would happen if the mothers didn't come to rescue their children.

The explosion was as unexpected as it was terrible. The force of it threw the jack-o'-lanterns into the air where they bounced like severed heads, flames darting out of their empty eyeholes, red-hot tongues bursting from their jagged mouths.

Fire! The nursery was on fire!

Janet awoke.

Or at least she thought she had.

Maybe she only dreamed she had awakened, because as she turned over and slid back into sleep, she could smell the stench of burning pumpkins and hear the roar of advancing flames as the children shrieked in horror.

Their mothers—where were their mothers?

Gina's hands moved urgently in Janet's mind. *Take the children to the beech tree*! came the order. *The beech tree. That's where the children will be saved.*

13

"I like that one," Ben said, pointing. "I was big on vampires as a kid." He showed his teeth in a leer and Janet laughed.

He had called her late on Friday, and now, on Saturday afternoon, the two of them strolled along Nassau Street, viewing the Halloween scenes that high school art class students had painted on the windows of stores and business establishments. In preparation for the weekend, the paintings had been completed and judged even though Halloween was still three days off. The project was an annual community effort that had been started years before to cut down on Mischief Night vandalism and had since become a tradition.

Janet studied the judge's card taped to the painting in question. "Somebody else agrees with your artistic taste—this won a third prize. Only it was probably the idea of a certain kind of victim and not the vampire which captured your adolescent imagination." The skillfully handled work showed a fanged, bat-winged monster floating through the bedroom window of a sleeping blonde who resembled Dolly Parton.

"Wrong, wrong, wrong," denied Ben. "The only thought on my mind was supernatural murder. The more gruesome, the better. Now, have a look at that one."

The next painted window showed insectlike creatures carrying cocoons to their spaceship. Protruding from the mummylike wrappings were human hands and feet.

"Yuck." Janet shook her head. "Was science fiction another one of your interests?"

"Was, is, and always shall be. Don't say you haven't been warned." Smiling down at her, he tucked her hand in his as they continued walking. Although the air was cold enough so their breath showed as frost, there was no wind and enough sunshine so that Janet felt comfortable wearing her coat open.

They viewed yet another painting of a bloody-fanged creature wearing a cape—this one presiding over a laboratory where modern guns and bombs were being created.

"It's well done, but more like a political cartoon," Janet complained. "Where's all the fun of Halloween?"

"Right this way, my lady." Ben tugged her hand. "I saw one earlier that has a theme I know you'll approve of."

"I bet." With a show of reluctance, she dug in her heels so he had to pull her along. "It's a werewolf, right? A werewolf with a laser gun?"

"No, this is old-fashioned Halloween. It's too bad it's not on the main street where traditionalists like you couldn't miss it."

He dragged her around the corner and into Palmer Square, where the historic Nassau Inn was located. Taking her past the famed bronze statue of the Princeton tiger, he led the way along Colonial-style storefronts to a brightly painted window.

"How's this?" he asked with a flourish.

The scene showed an old house on a hill, a graveyard, and the silhouette of a witch sailing across the face of a full moon. In the foreground, a huge black cat leaned against a pumpkin that had cutout eyes and a smiling mouth.

"Perfect, right?" he demanded. "No monsters, no X-rated gore, no threat of global or intergalactic war. Just old-timey stuff. Even a little ghost in a white sheet floating from behind a tombstone. As innocent as candy corn."

"Exactly my idea of Halloween," Janet agreed. "But look, it didn't even win an honorable mention. It's awfully well done. So what if it isn't so original? I would think..."

Her voice trailed off. After a moment of silence, Ben prompted, "You would think what?"

"Nothing really. The picture reminds me of something,

only I'm not sure what. Perhaps something to do with staying at the Renner house." Earlier, she had told Ben about "baby-sitting" for Rose.

"The cat maybe," he said helpfully. "Doesn't the cat in the picture look like the Siamese I found in the Renner yard?"

"Honestly, Ben! Where were your eyes? That Siamese wasn't black. It's a light tan."

"Oh?" He lowered his voice, teasing suggestively, "In the dark, don't all cats look alike?"

She shot him a glare of mock disgust, then returned her attention to the colorful window. "That pumpkin..." She stiffened. For an instant it seemed that the odor she had smelled at the Stocktons' party had wafted across her nostrils: burning pumpkins—the sickening-sweet stench of their scorching flesh. With a horrid, sinking sensation, she briefly relived the experience. Then the smell was gone and she remembered the jack-o'-lanterns in her dream.

"I've got it!" she cried, shrugging off the memory of the phantom scent of burning. "It was the Renners themselves that I dreamed about. About being with them in their garden or something—it was decorated for Halloween. Sort of a nightmare really."

"Oh, was I in it?" Ben repeated his Dracula face.

"I'm serious. You know how dreams are. Bits and pieces were all muddled together."

"If I don't remember a dream when I first wake up, it's probably gone forever."

"If that painted jack-o'-lantern hadn't jogged my mind, this one would have been gone too. Wish I could remember more. Not that it would make much sense. Seems like it was the kind of dream that didn't make sense even while it was going on."

Seeing that she was shivering, Ben admonished gently, "Better fasten that coat." He turned her around to face him and she stood with her hands at her sides, allowing him to draw the coat shut and loop the belt snug about her waist.

"Looks like you could do with a cup of coffee," he said. "Or, maybe hot chocolate."

"You sound like my sister. To her, hot chocolate is a cure-all, like chicken soup."

"She's probably right." He looked into her eyes. "There's a nice restaurant at the inn called the Greenhouse. We could go there, or we could go to my apartment instead." He paused, his expression questioning, saying more than his words. "It's only a few more blocks. You told me the other night that you missed my Arizona slides at the Stocktons because of a headache. I can fix us something hot to drink and show you the slides this afternoon."

A lock of his crisp-looking hair had fallen over his forehead and she found herself again wondering if it would feel soft to her touch. She felt a rush of physical yearning at the thought of being alone with him and her voice was suddenly unsteady. "Is this an invitation to see your etchings?"

Her coat collar was still open at the throat. He drew it closed and held his hands gently against her face. "I suppose it's just an invitation."

She liked very much the combination of self-confidence and honesty that she read in his warm, gray eyes. Gazing at him, her blood seemed to race with a quickening, breathless thrill, but then her eyes shied away from his. It was too soon: such a short time since the ending of her marriage, such a short time since Becky's death. She needed time to know him and to know herself as well. Too soon, too soon.... Words sung around her ears like the autumn wind, a Gypsy incantation that would keep her safe from future pain: don't ever again risk becoming a lover without first becoming a friend.

"Suppose we take a rain check for now," she told him softly, making the "for now" a new promise: not right now, but later—later when we know each other better... when the time is right.

He looked ready to argue, then didn't. "The Greenhouse it is." Swinging an arm about her waist, he led the way to the inn.

Over coffee, he explained with chagrin that he would be leaving for Pennsylvania the next day. A problem on his job had developed and he wouldn't return until the end of the coming week. "I've had to call everyone and cancel my second adult-school session." He grinned. "Hope you won't publish a newsletter article about my unreliability."

The lift of her brow emphasized the exotic tilt of her eyes as she teased, "Seems you're awfully concerned about what I'm going to write."

"Hey, I really wasn't, but now that you've said that, I am."

"To be honest, I've put nothing on paper yet."

"How about more research on the subject—over dinner tonight?"

"Oh, I can't. Fran planned one of her special meals." It was true enough but she was relieved for a ready excuse. Ben made her feel altogether too vulnerable. Extending their time together into the evening wasn't wise, she was sure of it.

"All right." His eyes were measuring, alert to possible evasion. She felt she juggled her defenses like Indian clubs and he was trying to slip them away from her, one by one, without causing a break in her rhythm. He asked, "How about lunch tomorrow?"

"I thought you were leaving for Pennsylvania."

"Not until the middle of the afternoon. I'll pick you up at noon. We can have lunch, then drive out for a look at my company's latest house. All energy efficient and on a terrific building site."

"Terrific, huh?" She was thinking it sounded safe enough.

"Yeah." His grin told her he was sure she was going to agree.

"Okay." She smiled back at him.

When they parted in Palmer Square he gently brushed her lower lip with a fingertip, a soft, butterfly stroke that left her flesh tingling. His voice was low, as soft as his caress. "See you tomorrow at noon."

Heading home, lips warmly remembering his touch, she

wondered, as she knew he had intended, what his kiss would have felt like instead. She suppressed the direction of her thoughts, reminding herself of the wisdom of taking things slowly—advice she wished she had followed during her first few months in college.

Back then, so abruptly, so marvelously free of Fran's constraint, she had eagerly flung herself into whatever experiences life had to offer. Almost at once, she met Clay, a devastatingly handsome honor student with an air of superiority that held her awe-struck.

When he led her back to his room after their first date she never questioned that giving him her virginity was anything but fated. Neither did she question his jealousy, his short temper, or his explanation that he had few friends because his intellectual gifts and serious interests were misunderstood by others, who only wanted to waste time on frivolous pursuits.

Janet's friends didn't like Clay, but they fervently approved of her taking a lover. After all, if a woman found a man attractive, why not? The only puzzle was why she'd waited until college. *Enjoy*, they had encouraged over Cokes and pizza. *Indulge*. These were modern times, not the almost forgotten age when a "good girl" believed she had to be in love before she could enjoy good sex. But Janet, a modern good girl, unwittingly believed that once she had found good sex, why then, she must have fallen in love! And sex with Clay had been very good indeed. Drugged by rapture, they went into marriage thinking they knew everything about each other, but the only thing they had known was the intensity of their physical relationship; an intensity that faded quickly once Clay entered the world beyond the classroom. There he discovered he was the sun, moon, and stars to no one except his widowed mother and Janet, who soon became the scapegoat for all his frustrations.

Had he not brutally cast her aside after Becky's death, Janet supposed she would have been with him yet, hopelessly trying to satisfy his impossible needs, still believing her failure to do so was all her fault. Time and distance had lent perspective, but her marriage had taught her to deeply distrust quick attraction. How ironic it was that if Ben had appealed to her less, she would have trusted him more—or perhaps, trusted herself more. She frowned, suddenly doubtful. Seeing him two days in a row might not be wise after all.

Deep in thought, she reached her sister's street, not seeing Gina playing on the Stockton lawn until the child, throwing aside a small bamboo rake, ran to her.

"Gina . . . hello!" Janet said, surprised and pleased to be greeted like an old friend. She was even more pleased when Gina shyly reached for her hand. Delighted, she tucked the small, sweaty hand into her own. "Have you been working, Gina? Raking leaves?"

Nodding proudly, the little girl brushed strands of dark hair from her face. Her cheeks were flushed and her eyes, a deep, melting brown, sparkled with life.

Hailing cheerfully, Veronica came from the house. "Janet, so great to see you again!" The curving ends of her hair, worn pageboy style that afternoon, partly concealed the substantial width of her jaw. "Your sister tells me you're now the editor of the adult-school newsletter. I planned to take the class in French cuisine. Every year I say that, then I get so busy with other things!"

Although Veronica was gushy, the ensuing conversation was down-to-earth. Janet remembered Fran saying she was always more bearable when her husband wasn't around. But then, noticing the way Gina clung to Janet's hand, Veronica scolded, "Sweetheart—don't hang on people! Think of how dusty and rumpled you are. Go inside and tell Mrs. Ousler to get you washed for dinner."

The child flashed Janet a smile and obediently ran off. Pagoda, who had been hiding under the shrubbery, raced her to the house and both cat and little girl disappeared inside together.

"I'm sorry," Veronica apologized, tone exasperated. "She just *hangs* on people."

"I certainly didn't mind." Sparks of annoyance crackled

over Janet as if Veronica's words had stroked her the wrong way.

Sensing the reprimand, Veronica defended, "She needs to touch to communicate, I know that. But not everyone understands." She gave Janet a sharp look. "You are aware of her handicap, aren't you?"

"My sister told me she can't talk," Janet answered shortly. She hoped Veronica would deny Fran's contention, but instead, she nodded.

"It's a result of shock. Tommy and I had thought—had even been told—that she would come out of it when she felt secure again, but we've had her for almost two years."

Janet's conviction that the child could at least whisper remained unshaken, but all she said was, "Well, it's obvious she has no trouble understanding things."

At last Veronica gave evidence of pride. "She's really a bright little girl. Her tutor says she's learning to read and write very well considering that she's had to learn a new language." The smile that had softened her features suddenly thinned and grew critical. "Still, there's no denying the handicap. And it will only become a greater problem as she grows older."

Problem for whom? Janet's thoughts were not kind. It sounded to her as if Veronica was mostly concerned about social impressions. She and Tommy had been promised that their daughter would someday be perfect, yet here the child was, making a nuisance of herself, "hanging" on people. Janet wished the couple could be made to see how precious Gina was—to understand what a treasure it was to have a child.

On impulse, she spoke up, hardly knowing what she was about to say until hearing herself. "How about letting Gina spend tomorrow afternoon with Ben Yates and me?"

Veronica looked startled to think anyone might deliberately seek Gina's company. "You mean take her someplace?"

Janet struggled to hide her irritation. "Just for a few hours—a bit of an outing."

"Well, I suppose . . . if you're willing." Veronica still

sounded nonplused. "This is very nice of you. What time should I have her ready?"

"About noon." Janet outlined a sketchy plan. "For lunch, then a Sunday drive. As I said, only a few hours."

The women talked a few more minutes, then parted. Continuing on home, Janet realized she should have okayed things with Ben first. Well, it was too late now. She squared her shoulders. Veronica and Tommy had to be shown that Gina was not an embarrassment, and if Ben refused to go along with her impulsiveness, she would stay home and find a way to entertain the little girl herself.

When she reached Ben by phone later that evening and explained about her invitation to Gina, he was silent a moment, then, "Sure. Why not? Sounds great."

Relieved, Janet blurted, "You're not annoyed, are you?"

He chuckled. "Maybe I'm even flattered."

She was puzzled. "Why?"

"To think you feel you need a chaperone."

"Oh." She supposed he had a point. Although she hadn't consciously reasoned it out, inviting Gina along had relieved her mind on two counts. And seeing it, Ben had understood. When she replaced the receiver, she was smiling. Without a doubt, Ben Yates was a very nice man.

14

Janet took her place in the passenger seat of Ben's Subaru, while Gina, dressed in a pink hooded sweatshirt and candy-striped corduroy slacks, settled in the rear as if she belonged there, not casting as much as a glance back toward her house as the car left her street.

"She's a cute kid," Ben observed. "A friend of mine,

Edgar Lightfoot, works for the church agency that helped place her with the Stocktons. He told me she was a charmer." He shot Janet a grin. "I'll have to introduce you to Edgar sometime. I owe him my thanks. It's because of him that you and I met."

"How so?"

"He once invited me and the Stocktons to the same party and we started discussing ecology. It led to Tommy and Veronica asking me to give that talk at their house"—his smile became meaningful—"which I now think of as my lucky night."

"Oh." The personal note caught her off guard. Looking into the back seat at Gina, she found herself trying to shift the emphasis by including the little girl. "I guess I have to thank Edgar too. Gina and I are really looking forward to this afternoon."

Ben's eyes twinkled. "And do you and Gina have any idea where you'd like to have lunch?"

Janet was amused. He was a sharp one, all right. She would have to watch her step. "I haven't been here long enough to know the local restaurants," she said. Then, surprisingly, the thought of the perfect spot popped into her mind. "Wait—if we keep on this road a few miles, we'll come to a place Gina really likes."

"Sounds good," Ben agreed cheerfully.

Janet found herself frowning. How had she known about the restaurant? She decided that Veronica must have mentioned it the previous day. Turning in her seat, she met Gina's sparkling eyes.

"Oh, you heard us?" she teased. "Heard we're going to stop at your favorite eating place? Bet you already know what you want. Either a hot dog or a hamburger, right?"

Wearing a tucked-in, mischievous smile, Gina gave her head a negative shake.

"Oh, am I to guess? Let's see..." Thinking of what a child might enjoy, she suddenly visualized Gina sitting before a plate of chicken fingers. She could imagine her lifting a succulent morsel of the crisply fried chicken as clearly as if it were happening before her eyes. She was positive she was right, but to come out with the answer so quickly would ruin the game.

"I know," she said, deliberately making another choice. "A tuna sandwich. With pickles. Right?"

Vigorously, Gina shook her head *no*.

"Ummm. Spaghetti? Spaghetti with meat balls?"

Gina's brown eyes danced as she again shook her head.

"This must be the place," Ben announced, pulling into the parking lot of a log-cabin-style restaurant.

"Looks nice." Janet was thinking that any place Veronica and Tommy frequented was bound to come up to a certain standard. She got out and had Gina's door open by the time Ben had circled the car.

Bending, he called inside, "Gina, if it's lobster you want, tell me now. I can't take shocks to my wallet without warning."

The little girl covered her mouth with her hands and shook her head in gleeful denial.

Pleased over Ben's easy manner with the child, Janet figured the game had gone on long enough. "I've got it! You want chicken fingers, don't you? Chicken fingers are your very favorite. Am I right?"

Gina's delighted expression showed that Janet had hit the correct answer. She scrambled out of the car and into Janet's arms, giving her an exuberant hug.

An hour later, having finished lunch, the three arrived at the hillside where the construction site was located. The house was still at the framework stage. Seeing Gina's disinterested expression, Janet gave the child permission to go exploring. "But don't go any farther than that wall," she cautioned, indicating a tumbledown fieldstone wall bordered with thickets of milkweed and scarlet sumac along the property line.

Enthusiastically, Ben ushered Janet into the unfinished structure to give a grand, guided tour, his booted feet thumping across the boards with a confident familiarity that testified to his deep involvement.

It became immediately obvious that he was showing off his dream house. If he didn't plan to make it his someday, he at least looked forward to having something exactly like it in the future.

Standing in what would be the master bedroom, he waved a hand in the direction of rolling countryside. "See what I mean about this view? Imagine starting the day off like this! Who wouldn't wake up feeling wonderful?" Moving on, he pointed through an open wall to a private patio, and announced the future location of the hot tub. "Energy saving, of course," he amended.

"Come on," she joked. "A hot tub? After the way you criticized conspicuous consumption? You're just trying to justify sybaritic splendor."

"Not really. In winter, circulating water will be heated by the wood stove, which would be burning anyway. In summer, the sun's rays will do the job. Marvelously efficient. Besides, with no swimming pool planned, the tub isn't such an extravagance."

"Uh-huh."

He chuckled. "Hard to persuade, aren't you? Maybe you'll find the solar room more convincing. It opens off a fantastic kitchen. At the risk of sounding like a brochure, it really will lop dollars from the winter heating bill, yet keep cool all summer."

After they finished touring the house, Janet made sure that Gina was still harmlessly playing, then rejoined Ben, who sat on the sun-warmed deck, his long legs stretched out comfortably. A tilted sheet of plywood provided protection from occasional gusts of wind.

He smiled up at her, the slant of the sun casting intriguing shadows on the strong, irregular lines of his face, the muscular width of his throat made more evident by the open collar of his shirt.

Looking at him, she suddenly reviewed the implied intimacy of going to see a house under construction, that traditional sign of the nesting impulse. A stunning sense of longing flooded through her and she averted her eyes, fearing her thoughts must lie naked in them. Shaken, she realized she had been looking at him as if he might supply the answers for what was missing in her life. It frightened her. Her marriage had certainly taught the error of such thinking.

He beckoned. "Come on and sit down."

She did his bidding, but kept a distance between them, sitting with her arms wrapped about her drawn up knees. An awkward silence fell. The afternoon was shaping up to be a mistake, she decided morosely. It was exactly as she had feared. He was putting out all the signals of a man ready to get involved, but despite their mutual attraction, the timing was wrong. She was too burdened by emotional baggage from the past to do anything except move very slowly, and it wasn't fair to expect him to understand.

The silence suddenly seemed unbearable. Casting for something neutral to say, she asked in a strained voice, "So then, is . . . is this the type of housing project you're working on in Pennsylvania?"

He groaned. "Don't I wish."

When he volunteered nothing more, she couldn't help being curious. "Well, what is it that you're doing then?"

"Installing solar panels in an already inhabited condominium." He made it sound like hard labor with only bread and water.

She didn't know why he was being so cryptic. "What's so awful about that?"

"You wouldn't want to know."

"Why not? What are you talking about?" She was annoyed.

He grinned. "That's better, yell at me. I'm not so fierce. For a moment there, I thought you were afraid I would bite."

"I thought no such thing," she defended, her cheeks coloring as she realized he had deliberately led her on. "You're being ridiculous."

"See? Call me ridiculous, but do I get mad?"

She found herself laughing. "I'm going to call you worse

if you don't explain." She realized she felt more at ease and knew that's what he had been aiming for. Charm plus a knowledge of psychology—a dangerous man indeed. But in such a nice way. "Come on, what's so dreadful about the condo job?"

"It isn't so awful," he admitted, smiling. "It's just that a certain amount of labor has to be done from inside the homes. Trying to work around the homeowners' schedules has caused more holdups than I care to think about."

"And tomorrow will be more of the same?"

"Afraid so. But by Thursday, the crew should be able to finish up alone and I'll be free." Shifting position, he rested on an elbow as he gazed at her, his expression open and warm. Janet felt she had never known anyone else with eyes exactly his shade of gray, so clear, with such depth. He said, "Since I'll be home in time for the weekend, I was wondering if—"

Whatever he had intended to say was interrupted as Gina rushed up, bringing a fistful of pebbles.

"Oh, how pretty!" exclaimed Janet, glad for the distraction as the child spread the stones on the wooden surface of the deck. It was obvious that Ben wanted to make plans for the coming weekend and she didn't know how she wanted to respond. She reached for one of the stones. "Look, Gina, a piece of quartz. See how clear it is? Look, when you hold it to the sun, you can see rainbows in the light." As the little girl squinted through the cluster of crystals, Janet noticed Ben watching her. It made her feel as transparent as the quartz. She quickly picked up another stone. "Look, honey, see these sparkling glints? This is mica. Isn't it pretty?"

When the child scampered off to find more stones, Ben observed, "You're good with kids. Come from a big family?"

"No, just me and my sister." She was relieved he had tabled the subject of the weekend. Her thoughts went to his question. Because of the newsletter interview, she knew something about his family: his parents, who had lived near Cranbury, New Jersey until retirement in North Carolina; his sister, presently in Germany with her husband, a career

Army man. The interview had gotten the information more or less flowing in a one-way direction.

"There were some aunts and uncles on my father's side," she explained. "All much older than Dad. We never kept in touch." Lightly, she discussed her growing-up years, emphasizing the good parts, skimming over the bad, taking pleasure in Ben's appreciative responses when she related some of the funny things that had happened.

There was a silence, then he hesitantly ventured, "Tell me, what happened when your—"

She winced and turned her head, feeling all her contentment of the last few minutes drain. She didn't need a crystal ball to know he had intended his sentence to end: *when your baby died*.

"Janet..." He reached for her hand. She tried to pull away, but gently, firmly, he refused to let her go. "Janet," he ordered softly. "Janet—look at me."

Reluctantly, she did as he asked.

His smile was gentle. "It's okay," he whispered. "It's all right, really it is."

He relaxed his hold so that she could have moved her hand away had she wanted to, but it suddenly no longer seemed necessary. She gazed at him, his words echoing in her mind: *It's okay. It's all right*. Simple phrases that could be virtually meaningless, yet when combined with the way he had spoken them and the tenderness in his eyes, they had told her all she needed to know about his patience and understanding. A sweet confusion of emotions rushed through her—she wanted to sing, yet at the same time, she felt close to tears. There had been no need to feel apprehensive about their afternoon together, she realized that now.

Smile tremulous, she said, "About next weekend—"

"Hey—" He grinned. "Lady, are you trying to maneuver a date?"

She laughed. "Something like that."

"Ummm. Sounds good to me. I like aggressive women." His voice was teasing. "Any ideas of what to do?"

She shook her head.

"Okay, tell you what," he said, giving her hand a squeeze. "Starting Monday, I'll call you every night next week. By Thursday, we should have figured out something. How's that sound?"

She laughed again. "It sounds fine."

"Okay, then, it's a promise." Standing, he pulled her to her feet. "As much as I hate to say it, it's almost time to go. But there's one more thing I want you to see." His arm slipped easily about her waist. "There's a perfect spot for a gazebo, a view that can't be seen from inside the house. An extra dividend to the site."

Feeling more free with him than she would have thought was possible, they had started walking when she abruptly stopped. "Wait a second. I'll be with you in a moment, but Gina wants me."

Leaving Ben, she headed toward the property line, picking her way around fallen stones that would be gathered and reassembled when the landscaping was begun. Nearing the wall, she frowned, unable to find the little girl. Then, the pink-garbed figure jumped into view from the other side.

"What did you find?" Janet called.

Gina held up a pebble pinched between her fingers.

"Let's have a look." Going closer, seeing the clarity of the stone, Janet feared she would have to tell Gina her discovery was only a weathered chip of glass. But upon close inspection, it indeed proved to be quartz, the color faintly tinted with rose. "Maybe you should save that, honey," Janet advised. "Someday in science class, you'll study various kinds of rocks. Your teacher will talk about this kind and you'll have your own sample all ready to show."

"What's up?" Ben asked, reaching them.

Gina happily displayed her treasure.

"Very nice," he approved. His voice was warm, yet to Janet's ears it also held an odd note, one she couldn't define. "Hate to call things short," he reminded her, "but as soon as we take a look at the gazebo view, we'll have to be on our way."

"All right." She turned to Gina. "If you want to keep any of the other stones, you had better get them now."

Puzzled, Ben looked after the little girl as she hurried off. His gaze shifted to Janet. "How did you know she wanted to show you something?"

Janet thought back. "She must have motioned. I guess I saw her out of the corner of my eye."

"But I was on the side closest to the wall and there was no sign of her." He frowned. "I don't know how you could have seen her at all."

15

Janet was finishing her lunch when she heard a siren close by.

Carrying her mug of tea, she went to the front door and looked out. The street was now silent, with no signs of a police car or ambulance. Whatever the emergency vehicle had been, it must have gone on by. The weather was a disappointment after the sunshine of the previous day. The afternoon lay chill and corpselike under a sky the color of lead. At least it was the right atmosphere for Mischief Night.

Returning to the kitchen table, Janet surveyed her folder of newsletter material with a jaundiced eye. Although she wouldn't need her interview with Ben for the first issue, she should have written it days ago. The better she got to know him, the harder it would be to prepare the informative, yet impersonal kind of article that was required.

With a secret smile, she remembered their afternoon together, then she shook her head. Get your mind back on the job at hand, she instructed herself firmly as she rinsed the lunch dishes. She would spend the rest of the afternoon writing that interview, even if she had to chain herself to the desk.

As if the vow in itself was an accomplishment, she felt self-satisfaction as she carried a fresh mug of tea into Warren's office and sat before the typewriter. Three uninterrupted hours stretched before her. By the time she had to start dinner, the interview would be on paper.

The phone rang.

The high-pitched, strained voice on the line was Muriel's, her jumbled words filled with apologies for her "imposition" and the fear that she was "taking advantage." Janet finally understood she was being asked to come over.

"Yes, of course I can come, Mrs. Renner," she said. Then, putting the siren she had heard earlier together with Muriel's agitation, she asked worriedly, "Has something happened to your sister?"

"No, I need someone to stay with her. Dr. Renner has suffered a possible heart attack. I must go to the hospital with him. I need someone to be with Rose."

"I'll be there in a flash." Janet hung up the phone, snatched her folder from the desk and ran for her jacket.

By the time she reached the front entrance of the Renner house, the stretcher carrying the doctor was being placed in the ambulance. The Oldsmobile sat ready in the drive, engine running. Muriel, wearing her peach-colored coat, met Janet on the porch.

"Forgive me, but I did not know who else to call upon." She pressed Janet's hands. Her complexion was pale, with a chalky undertone. "Dr. Renner's condition may not be terribly serious, but with his medical history, we could not afford risks. Please, there is no way to know how long I will be at the hospital." Eyes fearful, she glanced at the ambulance. The men were closing the rear doors. She gave Janet an imploring look. "I am imposing, I know."

"Don't worry, I'm glad to help. Now, go on to the hospital and don't worry about your sister."

"Yes, you are so good with her." Distracted, Muriel saw

that the ambulance was ready to leave. She seemed torn between the responsibility of her sister's welfare and attending to the care of her husband. "You will find Rose in the study. Fortunately, this is a day when she is interested in her picture collection. She—"

"If you want to go with the ambulance, you had better be on your way," Janet advised gently. "Don't worry about Rose—don't worry about anything here at home. Everything will be fine."

Janet watched from the porch as the ambulance pulled smoothly from the drive. As the Oldsmobile followed, Muriel cast a look back toward the house. Janet waved and smiled reassuringly.

Entering the house, she noticed that the paneled door to the left of the entry was open to the living room. Looking in, she saw canvas spread on the floor and two ladders. The air smelled of paint and paste. Janet conjectured that the Renners probably intended to decorate the entire house, room by room. When they were done, it would probably all look as magnificent as the master bedroom.

Casting a faintly wary glance up the staircase, she went through the dining room to the study, where Rose had magazines spread upon a card table. Her black head scarf was tied like a shawl across her shoulders and sagging bust. Working with blunt-tipped scissors, she was industriously cutting a kitten picture from an advertisement for cat food. When Muriel had said Rose was busy with a picture collection, Janet had mistakenly assumed she meant photographs. Perhaps snapshots from their home in Argentina.

The stereo played and the television was silently tuned to a soap opera, the screen showing a middle-aged blond actress with enormous blue eyes in bed with a man who looked like a teenager.

Rose looked up. Not questioning Janet's presence, she showed her gums broadly, her smile puffing up smooth apples in the wrinkles of her cheeks. "More for my room," she announced, indicating the picture, "more, always more."

"Yes, that's a nice one," Janet said, wondering if Muriel

had taken time to explain that she and her husband were going to the hospital. Maybe Rose didn't even realize that the man was ill. She decided to make a reference to it unless Rose brought up the subject herself.

The final clip of the scissors severed one of the kitten's paws. Unconcerned, Rose placed the cutout on top of several similar ones and lifted a fresh magazine from the pile.

Janet watched as the woman leafed through the pages, her gnarled, swollen hands surprisingly dexterous.

"More!" she crowed triumphantly, having come upon another ad for cat food. She reached for her scissors. It didn't seem to matter that the picture was identical to the one she had just clipped.

Curious, Janet asked, "Do you just like the pictures, or do you also like real cats?"

Rose cackled and spread her arms. "Open the doors and in comes the cat—surprise! Hide in cupboard, hide under bed—surprise!"

Janet could only gather that Pagoda had at one time successfully sneaked inside. "Oh, so then you had to chase it out again? Once, I saw you shoo a cat from your yard."

It didn't appear that Rose was about to continue the conversation, but then, in a tone that somehow managed to be sullen and sly at the same time, she muttered, "Doctor Herman be angry. If he goes, cat can come. Cat and little girl come all days."

"Little girl? You mean Gina?"

"Little girl, she won't talk."

Privately, Janet wondered, *won't* talk or *can't* talk? The distinction intrigued her, but what she said aloud to Rose was, "Why would Dr. Renner be angry? Doesn't he like cats?"

Rose cackled as if Janet had purposely made a joke. "Cats, he doesn't like. Children, he *hates*."

The turn of Rose's phrase seemed out of character. For a moment, it was as if a different person had spoken from her withered lips—perhaps the person she had been years before.

To that person, Janet said, "I don't understand. How could he feel that way? I thought he was a child psychologist."

Rose smirked and said senselessly, "He's retired. Retired." Then she added, "I say little girl—*go home*. Dr. Herman be angry. Now the whistle wagon rides him away. Little girl can come all days if Dr. Herman dead."

Janet realized that "whistle wagon" must be Rose's name for ambulance. The woman's blunt, matter-of-factness when discussing her brother-in-law's possible death was a shock.

"You shouldn't talk that way, Rose," she chided, realizing even as she spoke that Rose had detached herself from the conversation. Calmly, the old woman finished cutting the picture and added it to the others. The kitten's paws were intact, but the tip of an ear was cropped. Returning to the magazine, she resumed flipping through the pages. "Dog food," she muttered, as if she could command the magazine to produce the ad she desired.

Realizing that she still wore her jacket, Janet slipped it off and took a seat on the couch. On television, a chubby brunette puffed a cigarette and flirted across a restaurant table at a man. When he looked into the camera, he turned out to be the youth who had been in bed with the blonde. Janet opened her folder to the notes from her interview with Ben.

After about five minutes of trying to devise a lead for her article, Janet started thinking about the dinner she had intended to prepare for Fran and Warren that evening. There was no telling when Muriel would return. Perhaps she should phone Fran and suggest she bring home something already cooked from the Spoon.

There was a phone in the study, but it was next to a stereo speaker. The radio volume could be turned down, but there was no point in doing anything that might disturb Rose, who was contentedly clipping away.

"I'm going to use the phone in the hallway for a minute," she told the woman. Busy with the scissors, Rose gave no sign that she had heard.

In the hall, call completed, Janet started to return to the

study, then paused to look up the staircase. The polished mahogany leading to the top of the steps gleamed with a cold, austere formality in the sunless afternoon. The words *a beckoning chill* leaped from the dark casket of Janet's imagination: ominous remnants from childhood fright tales, ever lying in wait for weak moments.

Annoyed, she remembered her apprehension the last time she was in the house and decided it was time to put speculations to rest. It would only take a second to climb up and prove there was nothing odd about the upper hallway. She would do it now. Quickly, while Rose was safely occupied.

16

Halfway up the steps, she heard the sounds.

Soft, breathy rustlings.

The leaves, she reminded herself—leaves caught against the window screens, shifting gently in the wind.

She mounted another step. Peering through the banisters, she could see the smooth, polished wood of the second-floor corridor. A narrow Oriental-style rug ran down the center of the walkway. She remembered that the rug had been fringed on either end. Her gaze shifted to the large window on the end wall. On that overcast day, the light coming through the numerous panes had a hard-edged glare, as cold as the glow from an alien moon.

The sounds came again.

They held a certain distinctive cadence that she had forgotten. Her flesh tingled as hairs on her arms and the nape of her neck lifted.

What she was hearing didn't have the irregular randomness

of wind shuffling through trapped leaves. It was something different. Something with an eerie sort of rhythm.

Breath held, she strained to find a pattern to the soft sounds: Da-da-ta-ta-da-da. No, not quite right. The accent fell strongly on the fifth count: Da-da-ta-ta-DA-da? Yes, that was it.

Uneasy, yet curious, she tapped a finger on the railing like a metronome: Da-da-ta-ta-DA-da. She felt as if she accompanied a ritual chant. A chill slithered its way down her spine. There had to be a reasonable explanation for the sounds. The heating system must be creating vibrations. Yet, could steam and water coursing through ancient pipes produce so measured a tempo?

Cocking her head, she tried to be analytical. Imagination could transform even the mundane ticking of a bedroom clock into a message: tick-tock—wake up; tick-tock—get up. She tried to suppress the creative part of her mind. All she wanted was the bare skeleton of the sounds.

It suddenly occurred to her that she might be hearing something related to music from the stereo. Just as a distant marching band can sound all drums and no tune, whatever currently played downstairs might have base notes that were being carried through the house.

Listening intently, she became more and more certain she was right. She nodded to herself. Yes, some echo or trick of architecture made the sounds seem to issue from the second floor, but when she returned to the study, she would discover their origin. She would find that the song being played over the radio had bass notes matching the rhythm she'd heard. Probably a catchy kind of dance beat, probably something Latin.

But, by the time she returned to the study, a mellow love ballad, soaring with violin notes, had just begun. Disappointed, Janet leaned against the doorjamb, watching Rose thumb through yet another magazine. The woman gave no sign she was aware of anything outside her own narrow world. A program of children's cartoons had supplanted the soap opera. A redheaded giant in a gladiator's costume battled a flying dragon. Watching the colorful action on the screen without really seeing it, Janet impatiently waited for the next radio selection.

After another misty love song, a boisterous orchestral rendition of "Hello, Dolly" began. Janet's eyes sparkled. Vigorously tapping her foot, she counted out the energetic beat: *ONE, two, three, four; DA-ta-ta-ta*. Distinctive and easily identifiable.

Quickly, she left the room. Now, while the song had another minute or two to go, she would become a detective.

She reached the dining room arch and could still clearly follow the "Hello, Dolly" melody, but the moment she rounded the corner, the music cut off so abruptly that she stepped back to make sure the radio still played. It did.

Reassured, she began to ascend the steps.

Unconsciously, she sang the words, "Hello, Dolly! How are you, Dolly!" under her breath. Then, hearing herself, she stopped, feeling spooked. She had seen too many films in which a merry background tune gradually assumed ominous, minor notes, fraught with warning. She shook her head, annoyed with the sinister twist of her thoughts. Her goal was only a harmless investigation. She would go halfway up the steps and find that some auditory trick of the old house did indeed transmit the underlying beat of "Hello, Dolly." She would hear it and be satisfied. What could be more simple?

She reached the point where she could look through the banisters to the second-floor corridor. One hand on the railing, she stopped, listening intently.

There was only silence. Frowning, she caught her lower lip between her teeth. The sounds must have been from the heating system after all, and now, the furnace had switched off. Her theory about the radio had been wrong.

Then she heard it, and her heart caught in her throat.

That soft, breathy pulse. Not louder than before, yet somehow stronger. *Determined*. Da-da-ta-ta-DA-da! Da-da-ta-ta-DA-da! Nothing like the boisterous, lighthearted tempo of "Dolly." Nothing at all.

Janet clutched the railing, her fingers going white. Earlier, she had likened the sounds to chanting, then had dismissed the thought. But a chant was what the syllabic cadence most resembled. One composed of a multitude of small, soft voices in unison. Voices as soft as a whisper...

Whispering. Yes! Her blood froze. That's what she was hearing—whispers! A whispering chant, like the doxology of a phantom choir.

Fear crackled along her flesh like an electric current. Now that her mind grasped what she was hearing, the beginning words began to separate themselves, taking on meaning. "*We are—*" The rest dissolved into the incomprehensible: ... ta-ta-DA-da. "We are ta-ta-DA-da."

Suddenly, off to the left of the window she caught sight of a small, glimmering blur. She didn't know if the whisperings ceased in that instant, or if her senses were so transfixed by the glowing whirl of motion that everything else faded away.

The blur blossomed into a shapeless mist, then slowly coalesced, taking the form of a faintly illuminated pillar about two feet high. The pillar wavered, then began to drift toward the corner, away from the harsh daylight of the window. As it entered the shadows, details, like etchings upon glass, began to emerge from the misty vortex. Part of a face, a cascade of dark ringlets, the curve of an arm, a rounded stomach...

Janet stifled a cry. A small girl—a mere toddler—now stood in the corner of the hall. Her body, not fully materialized, seemed to be garbed in a shiftlike garment. And then, beside the girl—another glowing shape! Taller, congealing more rapidly.

With a fascination that was beyond fear, Janet watched spellbound as the second child came into view. Thin, and nearly naked, the belly swollen. A little boy.

The same little boy she had seen that night in the garden with Ben.

17

The vision before her was so beyond comprehension that Janet simply stared. The glowing shapes shimmered before her eyes a moment more, then were gone as completely as if they had never been. In breathless disbelief, she continued to stare, waiting for something to happen, something... anything... But there was nothing. She took a staggering step toward the gallery, then drew back in confusion. Her legs trembled, threatening to give way. Holding fast to the railing, she sank to a sitting position on the landing.

Ghosts, she thought, her mind still whirling. *This house is haunted—I've just seen two ghosts*. She realized she felt no fear. How could she be afraid of children? Ghosts, yes, but children all the same. The Renner house was haunted by ghost children.

She was still in a daze when she descended the steps. What was the meaning of what she had seen? What event in the house had caused it to be possessed?

Downstairs, she found Rose still at the table, lovingly stroking a cat picture as if her fingers could feel the soft texture of animal fur. Her expression was peaceful, but blank. Biting her lip, Janet studied the old woman. Reality, unreality—she probably made little distinction between the two. Besides, even if she were aware of the ghosts, she wouldn't know any history of the house to help explain it. Muriel probably wouldn't know either.

Janet suddenly thought of the one person who might have some answers: local historian, Kirby Orchard. If anyone should know the background of the Renner house, it was he.

Excited, she decided that after adult school that evening, she would lose no time in asking.

But during her ride home with Kirby that night, Janet found that her earlier enthusiasm had cooled. If she hadn't seen the ghosts with her own eyes, she wouldn't believe in them, so why should Kirby be any different? The memory of what she had seen was strangely special and she didn't want to hear it mocked. It just wasn't a subject to rush into headlong. On the other hand, assuming that such a house would have collected a reputation over the years, she felt safe in asking, "What sort of research have you done on Dr. Renner's place?"

"Well, I know its recent history because it's on the block where I grew up, but I've done no special study." Kirby gave her a curious glance. "Why do you ask?"

Surprised by his reply, she found herself prevaricating. "I—I was there earlier today and saw how the Renners are putting a lot of money into fixing the place up. It made me wonder about it."

She couldn't believe that no one had ever seen the ghost children in the past. Kirby's ignorance on the subject must mean the witnesses had kept their mouths shut. And it was probably smart for her to do the same. People gave queer looks to individuals who claimed to see the things that go bump in the night. Besides, as illogical as it might be, she felt that seeing those ghostly figures represented a mystical privilege. It was an experience she found that she wanted to protect. It was just as well, she decided, that her investigation— such as it was—had come to such a quick impasse.

Redirecting the conversation, she asked Kirby if he had lived in Princeton all his life.

"Until the forties," he said, seeming to enjoy the opportunity to talk about himself. "That's when I went off to study in Los Angeles, with a career as a film director in mind. I saw myself traveling importantly between Hollywood and Cannes, as dashing as Errol Flynn, as sardonic as George Sanders, as urbane as David Niven. And thin." He shot her a playful glance. "Take note that the three aforementioned gentlemen all had board-flat stomachs."

He talked of being drafted into the Army, being wounded, then coming home to finish his degree. "I was away for a dozen years, then came home, knowing that this is where I belong."

"And you live in the same house where you grew up?"

"The very same. It's small and perfect for an old bachelor like me. It belonged to my parents, and my mother's parents before that, bookish, sedentary people—scholars, educators, and ministers. And all plumpish. It's in our genes. As with them, my proper milieu is the classroom and the library. Over the years, I've made some dear friends in the cinema, but it's what's written on paper about films that holds me rather than the flickering images themselves."

Kirby's use of the words *flickering images* vividly re-created in Janet's mind the scene in the upper hall of the Renner house.

I've seen a ghost, she repeated to herself, still awe-struck with the wonder of it. And not one ghost, but two! She recalled her attempt to figure out what had illuminated the boy that night in the garden, and now understood that his small form glowed with an energy of its own. In the dark garden he had appeared flesh and blood, but by daylight in the gallery, both he and the little girl stood revealed as apparitional.

Closing her eyes, she smiled at the remembered images of the two spectral youngsters. Then, with jarring suddenness, came the intrusive memory of the chant. Mind's ear working like a tape recorder, it seemed she was hearing those eerie whispers all over again: *We are ta-ta-DA-da!*

Her eyes flew open. She had forgotten until now that there had been something profoundly disquieting about those measured sounds. So determined, almost threatening! She shivered. What were the rest of the words?

It wasn't until Kirby slowed for his drive that she realized they had reached Quince Street. His cottage was brick, with white shutters and a post lamp that made a bright circle of welcome by the side entrance. She previously had told him she would walk the few doors home, but in her present mood, the darkness hovering just outside the light took on the aspect of a lurking, pulsing thing. It was almost as if she could feel its chilling breath.

Turning off the engine, Kirby said, "Your mention of the Renners reminds me that this afternoon, I saw an ambulance on their side of the block."

Janet grabbed at the chance to delay her dark walk home. "I should have thought to tell you, you being a neighbor and all. Dr. Renner was taken to the hospital. I sat with Rose most of the afternoon, but Muriel came home with good news. Dr. Renner's EKG shows no new damage, although he's going to stay a day or two for observation. The Renners have been redecorating, and the doctor suspects that his attack was actually a reaction to paint fumes."

Kirby asked, "Was it being in the house today that made you inquire about it?"

The return to the subject of the house caught her off guard and she blurted, "Well, sure, after the things that—" Having revealed more than she had intended, she found her defenses crumbling. In a reversal of her feelings, she knew she wanted to share what had happened at the Renner house, or at least share a part of it. Her conversation with Kirby had convinced her she could trust him to lend a sympathetic ear as long as she didn't stretch credulity too far.

"Actually," she said, "I asked because I wondered if the place had a reputation. I mean, as a place where strange things have happened."

Kirby murmured in interest. With his double chin a soft roll above his collar and the lamplight glinting off his glasses, he looked like a spectacled Buddha. "You mean you've experienced something strange there?"

"There was something," she admitted. "Today was the second time I stayed with Rose. The first time, when I had to go upstairs, I felt there might be something . . . *disturbed* about the second floor." Her laugh was nervous. "Or maybe I get goose bumps too easily."

"What unnerved you? Something you saw, something you felt?"

"Not exactly. It seemed I saw flickers of motion out of the corner of my eye, but when I looked, nothing was there. And I thought I heard soft little sounds." She had been twisting the strap of her purse as she talked and now discovered she had nearly cut off the flow of blood to her hand. Untangling the strap, she worked the circulation back into her fingers as she concluded, "I decided it couldn't be anything except the shadows and sounds of dry leaves blowing across the windows."

"But is that what you really believe?"

Her throat felt suddenly tight. "I don't know."

"And what about today?"

"More of the same, I guess."

"Maybe I've missed something about the house." Kirby's tone was musing. "If you can spare a minute, come inside while I consult one of my area history books. We might find some interesting mention of the Renner property after all."

Janet agreed, making a mental note not to say anything that might lead Kirby to believe she was simply being overimaginative.

Inside, in the small, neat kitchen, an overweight little Boston bulldog wheezed in from an adjoining room as Kirby hung their coats.

"Oh, what a cute little dog!" Janet knelt. "Does she mind if I pet her?" Answering in doggy body language, the animal shoved against Janet's extended hand and grunted blissfully as her head was scratched.

"Let me introduce Trixie," said Kirby fondly. "She's eighteen years old, aren't you old girl?" He reached to pat the dog's rump. "Go on back to your bed now, Trix."

As the dog obediently puffed off, Kirby led Janet to his office. The room was outfitted with a roll-top desk and an overstuffed couch and sofa from a long-lost era. A handmade rag rug covered the floor. One wall was all bookcases and a table on the opposite wall was piled both above and beneath with papers and more books. The framed film posters over the sofa were originals: Fay Wray in *King Kong*, Shirley Temple in *Little Miss Marker*, Bogart in *The Maltese Falcon*. On the other large wall were faded family photographs in dark oak frames and a large map of Princeton Borough, individual houses marked along the streets.

"Sit anywhere," Kirby directed with a vague wave. As Janet pushed aside newspapers and made a place for herself on the sofa, he knelt to paw through the books under the table, his bald head reflecting light from the desk lamp. Even though he was dressed in a suit and tie, all Janet could think of was a monk rooting through scrolls in a moldering monastery library.

She said, "Fran told me that the people who sold to the Renners were named Fiorello. And the people before them—the ones who had a young relative who drowned, were named Mitchum. But I don't know about anyone before that."

"The folks before them were named Crammer." With a grunt, Kirby dragged out a box. "They moved in when I was away and I never really got to know them."

Now that she was here, Janet felt excited all over again about learning about the house. She noticed a folder on the desk with the name Stockton typed upon it. "Did Veronica and Tommy ask you to research their house?"

Kirby glanced to see what she was looking at. "No, that's another family, over in West Windsor. No relation. Tommy enjoys talking about the Stockton name being prominent in Princeton history, but he has no interest in researching his house. It's like that when people expect to relocate."

"Relocate?" Thinking of Gina, Janet felt distress. "Where do they plan to go?"

"Overseas. Tommy is with a company that installs data processing systems worldwide. His outfit has been working out a government deal, something to do with embassies. Tommy will become the company's chief foreign representative and he and Veronica will move abroad. From the start, they've been prepared to leave as soon as Tommy's new position is assigned. It's kept them restless, unable to put down roots. Oh, drat!" He peered up at Janet, his eyes round and sorrowful. "I just remembered where that book is. I lent it to someone."

"Oh, no." Janet felt let down. "Do you know who has it? Can you get it back?"

"Yes to both questions," he said with a grin. His knees cracked as he got up and sat in his desk chair. "A friend of mine has kept it for months." His expression was impish. "I'll give him a call for lunch, and guilt over keeping the book will have him picking up the tab. Speaking of food, would you like something hot to drink? And a slice of pie maybe? Dutch apple, I think. Anyway, the kind with raisins." He stood, placing a hand on a stomach that strained his vest buttons. "Or, at least, keep me company and make sure I don't sneak an extra slice. I'll repay your vigilance by telling you all I know about the Renner house."

Over pie and cups of lemon herb tea in the kitchen, Kirby kept his promise. "Now, when I was a kid, the first people I remember there were the Patricks. I started school with the Patrick kids. They moved when I was in the third grade and the house sat empty until the Roberts arrived. They didn't leave until I was away. Then, came the Crammers who, as I told you, left shortly after I returned home."

Hoping that Kirby would remember something significant as they talked, she asked, "Were they all young families?"

"You mean were the same kinds of people always attracted to the house? No, it doesn't seem so. The Crammers and Roberts were middle-aged. The Roberts moved in young, but stayed until after their kids were grown. Same for the Mitchums. More pie?"

When she shook her head, he said, "At least more tea then." He filled both their cups from what remained in the pot. "No, I can't see a common pattern among the residents of the house. Take the Renners now, three older adults—an unusual family in any case. I've seen the sister from a distance." He tapped his head. "It appears her brain has gone a bit soft."

Disappointed that the talk had come to nothing, Janet said glumly, "Then in all the years you've lived here, there has never been a hint of disturbance?"

"None that I know of, but of course, that book may turn up something." He nudged his glasses back into place. "Have others in the household noticed anything amiss?"

"Hardly. When I fished around the subject with Muriel, she didn't know what I was talking about."

"Well, not everyone is sensitive to psychic phenomena. The fact that Muriel senses nothing actually means very little."

Janet's look was doubtful. "That's hard to believe."

"Not if you think about it in somewhat different terms. I'll give you a common example." He fluttered a pudgy hand over the table top. "We could both agree that nothing but empty air occupies this space. But if we turn on a TV, we would discover that this 'emptiness' is filled with an energy that will cause a television to show images and messages. Just as a TV is sensitive to certain energy waves, some people are sensitive to other types of energy." He peered at Janet. "Have you had many psychic experiences in the past?"

"*Me?*" Having the focus shift from the house to herself confounded her. "What do I have to do with it?"

"Because in this case, you're like the TV. If paranormal energy exists in the Renner house, it's apparently passed unnoticed. But now, something may have revealed itself to you—making you as much a part of the puzzle as the house itself." Pushing aside his empty pie plate, he folded his arms on the table, studying her with lively interest. "Any former psychic episodes may lend us valuable information."

"But I'm not psychic," she argued. "You mean weird experiences since childhood, or just *knowing* things? No, I've never had experiences like that." Into her mind jumped the wry thought that she would have avoided a lot of mistakes in life if she only had the power to read a crystal ball. "All I'm curious about is the house." Her voice became reflective. "You know, the very first time I saw the place, it drew me like a magnet. That's when it was for sale this past spring. So help me, if the plans to move to another state hadn't been already set, I would have fought tooth and nail to make it mine."

"Is that the way you feel now? That if it goes on the market again, you want it?"

Janet examined her feelings. "No, I don't believe so."

"But didn't you once tell me you would like to settle in this area, near your sister?"

"Yes, but I wasn't considering that house." She twirled the spoon in her empty teacup. "I mean, it never crossed my mind to watch for the time when it might become available again." Not understanding herself, she knit her brow. "You'd figure I would have still wanted it, wouldn't you? With property adjoining Fran's and all? It's too big for me, of course. But last spring, it could have been four times as large and I can't tell you how I longed to have it. Funny."

"Maybe your attitude has changed because you now suspect it's haunted."

She shook her head. "No, my feelings about the house had changed before I ever went inside it. I remember how on my first night living here with Fran, I stared out the window at the house for a long time. It fascinated me because of what it had meant to me in the spring, yet my desire to live there had evaporated."

"Are you still drawn there regardless, or are you leery of going back inside again?"

Smiling, Janet ran a hand through her dark curls. "If I'm afraid, then I'm in big trouble! I promised Muriel I'd stay with Rose tomorrow afternoon while she visits her husband in the hospital. Of course, it won't be just Rose and me. Men will be working in the living room. Muriel wants the painting finished and the place thoroughly aired before Dr. Renner returns."

"Okay, so you're not fearful as long as others are around. But, do you still feel *drawn* to the house?"

"Only in the sense of being curious. It's a puzzle, and I want to understand—" Breaking off, she frowned at Kirby. "Say, you're still studying *me*, aren't you?"

His smile made twin moons of his fleshy cheeks. "Yes, but I promise to get that book back and also study the house. If anything in its history explains why it may be disturbed, we should have the answer within the next few days."

18

Janet had made sure she was home in time to receive Ben's call from his motel room in Pennsylvania.

"Happy Halloween Eve," he greeted warmly.

"I never heard it called that," she said, thinking how wonderful it was to hear his voice. "This is Mischief Night."

"Well, I didn't want you thinking of mischief unless I was around. Miss me?"

"Terribly." She spoke lightly, as if kidding, but actually, it was true. She found it hard to believe she had only known him for such a short time. "I had to see the adult-school director tonight—Kirby Orchard gave me a ride there and back."

Standing in Fran's kitchen, leaning against the ridiculously ancient refrigerator, Janet realized she had already decided to say nothing about the Renner house. It had been enough of a venture to confide a part of the story to Kirby. There was no telling what attitude Ben might take. The risk seemed too great. But she did tell him about Herman Renner's attack and how she had stayed with Rose.

Concluding, she said, "When Muriel came home, she brought me a huge gift basket of fruit from the hospital gift shop. When she wanted to write me a check as well, I wouldn't allow it. But when she insisted on paying whenever I watch Rose in the future, I agreed. The idea of accepting charity gets under her skin. I bet they had servants galore in Argentina."

Ben asked, "Who do they have to help out now?"

"Nobody. That's why she had to call on me. Fran says she's seen a cleaning service van parked in front of their house. But that kind of help is awfully impersonal compared with having a housekeeper live in. Muriel must do the cooking herself, and I know she does the food shopping. When people come from a foreign country, it probably takes a long time to find the kind of help they feel comfortable with."

It wasn't until after they hung up that she realized she had forgotten to tell Ben what Kirby had said about Tommy Stockton's career plans. The thought of Gina moving away gave her a hollow sensation. Maybe it was just as well not to mention it. Ben was aware that she hardly knew the child. Mightn't he think it foolish for her to have become so attached so quickly?

She went to bed still thinking of the phone call and the warmth of Ben's voice. Thoughts of the Renner house waited just outside the rim of her consciousness and she held them there. Her talk with Kirby allowed her to postpone the matter until he contacted her. Thinking only of Ben, she drifted into sleep.

In the middle of the night she was awakened by what sounded like babies crying. She knew at once that it was someone else's child, the small voice caught in that strange echo that seemed to multiply the sound. Although it faded quickly, she was sharply reminded of how things used to be and she couldn't get back to sleep for a long time.

She recognized that a part of her wakefulness was due to her growing interest in Ben Yates. Her attraction to him had allowed her to start closing the door to the past. It was something she wanted to do—had to do, if she were to have a future, yet the adjustment brought pain. Whether with Ben or with someone else, a new life would place her among those who could only know Becky as a photo in an album, as anonymous as the already yellowing birth announcement she had once proudly clipped from the newspaper. No matter how strongly she might desire it, no one would ever be able to share with her the love she felt for her lost daughter. Her feelings for Becky would remain an important part of her forever, but that small personality could now exist only within her heart. Assailed by a loneliness too deep for tears, she lay wakeful for hours.

Suffering in the morning from lack of sleep, she sat with Fran at the breakfast table glumly thinking ahead to her eleven-thirty appointment with the student who was the newsletter photographer. The student would run circles around her, she just knew it. She got an idea. "Fran, I need a confidence boost. Do you think Ida Aaron might be free this morning? I need to brush up on newspaper lingo."

Fran was delighted to be of aid. "No problem! Ida comes into the Spoon at quarter of ten every morning on her break. Since Warren won't need his car until later, why don't you drive out and talk to Ida in person?"

The plan was a good one, and later, at the school, thanks to Ida's guidance, Janet was able to use terms familiar to the director and photographer when discussing picture cropping, layouts, and typefaces. After lunch, as she walked to the Renner house, she still reflected with pleasure over the success of her morning. Everything had gone like clockwork, and as a special bonus, she knew she would especially enjoy working with the photographer, Annabelle Chu.

Of Chinese descent, Annabelle was a high school sophomore, a lively, pretty girl with extraordinary camera skills and an effervescent manner. When the newsletter talk was finished, Janet had admired the showy earrings the girl wore in her double-pierced ears, and Annabelle had responded with a dramatic sigh. "What I want is three earrings per ear, but my mother refuses. Three needle holes in an ear, and she calls it *butchering*. Ever hear anything so ridiculous? My great-great-grandmother had bound feet! My lobes could look like IBM cards and who should care? *Butchering*. Can you imagine?"

As Janet rang Renner's front doorbell, she wondered if

she weren't so taken by Annabelle's theatrics because it distracted her from thoughts of the afternoon ahead. Despite her brave words to Kirby, perhaps she felt apprehensive about being in the house again after all. A haunted house, a house inhabited by ghosts. She was thinking how unreal it sounded when put into words when Muriel opened the door.

"How's Dr. Renner doing?" Janet asked, hesitating only a second before stepping inside.

"He is fine, thank you," replied Muriel, looking harassed. Nervously, she fingered the white braid on her navy Chanel jacket. "I am sorry if I kept you waiting, but I have been trying to prepare instructions to assist the workmen when they return from lunch. All morning, they have had nothing but questions! It is a wonder they have made any progress, but as you see, they have."

She directed Janet's attention to the living room. The half-hung silk wallpaper was a delicate salmon shade and the woodwork had been painted in an eggshell enamel. "I think I will use a pastel Oriental rug," Muriel explained distractedly. "And perhaps couches and chairs in an off-white."

"It sounds lovely."

"I hope so, although at present, too much goes on for me to enjoy the project. I am not at my best. During the night, I was kept lying awake, fearing the return of the Halloween mischief makers."

"Oh, my," Janet murmured in sympathy, thinking that she and Muriel had apparently been companions in sleeplessness, although for entirely different reasons. "When I was out earlier this morning, I saw toilet paper draped on trees and pumpkins smashed along the street. Mostly nuisance stuff. Was any of your property damaged?"

"Apparently not." Muriel folded her be-ringed hands, as if in thankful prayer. "I understand it is a custom for young people to roam on that one evening a year. They must have been in my rear yard, shining flashlights at the house. I heard sounds and opened my bedroom door a crack—just enough to see their lights."

"Oh?" Attention sharpening, Janet was suddenly thinking of the light emitted by the ghost children. Could that have been what Muriel had really seen? But the thought slid away as Muriel raved on, showing far more expression than usual. "Halloween! What an unwelcome custom! Had Dr. Renner been at home, he would have been terribly distressed."

Janet ventured, "Your sister said he didn't care to have children in his yard."

Muriel shot Janet a surprised, almost furtive look. "The tree is an attraction," she explained defensively. "He worries that a child might try to climb it and become injured. He would not want that to happen, and then, in this country, there are also the lawsuits."

The phone in the hallway rang, and while Muriel answered, Janet peered up the staircase. She found it incredible that no chills went along her spine. All she felt was a sense of loss. Although she was positive of what she had seen, she wondered if in future years, she might look back upon the incident and say, "Yes, there was a time once when I saw two ghosts—or at least, I *think* I did." Shaking her head, she hoped that wouldn't happen. She didn't want to repeat the experience, yet neither did she want to lose the feeling that she had been granted a privileged moment.

When Muriel hung up the receiver, Janet asked, "Is Rose busy with her picture collection again today?"

"No. She seems content with her music, but perhaps you can get her outside for awhile. The air will be good for her. That was Dr. Renner's physician on the phone." The call seemed to have lifted Muriel's spirits. "Tomorrow, he will make the journey from Manhattan to perform his own examination. He is an outstanding man in his field, one in whom Dr. Renner places great faith."

"It's great that he's willing to make the trip," said Janet, wondering about the cost of having a top specialist travel to a patient rather than the other way around. Without stopping to think, she asked, "Since you came to this country to be near your husband's doctor, why did you settle so far from New York?" Then, embarrassed, she stammered, "I'm sorry. It—it's none of my business. Curiosity is sometimes a bad habit."

She half expected Muriel to loftily ignore her prying, but instead, the woman smiled faintly. "We have a furnished hotel suite waiting for us on Park Avenue. Dr. Renner visited Princeton only to meet with an old friend of his who was speaking at the university. After their reunion, they drove through the town, enjoying the sights. I was not with them, so how they came to this street, I do not know, but as soon as Dr. Renner saw this house, he wanted it."

Still wearing that faint smile, she gazed at Janet, the rare beauty of her gold-brown eyes seeming to hint at unfathomable secrets. "From that one brief look, this house became an obsession. He claimed it called to him. Nothing else would satisfy. Since it was available and waiting, there was no impediment. We shipped only a few personal things from our home in Argentina. The rest of the furnishings were left here by the previous owners."

She seemed to be waiting for a response. Janet, not sure what to say, glanced back toward the living room. Feeling awkward, she said, "Well, this is a lovely house and the work you're having done will surely show it at its best. Your husband will be very happy here."

"Really?" Muriel smiled mysteriously.

Janet thought the reply inappropriate, yet Muriel seemed to know exactly what she was saying. The entire exchange was as perplexing as Muriel's Mona Lisa smile.

Feeling she had been presented with an unsolvable riddle, she felt vastly relieved when a van stopped outside and the painters and wallpaper hangers, back from lunch, trooped inside.

19

It wasn't until later, as Janet sat in the study with Rose, that she realized Dr. Renner's feelings for the house sounded similar to what hers had been in the spring. *Obsession*. The word had been Muriel's, but it was accurate enough.

She wondered if the strength of his attraction would fade as hers seemed to have done. It probably would. Just when Muriel finished the last room exactly to her taste, old Herman would announce it was ridiculous not to live closer to his heart specialist. Not that moving to an already furnished Park Avenue apartment was a trip to lower Siberia.

Park Avenue. Janet let her eyes roam the study. There would be no room like this at the fancy Manhattan address. The bookcase and paintings surely belonged to the Renners, but the sagging brown couch, Colonial-print draperies, and rag rug must have been left by the Fiorellos. Rose's rocker, although good solid maple, needed refinishing. It looked as if somebody's dog had teethed on the rungs.

Of course, viewed in a different way, the study wasn't so bad. Actually, she thought, it was the gilt-edged art works that made a basically cozy, if ordinary, room look shabby by contrast. Exchange the rich, sepia oils for plainly framed country prints, put plants on the wide sills and toss around a few brightly colored corduroy cushions and the room would have a pleasant, lived-in appeal. In fact, that was probably how the Fiorellos had it. Fran had said they had five children. This had probably been their family room.

How warm and friendly it must have looked with a crowd of youngsters flopped on the rug before the TV. Except, perhaps, for the poor boy who Fran said was crippled. Maybe he had been in a wheelchair. Janet sighed at this reminder that she wasn't the only person to have lost a child. Maybe that's why the Fiorellos moved away—after their son died, it had hurt too much to stay.

She glanced at the TV, which advertised a home computer. Rose, who wouldn't know a computer from an electric toothbrush, kept her eyes glued to the screen as she rocked. Every once in a while, the workmen could be heard over the sounds of the stereo. Although Muriel hadn't asked Janet to check on their progress, she supposed she should stick her head in there now and then. Still, she didn't feel like getting up at the moment. She yawned. Muriel kept the house too warm, yet the high temperature was perhaps best for Rose and the doctor. She yawned again. Her busy morning had tired her. So far, she had been able to keep only a step ahead in her new job, and it was a strain.

Mind drifting, she thought how she looked forward to Ben's telephone call that evening. She would tell him about Gina ... about how Gina.... Startled, she straightened, losing the trail of thought. Blinking, she looked around, realizing she must have been on the verge of dozing. Gina. She must have been thinking about Gina, because the child was in her mind; fuzzy impressions, with no degree of clarity. Frowning, she remembered Muriel suggesting that Rose should go outside. It certainly seemed an ideal time for it. The fresh air would benefit her as well as Rose.

Rose evidenced no objection to getting into her coat. Tying her babushka herself, she shuffled along with Janet through the kitchen and out to the latticed porch. Janet unlatched the door and stepped out, then smothered a startled gasp. Gina waited at the foot of the steps, smiling as if she had known they were about to appear.

I must have heard her playing, Janet told herself, recalling how thoughts of the child had so suddenly popped into her mind. "Hello, honey," she called. "Miss Rose and I are coming down the steps. Please keep out of the way while I help her."

Making certain that Rose had a good grip on the railing, Janet guided the arthritic woman safely down. Belatedly, she realized they should have used the front entrance—she'd make sure to bring Rose back inside that way. When they finally stood on the brick path which led to the lawn, Janet gave Gina a tentative look.

"I'm glad to see you, sweetheart, but I really don't think this is where you should be playing."

"Okay—is okay," Rose stated. "Doctor Herman not here." Reaching out a tender hand, she touched the child's arm. The gesture surprised Janet until she remembered that Rose had spoken once before of the little girl being welcome when the doctor wasn't around.

"That may be so," Janet told the old woman, "but neither he nor your sister want the responsibility of children in the yard. They're afraid someone might get hurt."

"Nobody get hurt," Rose answered. "This America."

Seeing no purpose in responding, Janet said warmly to Gina, "You can stay for now, as long as I'm with you, but when I go inside, you must leave." The little girl nodded to show her understanding and Janet smiled. "You come here often, don't you?"

Gina nodded even more vigorously.

"Well, it sure is pretty here, I have to admit that." Walking Rose over to sit on a bench where the pines sheltered them from the wind, Janet looked around appreciatively. Even with most of the trees denuded, the yard retained a fairy-tale quality. The narrow opening in the privet suggested an enticing maze just beyond, and the thick evergreens could easily mark the beginning of an enchanted forest. As Muriel had pointed out, the copper beech, with its smooth gray bark and low-growing branches, begged to have someone climb it. Janet saw a place about seven feet off the ground where the arrangement of limbs offered the perfect setting for a treehouse. Enticing indeed. Now that she was outside, it was difficult to think of anything unnatural happening anywhere on the property, either inside or out. Memories of the scene in the gallery faded under sunlight.

When Kirby regained his book, would there be even the slightest clue to help her understand what she had witnessed?

Gina's cat, Pagoda, slunk from under the privet, shifting eyes large and inquisitive. A gust of wind stirred a leaf under the beech tree. Instantly, the animal crouched, tail switching. When Gina went over to stand watch with her pet, Rose said: "Girl. Like my Lili. Next time, keep very close."

Janet frowned. "You mean you had a little girl, Rose?"

"Lili. Long time, long time...." Voice fading, the old woman lapsed into an inward silence, her eyes becoming as opaque and unseeing as tarnished tinfoil.

Janet reasoned that if Rose had a daughter, she would now be middle-aged. Where was she? Or did Rose mean she had died years ago? A burden of unanswered questions and stale memories seemed to hover around the dark, bent shoulders of the old woman and Janet decided it was best not to probe further. Unsettled, she looked across the yard to where Gina and the cat stood under the beech tree. Eyes still fixed on the leaf, muscles rippling under its coat, Pagoda made ready to pounce.

Janet narrowed her eyes. *The beech tree. Hide under the beech tree... it will be safe under the beech tree...* She didn't know why the words came to mind, but the promise of safety was disquieting rather than comforting. She was relieved when Gina lost interest in the cat and came to the bench. She wore the same pink flannel jacket as on Sunday and her cheeks and the tip of her nose were red.

"Are you warm enough?" Janet asked. "Let's see—oh, you have a nice, thick sweater on underneath. But here, let me fix that hood. It's letting cold air in around your ears." Gina inclined herself forward as Janet fussed over her, smoothing her rippling, dark hair, retying the string under her chin so that the hood fit more snugly.

"There, now," Janet cooed. "Isn't that better?"

Sounds came from the street. Seeing a small clown and an even smaller Smurf skip along the sidewalk, trick-or-treat bags on their arms, Janet exclaimed, "Oh, look at the cute costumes on those children!"

"Children," Rose intoned. "They were with us, then they were gone. All gone."

"Yes, that's right," Janet agreed absently, leaning forward to follow the last glimpse of the children. "They've gone on down the street now."

With a grunt of effort, Rose got to her feet and headed toward the lawn. With the grass dry and most of the leaves blown away, Janet figured it would be safe to allow the woman to walk by herself. Keeping one eye on the aged figure, she smiled down at Gina. "What's your costume for Halloween, honey?"

Janet expected her question to lead into a guessing game, but then she saw a blankness on the small, triangular face that she hadn't anticipated.

An unwelcome suspicion edged into her mind. "Gina . . . you do have a costume, don't you?"

The child shook her head.

"Oh, my." Janet felt terrible. She had never considered that Gina might not be prepared for Halloween. Although the event received a certain amount of attention in public school, a private tutor might not think to do anything about it. Which left everything up to Veronica—who apparently hadn't thought to do anything either.

Gina's soft, chocolate-brown eyes showed troubled uncertainty. Janet realized that the child couldn't be totally ignorant of Halloween—not if she watched television. But perhaps she hadn't understood it was something she could be expected to take part in. *Until I opened my big mouth,* Janet mourned.

Suddenly, she brightened. Why not call Veronica for permission to take Gina around to a few houses on her own? Smiling in anticipation, she knew she could rig up a costume of some kind. Oh, she did hope Veronica would go along with it! She realized her happy smile must have conveyed something good, for Gina reached for her hand and smiled back.

They sat contentedly for a few minutes before Janet began to feel concerned about Rose. The woman had started out as if she were enjoying her stroll, but then she had begun that strange, hypnotic circling of the yard, the expression on her lined face anguished. There was no telling what went on in her troubled mind, but Janet couldn't believe it was beneficial. Far better for her to be peacefully rocking in her chair, lost in her music.

"I'm going to take Miss Rose inside now," Janet told Gina, getting up. "It's time for you to go home. I want you to promise that you won't come back in the yard after I've gone inside, okay?"

"All gone," Rose muttered, her words thick and guttural as Janet urged her along. "They were with us, then they were all gone. Hot, everything burning hot. They were with us, then they were all gone." The woman suddenly became aware of Gina, who still lingered by the bench. Jerking her arm free, Rose clapped her hands sharply. "Go home!" she ordered, her voice frightened. "The doctor will catch you! Go home!"

Although startled by this outburst, Janet managed to maintain a comforting tone as she told the old woman, "Gina is leaving now, see?" She called firmly to Gina, "I'll see you later, honey, but for now, *go*."

Gina scurried off and Janet had no further difficulty getting Rose around to the front of the house and inside even though she kept up a constant, unintelligible mumble. When helping her remove her coat, Janet finally realized the woman was repeating the word *dangerous*, the first syllables issuing from deep in her throat in a foreign way, the final *s* hissing because of her toothlessness.

"What's dangerous, Rose? What are you worried about?"

Becoming excited, the woman uttered a low, almost animallike wail. "Dangerous! If little girl comes, I must keep her safe!"

"It's all right," Janet soothed, beginning to fear that Rose was getting out of control. "The little girl has gone home now, remember? And the doctor doesn't know she was here. He's away in the hospital, remember? We will never tell him the little girl was here."

"Dangerous," Rose repeated, but then, to Janet's relief

she fell silent as the reminder of Herman's absence apparently percolated down into her brain. By the time Janet got her settled in her rocking chair, the woman's mood was restored to tranquility.

After assuring herself that Rose would be all right, Janet left her long enough to see how the workmen were doing. The electrician had just arrived. He was to replace the living-room ceiling fixture and needed to trace the original wiring, which had been installed through the floor of an upper storeroom. Carrying his toolbox, he mounted the main steps. As he neared the top, Janet found herself holding her breath, waiting for a hesitation or some other sign that he had sensed something amiss lying ahead. But his boots tramped firmly upward and he was soon lost from her sight.

Annoyed by a vague disappointment, Janet released her breath. From the dining-room archway she could see Rose still rocking peacefully, and she decided to take the opportunity to telephone Veronica.

When hearing the purpose of Janet's call, Veronica gushed, "Gina will have the time of her life!" She gave no sign of realizing that as the child's mother, she should have planned something for Gina's Halloween herself. "Are you sure you'll have something for her to wear? I could send Ozzie out to the store."

"No thanks," Janet answered, trying not to let her feelings shade her voice. "Homemade costumes are fun."

After it was decided what time she would pick up Gina, Janet hung up the phone, feeling an inward ache. Veronica's lack of true interest in the child was unmistakable. It was such a waste, a genuine tragedy. If only there were some action she could take. But if the Stocktons eagerly awaited relocation, it would make things hard for Gina if she became emotionally involved. She sighed heavily, thinking that being the child's friend was the best she could do.

Hearing the electrician pounding away upstairs, Janet gave a glance toward the study to reassure herself that Rose was still settled, then she was drawn up the steps. Peering through the banisters at the open door to the storage room, she saw boxes and loose odds and ends piled in the corner by the window.

When there was a pause in the pounding, she called, "Is everything all right? Were you able to reach the proper wires?"

"What's that?" called a startled voice. The electrician, a thin, bearded man, appeared in the doorway, his eyes a bit wide. "Oh, it's you. You surprised me." He glanced around. "I'm making a racket slamming rusty nails out of a floor panel. Didn't hear you come up."

"Sorry. Please remember not to leave anything lying in the hallway. An elderly woman lives here—I wouldn't want her to trip."

"No need to worry, ma'am." After another glance around, the man disappeared back inside the room and the pounding commenced.

Janet remained as she was, testing the atmosphere. Hadn't the electrician seemed awfully rattled? Maybe he had been aware of something odd after all. Intently, she stared into the darkest corners, finding nothing out of the ordinary. Once again, she experienced that strange sense of loss. Shaking her head, she waited a moment more, then returned downstairs.

20

When Ben called that evening at eleven, Janet bubbled with news of her adventures with Gina.

"Fran and I fixed her up like a little witch. She wore my black skirt over her shoulders for a cape and Warren gave us an old black fedora that we stretched into a pointed hat. With her face powdered white, and frowning eyebrows and a scowling mouth painted on, she looked terrific. Gina herself got the idea for the finishing touch—horrid big freckles drawn on her cheeks with my eyebrow pencil."

"Hey," Ben chided. "Why not a princess or a snow fairy? I thought you didn't like Halloween monsters."

"This is different. She looked adorable."

Ben's sound of mock despair traveled over the wire. "A spotted kid with a scowl and a weird hat? Remind me not to ask you if I ever need help with my appearance. How did Gina like trick or treating? She get lots of loot?"

"I forgot there were so many brands of candy," Janet said, thinking how much she enjoyed relating the events of the evening to him. "We only went to houses on this block, still, she made out like a bandit. Veronica was away when we got back, but the Stockton housekeeper—her name's Mrs. Ousler, only they call her Ozzie—was waiting for us. When I left, she was sitting with Gina at the kitchen table as she sorted everything out. I'm so glad we went."

"It would have been a shame for her to miss it."

"Oh, it would have! And it brought back so many nice memories of Fran walking me around on Halloween night when I was a kid. She's been a great sister, Ben. I appreciate her more now than ever." She laughed a bit ruefully. "Of course, that doesn't mean she's perfect."

"Ohhh? This sounds like complaint time."

"Not really. It's just that she can be such a know-it-all. It rankles, you know?"

"What's she done?"

Janet hesitated, then decided there was no reason why she shouldn't tell him. "Remember that night she hauled you off to tell you I had imagined hearing a baby cry?"

"Sure. And I realized it was that Siamese cat."

"Yes, only it *wasn't*. A cat's cry might resemble that of a baby, but not enough to fool anyone comparing it with the real thing."

"But, I thought—"

"Look, the first time I heard it, it seemed possible I dreamed the cry, but then I kept hearing it. Fran insists there's no baby around, but she's obviously mistaken." Janet twisted the phone cord as she talked. "Maybe someone cares for a child overnight only periodically. Anyway, this evening, when I was out with Gina—"

"Oh-ho!" Ben's laugh traveled over the miles. "I'm way ahead. When you and Gina went from door to door, you took an impromptu survey to find out which house had the baby. And now you're all primed to show your sister that she doesn't know everything after all, right?"

"Yes, only—" Janet's voice reflected chagrin. "I didn't get my bright idea until after we had gone to several places, so I must have missed the right one." She was warmed by Ben's understanding groan. "And I had dreamed up such clever ways to ask!" She was beginning to see the funny side of her failed scheme. "You would have been proud of me. I'd have made a marvelous spy."

"At least you've eliminated all the wrong houses," he consoled.

Before they hung up, Ben said he would be returning to Princeton late on Thursday. He would report for work Friday morning, but could take off early if she would be free. Smiling, she said she thought she could arrange it.

The next two and a half days passed uneventfully, and on Friday at three-thirty, Ben picked up Janet outside the Renner house, pulling his car up behind a parked van.

"Perfect timing," she said, climbing into the Subaru. Too eager to wait for him to come to the door, she had rushed out as soon as she saw his car. Despite how she had looked forward to being with him again, she was unprepared for the impact it would have upon her. She had forgotten how appealing he was, forgotten the strength of his face, the warmth of his smile. The force of his presence caught her unawares. For a trembling moment she was on the verge of throwing herself into his arms, then caution seized her. Abruptly backpedaling her emotions, she floundered for something to fill the awkward moment.

"It—it was such a good idea for you to meet me here," she told him, speaking too rapidly, stumbling over the words. "Muriel just... she just returned home from the hospital five minutes ago."

His knowing grin was gentle. "I missed you too."

Her breath caught in her chest. She wondered how he could do it, how he could see through her that way. "Oh, Ben..." Her voice was unsteady. Another thing she had forgotten was how clearly he made her see the barriers she had built about herself. He opened his arms, and this time, she didn't allow herself to hesitate.

"Oh, Ben, I did miss you," she confessed, her eyes closed, her words muffled against his shirt. "I missed you very, very much."

"That's better," he said softly. She could feel his breath in her hair. After a long moment, he released her, saying, "So what's this about the Renners? More trouble with his heart?"

"Partly," Janet answered with a shaky laugh, thinking that after the snug security of Ben's embrace, she was the one with heart trouble. Another thing she had forgotten was how wonderful it felt to be hugged. She reluctantly shifted her thoughts to the Renners. "He didn't actually have another heart attack, but he's a lot weaker than before. Muriel says his color is awful. His specialist tried to argue him out of coming home tomorrow, but his mind is made up."

Starting to pull his car out, Ben raised his brow. "I thought you and Mrs. Renner expected to have all the redecoration finished several days before her husband came home."

Janet saw he was looking at the van. "That belongs to the new electrician. The painting and wallpapering are done, but the electrician came only once, then never showed up again." A frown briefly marred her forehead as she once again wondered if the man's refusal to return could mean he had sensed something odd in the gallery. Continuing, she said, "Muriel asked me to phone him, and after mumbling some excuse, he hung up on me. She had to find somebody else to finish the job."

Over the phone, Ben and Janet had decided that he should show her more of Princeton, and now, wanting to change the subject, she said, "This sunny afternoon is perfect for my tour. I've often wondered about that huge stone building on Nassau Street—a library, I think. It looks so modern."

"You must mean the Firestone Library, at the corner of Nassau and Washington. It was built in the fifties, so for around here, it's practically brand new. They always have a book or photography exhibit on display. We'll go see."

After seeing the Ansel Adams exhibit at the library, they went on down Washington Road, where they strolled hand in hand around the sculptured fountain of the contemporary Woodrow Wilson School, the building's striking, tall-columned simplicity marking it as one of the architectural highlights of the campus.

"For contrast," said Ben, as they walked across the street and back toward Nassau Street, "we'll look at the University Chapel. It was dedicated in the twenties, so it's hardly ancient, but the Gothic style makes you feel you've stepped back into the Middle Ages."

"It's magnificent!" breathed Janet in a hushed voice a few minutes later, craning her neck to view the chapel's high, vaulted ceiling and awe-inspiring display of stained glass. "I don't think I've ever seen church windows as impressive as these. But this place is huge! It must seat almost two thousand." She looked at Ben, whose rugged, irregular features were intriguingly shadowed by the cool, greenish lights filtering through the colored glass. She rather felt as if she were looking up at him from under water. "When you said 'chapel,' I imagined some place tiny and quaint."

"For that," he answered, "I've got to show you Faith Chapel. My aunt used to belong when it had an active congregation, but now, it's been taken over by the historical society. I don't know if it's open to the public on weekdays, but I hope so—I'd like to see it again myself."

After a drive that took them out of Princeton Borough and into the larger, more sparsely populated township, Ben led

Janet up the steps of a steepled, Colonial-style brick church that was surrounded by a graveyard. Set along a country road, the old building reminded her of a church in a miniature village set, the kind placed under a Christmas tree with cotton batting snow and a mirror for a scenic lake.

The doors were locked, but fortunately, a custodian showed up to sweep and turn on the heat in preparation for the wedding scheduled for the following day. Letting them in, he told them, "You'll find it a pretty little church for a small ceremony." It sounded as if he thought that's why they were scouting out the place. Janet and Ben exchanged amused glances.

While the man did his work, the pair walked down the carpeted aisle which was flanked by oak pews that could accommodate no more than forty people.

"Now, this is my idea of a chapel," Janet said, throwing a smile at Ben, who leaned against a pew, watching her explore. Seeing a brass cross on the altar, she asked, "Which denomination built it?"

"Presbyterian, I think." Ben's voice resounded in a hollow way against the bare plaster walls. "Kirby would know for sure."

Janet neared the gray marble baptismal font. Looking over the prayer rail, she touched the font with reverent sadness and read the inscription. "This is dedicated to the memory of Gregory and William Hickok. Two little boys who must have been twins."

At first, the satiny marble was cool against her fingertips, but then it seemed she felt a warm vibration, as if the years of sacred service had invested the font with blessed power of its own. She remembered Becky's baptism, the child's eyes wide with wonder, the sprinkles of water on her downy head like droplets of holy dew.

Ben walked up beside her, bending to read the date: *1874–1877*. "They were only three years old," he mused. "They're probably buried in the churchyard outside. Want to go see?"

Janet shook her head. "No, I don't think so."

Thanking the custodian, they left. Ben drove back toward Princeton and on down Washington Road again, driving in and around a lake. He pulled off where there was a good view and stopped the car.

"All the maps and brochures call this 'Lake Carnegie,'" he said, "but I've lived in this area most of my life, and never heard anyone call it anything except Carnegie Lake."

Janet smiled. "That just goes to show that the natives never know anything." Seated on the lake side of the car, she opened her door to the warm sunlight. Neither of them made a move to get out.

Ben chuckled. "My grandparents were from around Grover's Mill, which is just a few miles from here, and I loved to hear them tell about the Orson Wells radio broadcast, the 'War of the Worlds.' Millions across the country believed that Martians, armed with death-ray machines, had actually landed there. Of course, most all the natives recognized it as just a good story."

"Is that how you got interested in science fiction?"

"I never thought about it before, but I suppose it is." He angled about in his seat. "Let me share some of that sunlight, lady." Putting his arm around Janet's waist, he moved her back against him as he adjusted himself comfortably, one of his long legs thrust out to receive the sunlight streaming through the opened door.

They sat as they were for a moment, then he said, "That bothered you in the church, didn't it—when I suggested we got out into the graveyard."

With her body leaning against his, she knew he must be aware of her sudden tension. "Yes, it bothered me."

"What was your baby's name?"

Her voice was no more than a whisper. "Becky."

"Tell me about her," he urged gently. "Tell me about Becky."

She was quiet for a long moment. "You couldn't really understand without knowing some things about Clay and me."

"Tell me. I want to know."

She was quiet again, then: "As soon as we knew I was pregnant, Clay bragged to everyone it would be a son. Modern science aside, I knew it would be a black mark against me if I failed to produce the desired male heir. But when Becky was born, Clay's reaction was poorly disguised relief. It dawned on me that he had only talked of a son because it was the macho thing, but actually, a daughter was proof of his manhood without being the threat that a son would have been.

"Becky was named after his dead mother, who had passed away recently, and there was something fiercely intense about Clay's love for her. I think he believed she would grow up expressing that same uncritical admiration for him that his mother had always shown, almost a sort of worship. I could see trouble ahead in his relationship with Becky, but while she was so little, it was a beautiful time for us. Except for when we were newly married, Clay and I had never been happier."

She shifted, feeling Ben's chest against her back. A band of sunlight kissed one ankle, bared beneath the hem of her slacks. She was aware of the cradling security of Ben's arms, the lulling rhythm of his breathing. Resting her head back against his shoulder, she closed her eyes, continuing to speak.

"When Becky was four months old, I went in early one morning and found her lying still and bluish in her crib. Her skin was unnaturally cold. I snatched her up and tried to force her to breathe, to force her heart to start beating again. I guess I screamed for Clay.

"The next thing I remember, the ambulance was there and the police. I didn't want to let Becky go, but they took her away, and the police started asking questions.

"They were very kind, very polite, but it was just a little backwoods Alabama town, with outsiders like Clay and me coming in because of new industry in the area. If any of the townsfolk had ever heard of Sudden Infant Death Syndrome, they figured it was a fancy excuse for an ignorant mother who either puts her baby to sleep face up and it chokes on spit-up milk, or she puts it to sleep face down and it smothers.'' She uttered a small, mirthless laugh. "Let me ask you, how could a person win either way? One of the policemen even said: 'We know how hard it can be on the nerves when a baby keeps fretting, depriving a mother of sleep. A mother doesn't really want to hurt her baby, all she wants is to get a little rest.' Nobody made any direct accusations, but still, I was an outsider. People don't want to believe an apparently perfect baby could suddenly die. It made them feel better to view me with suspicion."

With a shudder, she fell silent again. Ben caressed her arm, his touch comforting. Finally, in an unsteady voice, she continued. "Whenever things went wrong, all Clay knew to do was cast blame. In this case, it was pitifully easy to blame me. In shock, I had withdrawn and was seen by the town as cold and uncaring. Typical northern woman, I guess. Clay, however, was openly tearful and a thankful receiver of every empty religious platitude ever handed out. He was seen as their kind of people. I don't mean to make light of his suffering, but when he became the center of attention he wallowed in it. Suddenly, he was accepted, while I was not. It was his nature to try and ingratiate himself further by making sure they all understood that he saw me as an outsider too. A few months of that, and divorce was the only answer for either of us."

When Janet fell silent, she and Ben remained sitting quietly for some time, then, without discussion, they got out and walked along the lake. Neither of them spoke until they returned to the car, when Ben said he figured it was time to think about dinner.

He took her to a place he knew near New Brunswick which was quiet and pleasant and had excellent food. He did most of the talking during the drive up, and by the time their salad was served, Janet, more at ease with him than ever before, knew it was good that he had encouraged her to be open about the past.

It was dark and starting to get cold by the time he took her home and walked her to the door. It wasn't terribly late and Janet knew Fran and Warren were still up, but she didn't want to ask Ben inside and have to share him with anyone. They stood talking in the shadows, she leaning against him as he stood with his arms lightly encircling her waist.

"You'd better go in," he finally said. "You're starting to shiver."

"I don't feel at all cold," she said, realizing the moment she had spoken that her words could have a double meaning.

He chuckled. "You know, you're a lady I could become addicted to very easily."

"Addictions are a terrible thing," came her answer as she looked up at him.

"There are certain exceptions." He inclined his face toward hers.

His kiss was gentle and undemanding. She reached up, touching his hair. The texture was soft, just as she had known it would be. She felt a tremor of emotion and fervently wished she were the kind of woman who could be more open with her feelings: one who could say, *Benjamin Yates, I think there's a very good chance I'm falling in love with you.*

He smiled as if he understood her thoughts. This time, their kiss was lingering.

"Lord," he groaned, "I wish I could be with you again tomorrow instead of having to attend that energy conference I told you about. I don't know if I can last till Sunday."

Snuggling against him, she thought of his invitation for Sunday. "Dinner and then a party at the home of some friends, right?"

"Yes. I'm looking forward to showing you off. Hey, wear that light-orange dress, okay?"

She smiled. "Apricot."

He kissed the tip of her nose. "Right, that's the one. Okay?"

"Okay," she promised and went on inside.

As she closed the door, Warren came out through the kitchen and switched on the light. He smiled paternally as she blinked against the glare, instinctively smoothing hasty fingers through her tousled curls. Feeling like a teenager coming in from a date, she wondered if she had any lipstick left on.

"The phone just rang for you," Warren told her, "and I said to hold on because I thought I heard you coming in. It's Kirby Orchard. It must be important, because he's called twice."

21

As Warren returned to his study, Janet hurriedly picked up the phone in the kitchen, her thoughts focusing on the Renner house. The fact that Kirby had called twice convinced her he must have turned up something especially important.

"Kirby," she said, her words tumbling out. She hadn't realized she would feel so eager. "You got your book back, right? What have you learned about the house?"

"Hold on," he admonished with a chuckle. "My friend did return my book, but so far, I've found nothing exciting—nothing like a nasty family curse or an Indian massacre on the land before the house was built. Of course, we can always hope. Anything new with you?"

"No," Janet complained, disappointed by Kirby's lack of news, "and I've been there every day this week with Rose."

"Well, don't feel downcast," he soothed cheerfully. "After a bit more investigation, I may turn up something on the wild side yet. My book is a local record written by a Princeton resident just before the turn of the century. He mentions the names of former residents of the present

Renner house, which have directed me to other sources—genealogies, collections of letters and diaries. When you study houses, you're also studying people, and rarely is everything waiting in one neat package."

It sounded dry to Janet, but when Kirby asked, "Could you come over tomorrow morning?" she was quick to say she would. "But it will have to be early. Muriel wants me by eleven-thirty, when she goes to bring Dr. Renner home from the hospital."

"Then why don't we meet at nine? That should give us all the time we need."

Agreeing, she hung up with a smile. With Ben scheduled to be away all day at the energy conference, Saturday had offered nothing of interest except Dr. Renner's homecoming. Now, thanks to Kirby, the prospects had brightened considerably.

She had no sooner gone into the living room to exchange a few words with Fran when the phone rang again. Warren lumbered from his study, grinning and rubbing his beard in exaggerated perplexity.

"I don't know about this sister of yours," he said to Fran. "She's bewitching all the males in Princeton." Still grinning, he turned to Janet. "The phone is for you again. I'm done working in my study—go ahead and take it in there."

The caller was Ben, wanting to say good night. He and Janet talked for awhile, their voices low, their words punctuated with soft laughter. She went to bed starry-eyed, thinking only of Ben. But in the morning, as soon as she opened her eyes, she found herself looking forward to her meeting with Kirby, certain his information would solve the mystery of the gallery.

At nine on the dot, he was answering her ring at his door. "A bright and early hello," he greeted, letting her in. He wore rumpled flannel trousers and a flannel shirt that was a bright, leprechaun green. "I see you've brought a notebook. Excellent. Nothing like organizing facts and your thoughts about them on paper."

"I'm all set," she said expectantly, eager to get down to business. With Trixie in tow, she followed as Kirby ushered the way into his office and directed her to a seat alongside his desk. She was no more than seated when he excused himself to fetch a tray bearing a teapot, napkins, cups, cream, sugar, and lemon. Setting down the tray, he said, "Oh, forgot something," and started for the kitchen again.

"Let me help," Janet offered, hoping to hurry him along.

"No, no—only take a second." He returned with a fussy little ceramic dish which contained assorted wheat crackers and cookies. He held out a piece of broken cookie to Trixie. Wheezing and snuffling, the elderly bulldog investigated the tidbit thoroughly before daintily accepting it and waddling off.

Eyes following the creature, Kirby shook his head. "Would you believe that had I given that persnickety animal a whole cookie, she would have snapped it right up?"

"Animals sure can be funny," Janet agreed impatiently, feeling she would jump out of her skin if she couldn't prod him into getting started. "So did you find out how old the house is?"

"Not exactly," he admitted, pouring the tea. Done with the food at last, he sat and turned his attention to the books and papers on his desk. "But there is enough information for us to make an intelligent guess." He tapped the open page on his desk. "Elizabeth Parke—that's spelled with a final *e*, was an orphan who built the house with an inheritance from her adoptive father. He died at Gettysburg in 1863. From another record, I learned that eight years later, in 1871, the house was standing and occupied. So, we know Elizabeth must have built it sometime between '63 and '71."

"Doesn't its architecture help pinpoint the year more accurately?"

"Not really. The Queen Anne style was popular in England at around the time of the Civil War, and spread to this country a bit later. But it was all within the same general time period we've discussed. For a conservative estimate"—he inclined his head toward her notebook—"let's say the house was finished around 1870."

Janet dutifully recorded the date and then, pen poised, looked up expectantly. "So, Elizabeth Parke was the first resident?"

"That's open to question. Perhaps she never got a chance to move in. I have here a collection of letters, some of which are from a Parke family relative who resented that blood kin had been overlooked in favor of an adopted child in regard to the inheritance. In honor of the family who had taken her in, Elizabeth Parke erected the house with the idea of making it a home for orphans, or, as this letter snidely puts it: 'Elizabeth was set on frittering good money on bastards as undeserving as herself.'"

"Hardly charitable!" sniffed Janet in disapproval.

"No indeed, although you must remember we are talking of a Victorian society, where a traceable and unblemished lineage was judged as considerably more important than it is today. In any case, Miss Parke seems to have died before her dream came to fruition, for at a later date, a letter states: 'her life's blood spent on her folly, she expired of influenza, leaving her shelter for the lost to be bought by strangers.'"

The corners of Janet's mouth turned down. "How sad. Then Elizabeth never established her orphanage after all?"

"Apparently not. By 1871, the house was inhabited by a family prominent in the area—they were the ones mentioned in the book my friend returned. It was a reference to the fact that they purchased the 'Parke House,' that gave me the clue to search out Elizabeth." His modest tone was somewhat belied by the proud way he puffed out his cheeks. "I knew I had come across the 'Parke' name somewhere in a letter, so I searched my collection of old published letters until I found it."

He took a sip of tea and returned his attention to the materials on his desk. "So," he continued, "the Hickoks lived in the house for about ten years, and then—"

"Hickok?" Janet interrupted. "I just saw that name yesterday. It was inscribed on a baptismal font in a tiny chapel that Ben Yates and I toured. Could it be the same family?"

"Faith Chapel?" Kirby beamed. "Yes, it certainly is the same family. The Hickoks were responsible for a number of community efforts, including the establishment of that church. It finally fell into disrepair, but was then saved by the historical society."

"The Hickoks lost twin sons," Janet said. "Their names were on the font—it was dedicated to them."

"Yes, and if I recall correctly, their family monument is in the cemetery outside."

"Ben thought it probably was." She was remembering her feelings when she stood at the font: her thoughts about Becky and the later discussion with Ben. And then even later, being in Ben's arms.

Busily consulting his papers, Kirby nodded absently. "Okay, we have Elizabeth Parke and then the Hickoks. Next, somewhere around 1888, the Alexander Whitehursts were in residence. We know because it's mentioned in an old record that an Alex Whitehurst Jr., of that address, was one of those who lost his life in the blizzard of '88. After that, I found no reference until 1910, when an old map shows that a family named Goodsmith lived there. Oh, by the way, I forgot to mention that Elizabeth had named the place The Beeches."

Janet brightened. "There's a huge old copper beech in the yard."

"When I was a kid, there were two of them," Kirby reminisced. "Perhaps at one time, there was a whole grove, a grove of beechen green..." Leaning back, he quoted: "That thou, light-winged Dryad of the trees, in some melodious plot of beechen green, and shadows numberless, singest of summer in full-throated ease..." Voice trailing off, he looked faintly embarrassed. "Keats, *Ode to a Nightingale*. Anyway—"

He straightened in his chair. "From then on, my job was a cinch. A phone call established that the people I knew as a kid, the Patricks, bought the house from folks named

Granger. The Grangers were supposed to have been there for years. I think it's safe to assume they purchased the place from the Goodsmiths, so—" He inflated his green-clad chest with pleased satisfaction. "We've come full circle in the investigation."

Janet, who had been writing down the family names, frowned at her list. "But we really don't know anything about the people or things that happened there. I mean, we don't know anything that indicates why the house should be disturbed."

Kirby gave her a sharp stare that seemed out of keeping with his cherubic appearance. "Haunted—that's what you really mean. You're convinced it's haunted."

Flushing, Janet was defensive. "Isn't that why I brought up the subject in the first place?"

Nodding, he adjusted his glasses. "And you told me you *thought* you saw lights and you *thought* you heard sounds. You painted a rather vague and uncertain picture." He tilted his head inquisitively. "You know, there are people who overplay their experiences, but I have a hunch you do the opposite. Could it be that you've been holding something back?" His tone remained mild, yet there was intensity behind it as he said, "Suppose you tell me all over again exactly what you witnessed at the Renner house."

22

So, she told him. Told him everything about the whispered chanting and the ghostly figures, including the fact that she had earlier seen the image of the little boy in the Renner back yard.

Kirby listened with absorbed interest, his eyes never

straying from her face. When she finished, he was silent a moment, then said, "Janet, I don't want you to misunderstand what I'm going to say. I *do* believe you, but the fact of the matter is, the children and the phantom voices may not actually be real."

"I never claimed they were," she defended, bristling. "I mean, they were there, but they were ghosts—*apparitions*!"

He cleared his throat. "What I mean is, without your presence they may not exist. There are several theories concerning the appearance of ghosts. One of them holds that the medium's very presence is what causes psychic energies to assume specific form. This mysterious energy is real, but not necessarily the form in which it is perceived. Let me give you an example." He arranged his portly form in a scholarly pose. "Let's use the example of neon lights. Neon signs are made in various designs and letters of the alphabet, yet would we say that electrified neon is shaped like the letter *K*, or shaped like a fish? No, because we understand it's the glass tubing that determines the patterns we see. According to the theory I'm explaining, ethereal energy has no more intrinsic form than neon gas. It is you, or rather, the projected force of your subconscious mind, that encases and fashions the energy in the Renner house into children and chanting. Another psychic might perceive it as entirely different."

Dismayed, Janet bit her lip. "Then you're saying that what I saw is possibly a result of my own mental state?"

"Under this supposition, yes. To test it, we ask—do children figure in your life in such a way that the theory is logical? When I say, *little children*, does it have a deep and special meaning?"

Janet hesitated, unable to keep tears, those damned betraying tears, from springing to her eyes. "Earlier this year, my little daughter died. She—she was only a few months old."

"Ah." Kirby's tone was sympathetic. "I am sorry to hear that. Had she been sickly since birth?"

When Janet briefly explained, he nodded. "Then her death was a tremendous blow."

"Yes, it was."

Pursing his lips, he studied her speculatively. "This shock could be responsible for opening your mind to psychic awareness."

Janet hated the way his explanation drained the magic from what she had witnessed. "Didn't you say there were other theories?"

"Yes, although I hardly think they apply here. Hauntings may also be a psychic record of an actual past event. Say, a woman who hanged herself in a certain room might keep appearing there as a ghost. Without prior knowledge of the actual event, witnesses will give identical descriptions of the woman. It's as if the distraught suicide victim has caused the event to indelibly shape the psychic ether. What's created is a sort of psychic imprint."

Perplexed, Janet asked, "But does that sort of ghost actually communicate with people?"

"No, and that brings us to the third theory. In traditional literature, a ghost is a human spirit trapped in this world after death instead of moving on to the spiritual realm. Such a ghost exhibits an independent personality and often is said to communicate with mediums in a séance." Kirby rocked back in his chair, folding his hands across the mound of his stomach. "There is enormous evidence that intangible energy exists, yet few keys to help us understand its true nature. But at least in your case, we can be pretty certain we're dealing with the first explanation: the ghost children are most assuredly a projection of your own mental state."

It was clear that Kirby's mind was set, and for a brief instant, Janet wondered if he could be right. Then she shook her head. What she had seen had been absolutely real. But she couldn't blame Kirby for not believing her. Ben probably wouldn't believe her either. Thank goodness she had kept her mouth shut with him. Accepting the futility of further argument, she attempted a laugh. "Maybe it's the electrician I should talk to."

When Kirby tilted his head in question, she waved a hand, dismissing her words even as she spoke them, figuring there was no way Kirby would listen with an open mind. "It's just that the electrician Muriel hired only worked upstairs a few hours on one afternoon, then refused to come back."

"What were his reasons for not returning?"

"He didn't have a reason, at least nothing that made sense. When Muriel had me call him, he said he had a job elsewhere, only he made it sound like a religious avocation."

"Oh? What were his precise words?"

Janet shrugged. "You'll think it's crazy, and I guess it is, but it sounded as if he said he was *born to call*. That's what made me think of religion—you know, a religious calling. But he mumbled and I must have heard him wrong."

"Think back," Kirby encouraged, excitement creeping into his tone. "Instead of saying, born *to*, could he have said born *with*?"

"Yes, I suppose so." Kirby's unexpected interest surprised her. "But he must have been drinking. 'Born with a call' makes no sense."

"Not c-a-l-l." Kirby looked like a man who had won an unexpected prize. "It's c-a-u-l. 'Born with a caul' is also termed, 'born with a veil.' It refers to a baby born with the afterbirth membrane covering the face. In folklore, such a child grows up possessing second sight, or, what we term a psychic gift. It sounds as if the electrician was trying to tell you he believed himself sensitive to the unknown and had no wish to return to the Renner house."

Janet felt sudden hope. "If he saw the children too, then you would have to believe me!"

"But I *do* believe you. It's just that neither of us know how to interpret what you saw and heard. In any case, since your experiences have not recurred, there's no reason for you to feel wary."

"Who said I did? Or at least, I don't feel wary of the children. It's the chanting that sounded so threatening."

He pondered this. "The ghost children themselves... you weren't the least afraid of them?"

"Little children? Of course not!"

He was puzzled. "But isn't it the children who utter the chant? 'We are, we are...' Who else is the 'we' except the children?"

Unsettled, Janet drew back. "It-it's logical, but—well, I just never thought of it that way."

"Perhaps you hesitated to think of the children as the source of something frightening."

"I guess that's true." She looked at her watch. Although there was a half-hour before she was due at the Renner house, she no longer wished to continue the discussion. The idea of the children being the source of the chant had shaken her, but why try hashing it out if Kirby believed it was all only a figment of her imagination anyway?

Standing, she said, "I'd better be going. Muriel might need me early."

Kirby also stood. "What's the name of the electrician? Perhaps he'll be willing to talk with me."

His request encouraged her, and as she got the electrician's name from the phone book, she decided she might have judged Kirby too hastily. Maybe his mind wasn't such a closed door after all.

"You know," she said slowly, sitting down again, "there's one other thing I've begun to wonder about." She told him about the crying baby. "I figure someone in the neighborhood cares for the child on an infrequent basis, which is why Fran doesn't know about it. But to be honest, there's something weird about the cries. Although I've never heard them when I've been in the Renner house, could they have something to do with the ghost children?"

Then, before Kirby could reply, she shook her head and spoke again, "But no, I forgot—Gina heard the baby too."

"Gina? Oh, you mean the Stocktons' foster child." Kirby frowned. "I understood that she's unable to talk. An emotional trauma from being in an earthquake. And now she's recovered?"

"Not to a full extent." Janet spoke with sudden heat. "The Stocktons were assured her speech would return when she felt secure again, but they've done precious little to give her that needed security."

Kirby was thoughtful. "She's the little girl you brought to my door on Halloween night, isn't she? A lovely child."

Janet was pleased. "Yes, she is. And when the mood strikes her, she *can* speak, even if only a few words."

"Then, she's spoken to you on several occasions?"

"Yes, she . . ." Janet corrected herself. "No, to be strictly honest, I have to say it was only once. It seems more because we get along so well, but I guess there really was only one time. However"—she wagged a finger—"I really heard her, so don't start calling it some neon gas fabrication."

With a rumbling chuckle, Kirby spread his hands. "I wouldn't presume to argue."

At the door, he said, "I'll let you know if the electrician has anything interesting to add to this mystery." His tone grew heavy. "And a word to the wise. Regardless of the cause of an apparent haunting, one aspect seems to be common to all—the force of the disturbance tends to increase in direct proportion to the time a sensitive person spends in the area, dwelling upon it. Don't be afraid of the Renner home, but on the other hand, don't linger in the upper stairway listening and watching. Although your vigilance may be rewarded, you also may get more than you bargained for."

23

Although it had looked like rain earlier, Janet saw the sun emerging as she came from Kirby's house. She started along the pavement which ran down the short side of the block. Reaching the point where the view led across a series of back yards, she saw Gina and Pagoda once again playing hide-and-seek in the Renner's privet hedge.

Oh, my! Janet thought, envisioning the doctor coming home to see the child and practically suffering a relapse. Such lovely property, and then to deny children access—it seemed so wrong! Nevertheless, he was the owner and she felt a responsibility to see that Gina abided by his rules.

Cutting across the intervening yards, she called Gina's name.

The little girl turned, a smile illuminating her face.

Janet's heart melted like taffy, but she struggled to maintain a stern expression. "Gina—I asked you the other day not to play here by yourself. The man who lives in this house is coming home from the hospital. He becomes very upset when children are in his yard."

Ignoring Janet's words, the child ran forward to give her an enthusiastic hug.

"You little monkey!" Janet was unable to keep from smiling. Her session with Kirby had been draining, but Gina's cheery openness refreshed her spirits. She untangled the child's arms from about her waist. "You think you can charm me, do you? Head on home, now. I have to go inside and take care of Miss Rose while her sister's away. I'll see you later."

Gina peered up at her quizzically.

Janet laughed at the child's expression. "Yes, honey, I promise. I'll stop by your house later. I know how long and dull a Saturday afternoon can be when there's nothing special to do."

As she said this, she was thinking that spending time with Gina would be a lot healthier than mulling over Kirby's ghost theories. How dumb to have looked forward to the session when it turned out to be so upsetting. It made her angry to recall Kirby's belief that the ghost children were created by her mental state. Unfortunately, the supposition that they uttered the chant was harder to argue with. Those eerie, whispered sounds . . . she couldn't suppress a shudder.

Maybe the chant wouldn't sound so ominous if she could make out all the words.

She shifted her attention back to Gina. "When I come over, we'll go to the park, or maybe you can show me your schoolwork." Placing her hands on the child's shoulders, she turned her about to face her house and gave her a little push. "See you later, young lady, but for now—skedaddle."

With a quick grin over her shoulder, Gina raced off, Pagoda at her heels.

When Janet was ushered in through the Renners' front door, she saw that Muriel was dressed to go—a short mink jacket worn over a claret-colored suit, a matching fur hat pinned to her sleek black hair. Tan gloves, and black purse and shoes completed the ensemble of what a high-born South American lady wears to fetch a husband home from the hospital.

The woman seemed nervous over the homecoming. "I have persuaded Dr. Renner to make the trip by ambulance," she said, explaining how he had adamantly refused to allow a bed to be set up for him on the first floor of the house.

"He insists he will be comfortable nowhere except in his study with his books, so I thought it would be best to have someone to carry him directly upstairs. He does not realize how weak his stay in bed has left him."

Janet wasn't impressed. "What he should realize is how much harder that makes it for you to care for him."

Muriel gave her a look of cool reprimand. "I will manage." Changing the subject, she said, "Rose is in the kitchen with her lunch. Perhaps you would care for lunch also. I regret to warn you that her mood today is restless."

"Does she know your husband is coming home?"

"I have told her. But I think she is edgy because her sleep was disturbed last night—as was mine. Those mischief makers returned again." The woman's eyes reflected her anxiety. "I don't know how Dr. Renner will react if they persist. It will upset him terribly."

There was no longer a doubt in Janet's mind that Muriel must mean genuine Halloween pranksters. Doubly glad she had sent Gina out of the yard, she said, "If it happens again, Mrs. Renner, you should call the police. It's their job to take care of such problems."

Muriel shook her head. "When one is a foreigner, one does not call in the authorities."

"There's nothing to fear," assured Janet. "Besides, if kids get away with causing trouble, they become even more bold. If you're bothered again, ring up the police. You'll be doing the entire neighborhood a favor."

Muriel's wry smile was polite, but disbelieving. "Thank you. I will remember your advice." Glancing at her watch, she reached for the door. "Look for our return within the hour."

Leaving her jacket on the entry hall chair, Janet went into the kitchen where she found Rose noisily eating a bowl of soup. A white napkin tucked under her chin protected the inevitable black dress from spatters. Looking up, the woman blotted her mouth. "Good soup. You want soup?"

Janet saw that there was plenty left in the pan on the stove. Without having given much thought to it, she had decided to wait for lunch until returning home again. But if she was to spend time with Gina later that afternoon, it would be well to have the meal over and done with.

"Sounds good," she told the elderly woman, turning on the gas under the pan. After they both finished eating, Janet was clearing the table when Rose stood. "Music," she intoned. "I want my music."

"I heard your music playing when I came in," Janet said. "You can go on into the study by yourself, can't you? I want to wash these dishes. Your sister will have enough work without clearing up after us once her husband is home."

"Dr. Herman," Rose mumbled, such scorn in her tone that Janet turned to gape at her in surprise. "Dr. Herman," the woman repeated, then gestured as if spitting on the floor.

"Rose!" Janet scolded. "I hope you don't act like that when your sister is around. It only makes things harder for her."

"Dr. Herman," Rose repeated in that same derisive tone. Abruptly, she reached for Janet's arm, her manner becoming urgent. "Come, you see! Must see!"

Janet allowed the woman to lead her into the study, figuring she would settle her with her music and then go back to finish the kitchen chores later. Only instead of going to her chair, Rose hobbled to the rosewood secretary.

"Look!" she ordered, pointing to the upper bookcase.

"Yes, all right, I'm looking, Rose," Janet said patiently. "What do you want me to see?"

With a cackle, the woman reached around and triumphantly produced a key from behind the secretary.

"Look!" she ordered again, fumbling the key into the lock.

"Now, Rose..." Janet chided, not liking the situation. "If that bookcase were any of my business, it wouldn't be locked."

Ignoring her protests, Rose opened the glass doors and tore out a volume.

"No," objected Janet as Rose thrust the book at her. "I don't want that—put it back."

But with desperate intensity, the woman shoved the book forward and Janet had to take it to prevent it from falling. It was heavy, its glossy, textbooklike pages filled with headings and subheadings in a foreign language.

"This must be one of Dr. Renner's school books," Janet reasoned aloud, curious despite herself. "The language of Austria is German, isn't it? Are these his old psychology books?"

"Yes, yes," verified Rose, the *s* sounds hissing like steam from a boiling teakettle. She showed Janet another book that was much the same, then opened and presented the clothbound journal. As Janet had assumed earlier, the journal correlated the numbers on the books with titles, also written in German. The fading ink showed a mechanically precise penmanship, the sevens slashed in the European way. The words *Mutter* and *Kinder* were frequently repeated. A likely translation sprang to Janet's lips and she said, "Mother and child?"

Rose moaned in delight, as if Janet had successfully deciphered a Rosetta stone. "Yes, yes!" she agreed, voice cracking in excitement. "Mother, child—the love, all the time!"

Janet stared. It was to be expected that books on child psychology would address themselves to the love found in a mother-child relationship. Such feverish elation made no sense.

"All right, Rose, now calm down. I've seen what you wanted to show me, thank you." She returned the journal and books to their places and closed the glass doors. Finding a hook on the back of the case, she rehung the key. With a brisk smile, she turned to the old woman. "Why don't you go sit and relax a little after your lunch."

The tension that had been on Rose's face eased slightly. "Lunch. Soup was good."

"Yes, it was delicious," Janet agreed, grateful that the woman had been sidetracked so easily. With no further difficulty, she was able to settle her in the rocker. The TV showed an underwater cartoon and by appropriate coincidence, the stereo played "Octopus's Garden," by the Beatles. Janet stayed until she was certain that Rose was absorbed in the music, then quietly returned to the kitchen.

Not five minutes later, when she was hanging the dish towel to dry, she heard Rose's shuffling approach. The old woman entered the kitchen, the expression on her lined face as intense as before.

"You must see," she said, her tone emphatic. "You must know."

Supposing that Rose intended to trot out the books again, Janet's reply was equally emphatic. "I refuse to poke into what's not my business, Rose."

The old woman squinted her rheumy eyes and worked her mouth. Janet could almost see rusty gears turning in the cobwebby attic of her mind. With a suddenly sly smile, Rose mumbled under her breath.

"What's that?" Janet leaned forward. "I didn't hear."

"I use the stair lift," the woman declared, voice growing in confidence. "Sister says, no big steps—now I use the stair lift."

"Rose, that's wonderful!" Relieved they were off the subject of the books, Janet applauded as if for a child.

"You see me!" Rose moved to the rear staircase, beckoning Janet to follow. "You go stairs, I go lift. So easy!"

Indulgently, Janet went after her, watching as Rose settled herself on the stair-lift seat and pressed a button. With a grinding whirr, the chair started to move along its metal track.

"Come!" Rose leaned forward anxiously, gesturing.

"Don't lean over—you'll fall!" Janet hurried to catch up. "I'm coming, see?" Reaching the top, she expected Rose to reverse the action of the lift and go down again, but instead, with a grunt, she stood.

"What now?" Janet asked rhetorically, thinking that Muriel hadn't exaggerated when warning that Rose was "restless."

"Room." Rose moved along the narrow corridor. "Must look room."

Janet hesitated. If Rose intended to lead on to her own room, they would have to cross the gallery. She shrank from the risk of once again hearing the chanting. She remembered Kirby's warning: regardless of the source of the disturbance, her sensitivity to it might cause its force to increase. She studied the sun-washed head of the main steps with a wary eye. It was hard to believe anything ominous could happen there. Surely, anyone lingering in that spot would find only the caress of sunshine, as pure and warm upon the shoulders as liquid gold.

"See!" crowed Rose. Startled, Janet saw that the woman had opened the door directly off the narrow corridor. She found herself looking into the study that went on through to the master bedroom. Furniture had been adjusted to make space for the hospital bed. Suddenly, she understood what Rose had wanted.

"Oh, Rose—you wanted me to see the room that's been fixed for Dr. Herman, didn't you? It's very nice. Thank you for showing it to me. Now, let's go back downstairs."

But Rose proceeded inside. Frowning, Janet went to bring her back, only to find her unlocking yet another bookcase.

"Oh, come on!" Janet stepped purposely toward her.

"No, must look!" the old woman insisted. Her head scarf had slipped and lank gray strands hung about her sunken cheeks as she pointed like an oracle toward a shelf of manila folders.

"I'll not look at a thing," Janet declared, realizing that Rose had tricked her. "What can this stuff mean to me? Your brother-in-law surely doesn't want us here. Come along, now."

"No!" Rose snatched a folder from a shelf. A label bearing the initial *P* was pasted to the front cover. Her voice rose, cracking in excitement. "See! The love, always the love! Always, he look for the love. So very important."

Not understanding, but deciding it best in the long run to pretend cooperation, Janet opened the folder. A musty odor wafted up from typed sheets of brittle, yellowed paper. Each sheet bore a different name beginning with a *P*.

"What are these?" Janet asked irritably. "The doctor's old clinical records?"

Nodding, Rose rifled the pages with her eager, knobby fingers. "See? All gone. All gone!"

Half choking over the moldering smell, Janet closed the folder with a slap. At the end of her patience, she stared directly into Rose's time-blurred eyes.

"Listen," she ordered. "I don't know how to read German. I can't read a word. Do you understand? Nothing on these pages makes a speck of sense, and I don't want to see another thing. Understand?"

Rose looked ready to argue. Then her shoulders sagged.

Seeing this change, Janet decided she had finally struck the right degree of firmness. "Rose, we have no business being here and we're going to leave. Understand? We're going to put things in their proper places and then go downstairs where we belong."

Returning the folder, she closed and locked the door. As with the secretary, there was a hook for the key fastened to the back.

"All gone," Rose said mournfully, wringing her hands.

"Yes," Janet said. "They're all gone back on the bookshelf and locked away." She ushered the old woman from the room.

Meekly, Rose went down the lift and along to the study, but all the while, she continued a mournful singsong: "All gone. All gone. They were with us, then they were all gone."

Janet realized she had heard Rose utter those identical words before. Perhaps she was like a computerized doll with all-purpose responses to suit any occasion. Getting separated from her sister in the store, seeing children pass by the house, having the folders locked away—all described as "all gone." Or could it be that she actually referred to something else? Perhaps something from the past that stuck in her aging mind like a burr.

Janet was tempted to ask, but once Rose was back in her chair, she appeared so much calmer that it seemed foolish to risk stirring her up again.

24

Although Muriel had told Janet she expected to be away for only an hour, it was closer to two hours before she and the ambulance arrived home with Dr. Renner. Even then, things did not go smoothly.

Janet, who had thrown on her jacket and gone to help by

holding the front door, saw Muriel leave the parked Oldsmobile and climb into the rear of the ambulance. She assumed that Herman would be brought out momentarily, but instead, nothing happened. One of the ambulance attendants, a handsome, dark-haired man, saw her on the porch and came to explain the reason for the delay.

"The wife gave us instructions," he said. "We were to carry the husband in through the front door and directly upstairs to his room. Simple—one, two, three. Now he's telling her he's going to walk."

Janet frowned. "That may be risky, considering his weak heart. His doctor wanted him to stay in the hospital longer, but he refused. I guess he has a stubborn streak."

The driver, who had come up in time to overhear Janet's words, commented, "Invalids don't realize that walking in their own homes is a lot tougher than a nice level hospital corridor with a railing on one side and a nurse on the other. Still, letting him get steamed up over it may be worse than giving him his way."

Muriel must have decided the same, for she emerged from the ambulance, her expression defeated. A second attendant was with her. For the first time, Janet saw Muriel's hair in disarray, strands loosening from her chignon to fly around a face drawn with fatigue. Her diction, however, was as controlled as ever.

Head held high, she addressed the three men: "My husband,, Dr. Herman Renner, wishes to use the stair lift to his room, but I have prevailed upon him to be carried through the house to the lift location. Once on the second floor, he need walk only a few yards before reaching his bed."

"Is there furniture to clear out of our path?" asked the driver.

"There probably is." Muriel gave Janet a weary look. "I will stay with Dr. Renner. Will you please show the gentlemen the way?"

Janet led them in, pointing out the route through the dining room and kitchen. Rose emerged from the study and stood with her head tilted to one side, giving the strangers an intent and curious stare.

"Have to move the dining set, that's all," the driver decided.

"Right," agreed the dark-haired man, grabbing a chair. He said something to Rose, probably a caution to keep out of the way, for Janet heard her respond, "I move, yes, I move."

Having taken her jacket out to the entry, Janet was aware that the attendant and Rose had each spoken again, but she missed their words. The next thing she knew, Rose was hobbling back to the study as rapidly as her stiffened legs could carry her. The attendant frowned after her, his expression reflecting puzzlement.

Wondering what was wrong, Janet hurried after the old woman. She found her standing in the study, both hands clamped over her mouth. Her eyes were wide and frightened.

"Rose..." Janet went to her. "What's the matter?" With a moan, the woman began swaying from side to side, as if suffering some indescribable mental anguish.

Janet asked her if anything hurt, or if the man had said something to upset her, but Rose's only response was continued moaning. Not knowing what else to do, Janet led her to her chair. Once seated, the woman's moans subsided although she still kept her hands clamped across her mouth.

Finished in the dining room, the men went out to get Dr. Renner. Keeping one eye on her charge, Janet stepped to the doorway when the stretcher was carried in, the wasted carcass upon it blanketed to the chin. The bony outlines of the doctor's skull was revealed by his scanty, white hair, and his nose was a jutting prow of bone. In that gaunt, wax mask of a face, only his fiercely darting eyes seemed alive.

Withdrawing from the strange gaze, Janet slipped back into the study with Rose. Ten minutes later, she heard footsteps at the study door. She glanced up to see the dark-haired attendant beckoning.

As she moved into the dining room, he said with concern,

"We're ready to leave and I wanted to know how the old gal was doing."

"Yes, I wanted to talk with you too. She's calmer now, but what happened? What did you say to her?"

"Nothing much." The man was obviously perplexed. "All I said was—" He spoke a few words in a foreign tongue, then translated: "Good afternoon, Grandmother— that's all I said. As soon as I recognized her accent."

Janet was nonplused. "What part of South America are you from?"

The man laughed. "South America? No part. I'm Hungarian."

Janet was more confused than ever. "Then she couldn't have understood you. I wonder what she thought you said? Whatever, it apparently frightened her. Rose is from Argentina."

The attendant gave her a sidelong look. "Originally? Even with the teeth gone and the way she mumbles, she's got the sound of my old relatives from Hungary. And she knows the language because her answer was perfect. She wished me a fine afternoon. Then all of a sudden, off she runs, her face like death. There's something a bit strange about the old gal, that's for sure."

By the time Muriel came downstairs after settling Dr. Renner in his sickroom, Rose was rocking blandly before the TV, her troubled mind apparently having gone as smooth as the paraffin seal in a jelly jar. Janet made no mention of the upsetting incident, but her confusion remained after she left the Renner house.

Having been told that Rose was a native of Argentina, she had never questioned her accent. If it hadn't really sounded Spanish, she had unthinkingly attributed it to the woman's garbled manner of speaking and her own uneducated ear. There was no chance the attendant was mistaken. The way Rose had clapped her hands over her mouth told the story— her knowledge of Hungarian was a secret, and the poor woman had been trying to seal her lips after it was too late.

Let's assume, Janet said to herself, cutting through the privet hedge on her way to Gina's, that the sisters were actually from a poor Hungarian family, only that wasn't good enough for Dr. Renner. He not only wanted people to believe his wife had a more elevated pedigree, he wanted it to be more exotic. And to him, South America was exotic. With Muriel's dark beauty, the deception was easy enough, and so it was done. The doctor's wishes were clearly law in that household—Janet could imagine him ordering Muriel to scour away any hint of her accent, while poor Rose, "who could not be trusted," was bound to secrecy.

Nearing the Stockton house, she remembered the urgency with which Rose had thrust the doctor's books and patient records upon her. There had been such wildness in her eyes. Perhaps she believed his private papers held references to herself and Muriel. Janet supposed Dr. Renner was aware of how disturbed the poor woman was. Not that he hadn't looked plenty disturbed himself when being moved through the house. Janet reasoned it must be a helpless sensation to be carried strapped to a stretcher. He had probably been terrified that the attendants would drop him. That would explain why he had been so against being carried up the stairs.

Unless—she couldn't help smiling—unless he had been afraid of the front way because of the ghosts.

Her smile faded as she realized she might have struck upon something. Suppose the doctor had sensed an odd atmosphere in the railed upper gallery? Maybe it had been fear rather than reasons of health that had inspired him to install the back stair lift.

Reaching the Stockton front door, she realized she was allowing her imagination to get out of hand. Except for herself—and perhaps the electrician—everyone else seemed to consider the upper hall neutral territory. When she wasn't playing games, Rose even preferred the front way, and she had seen Muriel dash up and down there without a thought.

Mrs. Ousler answered the bell. Janet explained about

wanting to spend time that afternoon with Gina only to learn that the child had gone out with Tommy and Veronica.

"Of all days for this to happen," the motherly woman lamented. "The child does so enjoy your company."

Glad that Gina was having an outing, but disappointed for herself, Janet was about to leave when the housekeeper said suddenly, "Say, your first name is Janet, isn't it?"

"Why, yes."

The woman's laugh was jolly. "Then that explains this!" She handed over a piece of paper from her apron pocket. "Gina wrote this and tucked it into my hand as she left. Only I couldn't figure out until this minute who it was for."

Janet saw that the message started with the printed word, *Ganit*.

"See how she sounded it out?" prompted the housekeeper. "Because Gina and Janet start with the same sound, she thought they both began with the same letter, only it threw me off. She's a smart little cookie, isn't she? And the message is awfully cute too."

"Yes." Janet saw that Gina had carefully printed:

Ganit I sorry have must go away.
I love you. Love Gina.

Mrs. Ousler chuckled. "Isn't that just the sweetest thing?"

"Yes, yes it is." Touched, Janet swallowed the lump that had formed in her throat. "Do you know when she'll be back?"

"Late, that's what Mrs. Stockton told me. She's throwing a party tomorrow—a spur of the moment thing for all his company friends, so you'd think she'd be getting things ready, wouldn't you? Instead, she and the mister rush off with the little girl, when usually, they never seem to remember she's around." The woman shook her head over the futility of trying to figure out her employers.

Janet went home to an empty house. Usually, she didn't mind solitude, but on that afternoon she longed to hear a friendly voice. If only Ben were home! She thought of calling Kirby, but didn't want to start thinking about the

Renner house again. It was all crazy stuff—she'd be better off to forget it all, every scrap of it.

She worked the rest of the day on the second newsletter. When checking a word in the dictionary, she saw it had a German-English section. After a hesitation, she looked up *Mutter* and *Kinder*, telling herself the words had to do with Rose and Muriel and not the haunting. As she had suspected, they meant "mother" and "child." *Kinder*, she thought, as in "kindergarten." Into her mind leaped an image of herself being in charge of kindergarten, or rather, some kind of nursery group. It was something she had never done and she didn't know why such an image had come to her. One more odd thing in a very odd day, she told herself, returning to her work.

Much later, after a supper of crackers and cheese, she waited up for Fran and Warren only to fall asleep during an old war movie on TV.

Somewhere in the back of her mind she knew she was starting to dream. She saw herself standing in Herman Renner's second-floor sickroom, only it had been cleverly decorated with a bold painting of the beech tree, the broad gray trunk on one wall, the limbs and colored leaves twisting upward to brightly cover the ceiling. *Like a nursery*, she thought, still outside the dream and able to remember thinking about a nursery earlier.

Abruptly, she became an active participant and the dream seemed real. She saw that the room actually was a nursery. Instead of Dr. Renner's hospital bed, there were rows of children's cribs.

An unseen companion handed her a folder. As she opened it, the typed pages burst into flames. She cast the folder away with a cry just as another was thrust upon her. She wanted to refuse it, but then it was in her hands, opening by itself. Fire burst upwards. Another burning folder appeared and then another. Starting to sob in panic, she struggled in vain to protect herself as the folders flew upon her like birds with incendiary plumage, scorching her hands, her arms, the smoke starting to fill her lungs.

It was then she saw fire spring up from inside the cribs and realized in horror that the burning folders had ignited the nursery beds. Feeling her hair and eyelashes start to crisp in the searing heat, she frantically beat at the flames with her blistering hands, but it was too late. The temperature rose to the flash point and the curtains, walls, and ceiling exploded with a roar. The cribs became a sea of fiery tongues that cried out in agony—cried like lost children, abandoned, trapped, and burning.

25

On Sunday, Janet went with Ben for a light supper at a Rocky Hill tavern he knew, and then on to the party as planned. Although she had especially looked forward to meeting his friends, she found it impossible to keep her thoughts on the evening at hand. The manner in which the terror of her nightmare had tied in with Dr. Renner's sickroom and the folders Rose had been so desperate for her to see kept her strange experiences at the Renner house in the forefront of her mind. Noticing her distraction, Ben asked several times if she was all right. She assured him that she was, but then, on the way home when he asked her again, she felt remorse.

"I'm sorry," she apologized glumly. "I hope I didn't spoil the evening for you. Maybe I should have canceled out."

"No, honey—it's just that I can tell something is wrong."

It had been on the tip of her tongue to excuse away her mood by simply saying she hadn't slept well and leaving it at that, but the concern in his voice broke through her reserve. Suddenly, she was telling him about her dream as well as confessing her belief that the Renner house was haunted.

While she talked, Ben interrupted only to clarify a few points, and when she finished, he was silent, staring straight ahead as he drove through the night.

Unable to help feeling rebuffed, she said stiffly, "Well, you're a good listener, I'll say that." Bitterly, she regretted having told him a thing. Hadn't she known all along it would be a mistake? "I guess it's time to move on to a less wacky topic, right?"

"No, it's not that." His tone was unreadable. "I was trying to sort things out. You gave me a lot to absorb all at once. The Renner crew sounds difficult enough without the occult angle." After a thoughtful pause, he said, "I guess what really bothers me is that you never mentioned any of this before. You tell Kirby you think you might have seen ghosts and that you've been frightened by strange chanting sounds, yet you've never said a word to me."

His reaction caught her off guard. She hadn't considered that her silence might seem a betrayal of trust, which didn't necessarily mean he thought her story had any merit. Defending herself, she said, "I only told Kirby because it's a subject that interests him."

Looking over at her, Ben said softly, "A subject that interests me is *you*. If you've had upsetting experiences, I want to know about them." He reached across the seat, his fingers strong and warm as he clasped her hand. "Being able to share things—isn't that what caring for each other is all about?"

"Oh, Ben." His words and the touch of his hand moved her deeply. Voice unsteady, she said, "Maybe the fault was that I cared too much. The whole idea of claiming to have had a supernatural experience... I was afraid of what you might think."

He pressed her hand. "Don't ever be afraid, honey. Not of being honest with me. Maybe I don't understand what you've experienced, but I'm not mocking it."

She sighed, feeling as if a weight had been lifted from her. "I don't know what reaction I expected," she admitted.

"If you had shown wide-eyed enthusiasm, I guess I would have thought you too gullible."

"No pleasing some people, huh?" He smiled at her across the dimness of the car. "Actually, I have a more open mind on this than many people because of an experience when I was young."

"Oh?" She was immediately captured. "What happened?"

"When I was a kid, my mother made me take piano lessons. She and her sister Blanche had each studied the piano as girls, but Mom had a tin ear and gave it up after only a few months. Blanche, who died when she was only a young woman, had been quite talented. Mom hoped I'd take after my aunt instead of her."

"And did you?" Janet asked, wondering where the story was headed.

"No, but when my teacher gave a big, formal evening recital, I had to perform anyway. It was held in the school and one of the kids got nervous and threw up. It caused a panic. The stage was empty, with nobody ready to go on, so the teacher asked Mom, who was backstage helping, if she would explain to the audience that there would be a slight delay.

"Mom was always scared to death of being in public, but she managed to stammer something to the crowd. Then, as she was about to escape to the wings, she noticed a music book lying on the piano. She says it was as if she were suddenly in a trance. Feeling as if she were watching herself from a distance, she opened the book to a selection, sat on the bench, and placed her fingers on the keys. Now, this is a lady who had failed at learning to read notes and who had never successfully managed to play even the most simple tune. My father, who was in the audience, said it was the most amazing thing he'd ever witnessed, because there, in front of a filled auditorium, she played an entire classical selection perfectly.

"Afterwards, backstage again, Mom was a total wreck, laughing and crying. The piece she played—something complicated by Debussy, had been a favorite with Aunt

Blanche. Mom swore she had felt Blanche's presence, and that it was actually Blanche who had done the playing, through her. She had always been convinced that her sister's spirit had lived on after death and believed that on the night of the recital, she had finally been granted the long-awaited proof."

Finishing his story, Ben shrugged. "I don't know if there's a rational explanation for Mom's experience, but whatever, it was totally outside of the normal range of happenings." Taking his eyes from the road, his smile was gentle. "I don't know whether that's good enough for you or not, but that's what I'm talking about when I say I have an open mind."

Janet's throat was tight with emotion. "It's a beautiful story. I only hope it means what your mother thinks." After a silence, she added, "But that still doesn't necessarily mean you accept everything I've told you, does it?"

"God, love, what do you want me to say? Accept it on what terms? You've told me Kirby claims there are several possible reasons for what you've experienced. Maybe the Renner house really is haunted. I know nothing about things like that, but doesn't it make sense that you might see little children for personal reasons of your own?"

"I lost one child, Ben—a four-month-old daughter. Why should I see a little boy who looks several years older, or a little girl, a toddler with dark hair? Becky's hair was blond. She never would have been really dark. I have a feeling there were more children there too, only they never took on form. The chanting was definitely made by more than two voices."

"What about the baby you keep hearing?" Approaching a crossroad, he slowed the car. "It sure seems that nobody except you thinks it exists. Maybe the cries are related to the haunting."

His words stirred the doubts in her mind. Hadn't she already admitted there was something strange about the cries? She stared at the blinker light, a coy yellow orb like the eye of an invisible cat, slyly winking at secrets that only it and the darkness knew.

As Ben moved the car on, she spoke, her voice strained. "I was about to remind you that Gina heard the baby too. But then I start to think that maybe the crying *is* related to the haunting. It scares me. If it isn't a living baby that Gina heard, does that mean she's also aware of the ghosts?"

"If there are any ghosts. I bet Kirby would say that if one mind could shape an image, another mind could see it."

"Ben, that's awful! You think Gina might be hearing and seeing illusions from my mind? It's just awful. I don't see how anyone could even suggest such a horrid thing."

"Okay, okay. So maybe the phantom children fit into one of Kirby's other categories of hauntings. They sure don't sound like a happy bunch. All that crying. That's what you said about the little boy that night, wasn't it? That he was crying?"

Janet angled herself about to see Ben's profile against the side window. The lines were firm and strong: the face of a practical man. Yet, when he had spoken of his mother's experience, he had made room in his mind for a certain cautious belief in the unknown. Perhaps it wasn't fair of her to demand more.

"You never saw the little boy, did you?" she asked. "It seems impossible that he was so clear to me, yet you didn't see him at all. Didn't you even *sense* something?"

"I'm afraid I only sensed that if we didn't get out of where we didn't belong, we'd land in trouble."

Sighing, Janet settled back. "Trouble for me would be another one of those nightmares. Even after I was awake, it seemed I could still hear the children screaming and smell the smoke from the fire. I'm fairly sure there was also something about a fire in that other dream I had. You know, that vague dream that I told you about before. I only wish I could remember."

"Maybe it's better not to. Maybe our brains work out hurts and confusions in ways we can't always understand. When we poke around, insisting on making interpretations, maybe we interfere. It might be like constantly disturbing a bandage instead of letting healing take place on its own."

Hearing his words and his comforting tone, Janet wished she had shared with him all along instead of holding back. Mentally reviewing their conversation, she realized that being *believed* had only a relative meaning and didn't count as much as she had thought. Nothing had been solved, but what mattered was to talk things over openly with someone who cared.

She looked out the window. The car traveled through a rural area a few miles above Princeton, occasional mailboxes along the way offering the only clues to nearby habitation. It must be lonely living so far away from town, so desperately lonely . . .

Stunned, she realized the drift of her thoughts. She'd always felt that living far out in the country would be peaceful. What had made thoughts of loneliness suddenly cross her mind? It made no sense, especially not when she considered how very close to Ben she'd been feeling only a moment before.

Yet she *did* feel lonely. Depressingly alone. It was as if a dark fog had seeped into the car, poisoning the air, settling over her spirits like a black cloak, making it almost impossible for her to breathe.

Suddenly, from the depth of the suffocating darkness, the image of Gina's face appeared, the child's eyes swollen with tears. Janet moaned.

Ben looked her way. "Honey—what is it?"

"I—I saw . . ." It was hard for her to speak. Blinking, she realized that the image was gone. She could breathe again, but the depression, a sense of hopeless abandonment, remained.

"I saw Gina. She . . ." Struggling to free herself from the lost, lonely mood was like fighting quicksand. She reached toward Ben. The contact steadied her. "Ben." Her voice was hoarse. "There's something wrong with Gina. We must go to her."

"What do you mean? What are you talking about?"

She clutched his sleeve. "Gina needs me, that's all I

know." Her alarm was growing. "I must go to her, *now*. She needs me!"

Ben started to ask further questions, then paused, seeming to think better of it. "All right. We're only a few miles away." He stepped on the accelerator. "Hang on. We'll be there in a matter of minutes." Saying nothing more, he simply drove.

When reaching Quince Street, Janet saw cars lined up before the brightly lit Stockton house and remembered Mrs. Ousler speaking of a party. With a party going on, the Stocktons would have no time for Gina—she might have hurt herself and no one would know...

Janet was out of the car and running toward the house as soon as Ben stopped. A man stepped out on the porch to smoke his cigar, the sounds of music and laughter following him. Heedless, she pushed past him and burst inside. Seeing her, Tommy Stockton detached himself from the crowd in the living room.

"Janet, hi! Wait a minute, I'll tell Veronica you've heard our good news—"

"Where's Gina?"

The highly polished plastic of Tommy's handsome features wrinkled in momentary confusion. "Why, upstairs with Ozzie, I suppose."

Wheeling about, Janet bolted up the stairs. She reached the landing just as Gina shot from a dimly lit corridor like a bullet and threw herself into her arms.

"Baby, baby, I'm here!" Janet cried. Running her hands along the sweating, trembling little body, she started to sob in relief. Whatever was wrong, it was nothing physical. Gina, although clearly upset, was all in one piece, alive and well.

Mrs. Ousler appeared. "My goodness! I might have guessed you'd be the one she'd be wanting." She switched on a light. "What a blessing you're here. I haven't been able to do a thing with the poor lamb."

There was confusion downstairs as Ben arrived at the door. He and Tommy stared in bewilderment at the tableau at the top of the landing. Tommy disappeared for a second and returned with Veronica. They came upstairs, Ben following.

"I didn't know what was the matter," Janet was saying in a choked voice to the housekeeper. "I had such a powerful feeling that she needed me." By that time, she was seated on the window bench, Gina on her lap, the child's face buried against her breasts, crushing her dress.

"Gina!" Veronica admonished sharply. "What do you think you're doing?" Embarrassed, she tried to pry the child free, but Janet shook her head. "No, no, it's all right."

"Not really," Mrs. Ousler snapped, flashing Veronica a look. "She's been crying for hours."

"Oh, dear," wailed Veronica.

"That's a damn shame, poor kid," Tommy commiserated uncomfortably. "It's going to take her time to adjust. I guess things were sort of abrupt."

Janet, who had been stroking Gina's back, suddenly remembered what Kirby had said about the Stocktons. Staring at Tommy, she accused, "Your new assignment came through! That's what the party is all about, isn't it?"

The entire picture became clear to her in an instant. With their thoughts focused on the excitement of the move and the celebration with their business friends, Veronica and Tommy had never taken the time to give Gina the assurances she so desperately needed.

Hugging Gina even closer, Janet vibrated with outrage. "Did you think you could just spring such changes on the child? Just announce you were whisking her abroad, uprooting her from everything she's familiar with, and not leave her feeling confused and frightened? She's only a little girl, you know."

Tommy's tone was defensive. "We're not going to uproot her at all. We've found the perfect boarding school. It has a splendid atmosphere, and living with other children will be the best thing for her anyway."

Janet couldn't believe her ears. "You're not taking her with you?"

It was Veronica who answered. "We can't, Janet. We're

going to keep moving from embassy to embassy, country to country. That would be a lot harder on Gina, you must see that. It's much better to have her settled in one place."

"A very expensive place, I might add," boasted Tommy. "The best. We toured it thoroughly today and Gina will be extremely happy there." Someone called him from below. "I must return to our guests," he told Veronica. Giving Janet a frosty nod, he retreated down the stairs.

Veronica suddenly looked very forlorn despite her sophisticated hairstyle and sleek, emerald-green gown. Then, remembering that she should be in charge, she thrust out her jaw, demanding of Janet, "Just how are you involved in this?"

"Janet is Gina's friend," spoke up Mrs. Ousler. "The child was upset and wanted her." Perhaps unaware that Janet had not been invited to the party, the housekeeper had accepted her presence without question, and her statement led Veronica to jump to conclusions of her own.

"Oh, and so you called her over. Well—" She rubbed her hands helplessly, clearly in a situation where she was at a loss.

Janet could feel Gina's tension as her small body continued to burrow silently against her like a young animal seeking comfort. Not wanting to risk being asked to leave, Janet kept her tone moderate and her feelings to herself as she offered, "Suppose I take Gina to her room and see if I can get her settled for the night?"

Veronica hesitated, then nodded. "Thank you—it seems like the best idea. I—I must return to the party."

When Veronica left, Janet realized Ben was still standing there.

"Oh, Ben," she whispered apologetically, still stroking Gina's hair. "I'll probably be a while." She felt torn by two different needs. "This isn't fair to you—I can walk home. You might as well go."

He studied her and the child, a warm but curious expression in his eyes. "It's all right," he said softly. "Take your time. Stay as long as Gina needs you. I'll wait."

26

"You want her, don't you?" Ben said to Janet as he walked her home to her sister's house.

"Yes." Her tone was fierce. "I want her desperately." Deeply shaken by Gina's hopeless, forlorn sobs, she could think of nothing else. "She went to sleep in my arms, Ben, still crying, while they were downstairs attending to their guests. They have no idea what it means to be parents. They never should have taken her in the first place."

"Don't be so rough on them, honey. Taking her was a lot better than letting her stay in an orphanage. That little Italian town where the earthquake happened was already on the edge of poverty. With her handicap, Gina's future wouldn't have stood a chance there."

Janet's eyes widened. "That's right! I forgot you knew someone from the agency that placed Gina. Have the Stocktons adopted her, or is she still only a foster child?"

"As far as I know, she's still a foster child. I could ask Edgar and find out for sure."

"Oh, would you?" They had reached Fran's side door where a lone, out-of-season rose sprang from the trellis, small and delicate, appearing colorless in the yellowish glow from the porch light. Janet looked up into Ben's face. Tone suddenly uncertain, she asked, "Do you think I'm acting crazy, wanting Gina so badly?"

He shook his head. "No, I have no trouble understanding it."

"But how do you feel about it?" Her voice quavered. "I've been thinking so much about Gina, but not . . . not about us. She's important to me, Ben." She realized she had been trying to keep her feelings for Ben and her feelings for Gina on separate tracks, but circumstances had now placed the two interests on what might be a collision course. She searched Ben's face. "I want her, Ben, but even though I'm not ready to make a commitment, I—I don't want to risk losing you."

His arms folded around her. "You don't have to make a choice, love." His gentle voice was husky. "If she's that important to you, she's important to me too."

"Oh, Ben." Perfume from the rose, unexpected and incredibly sweet, wafted over them. Tears that mingled joy and relief made her eyes shine like stars. "You don't know, you *can't* know how wonderful that makes me feel." Fingers closing on the sides of his jacket, she pulled him closer, lifting her lips to meet his.

It was some minutes later when Ben returned to the subject of Gina. "Hon, don't get your hopes too high about Gina and get hurt. She's hardly being neglected in a legal sense."

"But she is!"

"She's deprived emotionally. What that means as far as the law is concerned, I just don't know. And we don't have much time to find out. Didn't Veronica say they're scheduled to leave in two weeks?"

"Oh, God, yes. Could you reach Edgar tomorrow?"

"I'll be working out at a site all day, but I'll try to reach him at lunch time. After work, I have to go directly to my adult class. Tell you what. After class, when I pick you up for dinner, I'll let you know what's happened." He touched her hair with a gentle hand. "Don't expect too much. There's no telling what Edgar will say."

"But you'll try to make him understand?"

"I'll do my best, love," he promised, holding her close. "With you, I'll always do my best."

It was Ben's promise that saw Janet through to Monday morning, which dawned bright and clear, the film of ground frost melting away swiftly under the first rays of the sun.

After breakfast she borrowed Warren's car and drove to the high school, where she met with the newsletter director and Annabelle Chu, who had the photographs for the first issue ready. After a half day spent getting the captions written and discussing the next issue, she dropped off the final material at the printer's.

Home again, she remembered to call Kirby and tell him that since she'd already met with the director, she wouldn't be needing a ride to adult school that evening.

"Anything new?" he asked. Her thoughts were so filled with Gina that it took her a moment to realize he was speaking of the Renner house. When she told him there wasn't, he told her he had phoned the electrician. "He was out but his wife will have him return my call. I'll let you know as soon as I hear anything."

Thanking him, Janet hung up, dismissing his words as her thoughts returned immediately to Gina, who was to have had school lessons that morning and a dentist appointment that afternoon. Mrs. Ousler had promised to call if there were problems. It was a relief to know there was an ally in the motherly housekeeper.

That evening, to Janet's delight, Ben had good news. Over his steak and baked potato, he explained he had reached Edgar and learned that the agency retained final authority over the foster children under its care.

"He told me that having foster parents go away and leave a child in boarding school had never come up before, but he personally feels it violates the agency philosophy, which is to place the child in a nurturing home situation."

"Can they take Gina back?" Janet asked eagerly, paying no attention to her food.

"Perhaps." Ben finished the salad she had pushed over to his side of the table. "But it might be best for you to deal with the Stocktons privately. If you're qualified as a foster parent—"

Interrupting, she asked worriedly, "Does Edgar realize I'm single? If the agency insists on a traditional home situation, I won't qualify."

"I explained everything. Because of her handicap, Gina's case is unique, and the special rapport you have with her should count heavily in your favor. The agency will probably back your efforts, but if they step in directly themselves, Tommy might put up a fight."

"But he doesn't really care about her!"

"He's a competitive guy. He might suddenly view Gina as a game point and battle hard not to lose." Ben looked at her untouched plate. "Hey, how about eating? I don't want you wasting away."

She picked up her fork, but her thoughts were far from her food.

Later, sitting with Ben on the couch in his apartment, she told him that the adult school director had informed her there was a full-time clerical position coming up, and that he'd recommend her for the job.

"Have you said anything yet to your sister about your plans?"

"About wanting Gina?" Janet sighed. "Fran either bucks me or tries to take over—I'm not going to say a word until I've found a place to stay."

"You could move in here—no strings."

"Oh, Ben, thanks, but no. I'm not—"

"I know, I know. You're not ready yet. But then at least let me help in the apartment search." When she hesitated, he added, "You have a tendency to act as if you're all alone in the world, having to make all the hard decisions on your own." He looked at her with eyes that were serious and filled with caring. "I'm saying that you're not alone. Janet, honey, I'm here for you."

Here for her. Peace flowed through her as if a soothing hand had quietly turned off her racing anxiety. It was true: he *was* here for her, real and dependable. She lifted a hand to touch his cheek, her love for him quickening her blood, her desire reflecting in her eyes.

"Ben," she whispered, "I want you to know I'm here for you too."

Later, much later, she remembered something he had said

at dinner. Relaxed in his arms, she asked drowsily, "What did you mean about Gina and me having a special rapport?"

He chuckled softly, his breath warm against the curve of her shoulder. "I'd call rushing through the night because of a powerful premonition that she needed you rather special, wouldn't you?"

"That *was* strange, wasn't it?"

"You're darned right—and it's not the only example." He pulled her closer, his tenderness showing that he knew his words would be disquieting. "That day at the house site, I swear she sent a mental message for your attention."

"No, no—I explained that. She beckoned or made some other move to catch my eye. Anything else is impossible, Ben."

"You still say that—after last night?"

Her answering tone was hushed, almost fearful. "There have been times when things about her have surprised me. Things I ignored. At the time, I didn't attribute them to anything unnatural."

"Because she's deprived of speech, maybe she's found other ways to communicate."

"Can things like that really happen?" As she spoke, a vague, dreamlike scene floated across her mind. Gina, dressed in black and white, hands sending secret messages... the beech tree, its branches spread protectively... The images fled as swiftly as they had come.

Her throat felt tight. "This talk makes me feel awful. Like you're saying Gina's a freak, and maybe I'm a freak too."

Ben's caress was gentle. "I'm saying she has a gift. Deprived of one sense, she's been granted another. And thankfully, you seem to be able to answer to it. I also think she's the answer to something else for you. Perhaps she helps fill that hollow spot left by the loss of your daughter."

"She could never take Becky's place."

"I know. But she could answer your need to love and protect a child. The need that right now is probably expressed in other ways."

She was uncertain. "You mean the ghost children?"

He nodded.

"And what if you're wrong?" she demanded with a sudden surge of emotion. "What if the apparitions are totally independent from me? Something truly real?"

"I don't know." His lips moved gently along her cheek. "I don't know what that would mean, but I don't think it's anything we have to worry about."

"Because you think you're right."

"Yes, honey, because I think I'm right."

It was late when Ben brought Janet home. It wasn't until after they parted at the door that she remembered his certainty about the ghost children. The memory rankled. Still basking in the blissful memory of his embrace, she knew that he was, for her, one man in a million, but that didn't mean he was perfect. Standing at the front door, she watched his car drive off and thought that maybe his theory about the haunting was right, but maybe it wasn't—so how could he sound so dratted *sure*?

Turning, she walked quietly through the darkened house to the back, mindful of not awakening Fran and Warren. In the kitchen, she went to a rear window. Her breath made a white mist on the pane as she looked out to find the outlines of the beech tree, the tops of its bare limbs swaying gently above the dark peaks of the Renner rooftop. Was the house truly haunted, or were Kirby and Ben right about the disturbance being solely a product of her mind?

On impulse, she opened the back door and stepped out into the night. Snapping the catch so the door wouldn't lock behind her, she went stealthily across the back lawn. Crisp, frozen blades of grass crunched under her feet and she could feel the clammy midnight air deep in her lungs.

Heart beginning to thud, she reached the row of pines and breathlessly stared into the Renner yard. For an instant, it seemed that she glimpsed fireflylike movements amidst the branches of the beech tree. The words of the poem Kirby had quoted came to her: *thou, light-winged Dryad of the trees* . . .

The cold began to settle around her. Shaking her head, she decided she saw no creatures of any kind, neither of this world nor the next, but rather, only glimmers of frost catching the starlight. Belatedly drawing her coat collar up around her neck and ears, she gave one last regretful look into the Renner yard, then turned away to retrace her steps to Fran's house.

She had just slipped inside the door when a soft touch against her ankle turned her to stone, a scream strangling in her throat. Then she heard the soft, plaintive cry.

Pagoda. Shaking with relief, she reached down to lift the cat into her arms. "Oh, my," she murmured against the animal's soft fur. "What you did to my nervous system!" Pagoda mewed again, then started to purr.

"You sneaked in when I held the door to snap the lock, didn't you? Well, now, you're going right outside again." She deposited the animal on the stoop, locked the door, and tiptoed upstairs.

In bed, still chilled from her midnight escapade, she thought of Ben. Slowly, she felt her body heat begin to radiate. Smiling in the darkness, she remembered how she had so urgently ordered him to take her to Gina the night before. He had asked no questions, but simply drove—doing what she wanted because it had been important to her.

A very special man, she thought, remembering again the warmth of his arms. Cozy now, her thoughts began to drift. What had she expected to find in the Renner yard—the spirits of the ghost children dancing under the safe shelter of the copper beech? *The Beeches*. Kirby said that had once been the name for the Renner house. She wondered where the thought that the beech tree provided safety had come from. From her forgotten dream, perhaps?

She stirred restlessly, recalling her strange feelings that day she had watched Gina playing under the tree. Gina, who went too frequently to the Renner yard. *Dangerous*, Rose had warned. Janet turned over in bed. Starting to shiver, she drew herself up into the tight ball. She would protect Gina. If there was danger, whatever it was, she would protect her.

* * *

It was not until the next evening, after another long talk with Ben and a meeting with his agency friend, Edgar Lightfoot, that Janet told Fran and Warren of her hopes to have Gina placed in her care.

"Ben has come up with a lead to an apartment, and so far, things seem to be falling into place. I know I'm doing the right thing." She then told them how Mrs. Ousler had phoned that afternoon as soon as Veronica left on a shopping trip. "You should have seen the look in Gina's eyes when I went over—she thought I had forgotten her too." Pain was in Janet's voice. "I told her that her parents might get upset if they saw me around too much. I don't dare do anything that might antagonize Tommy and Veronica."

Fran, whose expression had grown more and more guarded as Janet talked, spoke up. "I can see that boarding school would be bad for the child, but what about you? You shouldn't be talking about moving out and taking on the responsibility of a stranger's child, especially one with problems." The usual clear blue of Fran's eyes were clouded with concern as she gazed at her younger sister. "This is all wrong for you at this stage of your life. Besides, there's no reason to believe the agency will consider you as a foster parent. You're getting your hopes up for nothing."

"I told you, I've already spoken to Mr. Lightfoot," Janet answered patiently. "He told me it wouldn't be unheard of to place an older, handicapped child in a single-parent home."

"But, Jan," Fran objected. "I don't see how I can let—"

Clearing his throat, Warren interrupted. "I don't know as Janet is asking our permission, sweetheart." Hunching his burly shoulders, he added quietly, "She's certainly given the matter careful thought, and if it's what she wants to do, I think we should support her."

Braced for further argument, Janet was surprised and relieved when Fran, after a thoughtful silence, nodded. "You're right, of course. Jan, I'm not going to say I'm wholehearted about this thing, that would be lying. But if it's what you want, okay." She squared her shoulders. Her eyes, which had been soft a moment earlier, turned flinty as she narrowed them. "What we must do now, is plan. We'll have to talk to the Stocktons. Veronica can be sensible, but Tommy's going to be tough. And we won't have much time to soften him up. The best thing is for me to have a private talk with Veronica first."

Hearing these words, Janet's relief turned to dismay. She recognized both her sister's look and her tone—Fran had just transformed herself from chief antagonist to top sergeant, taking over the campaign completely. Heavy-handed Fran. Janet flashed a desperate look in Warren's direction. She could imagine Fran charging over to Veronica's with all the best intentions in the world, innocently creating the very stumbling blocks they must avoid.

Warren, his thoughts apparently running along the same lines, spoke up. "Since Veronica's unlikely to be the problem, let's leave her out for the moment. Tommy's the one to work on."

"Sure, Warren," Fran complained testily, "but I never get a chance to see him."

"Maybe not, but I do. When he's in town, as he is now, I pretty much know when he'll be at his broker's office, keeping an eye on the market. I could wander into the office and ease into a discussion that points out the wisdom of having an interested local party—Janet, of course—keep an eye on Gina while they're abroad. Knowing Tommy, he'll quickly calculate how much cheaper it will be to have her in a private home rather than in a boarding school."

"Yes, yes I see!" approved Fran, her tone registering the surprise she always showed when someone presented a solution she judged as good as anything she might think of herself. "And once Tommy starts thinking that way, it would be only a short jump for the Stocktons to move Janet from being an approved guardian to appointing her as an official foster parent. Yes, it would work!" She turned to Janet. "Isn't it a wonderful plan?"

"Definitely!" Janet answered, uttering a silent thankful

prayer. Wait until she told Ben of the narrow escape! "I think you're right. We should leave everything up to Warren."

With Janet's immediate concerns placed in Warren's capable hands, her mind was free to turn to other matters when Muriel Renner phoned the next evening.

"I must take Rose out shopping tomorrow afternoon," Muriel explained. "Dr. Renner's recovery has been smooth, but I am not feeling peaceful about leaving him alone in the house. Could you come over for several hours?"

Viewing Muriel's request as a gift wrapped in gold ribbon, Janet agreed at once. Even before she had replaced the phone, a plan had leaped almost full-blown into her mind.

So Mr. Benjamin Yates thought he knew all about hauntings, did he? Well, she soon might have a surprise for him—a surprise that would badly dent his theory concerning her part in the disturbance of the Renner house.

27

On Wednesday morning, after learning that Annabelle Chu had a morning study hall, Janet finished the article about Ben and added it to those of two other new instructors. She then walked over to the high school. Explaining that she had newsletter business to discuss, she had the girl called to the office.

When Annabelle appeared, shiny black hair swinging to reveal there were still only two earrings per lobe, Janet gave her the names of the instructors who were to be photographed for upcoming features. That done, Janet got around to the real purpose behind her visit—asking the girl if she had a camera to rent.

Annabelle waved a hand expansively. "Rent? No, but you can borrow one. The school has several it signs out. What kind of pictures are you planning to take? Snapshots?"

"Not exactly," Janet hedged, wondering how Annabelle would react if she confessed she wanted to photograph a haunted house. She didn't even know if her plan was feasible although she had once see a TV documentary in which a camera had supposedly captured faint, ghostlike figures that had been invisible to the naked eye. Because of his film background, she would have liked to discuss the phenomena with Kirby, but when remembering his warning against dwelling upon the disturbance, she feared he might throw cold water on her idea regardless of its merits.

Giving Annabelle the story she had fabricated, she said, "I want to take interior shots of how some rooms are decorated, only there's not much light. And I can't use a flash. There are a number of mirrors, and reflections would be a big problem."

"I could lend you stands and lights."

"Thanks, but I don't want to go to that much trouble. I just need a camera and light-sensitive film. Something fast."

The corners of Annabelle's mouth pulled down as she shook her head. "You don't need fast film for still pictures of rooms."

Janet improvised. "I'm nervous with a camera and my hands tremble or something. My pictures are always coming out blurred. Anyway, that's what I want to try—something fast, and something that will allow me to catch plenty of light."

Shrugging, Annabelle led her to the media center, but the camera she thought most suitable had already been borrowed. She selected a substitute.

"This will make automatic adjustments for light, but you've got to watch the way the motor drive advances the film. Maybe I should disconnect it. It's a bad feature if you're shaky. You could end up ripping off a bunch of shots of the same thing before you know it."

To Janet, this sounded just fine. "No, leave it. And now, what kind of film should I get?"

Three hours later, with the freshly loaded camera making a lumpy outline in her shoulder bag, she arrived at the Renner house.

The morning sun had given way to threatening clouds. Rose was wearing a black London Fog that lost all its style the moment the woman pulled on her head scarf and awkwardly knotted it under her chin. Muriel was also prepared for foul weather, a veritable fashion plate in a mulberry-colored rain coat with gray boots and matching accessories. Her complexion was pale, with shadows of fatigue under her eyes, yet there was an anticipatory excitement in her manner as she stood in the entry smoothing on her gloves. Janet suspected that after several days of being cooped up with a husband issuing demands from his sickbed, she was more than eager to escape for a few hours.

More chatty than usual, Muriel pointed to her sister's feet. "See how thin the leather has worn? Today, we buy new ones. With her arthritis, it is not easy to get them perfectly fitted." She spoke as if discussing a child with an intriguing problem. Obviously relishing being the center of conversation, Rose smiled broadly.

Nodding to show her attention, Janet placed her bag on a chair and laid her jacket across it. As she listened to Muriel's speech, she tried in vain to detect an accent. A certain stiltedness and too perfect pronunciation marked her as not being native-born, but that was all.

The woman gave final instructions. "You should know that Dr. Renner's sickroom is at the rear of the house, near the head of the back stairway." She indicated a note pad on the phone table. "Here are the phone numbers of Dr. Renner's physician and that of the ambulance, although, you will of course, not need them."

"Should I check on him while you're away?"

Muriel's expression revealed sudden discomfort. She lowered her voice. "In about a half-hour, could you please pour a bottle of mineral water from the refrigerator and take it upstairs?"

Wondering why this was hush-hush, Janet nevertheless lowered her own tones. "No problem. Does he need it to take his medicine?"

Shaking her head, Muriel whispered, "Dr. Renner would be angered if he knew I asked you to look in upon him. He is a very self-reliant man. But if you tell him I instructed you to bring him a drink, that will be all right."

Janet nodded wryly, feeling she understood this kind of self-reliancy. Dr. Renner no doubt enjoyed being waited on hand and foot—Muriel's fatigue testified to that. What he wouldn't like was the suggestion that any weakness on his part made it necessary.

She asked, "Are there danger signs I should be alert for?"

"No. His recovery has been remarkable and at this time of day, he usually arises to work at his desk. Still, in case he needs anything, I must provide the opportunity for him to say so. He has a bell, but I suspect he would be too proud to ring it."

Muriel's manner suggested she felt she imposed upon Janet's good nature, but Janet was delighted. She had planned to carry the camera up the front staircase, creeping along, hoping against hope that the doctor wouldn't hear her prowling. Now, she had a justifiable reason for being on the second floor.

After the two women departed, Janet took the camera into the study. She reviewed its workings and her plans to use it: going up the back stairs from the kitchen, she would carry the water to the doctor. After leaving him, she would head for the railed gallery. He would, of course, hear her, but coming up one stairway and going down another was certainly nothing to question. Even if he kept his door open, the lack of a flash would do nothing to draw his attention, and the electronic advance would enable her to simply point the camera and sweep its eye smoothly along the gallery, taking pictures in rapid succession. She would then proceed downstairs, her mission successfully completed.

As easy as it sounded, she still felt nervous butterflies in her stomach. She hadn't realized the house would be so quiet without Rose's music. The silence increased her edginess. After returning the camera to her purse, she noticed that the front of the rosewood secretary had been dropped down to form a writing surface. A bound, untitled book lay there. Curious, she went to look.

A glance into the bookcase showed several empty spaces. There was no sign of the ledger. She reasoned that the doctor had called for his records so he could request certain books. The one on the desk either waited to be taken upstairs or had been brought back because he had finished with it.

Feeling no restraint against examining a volume left in plain sight, Janet leafed through, finding a slip of paper listing the book she held as well as other titles, the doctor's code numbers carefully written by each. Impulsively, she copied the foreign titles. Although Rose had testified that the books were the doctor's school texts, the titles might prove interesting if translated.

Twenty minutes later, when she was in the kitchen opening the mineral water, Janet glanced out the window and saw Gina and Pagoda playing. Seemingly unmindful of the worsening weather, Gina was bareheaded, her dark hair pulled back in a pony tail, the style emphasizing her soulful, dark eyes. Although she was dressed in a sturdy costume of jeans and a red slicker, Janet was keenly aware of the child's vulnerability. Her heart twisted. Because of the doctor, instead of greeting Gina warmly and spending time with her, she must immediately send her away. Would the little girl understand, or would she feel that once again, someone she trusted had rebuffed her?

Raindrops spattered against the window. Almost at once, the glass was sheeted. Peering through the wavy wetness, Janet could barely make out the cat darting off with Gina in tow. The last glimpse of the red slicker disappeared into the rain as the small figure tore off in the direction of her own property.

Able to smile again, Janet slipped the bag containing the camera over her shoulder and took the tumbler of mineral water and a tray and napkin up the back stairway, making enough noise to alert the doctor to her imminent arrival. In the narrow corridor, she let the bag slide soundlessly to the floor. Drawing a deep breath, she stood like a servant at the door and knocked.

"Yes?" The doctor sounded testy, annoyed at being disturbed. His voice was stronger than she had expected.

"It's Janet Fairweather, Dr. Renner," she answered, suddenly timorous. When he said nothing more, she cautiously pushed the door open.

The doctor was seated at his desk, pen in hand. As he peered up through his trifocals, his expression was barely cordial, no warmth reaching his eyes. He wore a rust-colored woolen robe, the long sleeves enveloping bony wrists that seemed as if they could be snapped like matchsticks. Although a lamp illuminated his work space, his gaunt, cadaverlike face was in shadow. The outline of his head, eerily backlighted by the window, made his skull appear semitransparent and as fragile as an egg. Before him on the desk lay outspread folders, and Janet saw he must be reviewing his old patient files. Off to one side was the ledger.

Stepping in, she nervously explained, "Mrs. Renner asked me to bring you this mineral water." Looking for a place to set the tray, she saw a side table with an open book upon it.

Following her gaze, the doctor's face hardened. Quickly, he reached to close the book. It had shown a diagram and Janet got the distinct impression he hadn't wanted her to see it. Whisking the book away, he directed, "Put the tray here," and gave her a smile that was conspicuously false, his long, yellowed teeth catching the light. From a forgotten fairy tale, silent words popped into Janet's mind: *Why, Grandmother—what big teeth you have!*

She set down the tray, aware of the intensity of his stare. It seemed as if the force of his personality was a tangible thing. The atmosphere of the room felt as if it were thickening, making it hard for her to breathe.

"Is there anything else you need?" she asked, looking up, trying not to flinch. When he made no reply, she stammered awkwardly, "If not, then . . . then I guess I'll go."

He nodded coldly and returned his attention to the pages on his desk.

Out in the corridor, Janet still found it difficult to catch her breath. She would not have believed she could be cowed by someone so frail and infirm. No wonder Muriel showed him such submissive respect.

It wasn't until her foot knocked against her shoulder bag that she remembered the camera. Lifting the bag, she was momentarily tempted to postpone her plan, then her resolve stiffened. She was upstairs now and only a few steps from the railed gallery—what time would be more fortuitous?

Putting the camera to her eye, she focused on the gallery ahead, mentally reviewing her planned course of action.

"And what do you think you are doing, Miss Fairweather?"

With a gasp, Janet whirled, the camera clutched against her chest. The doctor stood in his doorway.

"I did not hear you leaving, and so I wondered," he explained mildly. To her immense relief, he did not seem angered, only curious. His eyes fastened on the camera.

"Were you perhaps thinking to take my photograph?"

"No, no! I just wanted—" Frantically, Janet tried to think of some excuse. She could hardly tell him what she had told Annabelle. Nothing in the upstairs had decorations worth photographing, except the master bedroom, of course, and saying she planned to take pictures of such private quarters would hardly get her off the hook.

"The . . . from the window," she stammered, pointing over her shoulder in the general direction of the large window in the rear gallery wall. "There's a good view from that window. I can see my sister's house and the yard. I thought it might make a pretty little picture."

He nodded. "Ah, yes, and a rainy day is so ideal for an amateur to take a few harmless snapshots, isn't it?" Even in biting sarcasm, his tone remained mild. "May I see your camera?"

Wordlessly, she handed it over.

His hands, with their thick, horny nails, turned the instrument as he examined it from all angles as if it were a rare thing. "Pictures of the yard, you say? My yard?"

"Well, more across your yard. I—" Her words ran out.

He looked at her and merely waited.

She found herself babbling. "A friend of mine on the newsletter is a photographer and I thought I could take a few shots and she could tell me what was really good. I mean..." Her laugh trembled like a thin wire. "Like you say, I'm just an amateur." She waved a hand. "Rainy day and all. You're right. Not a good time at all."

He nodded. "Perhaps not the best time, but as good a time as you thought you might get, hmmm?" His smile was almost benign, his tone cajoling. "Who is your newspaper friend? Someone local whom I've met unknowingly, perhaps? And of course, he knows others of his ilk. Journalists— so hungry, sniffing like hounds for greasy tidbits."

"Not newspaper," she corrected, repelled by the nasty turn of his phrase. "*Newsletter.* The adult-school newsletter. It's for news about the night school."

Shrugging as if she hadn't spoken, he returned his attention to the camera. "Made in Japan. I remember a time when all fine optical equipment was from Germany." Shaking his head, he peered at her sadly. "I live in the past," he lamented. "Too much in the past."

In that moment, he looked so pathetically ill and wasted that Janet wondered how she could have ever found him intimidating. A strange clicking and whirring sound suddenly startled her. Momentarily, she felt only confusion, then she realized the noise issued from the camera.

"Oh, no!" she cried, belatedly realizing she was hearing

the motor drive. Never having experimented, she had no idea it would be so loud. "The pictures! You're pressing the shutter, the film—" She grabbed for the camera, but he twisted about, holding it from her.

"The film!" she repeated, snatching again for the camera. As the last sound faded, he released the instrument into her hands. She looked at the counter, then gaped at the doctor in disbelief. "You used the film. It's all run out. Twenty-four pictures—you used them all!"

"Did I?" He mimicked surprise. "My, my—twenty-four pictures, and all of the floor?" His lips exposed his teeth in a feral sneer. "I wonder what your newspaper friend will say."

"Not *newspaper*," she insisted, upset and confused, but sensing that it was important to explain. "The newsletter is only for the high school, for their evening teaching program for adults. It's—"

Her words broke off as she saw that instead of listening, the doctor stared into the hall beyond her, an unreadable expression on his face.

Thinking that Muriel had returned and had come up the front stairs unheard, Janet turned, but instead of Muriel, she saw pinpoints of light. An icy fist clutched her stomach as ever so faintly, she heard the whispered chant:

"We are ta-ta-DA-da. We are ta-ta-DA-da!"

The sounds breathed through the corridor ahead like a restless sigh as more and more shimmering lights appeared. With a flickering, misty swirl, one of the lights began to congeal.

All at once, Janet saw the toddler—the small, dark-haired girl, garbed in a shiftlike garment. As before, the figure did not seem to take complete form, but then, aghast, Janet saw the reason: the child *was* fully materialized, it was her body that was not complete. One shoulder and arm were perfect, but the other arm stopped at mid-elbow in a bone-jagged line of torn, bloodless flesh. As if aware of Janet's horrified observation, the child turned in her direction.

Janet uttered a choked scream as she saw that one eye,

the left one, was wide and bruised. But there was no right eye. There was no right side of the face!

Then, beside the toddler, appeared the little boy. His nearly naked body was not as thin as Janet had remembered, but his bloated belly still gave evidence of malnourishment. Although he stood on both legs, one of them was bent in an unnatural angle, as if it had been broken. No longer crying, his eyes were clear and his lips moved as if he were about to speak.

More ghost children leaped into view. Youngsters huddled together, some of them holding infants. And all of them were damaged—arms broken, bodies contorted, faces disfigured. Maimed. All of the children were *maimed*.

And then she heard the chant again, the sounds suddenly becoming clearer: "We are ta-ta-DA-da! We are growing-DA-da!"

Yes, that was it—"growing." That was one of the missing words! *Growing*. With a sense of benumbed shock, Janet listened, finally hearing the last word, finally hearing the chant in its entirety: "We are growing stronger."

The rhythm steady and unstoppable; the chorus of the phantom children:

We are growing stronger!
We are growing stronger!
WE ARE GROWING STRONGER!

28

Janet had no idea for how long she stood transfixed by the specter of the mutilated children, their eerie, otherworldly chanting dinning against her ears. She lost all sense of time.

Then, other sounds intruded: a strangled, wheezing from behind her and a hollow thud.

With effort, she tore her gaze from the gallery and turned to see the doctor slumped against the wall, a feeble hand extended in an inarticulate plea for aid. His complexion was bluish, and as she watched, his eyes started to roll upward.

With no time for thought, she lunged to support him as his body sagged, a dead weight in her arms. As she struggled to lower him to the floor, his head rolled lifelessly, and she felt a drooling wetness on her shoulder.

He's dead, went through her mind. *He saw the ghost children, and his heart stopped—he's dead from shock.*

With that thought, she managed to look back toward the gallery. There was now nothing to see except the walls, the window, and the end of the railing which flanked the front stairs. *Nothing*. And, except for her own labored breathing, nothing to hear.

The doctor groaned and Janet felt his legs weakly scramble for renewed footing. With a thick, guttural muttering, he lifted his head and attempted to stand on his own. He looked at Janet without recognition and mumbled again.

"Go easy!" she cautioned, holding him propped against the wall, still certain he had suffered a heart attack. "Just slide down to the floor and sit. Don't try to walk."

With surprising strength, he freed himself. Tottering, he turned toward his room. There was nothing for Janet to do except hurry along at his side, making sure he didn't fall. By the time she had assisted him to his bed, the awful blueness had left his face although he still sucked air in wheezing gasps. As she lifted up his feet and pulled a blanket over him, she began to realize his collapse might have only been a faint.

"Muriel . . . my wife, where is she?" he demanded with effort, still viewing Janet without apparent recognition.

It took Janet a moment for her to get her thoughts straight, to think of people doing ordinary things in ordinary ways. "She's gone to the store," she told him. "She went to buy shoes for Rose."

He stared. "Miss Fairweather? What are you doing up here?" His speech was easier now. He lay back against the pillow. "I was working at my desk." He closed his eyes, murmuring, "At my desk—that's where I was. Working at my desk."

She realized he was saying he had no recall of finding her with the camera. Or of seeing the ghost children.

The ghost children.

Leaving the doctor, she hurried to the door and stared once more down the corridor. Nothing there. But there *had* been. Those disfigured forms—*they had been there*. And the doctor had seen them too. Whether he was admitting it or not, he had seen them.

She heard the front door open. Muriel's voice floated up. Stopping only to gather her bag and the camera, Janet flew downstairs.

"Dr. Renner might be having a little problem," she said hastily to Muriel. Muriel, dropping the shoe box she carried, rushed upstairs. Hands shaking, Janet helped Rose off with her wet raincoat and guided her into the study.

When Muriel reappeared a few minutes later, she said that her husband seemed to be a bit tired, but otherwise just fine. "He did admit to lightheadedness," she told Janet. "He thinks he may have gotten up too quickly after working at his desk, causing the blood to rush from his head. He thinks he lost consciousness for a minute of two."

Feeling somewhat lightheaded herself, Janet decided that if that was what the doctor wanted his wife to think, she would go along with it. Mumbling that she was glad his spell hadn't been serious, she smiled and nodded mechanically as she was shown Rose's new shoes and heard about the shopping excursion. As soon as tactfully possible, she left the house, unmindful that the rain still fell heavily. It was only when she reached the Renner back yard that she began to experience the aftermath of shock.

The emergency of the doctor's collapse had for a time blanked out the horrifying appearance of the children, but now, when standing in a world that was so very real, raindrops upon her face, wind singing in the pine tops, the full impact of the dreadful vision settled upon her.

Swaying sickly, she leaned against a tree, her head spinning.

Children—ghost children—not two or three, but at least ten or more. Children of various ages. Damaged. Bodies twisted, starving, swollen. Grotesque. Parts missing, eyes gone—limbs broken, torn away. Like the leavings of some hideous accident.

And, what had the chant meant? *Growing stronger.* Growing stronger in number? More children to join their dreadful little band?

Children from where?

From what source had the ghost children been assembled?

And why were they at the Renner house?

Lost in confusion, she leaned her aching head against the tree, heedless of her rain-soaked hair and the rivulets of water running down her collar. She knew it was impossible to reach Ben on that particular afternoon, but oh, how she yearned for his comfort. Even if he couldn't help her make sense of what she had seen, she desperately wanted to be with him, to talk with him. Close to tears, her thoughts spun disjointedly. Good old beech tree... She felt the smooth hardness of the wet trunk against her forehead. Safe. So safe under your branches.

Beech tree. *The Beeches.*

A thought nagged. She stepped back, craning her head up to see the great branches twisting above her. Slowly, she turned to view the house. Seen through the grayness of rain, the tall pointed gables, the decorative trim, and once-cheerful yellow paint had lost their charm. The house was transformed into a brooding hulk—a witch's house with the gingerbread and sugar masquerade finally melted away.

The history of The Beeches came to the forefront of her mind, and suddenly, with horror, she knew—

She knew who the children were, and especially, she knew why they made the Renner house their home.

29

Janet's frantic pounding brought Kirby Orchard to his door.

"Janet!" His round face showed alarm as he stepped back to let her in. "You're soaked!"

"The children..." She stood in his kitchen, dripping, shivering violently. "I saw the ghost children, heard them..." Her words ran together unintelligibly.

"It's all right, it's all right," Kirby soothed, patting her arm. Trixie, not liking the commotion, whined for attention and did an agitated toe tap on the tiles.

When Janet, teeth chattering, tried to explain again, Kirby decided, "It can wait. First, get yourself warm and dry."

He hustled her down the hall to the bathroom where he switched on an electric heater and opened a linen closet. "There's plenty of towels. And here, look—a nice thick terry robe. Put it on and leave your wet clothes in front of the heater to dry." Moving to the door, he ushered out Trixie, who had tagged along, and promised, "I'll have a hot drink waiting for you in my study."

When Janet, robed, her dark hair still damp and curling tightly about her face, met Kirby in the study, she was calmer, although the undercurrents of panic still ran close to the surface. She told herself that while Kirby couldn't give her the comfort she so desperately needed, he would understand what she had to say far better than Ben. Sitting on the couch, she accepted a hot, rum-laced mug of tea with a trembling hand.

Kirby watched with concern as she tucked up her feet and took an unsteady sip of the tea. "I've just gotten home after my last film class," he said. "Got into as much bad weather as you, but at least I was wearing rain gear."

She managed a weak smile. Seeing she was recovering, he leaned back in his desk chair. "From what you said at my door, am I to assume you've persisted in investigating the Renner house?" His tone was chiding, but gentle.

"Oh, I remembered your warnings all right." She drew a shaky breath. "I also remembered how convinced you are that the apparitions only take the shape of children in my own mind. That's why I went over with a camera—to gain evidence to show to you and Ben."

"You took photos?" Kirby couldn't hide his interest. "They might not show what you hope to see, still, there are cases where films have recorded unusual signs—"

"No, no," Janet interrupted. "What happened with the camera is another story—but, oh, God! If I'd only had the camera ready when those children appeared today."

"You saw them again?"

"Saw them and a whole lot more. Ten at least, and a number of them were babies." She started to lose control again. "Babies, Kirby, innocent babies! And I heard them—that awful chanting... Kirby, if only you could have been there!"

"Now, now," he said, moving his chair closer.

"It wasn't just that there were so many of them, Kirby—it was their condition. This is going to sound incredible, but the ghost children are damaged—*mutilated*."

Taking a deep breath, she described the horror of what she had seen.

"My Lord!" Kirby had gone pale. "I've never heard of anything like that. Never."

She pushed a hand through her hair. "That wasn't what sent me running over here like a madwoman. What happened was, I suddenly realized just who the children are." Her voice lowered. "Kirby, they're victims of the house. The ghosts are the captured spirits of children who have lived and died in that house."

He drew back. "Victims of the Renner house? I don't understand. Where did you get such an idea?"

"From the very history we've discussed. I've finally figured out the common denominator among the residents. We didn't think there was one, but there is—time after time, people have moved in there, and then lost a child. Don't you see? The house lures families, kills their children, and holds fast to their spirits. And I can prove it. Remember the boy I saw in the garden, the crippled boy I later realized must be a ghost?" Her eyes held a challenge. "Think about the last child who lived at that address, the Fiorello boy. What do we know about him?"

Looking pained, Kirby admitted reluctantly, "Timmy Fiorello was crippled."

"And what eventually happened to him?"

Kirby waved in protest. "He died. But the house wasn't responsible. He was afflicted from birth with a muscular disease that progressively worsened. When the family came here, he already suffered from it."

Frowning, Janet set that objection aside. "The important thing is, the house is where he died. And now it has him forever."

"That's an unhealthy idea, Janet, and totally without foundation. You shouldn't even explore such a notion."

"Why? Because it's so frightening? Ignoring the truth doesn't change things. Think of the family before them—the Mitchums. A child came into the house with them, and shortly thereafter drowned."

"But not on the property, Janet. It was on a school outing, if I recall."

"The child had lived there. It was her home, and when she died, it had a claim on her—or, at least on her spirit." Janet's tone was certain. "And she's still there, along with the other victims. I know it."

Disgruntled, Kirby sat back in his chair. "All right, so two children at that address have died. Children do die on occasion, sad as that fact might be. That hardly means their homes keep their spirits in bondage."

"Oh, but The Beeches is special, remember?" Janet spoke with bitter irony. "*Dedicated* to the care of children, right?

Examine your notes. Back in the 1800s, Elizabeth Parke built it as a home for orphans—a shelter for the lost. Remember how self-righteous and cruel that relative was when writing about her? Elizabeth was an orphan herself, a bastard, despised and scorned in her stringent Victorian world. How she must have suffered! It would be enough to drive her insane, and I think it did. When she died before her house could fulfill the purpose for which it was built, I think she continued her mission from beyond the grave. The house now carries on as she intended, only in a sick, twisted way, because the lost children it now shelters are ghosts. And to gain them, living children become its prey."

The expression on Kirby's round face was dour. "Even if you're right about Elizabeth being mad, I can't believe it would have the effect on the house that you claim."

Janet put her empty tea mug on the table and pushed it aside. "Can't you? Look at what's happened to the families there. The Hickoks, the very first residents, lost three-year-old twin sons."

"You're claiming they were the first victims?"

"Exactly. And after them, the next family lost a son to a blizzard."

Goaded, Kirby found his notes. "All right, yes. The victim was an Alexander Whitehurst Jr. But that doesn't mean he was a child. 'Junior' doesn't tell us his age. He could have been an adult."

Janet remained adamant. "And he could have been a five-year-old, gone out to feed his pet pony in the barn, lost in the snowstorm and frozen to death before he could be found."

Kirby scrubbed a helpless hand through his scanty fringe of hair. "But you just made that up. We have to deal with facts."

"Facts? Come on, Kirby. The first residents lost two children, the second residents lost one, age uncertain, and the last two families lost one child each. That's four dead children for sure. How's that for facts? Let's look at the other families." Leaping up to see the list, she pointed to a name. "After the Whitehursts came the Goodsmiths. What about them?"

"We don't know if they lost any children or not." Kirby's manner was stubborn. "But there's one thing I can tell you—the people living here when I was a child suffered no such tragedies. Their children were my playmates."

Janet narrowed her eyes. "The Patricks and the Roberts, right?"

"Indeed. As for the family the Patricks bought the house from—the Grangers, we know nothing about them. You may have found a few coincidences, but nothing to build a sound theory upon."

"No? Suppose we take a closer look at the Grangers." She jabbed a finger at their name. "You've written that they lived in the house from about 1910 to 1924. That's not the Dark Ages. Having lived here most of your life, you must know some senior citizen who remembers them."

"I do. The old lady who lived next door to them is now in a nursing home. Nettie Laine. I paid her a visit only a month ago."

"Fine. Then give her a call."

The corners of his mouth suddenly turned up impishly. "Pretty sure of yourself, aren't you?" He reached for the phone. "Don't be surprised when you're wrong."

Resuming her seat on the couch, Janet folded her arms as Kirby greeted his old friend. After a moment of folksy chatter, he inquired about the Grangers. "Do you recall them, Nettie? I'm researching a genealogy and a question has come up. Would you know if the Grangers had any children who passed away?"

As he listened, Janet saw his face slacken. When he hung up, the eyes he turned to her showed baffled shock. "Mrs. Granger lost a child to diphtheria."

Janet showed dark triumph. "I knew it!"

"There's more. When the child died, Mrs. Granger was pregnant. Grief apparently sent her into early labor and the infant died soon after birth."

"Then, that baby was one of those that I saw!"

"The thing is, now I remember something else." Shoulders sagging, Kirby drew a heavy breath. "I insisted there were no deaths of children in the families I knew. But, when I was little, the Patrick kids were supposed to get a new brother or sister. I remember Mrs. Patrick looking very fat. Then I was told there would be no baby after all. It didn't mean anything to me then, but now, I realize the baby must have died."

The full implication touched Janet like a clammy hand. Her voice dropped to a whisper. "Now we've traced two of the infants trapped with the other children in that house."

Kirby mused, "Then, could they be the ones you've heard crying—" He snapped his lips like a rubbery trap, pinching off the words. "Drat!" he cried. "Now you've got *me* tangled in your yarn!"

Janet leaned forward. "Open your mind Kirby! What if you're wrong about the children being figments of my imagination? If they exist, they had to originate from somewhere."

"I suppose you have a point," he admitted, then scowled. "I still don't know. As far as I can recall, the Roberts lost no little children. A few years ago, I did hear that the oldest daughter, Meg, had died. But that was the result of an accident in the place where she worked, and it happened long after they left here. She was nearly my age."

Janet speculated, "Maybe she isn't a ghost then, or maybe age doesn't matter. Suppose that what counts is that the house was her home when she was little? Could the house somehow retain a part of her after death—the childish part of her spirit?"

Kirby grunted. "Unlikely, I'd say." He pursed his lips. "You told me that at one time, you were desperately eager to live there yourself. Had you done so, the death of your baby might be another point for your argument. But you didn't move in and your baby died anyway." He hesitated. "Do you believe the house had something to do with your child's death?"

Becky? The question stunned her. After a silence, she said, "Maybe I was wrong about the house actually killing the children. Maybe it senses those who are doomed. Maybe that's why the house called to me—it sensed that Becky had a problem and would die." Her eyes grew haunted. "It's hard now to recall my enchantment with that house. At the time, had you told me that standing under that beech tree meant anything bad, I would have been outraged. I felt enfolded by something that was rare, magical, and unbelievably beautiful, like in that poem you quoted: *some melodious plot of beechen green.* . . . I stood under its shelter, holding Becky and wishing the moment would never end."

She clasped her hands, which suddenly felt icy. "But now I know that had I moved in, Becky would have become part of the house's terrible history." Swallowing, she added fiercely, "But I didn't move in, so—thank God, she was at least saved from that."

Kirby searched her face. "You don't feel she's there?"

"As one of the ghost children? God, Kirby—definitely not! Believe me, I would *know*." After a long, agitated moment, she got herself under control. Her eyes enlarged as a new thought came to her. "Kirby, I think the loss of my desire to live there is significant. Once I no longer possessed a child it wanted, the house no longer tried to attract me."

"You speak as if it has a personality."

"Perhaps through the spirit of Elizabeth Parke, it does."

"What about the Renners? There's your exception to the rule—they have no children."

His comment gave her pause. "Yes, and that's puzzling because he was apparently drawn to the house much as I was." She explained how Muriel had described the doctor's strong attraction. "An *obsession*, she called it." Thoughts of the camera returned to her mind. "He's a strange man. The reason I wasn't able to use the camera today was because Dr. Renner appeared and stopped me."

"Oh, so that's what happened."

"Yes. He got the idea I wanted to photograph *him*. I've learned he has secrets to hide." Her tone downplayed the awesome force of the man's personality. In some odd way, she felt that to acknowledge his power might pop the cork from a crusted bottle and release the foul, oily smoke of an evil genie into the cozy room. "I found out that Rose and Muriel probably aren't from South America at all, but from Hungary. For reasons of his own, the doctor has them living a charade. It's a wonder they stand for it. Rose makes no secret of despising him. She spent most of an afternoon trying to discredit him in my eyes, only I never understood what she was trying to get across."

Remembering the book list, she pulled it from her purse. "She insisted on showing me his old textbooks. I thought she confirmed my guess that they were on child psychology, but maybe I didn't understand. I copied down titles. If some are in a different field, Rose might have been trying to indicate he's flying under false colors."

Shoving his glasses into place, Kirby studied the list. He consulted a dictionary for several words, then peered up at Janet, expression puzzled. "I suppose these books are indeed in the doctor's line of interest, only they study a peculiar type of abnormal psychology."

"Found in children?"

"Not likely. They're cases in which the victim believes he or she suffers from supernatural afflictions—possession, clairvoyance, thought transference—that kind of thing. Of course, Freud and Jung showed some interest in the occult, so there's a certain amount of tradition for this."

Janet's brows knit. "The doctor had a book in his room that he didn't want me to see. It showed an odd diagram."

"How did it look?"

"Sort of a star, with writing on the various points."

An inspired light suddenly gleamed in Kirby's eyes. He jumped up and pulled a book from a shelf. "Like this?"

She didn't understand his excitement. "Something similar. I didn't see it well."

He showed her the title: *Encyclopedia of Witchcraft*.

Janet's mouth dropped. "Dr. Renner is weird, but not *that* weird."

Kirby spoke excitedly. "Suppose it was the doctor's study of the supernatural that drew him to the house in the first place? He's presumably had his books a long time, so it's not a new interest. Suppose his occult studies enabled him to sense its paranormal atmosphere from the start?"

"You mean his so-called obsession could have actually been intense curiosity?"

Kirby beamed. "Why not? Starting before the Second World War, there was a resurgence of the occult in Europe. It's well documented that Hitler consulted astrologers. There were even rumors that he hoped to tap unseen mystical powers to help him gain world rule. With this sort of thinking in the air, Dr. Renner could have gotten caught up in it in his youth." He flourished the book list. "I bet he's been going through his books anew in the attempt to understand the aura within the house."

A mental picture of the ghosts came into Janet's mind. Except for the boy who had been crippled, there was nothing in the history of the residents to explain why the children had appeared as mutilated. She winced from the sickening memory, thinking it was almost better to believe that Kirby was right about her perceptions being distorted than to believe what she had seen. Remembering the chant, she realized she hadn't told Kirby that she had finally heard all the words.

"*We are growing stronger*," he echoed reflectively after Janet had explained. "But whatever does it mean?" His next questions pinpointed the thoughts that had lurked in Janet's mind like loathsome intruders ever since her experience that afternoon. "Growing stronger in what way? And for what purpose?"

30

Janet arrived home to find her sister impatiently waiting.

"Lord, girl!" the blond, older woman exclaimed. "I

rushed back here early with good news and then had no idea how to find you. When I called Mrs. Renner, she said you had left an hour ago. At that time it was raining cats and dogs. Where did you disappear to in the middle of a storm?" Not waiting for a reply, she rushed eagerly on. "Just wait till you hear!" She sat Janet down at the kitchen table and excitedly revealed she had had lunch with Veronica at the Spoon.

Oh, no, Janet thought in dismay, her stomach seesawing. Fearfully, she listened as Fran said, "She came in just by chance. I knew Warren had been working on Tommy, so I figured it was time to bring up the subject with her."

Everything discussed with Kirby went out of Janet's mind in the immediacy of the moment. Had Fran unknowingly undone whatever progress Warren had made?

"You told her I want to have Gina?"

"Right. And I think she was relieved to discuss it. She knows she and Tommy haven't done right by the child. When she told me that they had been reviewing possibilities other than boarding school, I knew that Warren's talking had done some good. She and I talked, and now, just a little while ago, she phoned. She says she and Tommy have definitely decided to make arrangement to leave Gina in your care. We're to go over to their house tonight and discuss the details."

Janet felt limp with relief. "Oh, Sis—you did a good job." She couldn't wait until Ben heard the good news.

Fran rubbed her hands. "Big sister sure doesn't let the grass grow." Her self-satisfied expression suddenly puddled and slid. "But, oh Jan—am I doing the right thing? I know it's what you think you want, but will it work? Taking on a handicapped orphan... Jan, it's going to be terribly hard."

Lovingly, Janet reached across the table to touch Fran's arm. "It is the right thing, Fran. Not only for Gina, but for me too."

But despite her gladness, the reminder that Gina was an

orphan had her remembering the orphaned Elizabeth Parke and the Renner house. Kirby's contrary opinion hadn't shaken her conviction that its dedication as a shelter for lost children had become horribly perverted. All she had to do was remember the appearance of the ghost children to be sure of that.

As she called Ben to tell him of her meeting with the Stocktons, she found herself wondering what direction the thwarted desires of the house might take with the childless Renners as residents. A horrid question forced its way into her mind: had Gina's frequent visits to the property put her in jeopardy? *Dangerous*, Rose had warned. Did Rose mean danger from the house itself—a danger for Gina?

It suddenly seemed doubly important to talk to Ben, and Janet was dismayed to learn that he and his boss had left the office for an unexpected dinner meeting. Replacing the phone, she realized how much she had come to depend upon his calm, sensible outlook. She herself was too inclined to think with her heart instead of her head—especially where Gina was concerned. She decided to try her best to avoid thinking about the Renner house until she could discuss the latest happenings with him.

That evening, sitting in the Stockton living room, Janet was delighted to hear the couple say they had come fully to terms with the idea of transferring Gina's care to her.

"After all," Tommy pointed out righteously, "it's hardly as if we adopted her and changed our minds. But even if she's only been a foster child, we still want her to have what's best. The agency has given you its approval, Janet, and we agree that you're the best one to step in and take over for us."

Veronica nodded. "Yes, there's absolutely no doubt in our minds."

And so it was settled, and with remarkable ease. The following conversation was mundane and Janet allowed her mind to drift, thinking that Gina had undoubtedly been put to bed already by Mrs. Ousler. Projecting her thoughts, she imagined the time when the precious job of tucking the child in for the night would be hers.

Suddenly, she thought she heard herself softly being called. She glanced around, half expecting to see Mrs. Ousler. There was no one in sight and the conversation Warren and Fran were having with the Stocktons was drawing to a natural conclusion. After another minute everyone was on his or her feet and heading toward the door as the meeting ended. Janet heard the call again, but no one else seemed to react to the sound.

So strange, she thought, casting around another puzzled glance. Thinking I hear someone calling me when no one else seems aware . . .

They had reached the door and stood near the foot of the steps when Janet felt it happen again. *Felt*, not heard. In some strange way, totally apart from normal conversation, she realized she had been beckoned. It was as if a voice inside her mind had softly yet urgently issued a summons.

There came a pattering of footsteps and Gina appeared at the top of the stairs, eyes sparkling. Dressed in a white nightgown, she so resembled one of the ghost children that for a moment Janet felt her heart almost stop. The child danced down the steps and straight into her arms.

"What's gotten into that girl?" Mrs. Ousler demanded rhetorically, coming into view upstairs. "I'm sorry, but I thought she was asleep. All at once, she was out her room and down the steps."

"Seems as if some little person had been listening to grown-up conversation," said Tommy in a hearty tone. "It's good to know she's happy with this arrangement. Can't blame her for a little eavesdropping."

But Janet, holding Gina close, was aware that there had been no "eavesdropping"—at least, not of a physical kind. Stunned, she realized that everyone else had been right all along. Gina was indeed mute. That first night, those words: *I heard your baby crying*, had been spoken directly into her mind.

* * *

Returning home, Janet was finally able to reach Ben. She told him that the Stocktons had agreed to relinquish Gina, but she held back everything else. When he arrived to pick her up, he had no more than gotten out of his car when she ran down the walk to meet him and flung herself into his arms.

"Janet, love—" The hug he gave her was joyful. "So it's all settled about Gina?"

"Yes," she answered, burying her face in his coat collar, savoring the strength of his embrace.

He laughed aloud. "How shall we celebrate? Want to go out—or maybe a more private celebration sounds best." His tone made it clear that's what he preferred. "I stopped and got a bottle of champagne, all iced and ready to drink."

"All I want," she said, "is to be with you."

"Hey, is something the matter?" Gently holding her arms, he stepped back, studying her face in the dim glow from the street lamp. "Everything *did* go all right, didn't it?"

"Yes, it went fine. We're to go to Edgar's office in a few days to sign documents that will make it official. Only—"

"It's cold out here," he said. "You're shivering. Let's get into the car and then we can talk."

As they drove the short distance to his apartment, Janet explained how Gina had come plummeting down the steps and into her arms.

"You've been right all along, Ben. There is a strange connection between Gina and me." She spoke with wonder, still adjusting to the fact. "Kirby has said that severe shock can enhance psychic abilities, and being caught in an earthquake should certainly qualify. It explains any number of things that have happened to her. The bond between us must have started the night of the Stockton party, when Gina somehow sensed I would be sympathetic to her."

Reaching his apartment, Ben pulled to the curb. "I wouldn't be surprised if we all don't have flashes of psychic insight now and then," he said, his tone thoughtful. "It just must be a lot stronger in Gina because of being unable to talk, and also, there's her great need. With the Stocktons for parents, she badly needed a loving friend." He switched off the engine and the headlights. "And I guess this also solves the puzzling question of the crying baby. Gina never actually heard it. She simply tapped into your strong emotions at the time."

Janet stiffened. "What do you mean, she never actually heard it?"

"Well, it was just something she picked up from you, right? When you met her upstairs in the Stockton hallway, she tapped into your feelings and mistakenly assumed you had really just heard your own baby crying. Your emotions were projected so powerfully that it must have seemed to Gina that the crying was real and that she must have heard it too."

Janet stared across the darkened car at him. "Okay, so she thought the crying baby was mine because Becky was so much in my thoughts. But we each heard the crying independently."

"Honey, I really don't think so." His tone was patient. "Remember what you told me—how you felt ill at the Stockton party and started thinking about Becky? You felt depressed and thought you heard a baby crying. So when you went upstairs and met Gina, you were in a heightened emotional state. She simply picked up on it."

Janet shook her head. "You've got it backward. The sound of crying came first. I went outside the Stockton house, heard the sound of the baby, and *then* started thinking about Becky."

Ben shrugged uncomfortably, obviously unwilling to pursue the matter any further. "Either way, it doesn't really matter, does it? What counts is that Gina will soon be an official part of your life."

Janet said nothing more until they were in his apartment, then, after he had helped her off with her coat, she turned to him, putting her face in his shoulder.

"Hey, hey love," he murmured softly, his arms enclosing her with warm firmness. "What's this? A reaction after finally winning Gina?"

"No, Ben, I'm scared for her." Knowing he didn't understand and resenting him for it even though it wasn't his fault, she moved away. Trying to keep her voice steady, she said, "I tried to explain the other night—if the crying sounds are related to the haunting, the fact that Gina's heard them means she's in unconscious contact with whatever possesses the Renner house."

Ben looked pained. "Honey, isn't it obvious to you what's really been happening? It's just as Kirby said: the loss of your daughter has gotten mixed up in your mind with the history of the Renner house." His tone became grim. "And a big part of the blame goes to Kirby. I know he's all wrapped up in this stuff, and maybe there's merit in his theory about free-flowing psychic energy. But he should have been able to see that his theories were only encouraging you in the wrong direction."

"Oh, God, Ben—you're so wrong!" Urgently, Janet pulled him down to sit with her at the kitchenette table. "Let me tell you what happened there today."

The retelling of the horrid, second sighting of the ghosts and her dreadful conclusions about them exhausted her. When she was finished, Ben's reaction was to get up to heat water for coffee. Feeling resentment, she looked at his broad, muscular back. This was the man who was *here* for her when she needed him? Feeling abandoned, she stared woodenly as he filled the cups and sat down.

Correctly reading her manner, he reached across the table, his caressing touch offering comfort as well as strength. "I'm trying to understand," he said. "But somehow I got stuck when you started explaining that the house was evil. Even if Elizabeth Parke was insane, which you can't prove, that hardly establishes the house as wicked."

Her hand tightened on his. "Oh, Lord, Ben! People move in there, their children die, and the spirits of the children stay in the house. Children, tiny babies . . . I've seen them and it's horrible! What more do you need to start looking for evil?"

"I don't know." The lamp hanging over the table cast

solemn shadows under his high cheekbones, making him look wise.

She released his hand. "You sound like Kirby."

"He feels the same way?"

"Just about. Only neither of you can judge because you weren't there. If you had been, you would've realized something unspeakably wicked has afflicted those children. It was as if they were victims of some diabolical creature."

Ben cocked an eyebrow. "Why not a fire?"

"Fire?" She spoke as if it were a foreign word. "Why fire?"

"Because several times you've mentioned catching whiffs of phantom smoke. And you dreamed about a fire."

"Oh, where the folders burst into flames."

"Yes, along with some cribs. It seems to me that nursery beds should symbolize children."

She blinked. "I don't understand my dreams, but Kirby's research would have shown if there had been a serious fire. Besides, a fire would have only harmed the children of whichever family lived there at the time, but all the children are damaged, Ben, not just one or two."

"I have a tough time believing in disembodied evil. Evil is something that people do. It doesn't exist on its own, as a force."

"Ben, how can you say that? Of course, people may not want to believe in it, but—"

He interrupted. "Actually, I think the vast majority love believing in evil forces. It's such a handy scapegoat. But that argument is neither here nor there. Right now what I'd like to learn more about is Dr. Renner. His dread of photographs and his assumption that you were a reporter makes it sound as if he's hiding something newsworthy."

Janet realized he was deliberately turning the subject from the haunting. Tone stubborn, she said, "One of the things he's hiding is knowledge of the ghosts."

Ben stuck to his own line of conversation. "I never met the man. What's he like?"

Admitting defeat for the moment, Janet answered his

question. "Despite being infirm, he radiates a kind of power, a force. Even when he's trying to be charming there's a creepy sense of it, and this afternoon—when he wasn't being charming at all, he was downright frightening. It's no wonder Muriel walks the line."

"If she's actually a native of Hungary she has secrets of her own. A lot of things happened during the war."

"Fran says he claims to have left before it started."

"He still could have left under a cloud. For that matter, maybe he didn't even leave Argentina because of his health. He could have been fleeing trouble."

"No, he's really ill, Ben."

"You thought he faked that faint."

"No, the faint was genuine. I said I thought he was faking when he acted as if he didn't remember finding me with the camera or seeing the ghosts. Those were issues he didn't want to deal with, so he pretended his memory had blanked out."

"So, we've gone full circle," observed Ben with a bleak smile. "We're back to the ghosts, with you insisting that Renner saw them."

"Definitely. I also feel Kirby was right about why Dr. Renner bought that particular house. He sensed the haunting and *had* to move in."

Ben's mouth tightened. "And naturally, he did this because he was compelled by mysterious forces."

Janet glared. "I don't like Dr. Renner. There's something strange and scary about him. But as little as I care for the man, I think I'd get further talking to him than either you or Kirby." She jumped to her feet. "Don't you understand, Ben? Haven't you listened to a thing I've said? The house feeds on little children. Ever since Elizabeth Parke's death, the house has been a mortal danger to youngsters, but never more so than it is today. It's hungry, Ben—hungry and thwarted, because for the first time in generations, the family living in it has no children."

"Sweetheart, listen," Ben said, getting up himself. "Don't you see that you've disproved your own theory? A house that hungry for victims wouldn't settle for anything less than a family with little kids. A power to attract should assure an equal power to repel. If that pile of wood is as conniving as you say, it never would have allowed the Renners to move in. How can you explain that kind of goof?"

Janet bit back a sob. "Ben—can't you see that's what terrifies me? The house made a mistake, but it won't have cheated itself if it can take Gina. If it can somehow draw her in, the house will have its prey after all!"

31

For Janet, putting her fears into words was like hatching a clutch of leathery eggs, releasing scaly horrors into the light and air where she could no longer pretend they did not exist. Her concern for Gina—was it justified or not? Starting to cry, she collapsed in Ben's arms, and it was a long time before she was calm enough to speak.

"Maybe you're right about everything," she told him, her voice hoarse from weeping and muffled against his chest. "Maybe I'm seeing everything in a distorted way. Lord knows I want to believe Gina's not in danger."

"She isn't, I'm sure of it," he soothed, stroking her hair. They had moved to the couch and he held her, cradling her protectively. "Today's been an emotional roller coaster for you—your session with Renner at his house, then the meeting tonight with the Stocktons—things are happening so fast. Despite how much you want Gina, there's been no chance to adjust to the idea of getting her."

Sitting up, Janet blew her nose and managed a wan smile. She couldn't miss how he had bypassed the question of the ghosts entirely. There seemed no point in arguing; besides, wouldn't it be wonderful if he were right? "So, you think my fears are mostly a reaction?"

He kissed her. "I don't want to sound like a pop psychologist, but yes. Instead of confronting true concerns, I think your mind has focused on imaginary ones. What threatens Gina are her built-in problems, not supernatural horrors from the Renner house. In a way, your sister is right. You are taking on a big responsibility—but it's not one you have to handle all on your own." His voice deepened. "Don't you think it would be a good idea to offer Gina a home with two parents?"

"Two?" Janet echoed blankly.

"Sure, you know—male and female, two by two, like in the ark." His eyes were the soft gray of the sky after a storm. "In case you haven't guessed, I've fallen in love with you, lady. This is a marriage proposal."

"Oh, my," she said.

"Is that an acceptance speech?"

Her lips curved in a tremulous smile. "It was a bit wordy, wasn't it?" She felt as if she were going to cry again, only this time, it would be for joy. It was hard to remember she had ever doubted her feelings for him. Laying a hand along the strong, lean planes of his cheek, she lifted her face to his, knowing how dear he was to her. "Oh, Ben, yes, I accept."

Her fears had receded like whipped dragons. It was as if Ben's words, his touch, and his nearness had driven them all away. It was not until later, from within the safe circle of his arms, that she teased: "I haven't forgotten your story about your Aunt Blanche and how you have an open mind, but are you sure you know what you're getting into?"

Pouring the last of the champagne that he had finally opened after all, Ben nuzzled her cheek. "You planning for you and Gina to use thought swapping to gang up on me? I'm prepared. I was the one who noticed you two put new meaning into the phrase, 'being on the same wave length,' remember?"

Janet snuggled against him. Despite the November night

outside, she felt warm and blissful, as if it were a summer afternoon filled with the sweet scent of honeysuckle and the gentle buzz of bees. Her words drifted lazily. "Oh, yes, at the house site. And I refused to believe you."

"What's it like?" he asked. "Like you hear her speaking inside your mind?"

"Sort of. Only, it's not language as much as it's complete thoughts. It fools me." She laughed softly. "Actually, I suppose Gina could communicate in her native Italian and I'd understand even though I don't know a word. Although I think I'm hearing actual words, it's more like something I *feel*. It's as if the thoughts themselves are tangible, and invisible fingers place them in my head."

She sat up abruptly. "My dream—I remember it now. Gina was a nun who had taken a vow of silence, only she had a special sign language. Her hands moved in a person's mind."

Ben whistled softly. "Then, something in you recognized her abilities all along. Even when you insisted she had spoken aloud, something inside of you recognized the truth about her."

"Yes, the special sign language in my dream was really her telepathy." Janet's tone was filled with wonder. "Ben, now I remember it—all of it! It's as if that memory of Gina acted like a key."

Eagerly, she related the dream, which was suddenly as vivid as it had been the night it had occurred. "The school building looked like a concrete-block government project, and after Dr. Renner marched me inside, Muriel assigned me to work in the kindergarten. That's where Gina was. The children were restless but Gina was supposed to be especially good with them because of her unique method of communication."

"The children?"

"Yes, and the nursery was all—"

"I thought you said it was a kindergarten."

"Well, it was, only I said kindergarten because that sounds more like a class in a school. But it was really a kind of nursery for little children, with cribs for their naps. All those cribs..." Her voice trailed off.

"You dreamed about cribs another time."

"Yes." Her face had tightened. "The cribs were placed under the beech tree."

He didn't catch her changed mood. "If the dream held clues about Gina, maybe it also holds other clues. *Kindergarten*—"children's garden" in German. So the nursery was actually in a part of the Renner property?"

"Yes." Her voice dropped to a rough whisper. "The garden was decorated for Halloween, with jack-o'-lanterns. The first time I smelled that awful burning odor, I thought it was the jack-o'-lanterns, remember? The horrid, smoky stench, those distorted little carved faces, all afire. Ben, there was a fire in this dream too—again, in a nursery. I heard the children shrieking, their cries terrified, filled with pain. Screaming, screaming..."

"Hey, hey!" Becoming alarmed for her, he gave her a shake. "It was only a dream. Nightmare, really."

She turned on him fiercely. "Only a dream? You just said that my dreams might hold clues to the truth, and you're right. And you're also right in thinking they have something to do with the Renners' house." Her voice shook. "I dreamed the children in the nursery would be safe under the beech tree, but that's not so. The truth is the direct opposite. That tree represents the name Elizabeth Parke gave to the house and the property: The Beeches. And it's not a place of safety. It's where the danger is for Gina."

"Honey, we've just been through all that. Gina's not in any jeopardy."

Janet looked at him with haunted eyes. "Then, why do I feel so desperately that she needs to be protected?"

"Because you care so much, love." Ben caressed her, his kiss tender. "You've already suffered the loss of a precious child. It's only natural to fear that it might happen again. It takes time to heal, time to trust life again. Give it time, my darling, give it time. And remember, I'm with you all the while."

32

Had it not been for a lingering taint of fear about the Renner house, the next few days would have ranked among the best in Janet's life. She and Ben found a furnished apartment and he was warmly welcomed by Fran and Warren as a future family member. At a weekend meeting with the Stocktons at Edgar Lightfoot's office, Janet was swiftly and easily appointed Gina's custodian—effective on the date Tommy and Victoria were to leave for Europe. There would be a waiting period before she could apply for adoption, but by that time, her divorce would be final and she and Ben could marry, making things work out perfectly.

There was but a single holdup. With the apartment ready, Janet felt it safest to immediately remove Gina from the vicinity of the Renner house, but Tommy, in a trumpery of paternal devotion, had insisted that Gina stay under his roof, until, as stated in the legal agreement: "that sad day, when my wife Veronica and I release her into the care of Janet Fairweather."

He would not be budged from this, and what could Janet say—? "But Mr. Stockton, as long as she stays on this block, she may be in danger from the ghost children." She had no doubt that such a statement would have Edgar Lightfoot viewing her with entirely new eyes.

"Wicked little ghost tykes, Mrs. Fairweather?" he would question. "Ahem. Perhaps we should discuss this a bit further before continuing with the proceedings."

And so, although Janet still feared that the haunting might have an adverse influence on Gina, she bit her lip and said nothing.

On Monday afternoon, Kirby phoned in a jovial mood. "In case you weren't already aware, Princeton can be quite the small town. The grapevine informs me that you and Ben Yates plan to marry and start off with a ready-made daughter. Congratulations."

"Thanks, Kirby. Everything seems to be working out so very well, except—" She hesitated, and Kirby guessed the reason at once.

"Your mind is still on that house?"

With an uneasy laugh, she admitted, "When I heard your voice, I hoped you were calling with fresh information."

"Actually, I've been juggling around the facts we've already uncovered. You know—examining things from a different angle."

Her eyes brightened. "You've found something new after all?"

"If you can call a different approach new, yes."

"Oh." Janet knew what that meant—a new way to persuade her that she should simply erase the matter from her mind.

When Kirby suggested that she and Ben come home with him that evening after adult school "just for a chat" she begged off, explaining that she and Ben were having dinner together after his class. She was glad for the excuse. The idea of the two men ganging up to "talk sense" into her was more than she could bear.

The call completed, Janet nearly dropped the phone as she went to hang up. Her hand had broken out in a nervous sweat and she realized how much the discussion of the haunting had upset her. She was suddenly angry. For how long was she supposed to go around with the question of the ghosts unresolved? It was time to find some answers, and if Kirby couldn't help, she thought she knew who could.

Lifting the phone again before she could change her mind, she dialed the Renner number. The one person who would take her concerns seriously was Dr. Renner. He might have his secrets and his strange, frightening manner, yet he had not only witnessed the ghost children—he apparently was making a study of the phenomena.

Determination increasing, she listened to the phone ring. Due to the misunderstanding about the camera, she figured there might be difficulty in getting an interview, but once he understood her mission, he would probably be as eager to speak with her as she was to speak with him. First, she would explain the situation to Muriel. Half the battle could be won, she felt, by enlisting Muriel's aid. As intimidating as the doctor could be, his field of child psychology surely testified to a deep concern for children. Janet couldn't believe he would turn his back once she explained her concern that the house might pose danger for living children in the neighborhood.

As she had anticipated, it was Muriel who answered the phone. To her delight, the woman was surprisingly receptive to a meeting. So receptive in fact that it almost seemed to Janet as if she were part of Muriel's plan rather than the other way around.

"But let us not meet for lunch," the woman said in response to Janet's invitation. "It would be too difficult with Rose. Suppose we go for a drive?" Her refined tone was low and guarded, as if she feared being overheard. "Would it be possible for me to pick you up in about an hour?"

An hour later, Janet was climbing into the Oldsmobile. She responded to Muriel's quick, nervous greeting, then looked into the rear to say hello to Rose.

The elderly woman sat with her radio clutched against her black-coated midriff, her eyes as blank and faded as the painted eyes of an ancient doll. She stared out the window, seemingly unaware of Janet or anyone else. A thin wire ran from the radio to lightweight, orange sponge earphones, a comical anomaly when compared to that wizened, babushka-framed face.

Muriel eased the car from the curb. "We will park near a main street. Rose can watch the traffic and pedestrians while we talk."

Once again Janet had the feeling that Muriel was as eager for the meeting as she. Puzzling this, she said nothing more as the black car rolled toward the center of town past neatly kept yards and houses, the ride so smooth and effortless that the wheels might have been magically pulled along a pre-destined route.

Fortunate to find a space on Nassau Street, Muriel parked where Rose could observe patrons bustling in and out of a row of shops. She switched off the engine. Then, with a spasmodic gesture, she switched it on again.

"It is too cold not to have the heater running. It is such a terrible thing to be cold." She fluttered a slender hand apologetically and fell into an awkward silence, staring at Janet with wide eyes that held the expression of a long-caged animal who still had moments in which she remembered freedom.

"Mrs. Renner," Janet began, but Muriel held up a hand, stemming Janet's words as she spoke herself, reeling out what was obviously a well-rehearsed speech:

"Miss Fairweather, you have been a great help and comfort to me and my sister. We have appreciated your kindness, but Dr. Renner will no longer allow outsiders inside our house."

At the abrupt announcement, Janet stared dumbfounded, able to think of nothing except her thwarted plans. Then, remembering the doctor's reaction to finding her with the camera, she asked boldly, "Does his rule really include everyone, or just me?"

A flush stained Muriel's olive complexion. "He is not well," she excused. "For no apparent reason, he forbade me to call upon your aid again. I thought it was a whim, but it apparently is not. I felt I owed you an explanation." Before Janet could explain what had happened regarding the camera, Muriel added, "There is another matter we must discuss." The caged look in her eyes had intensified. "Do you remember my complaints about the mischief makers?"

At this turn of conversation, premonition rippled along

Janet's spine. "The flickering lights, the sounds... Have they troubled you again?"

"Yes." Muriel's voice dropped to a whisper. "I do not think they are neighborhood pranksters as I once believed." The smooth oval of her perfect face looked carved from marble, beautiful, but bloodless. Her lips barely moved. "I think they are not of this world."

At Janet's gasp, Muriel's eyes sharpened. "Ah, Miss Fairweather, then you know of what I speak!" Eagerly, she leaned forward. "This is the other reason I needed to see you. Something incorporeal has possessed my house. You have been there—you know it is true, is that right?"

"Yes, yes," agreed Janet, trembling with relief to know that Muriel was also aware of the ghosts. At last, here was proof that the haunting truly existed outside her own perceptions. Now, more than ever, it was crucial to meet with Dr. Renner. Perhaps Muriel didn't know that her husband was equally aware of the haunting. But once she realized his knowledge of the occult might protect the children who came under the influence of the house, she would surely arrange a meeting as quickly as possible.

Trying to suppress her excitement, Janet sensed it was still important to pick her way carefully. "In the upper gallery, and perhaps also in the back yard, there is something," she said, pausing to gage Muriel's reaction. Then she added, "But especially in the gallery."

"And what did you see?" Muriel's gaze, watchful, intense—cat's eyes, tiger's eyes—waiting, as if their owner were ready to pounce.

"Children," Janet whispered.

"Yes," breathed Muriel, nodding. "Yes, wraiths of long-dead children."

Janet swallowed, knowing there was no reason to hold back any longer. "I saw a small boy, and a smaller girl, along with others." It was morbidly comforting to share the experience. Words burst from her. "*Mutilated*. The spirit children's bodies were mutilated!"

She expected Muriel to confirm this horror, but instead,

she drew back with surprise. "No, I saw nothing like that."

Janet was confused. "But you must have! The boy was crippled! And the little girl, her one eye was gone, *one entire side of her face.*"

"A bruise perhaps," said Muriel. "A slight bruise on the side of her cheek. But two eyes, definitely, for both shone brightly."

"But the damage was there," insisted Janet, her voice rising. "I saw it clearly. And the other children were harmed as well, even the babies—bodies crushed, limbs torn..."

Muriel gave her a cautioning glance. After checking to see that Rose had not been disturbed, she conceded quietly, "There were many children, you are right. In my state of alarm, I did not study them closely. I was too stunned, you understand?" She was clearly reluctant to argue. "The harm you saw, it is probable, only I did not notice. But we can agree we have seen the ghosts of children, can we not?"

"Yes," Janet answered. "We can agree."

The air in the overheated car was claustrophobic. The conversation was not going as Janet had anticipated and she wondered how two otherwise sane women could be sitting along busy, modern Nassau Street discussing a haunted house. It was unreal. A glance from the car window showed a woman with a red muffler and a brown coat emerging from a travel agency. Despite knifelike gusts of November wind, her smile was blissful, as if she envisioned herself already off on some tropic holiday. She carried a canvas purse and Janet wondered if there were ticket reservations tucked inside. Oh, if only she could go scoop up Gina and run with Ben to some faraway safe place!

She asked Muriel, "Did you hear the words the children chanted?"

"I heard rhythmic sounds, but not words."

Janet repeated the chant and Muriel shook her head. "I heard nothing clearly enough to understand. What you say is strange. For what purpose do they increase in strength? Does it mean an increase in number?"

Janet twisted the strap of her purse. "That's what it

sounds like to me." She related the history of The Beeches, telling about the resident children who had died there over the years. She then revealed her dreadful certainty that the misguided wishes of Elizabeth Parke had endowed the house with an evil that distorted the spirits of the young victims it held.

She concluded, "I think you're right about the ghost children wishing to increase their number. Denied the child of a resident, they now might seek—" She was unable to voice Gina's name in this context. "They might seek some other child to join them."

Falling silent, she realized that for some incredible reason, Muriel seemed to have been calmed by hearing the history of the house. The tension had eased from her face and her eyes were almost tranquil. Arching a perfectly shaped brow in thought, she asked, "Then this haunting apparently results from a long-existing pattern . . . one dating back almost to your Civil War?"

"Yes." Janet couldn't understand Muriel's bland reaction. To her own mind, one of the most dreadful aspects of the haunting was that the deaths had continued undetected for so many years.

"Ah . . . for so very long, over a century." Muriel's sigh sounded strangely satisfied. "No concern of ours then."

Janet couldn't believe what she was hearing. "Oh, but it's very much our concern! There may be some way we can stop the tragedy from ever happening again." Sensing it was the time to put Kirby's theory to the test, she asked urgently, "Mrs. Renner, has your husband ever studied the occult?"

The question jolted Muriel from her complacency. "Why ask such a question?"

"Because I think it explains why he bought the house. From the first time he saw it, he must have sensed it was haunted. The desire to explore it must have proved irresistible."

Muriel wet her lips as if about to argue, then after a hesitation, said thoughtfully, "You may be right. It is true that he has studied the psychic realm. An interest from his younger days, shall we say?" Her smile was mirthless.

"The location of the house was impractical, so far from his physician. Why would he make such a move? But your theory explains the mystery. As you say, it would have proved irresistible."

Encouraged, Janet eagerly pressed on to the moment she had been waiting for. "If your husband has studied the haunting, he may have gained knowledge, even influence, over its powers. That's why I wanted to see you today—to ask you to arrange a time for me to speak with him. He may be able to help me."

"Help you?" Muriel's amused laugh was like an old gate swinging in a lonely wind. "He can help no one, Miss Fairweather. He is beyond help of all kinds."

"You don't understand. It's desperately important that I talk with him. Once I explain—"

Muriel cut her off. "He would not see you. Have I not already made that clear? You, of all people, he would not see." Her tone was adamant. "He is a man with a great need for privacy."

Thrown into confusion, Janet couldn't fathom Muriel's reactions. The woman knew her house was haunted, and certainly could see it held potential danger. Could she be so self-centered that she saw danger only when it threatened her personally? Suddenly furious, Janet knew she wasn't going to accept a runaround. If she had to act tough, that's exactly what she would do. "He needs privacy all right, Mrs. Renner, privacy to keep his secrets! Only some of his secrets are out." Her eyes bored into Muriel's. "For example—you, Mrs. Renner, are not as he claims. He tells everyone you're a high-born South American lady, but that's not so. Your homeland is actually Hungary, isn't it?"

Muriel stared at Janet as if some evil moon had risen and transformed her. "Oh, God," she whispered, clutching her heart. "How did you know? Rose . . . you learned this from Rose!" She gestured in despair. "Her speech is so unclear, and for so many years she has never allowed anyone close to her. Never . . . until you." She reached out, the gesture imploring. "Are others also aware?"

Shaken, Janet decided that the ambulance attendant hardly mattered and that the information was safe enough with Kirby and Ben. "No, I'm the only one." In the face of Muriel's distress, she was ashamed of her ruthlessness, yet determined all the same not to lose her advantage, not when Gina's safety might be concerned.

She spoke with a calculation born of need. "Everyone else believes you're from South America, born in Argentina, just as they've been told. There's been no question." Her tone softened persuasively. "But since I've guessed, well, I've been so awfully curious about you and your husband..."

Her voice trailed away, implying that she needed only to have her curiosity satisfied and she would agree to hold her tongue. But her mind was on future payments: once the doctor's secrets were revealed, he would have no further reason to refuse a meeting. And she would have leverage to insist upon it.

Muriel closed her eyes briefly, then reopened them. When she spoke again, it was as if a burden had been lifted from her. "Yes, I will tell you. It has not been healthy to bury the past, to pretend it never existed. That has been wrong, so very wrong..."

Breathlessly, Janet waited to hear more.

33

Muriel glanced to assure herself that Rose was still absorbed in her music. The old woman's earphones were in position, her faded eyes fixed on the traffic and passersby as if her window were a flickering screen rather than reality.

Turning back around, Muriel started to speak, a soft

radiance suffusing her lovely face, her voice holding a faraway tone. "We lived in Hungary, near a city where my father was a professor at the university, but we also knew the country, for our holidays were spent at the villa of my grandparents on Lake Balaton." Her smile was reminiscent. "There, fields of lavender lay full on the hillside. Oh, to smell them again! We were seven, two girls and five boys, Rose the first born, I, the last. Pretty bookends, Papa called us. Life has taken its cruel toll, but when young, Rose was pretty indeed, although not in a popular way. Shy and nervous, she felt ill at ease mingling with those her own age. Since there were sixteen years between us, it suited her to occupy herself with me like a mother." She shook her head sadly. "It was to my benefit that she gave me her youth."

The picture Muriel painted of a richly coddled childhood was vastly different than the one Janet had visualized, yet she immediately recognized it as truth. Every gesture of Muriel's was one to the manor born. An educated father, wealthy grandparents—a child loved, even pampered by an adoring older sister—yes, it all rang true. How could she have ever thought otherwise?

"At that time," Muriel continued, "our nation was caught between the powers of Russia and Germany. Many leaned toward the fascist thought, and in an outbreak of ugliness, one of my brothers and his best friend, who later became Rose's husband, were seriously injured. My father sent them to Vienna, where he had a trusted colleague, to recuperate. Rose went along as a nurse, taking me with her. It was there, in the spring, that we met Dr. Renner.

"An acquaintance of my father's colleague, he and his wife were house guests. Even though I was barely on the threshold of womanhood, I was aware of Dr. Renner's particular attention, his gaze fastening upon me constantly. He was extremely handsome, very masculine. Young as I was, I was flattered, and found it pleasing to think that his fair-haired wife, so pink and white and rounded, resented the notice I received." Anxiety darted over Muriel's face as she hastily amended, "You must understand that I imply nothing improper. He rarely spoke to me directly. The most personal moment was when I once overheard him telling my father's friend that I would someday be a lovely woman. That was all.

"Matters quieted at home and by the winter, we had returned. Two years passed, then things changed abruptly. Restrictions clamped like iron. We could go nowhere, do nothing, without special permission. Because of the annexation of Austria, Germany was our neighbor. Their rules became ours. Some found ways to leave, others tried to fight. My brothers and their friend, by then, Rose's husband, were accused of working with the communists. They were taken for questioning and never returned. On her own, Rose, so courageous and resourceful despite her shyness, wrote to Dr. Renner, asking if he might use his influence to help us." Color stained Muriel's face as she added, "She enclosed my photograph.

"If Dr. Renner responded, we did not have time to learn of it, for my father, terrified by the disappearance of his sons and son-in-law, arranged train passage for Rose and me to friends who promised protection. Our parents, my brothers' wives, and their children were to follow the next day. We never saw any of them again.

"Our train was stopped by the Gestapo. Rose and I, along with others, were taken to a small village which had been emptied and given over as a holding place for refugees. There, we were kept for some months."

"Kept?" asked Janet, incredulous. "You mean, like prisoners?"

Muriel seemed amused by Janet's tone. "I do not think you can understand. We were guarded. We had been stripped of everything except the clothes on our backs. The only thing we had left of value was each other."

Her eyes darkened. "Since the disappearance of her husband, Rose's mind had grown increasingly unsound. In the village she met a man whom she fantasized was her husband returned to her. She became pregnant but had not yet begun to show when troops arrived. The elderly and the infirm, mothers and young children, were gathered in the square. All those able to work were forced into trucks. The last of us to leave saw the remaining soldiers firing their guns at those huddled in the square." Ignoring Janet's horrified gasp, she continued: "It was winter—many died on the way, including the man Rose believed was her husband. During our stay in the village, we had heard frightening tales of where people like us might be taken. When the trucks finally stopped, we thought the worst had come true, that we had been brought to Auschwitz."

"Auschwitz?" It was a word Janet had heard, but until that moment it had never seemed real.

This time, Muriel gave attention to Janet's horror. She arched a brow, her smile cool, and blade thin. "Yes. Have I neglected to mention the crime of our little band? Our sin was being Jewish."

Once heard, Janet found this truth also self-evident. There could be no other explanation for the inhumanity Muriel described. In some confusion, she asked, "Then, Dr. Renner—is he Jewish as well?"

Muriel's eyes glittered. "No, he is not. A far different story if he were. Rose and I are both his glory and his shame." Without enlarging on her cryptic comment, she went on.

"We found we had actually been transported to a work camp for a munitions plant. To describe the conditions, I only need say that new workers were brought in daily to supplant those who died during the night. As to Rose and me, our situation became reversed—although I was fifteen to her thirty-one, I became the senior sister. I managed to help her hide her pregnancy although it was to no purpose. The delivery of the child would automatically end both their lives.

"Then, what seemed a miracle intervened. I was called by name to the commander's office. When he was satisfied as to my identity, he said I was to be moved to a new location. I remember crying that I could not be separated from my sister." She gave her head a helpless shake. "Whatever was I thinking? To imagine anyone would heed my tears! My mind as well as Rose's must have become unhinged.

"The commander laughed and had Rose brought to him. Anyone who really looked at her could see that she was pregnant. I realized my foolish plea had signed her death order." Remembered wonderment crept into her voice. "Yet, within the hour, we were taken to a car. Coats were given to us." Unconsciously, she stroked the coat she now wore. "They were coarse and dirty, but they felt like the richest fabric. The vehicle was heated. I had forgotten such luxury could exist."

Breaking off, she smiled strangely at Janet. "You have guessed so many things expertly. Can you guess the name of our savior?"

Janet moistened her dry lips. "Dr. Renner?"

"Ah, yes. But that wasn't really so difficult, was it? I gave you so many clues. Yes, Dr. Renner. He had received Rose's letter, but his inquiries to locate us failed. His interest was piqued, and he redoubled his effort. He is a man who dislikes being thwarted. Thoughts of us began to occupy his imagination. Learning our fate had become a quest."

It was clear to Janet that it was Muriel herself who occupied the man's imagination. As Rose had cleverly planned, the photograph had done its work. A lovely child had become a breathtakingly beautiful woman, exactly as the doctor had predicted. He had to find her again. It was a romantic tale, especially when viewed against the backdrop of the brutal Nazi regime—romantic despite his lies about Muriel's background and those of having left Europe before the war.

"The doctor had friends, important connections," Muriel continued almost dreamily. "His search was aided by the fact that detailed records were often kept. Eventually, his search was rewarded. Through special influence, he had us moved to the place where he was."

"And so he helped you escape the country?"

"Yes, but not immediately. Such things take time. He had to be careful not to arouse suspicion. Getting the proper papers, shipping his books and records, tying up loose ends, gathering sufficient funds." Muriel's smile twisted as she repeated with irony, "Ah, yes—the tying of loose ends and the gathering of funds."

"And Dr. Renner's first wife?" Janet remembered reading of the bombing of German-held cities. "She died in the war?"

Muriel's shrug was oddly unconcerned. "Much was lost in the war."

A bell rang in Janet's mind. Ben had speculated that the doctor left Europe under a cloud. From what Muriel was saying, the doctor fled Germany while war still raged. Smuggling out his belongings, gathering "funds," which Muriel seemed to hint might not have been his to take—that, plus possibly leaving a wife behind... The doctor's deeds could have won him bitter enemies—enemies who would not, even after all these years, forget.

Still, there was the romance! The influential German doctor smitten by the lovely Jewish girl—she, so adoring of her knight in shining armor. He had not only pried her from the jaws of certain death but was also willing to rescue her demented sister. Muriel must have worshiped him. Yet it was clear her feelings had changed over the years. She gave him care and obedience, yet Janet had never seen evidence of warmth. What had gone wrong?

In some corner of his mind, had the doctor despised himself for loving Muriel? Raised in an anti-Semitic society, he might have disdained the attraction he felt. Also, Renner and Muriel had known virtually nothing of each other before fate and circumstances bound them together. He saw only her physical beauty, while she saw only his power to act as her deliverer. When their illusions faded, there might have been little left to build on. Yet, they had stayed together. Muriel's clothes and jewels showed his continued pride in her loveliness; and if for no other consideration than Rose, Muriel owed him a great debt.

Abruptly, Janet asked, "What happened to Rose's baby?"

Lost in her thoughts, Muriel was startled. Turning her head, she stared blankly out the window. "After its birth, it died. That was the finish for Rose. Her mind became then as it is now."

Janet felt an anguished pang, understanding how destructive the forces of grief could be. Then she reminded herself that she had chosen to escape that destruction and fasten her concerns on the living. Enough of old history. It was time to return to her reason for wanting to learn more about the doctor in the first place.

Straightening her shoulders, she offered a proposition to Muriel, "I'll hold everything you've told me in the strictest confidence, but I urgently need to talk with your husband. Not about the past. That's private between the two of you and can stay that way. But I need to talk with him about the house and the fact that it's haunted. You said that in his younger days he studied the occult—"

Muriel cut her off. "Yes, long ago. It need not be discussed."

"But it must be!" cried Janet, desperate to keep victory from slipping from her grasp. "We've already agreed it explains his interest in moving into that particular house. Listen, please—I must make you understand. There is a child in the neighborhood, one who has been repeatedly drawn to the property. She—"

Again Muriel interrupted. "The little girl who has that cat? Such an annoying animal!"

Janet blinked. "Well, yes. The girl's name is Gina, and—"

Her shoulder was gripped from behind. She whirled to see Rose sitting on the edge of her seat. Unnoticed, the elderly woman had stirred and the earphones now hung loosely about her wattled neck. She leaned forward, her face only inches away.

"Dangerous!" she hissed. "Dangerous." Flecks of spittle landed on Janet's cheek. That knobby, arthritic hand gripped with a force that must have been as painful for its owner as it was for the one who was held. "The little girl! If she comes, this time, I know what to do. This time, I keep her safe."

Coming to Janet's aid, Muriel tried to loosen her sister's grip. "It is all right, Rose. It is all right."

Rose stared at her in blind confusion, peering down the dingy chambers of a long lost past. "The children. All gone."

Succeeding in lifting the hand, Muriel clasped it between the both of hers, gently, as if holding and comforting a frail bird. "Hush, now, do not worry."

"All gone, all gone! They were with us, then they were all gone!"

"Yes," Muriel soothed, stroking her sister's hand. "But now it is all right. We need not worry about them anymore."

"No," protested Rose, struggling to free her hand. "No, no . . ."

Seeing that the old woman was on the verge of getting out of control, Janet quickly spoke up. "Mrs. Renner, perhaps you should get in the back. I'll drive the car home."

"Yes, thank you," the woman said gratefully, swiftly moving to do as Janet suggested.

By the time Janet pulled the vehicle to a stop before the yellow house, Rose had quieted. Muriel, who had been crooning to her in a foreign tongue, allowed Janet to assist them from the car. Then, at the front driveway, she said in a dismissal that was distracted rather than rude: "Thank you, but we are all right now," and proceeded to take Rose into the house.

Helplessly, Janet watched the door close behind the two figures. Feeling upset and frustrated, she returned home, but no more than twenty minutes later, Muriel phoned. Without preliminary, she said, "Miss Fairweather, I have been giving thought to your concerns. It may be possible that my husband might be persuaded to speak with you after all."

"Oh, Mrs. Renner, thank you!"

"I promise nothing," Muriel said quickly. "It will be no easy task. As I have explained, his mind is most set against you. If you desire this meeting, you must be patient. Can you be that?"

"Yes, of course. But—"

"Good. I cannot talk further at this time. I will do my best. Please, I beg of you, be patient."

The phone clicked softly in Janet's ear as Muriel broke the connection.

34

That evening, Janet expressed disbelief when Ben led her into The Black Swan, the most elegant of the restaurants housed in Princeton's renowned Danish hotel and convention center, Scanticon. "We're having dinner here? Did you come into an inheritance—what's the special occasion?"

He grinned. "From the way you sounded over the phone, I felt we needed something extra special to fortify us when you tell me the details of your meeting with Muriel."

The formally garbed waiter ushered them into the red and black dining room where the centerpiece on each table was a tall crystal vase of cut tulips, the velvet-black stamens dramatic against the scarlet petals. After ordering, Janet began telling Ben of her experience that afternoon.

"One of the most significant things I've learned is that Muriel's aware of the ghosts too," she said quietly. "They're there, whether you and Kirby believe me or not."

Ben frowned. "Okay, so something in that house is strange. I guess I can't really argue with that. I mean, I believe such things might be possible. But did you and Muriel actually see the same things?"

"Children, Ben. She said 'children,' without any prompting from me."

Although she wanted Ben to know that Muriel confirmed the presence of the ghosts, Janet had already decided not to press that point too hard. Muriel's promise to arrange a talk with Dr. Renner had lifted a weight from her. Dr. Renner not only knew about the ghosts—he also might have some way to exorcise their threat. At the moment, whether or not Ben truly believed in the haunting no longer seemed quite so important.

After their food arrived, she said, "Let me go on to what Muriel said. The things she and Rose experienced during the war were horrible, and I know there was plenty more she left out." She related the story Muriel told her, ending with, "It's a wonder any of the survivors found the courage to live again. And you sure were right about Dr. Renner having reasons for hiding. Maybe 'Renner' isn't even his real name."

Ben said, "If he's Herman Renner, Viennese child psychologist, his professional credentials are in order."

Janet's eyes widened. "You checked on him? What did you find?"

Ben looked pleased with himself. "Nothing except that he's who he claims to be. Which still means he could have loaded a Swiss bank account with stolen funds and knocked off his first wife before leaving Europe."

"Ben!"

"*Ben!*" he mimicked good-naturedly. "Think of what Muriel told you—the last thing the doctor did before leaving Germany was to tie up loose ends."

"Murdering a wife could hardly be described as 'tying up loose ends.' Muriel couldn't have meant anything like that."

"Are you so sure? I get the impression she drops veiled hints instead of saying things straight out. The way the doctor reacted when he found you with that camera proves he's guilty of something."

"Oh, yes, about the camera. I had intended to tell Muriel about that, only it was forgotten when Rose became so upset." She knew she was returning to the subject of the haunting, but she couldn't help herself. "Tomorrow, I'm calling and explaining my real reason for having the camera. Once Muriel tells Dr. Renner I was after pictures of the ghosts, it should make it a lot easier for her to persuade him to see me."

Ben looked up from his steak au poivre. "I wish you'd stop thinking that Gina is in danger."

"I don't really know if I believe that anymore. Or maybe I just don't want to believe it. But I can't deny that today is the second time that Rose gave me a warning."

"Honey, the woman's mind isn't sound. She probably has Gina mixed up with someone from her past." His tone was persuasive. "It doesn't matter what's happening in that house—whether it's haunted or not. Next Tuesday, the Stocktons leave and Gina will be yours. The new apartment will be waiting, and that night, Gina will be sleeping there safely, blocks from the Renner place. Only a week more to wait."

"Eight days," Janet corrected, but privately, she admitted that he was probably right about Rose. The woman was hardly what she would call reliable. Thoughts veering off, she considered how different life soon would be for Gina. Instead of having a tutor, the little girl would attend a public school program for the handicapped. Edgar had agreed that having Gina attend classes with other children would undoubtedly be beneficial. He had also reviewed agency medical reports which assured that Gina should someday speak normally.

Looking at Ben, Janet said, "You know, when I was talking with Edgar, I realized that even though I kept insisting that Gina had spoken, I never once tried to coax her into talking to me again."

"I figured you just felt it best not to pressure her."

"I guess that's what I told myself, but I think I feared proving she really couldn't do it. But now, I've brought up the subject with her. I've told her that someday, the words will just start popping out. She hates being different—she wants to be able to join in with the other kids. But I also made it clear that no matter what happens, she's okay in my book."

"Did you make any mention of the mind reading?"

"No. I doubt she realizes it happens. Or perhaps she assumes it's an ability everyone possesses. I don't understand enough about it myself to attempt a discussion." Strain came into her voice. "I don't understand any of this, Ben. Don't you see that's why I want to talk with Dr. Renner?"

Ben's ruggedly handsome face reflected sympathy, yet his answer was emphatic. "No, I don't see. This very moment we're sitting in a restaurant located on grounds belonging to Princeton University, a world-famous institution of learning. The Forrestal Research Campus is here, packed with engineers and scientists. Then there's all the other university schools, plus the Institute for Advanced Study—that's where Einstein was, for God's sake. If you want to investigate, Kirby Orchard could probably find you scores of people who know more about the supernatural than Renner ever dreamed of."

"But they wouldn't know about the haunting, Ben. They wouldn't know about that particular house."

"And you think that paranoid bigamist does? The house may be disturbed, but I doubt that the doctor or anyone else has power over it. Nor do I believe that ghosts have powers over the living. I admit there may be something odd about the number of resident kids who have died there, but Gina's occasional romps in the yard hardly put her in that category. You're worrying for nothing."

Expression suddenly contrite, he reached over to place his hand gently upon Janet's, his gray eyes showing love and concern. "Honest, honey, I'm not making light of your concerns, but I just don't believe there's any reason for them. Now, how about finishing your shrimp Copenhagen and then let's have a look at the dessert menu."

Janet discussed the matter no further with Ben, but the next day she followed through with her plan and phoned Muriel to explain why she had taken a camera into the house.

Muriel was silent a moment, then: "Ah, yes. Now I understand. I will explain this matter to him. But he must be in the proper mood before I make the attempt. Do you understand?"

"Yes, but you will explain?"

Muriel's response was testy. "Have I not told you so? Again, I ask you to be patient."

Not satisfied, yet feeling there was nothing else she could do except trust the woman, Janet tried to turn her mind to other matters. Even though there was no word from Muriel during the rest of the week, everything else proceeded so smoothly that almost despite herself, she began to relax.

On Saturday, she and Ben took Gina over to the apartment. Janet had already moved some of their things in, but it was the first time Gina had seen the place. Mrs. Ousler had gotten a few of the child's extra clothes together so that she could hang garments in the closet that would be hers and put underwear and night things into the drawers. There were also a new toy and a game that Ben had gotten to surprise her.

"The things you selected were perfect," Janet told him as they left Gina playing.

He grinned. "I think maybe I'm an expert in eight-year-olds. The presents I mailed to my nephew on his eighth birthday made a big hit too. When Gina gets me for a father, she's getting someone with a proven track record as a gift selector."

"Oh, Ben, I do love you," Janet said, wrapping her arms about his waist. "To think I ever worried I'd have to choose between you or Gina."

He held her close. "Never, love. The two of you are a package deal as far as I'm concerned. I couldn't ask for anything more." He hesitated, then added, "Except, maybe someday, a baby brother or sister for Gina?"

Janet rested her head on his chest. "That sounds good, Ben," she said softly, knowing that she no longer feared the slipping away of the past as she began her new life. "Yes, that sounds very good."

Later that afternoon, the three of them drove to the Quaker Bridge Mall and shopped for linens, kitchen items, and a rug for the master bedroom. The store windows were decorated for Thanksgiving, with displays of squashes, apples, and nuts spilling in abundance from giant cornucopias. Eagerly, Janet found herself looking forward to the first holiday meal that she, Ben, and Gina would share as a family.

Although Gina couldn't be with them on Sunday, it was yet another blissful day: Sunday dinner with Fran and Warren and the families of two of Warren's married children. All in all, a perfect weekend, thought Janet.

That evening, she fell asleep with nothing except good thoughts on her mind. As she started to dream, it first seemed an extension of her contented mood. She, Gina, and Ben were once again walking through the mall, looking at the rich heaps of produce in the Thanksgiving displays. In her dream, she turned to speak with Ben, but he was gone. Gina and all the other shoppers were gone as well. Janet found herself alone before a window that showed a cinder-block wall. In front of it were crates of turnips and cabbages, and a wheeled cart heaped high with knobby, orange-red squash.

Strangely fascinated, she moved forward. Abruptly, she was on the other side of the wall and inside a crude room. As a hint of sulfurous smoke curled from a secret corner, Janet saw that the room was filled with children in their cribs. They slept restlessly, the night broken here and there by a plaintive cry.

Like my dreams, Janet thought, knowing even as the thought formed that this was also a dream. The nursery, the children's restless cries, the smoke . . . all from her dreams. Yet it also seemed that she remembered crying children and the smell of smoke in real life as well. A shadow of fear fell over her. She suddenly sensed that something bad was about to happen, something her other dreams had warned her about, something terrible...

The force of the explosion slammed into her like a fist, numbing her, turning her into stone. With a thunderous roar, a corner of the room collapsed. Trapped in their cribs, the children screamed. Aghast, Janet watched helplessly as the ceiling fell, timbers and rubble tumbling down upon the victims of the nursery, tearing flesh, smashing bone, caving small skulls.

Where are their mothers? a voice inside Janet shrieked. *Why haven't their mothers come to save them?*

Flames leaped with a deafening roar. Through the exploded wall spilled the orange-red globes of squash, rolling and smashing into the thick of the fire, filling the air with the pumpkinlike stench of the burning squashes.

Where are the mothers?

A searing light erupted. All went dark.

There was only the dark, the acrid smoke, and the fading screams of dying children...

Then all was silence. Silence as deep as a grave.

Janet slept on.

In the morning she awoke with a vague sense of unease. *I must have dreamed*, she thought. I must have had another nightmare. Still lying in bed, she tried to recall the nightmare, then she remembered Ben saying that it was probably best to allow troubling dreams to lie undisturbed.

Ben's right, she said to herself as she arose. There was only one more day to go before Gina officially became her child, and she didn't need the aggravation of mysterious night phantoms. As she dressed, she glanced out the window and saw the yellow paint and white latticework of the Renner house peeking through the bare limbs of the copper beech. Ben was right about a lot of things, she decided. Whatever went on at that property had nothing to do with her or with Gina. If she wanted to concern herself with the welfare of its future residents, she'd have plenty of time for that after she heard from Muriel. For the time being, she had enough concerns of her own, thank you.

Later that day, Kirby phoned to suggest that she and Ben drop over that evening. "Ben tells me that after class, you two will go out for dinner, but afterwards, there's no reason why you can't stop here for a nightcap," he said winningly, then added, "if it's all right with you, that is."

Janet remembered his previous invitation had been to come and discuss the Renner house. She had no doubt that the reason behind this invitation was the same. *What a schemer*, she thought, seeing his plan had been to rope her in by gaining Ben's approval first. And if she agreed, she'd end up listening to the rotund little man parade forth additional reasons as to why the Renner house couldn't possibly be haunted.

But then, in an indulgent mood, she gave in. "All right," she said. "Ben and I will drop by."

She was thinking that even though Kirby was all wrong about the house, he had been a good friend. Since he really seemed to want this meeting, she supposed it would do no harm to go along.

35

On her way to Kirby's that evening, Janet was on cloud nine, able to think of little except the fact that by early the next morning, Gina would officially become hers. Even the unexpected call from Ben's boss, which had disrupted their dinner plans, didn't take the shine from her giddy mood. In her frame of mind, she was more inclined to tease Ben about his late-hour meeting than anything else.

Mischievously pressing against him as he rang Kirby's

doorbell, she said, "I've got your number, Ben Yates. Last week it was dining at Scanticon, while this week it's a quick bite at a neighborhood deli. Now you claim you have work to do and leave me at the house of another man. Clearly you've grown bored and you're trying to let me down easy."

Laughing, Ben gave her a hug. "Gosh, and I thought I was being subtle."

When Kirby answered the door, Ben explained why he wouldn't be back until later. "I hope I won't be long, but I won't be able to get away until the meeting is over."

"Don't hurry on our account," Janet purred sweetly. "Kirby and I get along just fine."

Looking at the other man, Ben shrugged helplessly. "She's been a handful all evening. For dessert, she wanted pickles and ice cream."

Kirby beamed. "Oh, yes, Janet—tomorrow you become a mother. Are you and Gina going with the Stocktons to see them off at the airport?"

"No, I'm to meet them at their house early tomorrow before the limousine picks them up. We'll say our goodbyes and Gina and I will become a family." Joy sang through her voice.

Hanging up her coat after Ben left, Kirby asked, "Did you already have dessert?"

"No, there wasn't enough time." Janet giggled. "And even if there had been, I wouldn't have had pickles and ice cream."

It wasn't until after Kirby had served slices of chocolate cake and they adjourned to the study that he introduced the subject of the Renner house.

Expression on his round face earnest, he said, "I told you over the phone that I had a new slant, a different way to interpret the deaths of those children. I think we looked at things from the wrong angle."

Settled comfortably on the couch, Janet was so sure she could anticipate what he was about to say that she decided to beat him to it. Brightly, she announced, "During the past few days, I've decided just about the same thing. Regardless of what's happened over the years at that house, or what's there now, it has nothing to do with me, and it certainly has nothing to do with Gina. You tried to convince me of that and so did Ben. Finally, I've accepted that you're both right."

"Oh, my." Kirby pursed his lips into a pout. "I feel like I'm in an O'Henry story—the one where she sells her hair to buy him a watch chain, while he sells his watch to buy her combs."

"Oh? What's that mean?"

Kirby shifted his bulk in his chair. "First, that I owe you an apology. I finally reached the electrician, and you were right. There's more to the haunting than just your own perception of it."

She was suddenly wary. "You're saying he saw the ghosts too?"

"What he had was a strong feeling of being watched. He said he kept going to the hallway outside the room in which he was working, and on each occasion, he felt he had just missed a glimpse of some movement out of the corner of his eye. He also complained of hearing sounds. He described them as being very faint, and similar to singing without actually being a song."

"You mean the chanting." Her voice was flat. This wasn't what she had expected to hear from Kirby and it certainly wasn't what she wanted to hear. Not now, not when she wanted to devote her attention to other matters.

"Yes, I asked him if it could have been a chant, and he agreed that it might have been."

Reluctantly, Janet asked, "What did he see?"

"Apparently nothing meaningful." Kirby adjusted his glasses. "Or maybe he didn't want to admit what he really saw. He did say that if he were his Irish grandfather, he would think the house bewitched by wee folk. That means fairies, of course, but I suppose he could also have meant ghost children."

Lighthearted mood destroyed, Janet closed her eyes. "That's what he meant all right. I haven't told you—I didn't think there was any point, but Muriel has seen the ghost children too."

"Ah, and you kept quiet because you didn't think I'd believe you?"

Her eyes opened. "And you wouldn't have! All you would have done is argue. When I told Ben, he seemed to think Muriel and I were simply trading hallucinations." Distraught, she put a hand to her head. "In the past few days my fears have seemed to evaporate. I criticized Muriel because she wasn't concerned enough about the haunting, but now I understand. She has enough concerns in real life and so do I. All I want to think of is having Gina, getting married to Ben, and being happy and now—" On the verge of tears, she suddenly became furious.

"Why did you stir this all up again right now, Kirby? Okay, so the ghosts exist apart from my own imagination. Terrific. I knew that all along. But it doesn't matter. Regardless of what's in that house, the influence doesn't extend beyond the property. That's what counts."

Kirby leaned his portly body forward. "But the last time we talked, you were concerned over a possible threat to Gina. My new understanding of the haunting should relieve your fears."

"I don't have any fears. And even if I did, my worries will be over by tomorrow morning. That's when Gina and I move across town into the new apartment. Regardless of the powers of the ghost children, she'll be safe. There's nothing more to discuss."

"But I think there is," Kirby persisted. "Are you going to feel comfortable taking Gina to visit your sister when it's so close to the Renner house? Will you have secret dreads that the hours Gina has spent in that yard have harmed her? I want to dispel those anxieties." He paused, then intoned dramatically, "Janet, I hope to prove to you that the influence of the house is not evil, but good."

Her eyes widened, but before she could speak, Kirby handed her a sheet of paper. "Take a look. Listed in order, those are the names of the resident children who have died."

Janet wished she could just refuse the list, but she couldn't; the subject had been important to her for too long. A new entry seemed to leap from the paper at her. "What's this?" She pointed to the dates after a name. "You now have the age of Alexander Whitehurst Jr.—dead at age twenty-three. How did you discover that?"

Kirby couldn't restrain his cherubic grin. "Played a hunch. I looked in the graveyard of Faith Chapel. The Whitehurst plot wasn't too far from the burial place of the Hickok twins. Young Alexander was born in 1865 and died in 1888. If you look further down, you'll find something additional about the Crammer family."

Janet gasped. "They lost a daughter? But weren't they people you knew? You told me they had never suffered a loss."

"I never knew about it. The girl was born with problems and never mingled with other children. The family moved there when she was young and left after she died somewhere late in her teens. It all happened when I was away. I don't recall ever knowing she existed."

Janet stared at the list another moment, then looked up, her hazel eyes wise and shocked. "The Goodsmiths lost a child too?"

"A fully grown daughter, a widow who died during childbirth. Her infant, also a girl, thrived under the care of her grandparents at The Beeches and eventually married a senator from Virginia."

Janet was aghast. "Regardless of age, the Goodsmiths lost a daughter. That means that every family who ever lived at The Beeches lost one or more children. Every single family!" Her voice was shrill. "And to think you said you'd discovered no new information!"

"Had I revealed this without having time to explain the interpretation, you would have become upset."

Janet jumped to her feet. "And I'm not upset now? God, Kirby! Child after child, lured to that wicked house!" She brandished the paper. "Everything I worried about, everything you tried to convince me didn't exist is true. And there's no longer any guessing—here's the proof!"

Kirby remained as unruffled as a meditating monk. "Proof of certain deaths, but not necessarily of youngsters. What family does not have members who have died? And in any case, where is the proof that the house is wicked?"

"Isn't that self-evident?"

"No, it is not, and if you'll sit down again, I'll explain."

Sitting, she looked at the list again. Her face was pale. "You thought this would relieve my mind? Incredible!"

He leaned back in his chair, folding his hands across his ample paunch. "You were the one who gave me a clue as to what the truth might actually be. That, along with a reading of the letters written by Elizabeth Parke."

"I thought the letters you had were *about* Elizabeth. Written by a disgruntled relative."

"Yes, by one made angry because she spent her father's inheritance building The Beeches. If you think back, you may remember feeling sympathetic toward Elizabeth. The idea that she built a home to shelter children who needed help appealed to you."

"That was before I realized she was dangerously demented. Before I realized the house had become a torture chamber for the spirits of the children who died there."

"And did you believe the house actually killed them? Think back, now. Remember how you reacted when I asked if you felt the house was responsible for your own child's death?"

"I know what you're talking about, but I don't see the point of quibbling. I decided the house didn't murder the children outright—it sensed children who were doomed and drew them in by making their parents want to live in the house."

"Exactly. You said you felt that's why you initially found the house so appealing. You said the house sensed that your baby would die and so it 'called' to you."

"So? What really counts is that once the house had those

children, it wouldn't let them go. And what does any of this have to do with letters written by Elizabeth?"

Grunting as he reached over, Kirby passed an opened book across the desk to her. "Elizabeth had a friend named Thelma Flock. This is a collection of records from the Flock family which includes letters written by Elizabeth. In them, she comes across as a kindly, compassionate woman with deeply felt spiritual values. She wanted her life to count for something good."

"When she was young, sure, but that doesn't mean she didn't become crazy and vicious when older."

"She never had the chance to get old. She died of influenza at the age of forty-two, the same year in which one of her letters is dated. Elizabeth wasn't demented. The woman in those letters was incapable of creating the twisted legacy you ascribe to her."

"Then why all those dead children?"

"In part, you've already stumbled upon the answer. The house that Elizabeth built has the power to recognize children in deeply troubled situations. It may lure their families, yes. Beckon them, seduce them, if you will, but for a good purpose—to assure happiness for the children, to bless their lives." He hesitated, then added, "I know nothing of your past other than the loss of your infant daughter and the fact that you're in the process of divorce. Was your marriage secure, or did it need healing? Would it have provided for Becky the nurturing necessary for her happiness? Remember how you described your feelings as you stood in the garden with her in your arms? You said you felt surrounded by something rare and magical, that it was a moment of unbelievable beauty."

Remembering, Janet's mood shifted and she felt a lump in her throat. Reliving the experiences, she whispered, "Yes, I said that the moment was perfect. *Perfect*. I said that I wished it would never end."

"If your husband was with you, did he sense it too?"

"I think... Yes, Clay responded, I'm sure of it. For just that moment, yes."

Kirby spoke softly. "So I thought. And I believe that transcendent moment existed because of Elizabeth Parke's determination that the house be dedicated to the welfare of children. It reached out to you because of an unhappiness it wished to heal." He pointed to the list Janet still held. "The Beeches sheltered those children, my dear. Whether their time on earth was measured in months, days, or years, their childhoods were made beautiful. And I think I can prove it."

Janet's emotions were at war. On one hand, she vividly remembered the feelings of warmth which seemed to emanate from the house, yet the hideous conclusions she came to later seemed equally as vivid. She stared blankly at Kirby's posters, where Shirley Temple curtsied prettily and King Kong stared in bafflement at a miniature Fay Wray. Stiffening her spine defiantly, she said, "Okay, let's hear this oh-so convincing proof."

Kirby was undisturbed by her skepticism. "The last child who died here was Timmy Fiorello. I knew the family, and I can tell you that when they moved in, Timmy was the most unresponsive eight-year-old you could hope to find. He never smiled, he never showed interest in anything. Then, he began to change. Ask your sister, if you doubt me. His physical condition didn't improve, but his attitude did. On more than one occasion, I heard his mother speak of it as a miracle, for while living in that house, ill as he was, crippled as he was, Timmy became a happy child.

"And you're giving the house the credit?" demanded Janet, becoming angry again.

"Yes, because Timmy is not the only case. The little girl who later drowned, the relative the Mitchums took in, is another. She came from a neglected background, a child virtually raised on the streets. Eleven years old when orphaned, she already had a history of being in and out of foster homes and shelters for playing truant and shoplifting."

"At age eleven?"

"Yes, so the Mitchums were prepared for trouble. Only it didn't happen. The child responded beautifully to her new environment, did well in school, and made many friends. There were never any difficulties."

"Obviously, it was the Mitchums themselves who made the difference."

"Curious that you make the point, because when the Mitchums first moved in, they were a family in conflict. Nice people, but with short tempers and exacting expectations for their growing children. Had they still been like that when taking the little girl, there would have been war, I'm sure of it. As it was, as time went by, they seemed to learn patience and understanding. The conflicts ceased. Their own kids turned out fine. They're all grown now and leading good, productive lives. By the time the little girl entered their household, the Mitchums knew how to provide the environment she needed. I'm giving the house the credit, yes. And then there's the case of Dorinda Crammer."

Janet held onto her resistance. "The Crammer girl? I thought you didn't even remember her."

Kirby wagged a sausage of a finger. "Ah—indeed, I didn't remember. It was my old friend, Nettie Laine, who told me the story. After our last conversation, I paid her a visit at the nursing home and quizzed her about everything she could recall of folks who had lived at The Beeches. I learned that there were many troubled children from there whose futures turned out surprisingly well. For example, one of the Granger cousins would have been sent to jail had his aunt and uncle here not taken him to live at The Beeches. He straightened out, and now he's retired after a long and successful career as a lawyer. She also told me about Dorinda Crammer.

"She said that when the Crammers moved in, Dorinda was afflicted with violent spasms. She had suffered brain damage at birth that resulted in episodes in which she behaved like a wild animal, throwing herself against the floor, kicking, biting, and screaming.

"Because she was young, her parents could physically control her during these emotional storms, but they knew that when she reached her teen years, only heavy drugs could prevent her from harming herself or others. But, from the time they moved into the house, Nettie says Dorinda improved. Against all the expectations of her doctors, the number of spasms and their violence lessened. After a few months, they ceased altogether.

"Dorinda was never a normal child. Her mind wasn't right and she had severe respiratory difficulties. She was never able to withstand the excitement of playing with other children or going into public situations, but in the familiar surroundings of her home, she was at peace. She was, until the time of her death from pneumonia, a serene and contented individual."

Kirby tapped his balding head. "When Nettie called the beneficial changes in the girl miraculous, I started thinking. What happened to Timmy Fiorello had also been called a miracle, and perhaps the changes in the Mitchum family were miraculous as well. I began to see the house in a new light. Yes, some children who lived there died, but many others went on to enjoy full, productive lives. There is great evidence of happiness and emotional healing. Whatever the explanation, the way life changed for so many children seemed a fitting tribute to Elizabeth Parke's intentions when building the house."

Gazing at Janet, he said gently, "That's what I hoped to make you see—not only does the house hold no dangers for you and Gina, but that its history speaks of beauty rather than ugliness."

Janet looked away. She knew Kirby was trying to be helpful, yet everything he said increased her turmoil. She wondered what Ben would think about Kirby's theory. Sneaking a look at her watch, she wished he would hurry and rejoin them.

Shifting restlessly, she said, "Kirby, the trouble with your idea is that it ignores a very important point about the ghost children. Remember how I described them? Their bodies were torn, broken, mutilated." It made her feel sick to remember it. "How does that fit in?"

He pushed out his lower lip. "I guess it doesn't."

"Darned right it doesn't." She got to her feet. In the past few moments, a strange uneasiness that had nothing to do with the discussion had begun edging up upon her with the relentlessness of a dark tide creeping up a beach. Something was wrong, she thought. Had Ben run into some sort of trouble? Surely it was time for him to be showing up.

"I came to the conclusion the house was evil because of those damaged spirit forms. The house may appear to nurture troubled children—to introduce bliss into their days, but it's only an illusion." Her voice gained intensity. "Only an illusion, Kirby, because whenever these children die, something terrible happens to their spirits—something cruel and hideous starts feeding on them."

Kirby frowned. "You told me that Muriel also saw the ghosts. Did she also see them as damaged?"

"Yes." Janet's reply was emphatic. Then, remembering the actual conversation, she recalled that Muriel had only admitted to seeing bruises. From the poster, the darling Shirley-moppet showed a smile as dazzling as sunshine. Janet thought of the little girl whose face was partially battered away, her one eye completely gone. That couldn't have been the same little girl Muriel had seen as only bruised. And for some reason, Muriel had also missed seeing the crippled boy.

Angrily, she dismissed these discrepancies as irrelevant. Why waste time talking? She wasn't going to convince Kirby any more than he could convince her.

She said, "Muriel didn't see the children enough to examine their appearance. She was too frightened." She consulted her watch openly. "It seems like Ben should be here by now. I hope nothing has gone wrong."

Kirby stared. "But he's been gone less than an hour."

Her nod was brusque. The feeling of something being amiss grew stronger, as if she stood in deep water with scuttling creatures she couldn't see gathered about her feet, nagging, nibbling, waiting to draw the first blood.

"I think I should go home," she decided abruptly and headed for the hall. By the time Kirby jumped to his feet and caught up, she had nearly reached the kitchen.

"Janet . . . What's the matter?"

"After our discussion tonight, how can you even ask? It's late. I'm going home."

In the kitchen, she threw on her coat. Trixie, hopeful of some tidbit, stood by her empty food bowl, watching with round, protruding eyes.

"Why the rush?" Kirby reached for his coat. "I'll walk you."

"It's not necessary." She turned the doorknob. "When Ben arrives, tell him where I am."

Without waiting for Kirby's reply, she hurried outside, breaking into a jog as she reached the sidewalk. The air was frigid and she realized she hadn't buttoned her coat. Distraught, she found that the clear night air did nothing to calm her. She felt as if she were on a mad treadmill, the adrenaline racing without purpose through her veins. Was she upset because of how Kirby had defended the Renner house? His arguments simply made no sense. How could anyone imagine that a house with such a gruesome history could have a beneficial influence?

The cold air stabbed her lungs. Gasping, she slowed to a fast walk as she neared Fran's yard. Her thoughts revolved about the conversation of the last hour.

She considered all the families from The Beeches who had lost children. How well she knew the pain of such a loss. Those babies, all those helpless little children. She suddenly wondered if the older victims had somehow managed to escape the curse after death. The ghost children were so pitifully young! The crippled boy, who looked about four, seemed the oldest. She remembered Kirby saying that Timmy Fiorello was eight when the family moved in. How old had he been when he died? In any case, it seemed that the crippled ghost boy couldn't be the spirit of Timmy. She didn't recall seeing any twins, either. Of course, if the Hickok twins weren't identical, there would be no way of recognizing them.

With Fran's side door in view, she ran the last few steps. It suddenly seemed vital that she get inside as quickly as possible, but once she was there, she stared about the kitchen in confusion. This was not where she wanted to be, *needed* to be.

Fran, standing at the counter, setting the coffee timer for the morning, turned. "Oh, Jan, glad you're home. You're never going to believe what happened after you left. Mrs. Ousler called to say that the Stocktons had phoned from yet another party to say they're staying overnight with friends and leaving for the airport from there." She rolled her eyes. "Imagine! Their big farewell scene with Gina tomorrow has all been forgotten." She looked at the clock. "If you had gotten in earlier, maybe you could have had Gina tonight. But she's surely been in bed for hours."

Janet had no time to absorb this before the phone rang. Fran answered, and from her expression, Janet was positive the call brought bad news. She felt something vital give way inside her. She had been right—there *was* something wrong. Desperately so. *Ben*, she thought. She felt hollow, a cold wind blowing through. Something awful had happened to Ben. *Oh, Ben*.

Perplexed, Fran turned from the phone. "It's Ozzie again. She wants to know if Gina's been over here."

Gina? A new and different terror iced through Janet's veins. "Come here—in the dark?"

"Yes, but it's surely a mistake." Fran shook her head. "Ozzie has found Gina's bed empty and the back door unlocked, so she's afraid that—"

"Let me talk." Janet snatched the phone.

"Gina's not with me, I haven't seen her," she told Mrs. Ousler. "She can't have gone out at this hour—she must be hiding somewhere inside. I'll come help you hunt."

"No, she's gone out," Mrs. Ousler answered. "Her jacket and boots are missing. But if she's not with you, I bet I know where she went. Her pet cat hadn't come in by bedtime and I think she woke up, found it still missing, and went out to hunt for it. Naughty of her, but the last few days have been hectic and she finds the creature a comfort."

Fear slashed through Janet like a blade. All she could

think of was the Renner yard. "You say you know where she's gone?"

"Yes. There's a house on the next street with cats and we've found Pagoda there before. I'm sure that's where the child has gone. Why don't you come along? We'll probably meet her bringing the cat home."

"No—no, Ozzie." Janet could hardly speak past the fear that clogged her throat. "There's another place where she and Pagoda play. I'll check there instead." She now understood the reason for her powerful feelings of unrest: *Gina*. Gina was in trouble and calling out to her.

Cursing the peaceful days that had lulled her sure instincts of menace lying in wait, Janet was out of the house before Fran could ask questions. Heart hammering, she raced across the rear yard, heading toward the barrier line of pines.

36

Breath rasping in her throat, Janet emerged on the other side of the pine trees. The crisscrossing, starlit shadows cast by the beech limbs had transformed the Renner garden into a maze. Her eyes burned as she strained to make sense of the shadows. Nowhere in the tangle was there any sign of Gina or the cat, yet an increasing sense of urgency convinced her that the child was nearby.

As if responding to a silent call, she started toward the house then stopped, her heart squeezing as she heard a cry. *Gina*. But no, not Gina. Stunned, she recognized the cry of the baby. Or rather, the babies. The sound of their lonely wailing shivered in a night air that was suddenly clouded with a foul smoke. Smoldering pumpkins? No, *squash*. Orange-red globes of burning squash . . .

Her forgotten nightmare flooded her consciousness, the memory so vivid that it almost seemed to be happening again: the nursery beds, the helpless children, the devastating fire . . .

The night air cleared. The smell was gone. Gone also were the cries of the children. But the memory of the nightmare remained. Sickened, Janet tried to clear the vision of holocaust from her mind. Fire, as if from the very pit of hell. There was no record of fire at The Beeches. The Beeches—house of Satan. Had her dreams been a portent of the final evil the house would inflict: flames and destruction sweeping through a haunted nursery, devouring the last ethereal remnants of the spirit children?

Her eyes focused on a lighted kitchen window where Muriel stood at the sink. Like a quick cut in a film, Janet's mind moved from her waking nightmare to the here and now: the Renner house, and Gina. *Gina*. A conviction grew within her that the child must be inside the house.

Moving once again, she rushed across the lawn and up the steps of the latticed porch. At her wild rapping, the outside light came on. Recognizing her caller, Muriel opened the door.

"Miss Fairweather—Janet . . ."

"Gina's missing!" announced Janet, entering without awaiting permission. "The little girl who has the cat—is she here?"

Flustered, Muriel shook her perfectly groomed head. "Why, no." Dressed in a lace-collared, full-length lavender dressing gown, she looked like a portrait of Renaissance royalty come to life. "I have been downstairs all evening. Had anyone knocked, I would have heard."

"Gina wouldn't have knocked. Her cat is missing, but she couldn't have explained what she wanted." Janet thought of the allure open doors held for the animal. "Mrs. Renner, have you been outside? If you left the door ajar, the cat could have sneaked in. Gina could have followed."

"No, I have been inside all evening. Unless—"

"Yes?"

"When Rose climbed the front stairs to go to bed, her footsteps seemed oddly noisy. Then I thought no more about it. Now I am remembering that my sister enjoys both the little girl and the cat. I have cautioned her against encouraging them to come into the yard."

Janet's hope surged. "Could Rose have brought them inside?"

"I hardly think—"

"But that's what must have happened," Janet insisted excitedly, pressing forward. "She's taken her upstairs."

"But, no! Miss Fairweather, my husband cannot be disturbed. You cannot go up there." The restraining hand she held out was pushed aside as the younger woman moved relentlessly ahead. In the face of Janet's determination, Muriel changed tactics. "Miss Fairweather, we will go to Rose. We will inquire about the child, but you must be quiet. Quiet, do you understand? Come."

As Janet followed Muriel upstairs and onto the railed gallery, visions of fire pervaded her thoughts: flames and the final end for the haunted children. Did the house need Gina's presence before it could enact this last, dreadful curse? Her heart thudded painfully. She told herself that if Gina was in Rose's room, she was all right. The danger for her would be in the area near the window which overlooked the garden and the beech tree. There, the ghosts had materialized en masse, but as long as Gina stayed away from that area, she was safe. She had to believe that.

Opening Rose's door without knocking, Muriel led the way in. The room was empty. "She has taken pictures from her wall," she said softly, her tone puzzled. "The little cats, the puppies..."

A muffled thump sounded. Wide-eyed, Muriel looked at Janet. "That comes from the storeroom. It has a bed and bureau—could Rose be there with the child? Maybe that is why she took the pictures—to decorate the room for the little girl."

Convinced that was exactly what had happened, Janet felt panic close in at the thought of the storeroom. She reminded herself that the electrician, who had been sensitive to the haunting, had not complained about the room itself. The threats he had feared were outside in the corridor. If Gina was in the storage room with Rose, she was not in danger.

Unless there was danger from Rose herself.

37

Janet turned toward Rose's bedroom door, preparing to fling herself out into the gallery and down the hall, but Muriel reached to hold her back.

"Wait! The storeroom is opposite the ell which leads past Dr. Renner's sickroom. He often leaves his door open. Even with his sleeping medication, we must go quietly."

Although recognizing this wisdom, Janet impatiently jerked free. The light from Rose's room behind her cast her shadow forward, making a misshapen, brooding outline. Instinctively edging closer to the wall, she became aware of the oppressive atmosphere. Muriel had switched off the entry hall lights as they ascended, and the staircase on the far side of the railing yawned with dark menace. Ahead, the uncurtained window which overlooked the garden by day now presented an expanse of impenetrable blackness. With Muriel close behind her, she glanced down the doctor's inky corridor, finding no clue as to whether his room was open or not. She neared the storeroom. No sounds issued from it, but a band of light showed beneath the door, a pale ribbon of promise.

With the taste of fear sharp in her throat, she opened the door. What she saw inside was an answered prayer. The pale lamplight showed Gina, sleepy-eyes but smiling, curled upon a battered maple bed. Rose sat beside her, holding Pagoda on her lap. The child looked up in delight as Janet rushed to gather her into her arms.

"Oh, Gina! Baby, you're all right!" Tears wet on her cheeks, she held the child close. Gina reached up to touch her face and Janet felt thoughts move and shift in her mind, thoughts like pictures, placed as if by phantom fingers: the ending of the little girl's lonely search for her pet, the invitation into the nice old lady's house. The pictures increased in pleasure. In her mind, Janet heard the purring warmth of Pagoda, Rose's soft crooning, tasted the sweetness of chocolate . . .

Janet smelled chocolate. The mental connection broken, Janet held Gina away from her, seeing chocolate at the corners of the child's mouth. Sticky smears also marked her fingers and the lacy bib of the nightgown she wore under her unzipped jacket.

"My, you've had a feast!" marveled Janet, her laugh shaky. Still reeling from the stunning oneness with Gina's memories, she blinked her eyes, seeing the empty candy papers on the bed and the floor.

"Lili. Chocolates for my Lili," crooned Rose, stroking the cat, but showing a fond, toothless smile at the child. "Chocolates, so good. Never when she my little baby, but now, always. For Lili, always."

Muriel, who had remained standing near the door after quietly closing it, shook her head. "Not Lili," she corrected gently. "The little girl is not Lili. She is a neighbor child."

"My Lili," Rose repeated emphatically. "A big girl now."

"That was her baby's name, Lili," Muriel explained to Janet, her soft voice filled with regret.

Pagoda tensed its wiry body skittishly, giving Muriel a suspicious glare as she stepped around a stack of piled cardboard boxes and came nearer. Placing a loving hand on Rose's shoulder, Muriel said to Janet, "She only wanted the child's company, do you understand? She did not intend to cause you distress."

Janet gazed upon Rose's nutcracker face, the sharp lines shadowed harshly by the folds of her black head scarf. For a moment, the wrinkled form transformed into the witch with the gingerbread and candy house. "Come in, come in," the old crone had beckoned, and lured by sweets, the unsuspecting child had answered her wicked call.

The fanciful image faded, leaving only a bewildered old woman who had desperately grasped for a lost dream. Gina, content now that Janet was with her, was drifting sweetly toward sleep, one small hand, palm up, resting trustfully upon Rose's lap.

Janet's gaze lifted to Muriel. "I understand. She meant no harm."

Speaking in a singsong, the old woman stroked Pagoda's sleek coat. "Sister say, no cat inside. So soft and nice, but sister say, no cat. Sister say, no little girl." Her emotions burst forth and her chin jutted. "This time, children safe. This time, Dr. Herman knows nothing!" She moved her hand from the cat to Gina, who opened her eyes briefly to give her a sleepy smile. "Mother, child," crooned Rose, her voice cracked and tinny. "Love, always love. My Lili come back safe with me. Safe. I keep her safe always."

At these words, Janet darted Muriel a swift and anxious look and the woman repeated, "There is no harm."

Gina was now clearly asleep, the blue tracings of veins delicate on her closed eyelids, the lashes, long and thick. She shifted, burrowing her body more comfortably between the old woman and the young one, drawing up her legs, the red plastic rain boots she wore on her stockinged feet showing under the hem of her nightgown.

Janet whispered to Muriel, "Does Rose believe Gina is her child returned—as she once believed a stranger was her husband?"

"Apparently." Muriel gave her sister a tender look. "We may speak before her. There are blessings to her condition. She is content with the child and cat and for the moment they have become her entire world." She focused back on Janet, whose expression had remained anxious. "Do you still worry about the child?" A strange smile iced her lips. "Ah, my little American friend, have you never faced real danger that you must run from phantoms?" Moving from Rose, she stood near the closed door. "Once, you asked about Dr. Renner's study of dark mysteries. You were insistent in thinking he could help you. To hold you off, I said I would consult with Dr. Renner about this. But I had no intention of doing any such thing."

"It's all right," Janet excused, finding she didn't care about the woman's lie. "You had your reasons." With Gina safely found, all she wanted to do was leave, but Muriel was in the way.

"Yes, I had my reasons. But it is now time for you to learn more."

"No, it's all right," Janet repeated, starting to get up, her desire to leave quickening as she became aware of the vengeful note which had crept into Muriel's voice.

"But you must listen," Muriel insisted fiercely, now clearly blocking the door. "Sit down again. I will tell you what you wanted to know and you can judge for yourself the help he would be."

"No, really—" protested Janet, but Muriel's look quelled her.

"I must begin in the past," the woman said, her eyes glittering with a light that struck a coldness through Janet even while holding her spellbound. "There is more I did not tell you about the place where Dr. Renner had Rose and me taken during the war. The car took us to a compound where he had his quarters. Now I tell you that in his work with children, he had come to believe in a strong psychic bond between a mother and child. He developed a theory that a mother and young child communicate through psychic channels and he wished to prove it." Her voice sounded as if chips of glass were in her throat, grinding, cutting her words. "You may have heard of other doctors during the war who wished to prove similar theories about twins."

Instinctively, Janet drew the sleeping child closer. "I've heard of hideous, unbelievable experiments."

"Ah, but believe them, for they are true," answered Muriel softly.

"You don't mean that your husband—"

"Not medical experiments. But in its own way, no less cruel."

Janet's thoughts whirled. "Then, how could you marry him!"

Assured now of Janet's attention, Muriel moved to sit on the bed. "I knew nothing of this work until I came upon his record folders after we were in Argentina." Her sigh was like the sound of sand sifting through an hourglass and her fierce tone had changed to one of poignant regret. "By then, we had been together for over twenty years."

"You mean those folders that are now in his upstairs study?"

"You know of them?" Her smile was thin. "No wonder he wished to keep you away. By the time I learned the truth, it was all part of the past, the same past in which he had saved Rose and me. How could I compare those dry written records with my vivid memories? Or with my gratitude. Perhaps I have not told you that the compound was outside a death camp. There was a wall between the camp and us, yet no walls could keep out the distant screams or the constant stench of death. Is there any way I can make you understand my fear? I was only fifteen, and from all that horror, he had delivered me. And he had also delivered Rose. Life with him was all I knew. He had become my life."

Janet looked at the woman before her, her face still unlined, every strand of her blue-black hair perfect. Could an individual pass through what Muriel spoke of and remain sane? Vocal cords strained with tension, Janet asked, "Then, he was a Nazi?"

"He did not consider himself political. He thought of himself as a scientist who benefited from the military machine. Through high-ranking friends, who believed his theories might have military implications, he had been allowed to set up a laboratory. He called the laboratory his 'nursery.' He had Rose placed in what he assured me was a safe hospital for the birth of her baby, while I lived with him in a private apartment."

"Did his wife know about you?"

"His wife?" Muriel's tone suggested that the question was irrelevant. "She had already left him to marry another man."

"But, I thought—" So much for the theory about him leaving behind a wife, either dead or alive, when he fled Europe.

"But, it is interesting," mused Muriel, "that you ask about her, for the blow of her betrayal had changed him from the man I had met as a child. Only when we were together privately could he reveal his softer emotions. Years before, he had developed a passion for me, the strength of which had never waned." Her tone became ironic. "Perhaps, only because I was Jewish, and not quite human in his mind, could he reveal the weakness of feelings. I was a pet, like a dog or cat, before which one is never ashamed. Odd that he should have turned so cold in all other respects, for his research depended so strongly on emotion."

"The love between a mother and child?"

Muriel's golden-brown eyes flickered and her voice dropped ominously. "From his records, I learned he had snatched mothers with young children from the gas chambers and thus considered their lives his possession. He put them in separate, soundproofed rooms, then, stationing himself to secretly view both subjects, he would order his assistants to subject either the child or the mother to distress. He studied the other party for possible reaction. The aim, of course, was to see if messages could be transported by psychic means."

Janet's voice quavered. "Messages of distress?"

"Yes, on the theory that the primitive reactions to pain and fear were the strongest of all emotions, and therefore, the most efficiently communicated."

"What—what sorts of pain and fear?"

"He employed simple measures, like leaving hungry infants to cry in isolation for hours, or pricking tender flesh, or placing a suffocating hand over a baby's face until it was in a panic, starving for air." Muriel's emotionless tone only increased the sickening impact of her words as she continued.

"With the older ones, he employed more sophisticated techniques, such as having masked attendants awaken the little ones in the middle of the night. Skillfully, he created for them an existence of living nightmares. The methods used on the mothers were similar. In torment and fear, we all become as little children."

The intensity of her gaze held Janet in thrall. "His studies proved that a powerful psychic bond flowing between both mother and child was very rare. Unknown distress in one party caused no consistent response in the other, *except* in the case of extremely young infants. He became convinced such infants react to stress which alters their mother's heart rate and the amount of oxygen in her blood. The sound of the mother's heartbeat and the richness of her blood are meaningful to the unborn child. He thus deduced that a response to these factors persists for some weeks after birth."

Smile twisted, she said softly, "It was all scientifically done. No one could fault the carefulness and the details of his research."

Mesmerized, Janet asked, "And he was able to hide this from you?"

"I believed him when he said he was using psychiatry to help the children he had saved. I had visited the nursery and saw how the children adored him. The babies in their cribs turned eagerly toward the sound of his voice and toddlers rushed to cling to his legs when he entered the room. They had no idea he was the father of their pain. They loved him. And perhaps, in an odd way, he loved them too. I know that the memory of their suffering has haunted him, never allowing him to rest." Again, that twisted smile. "Perhaps, because with the children, as with me, he felt safe in revealing tender emotion."

"Tender emotion! When he tortured them?"

Muriel seemed to savor Janet's revulsion. "I do not explain it. I only tell you that the memories have never allowed him to rest."

"What of Rose and her baby? Were they also part of this—this experiment?"

"Yes, but with her mind as it was, she was incapable of telling me about it. Perhaps she only cared that there were times when she and the infant were allowed to be together."

"But the baby eventually died?"

Muriel's face was old now, still perfect and unlined, yet ages old, her eyes empty of all but pain. "There came a time when men like Dr. Renner realized the war had turned against Germany. His research had been completed to his satisfaction and he wanted only to escape. He, along with others in his position, had used funds robbed from war victims to establish fortunes in foreign banks. His dilemma was to leave before the Allies arrived and yet not appear to be a traitor.

"His original plan was to send me on ahead, but I refused to leave without Rose. He finally allowed this, but he kept the child, saying he and a nurse would join us later. When he arrived, he was alone. He said that the Russians had attacked, firing upon his laboratory, destroying the nursery.

"Only later did I learn that he himself had destroyed the nursery with explosives, buying time for his escape by making it appear that he was dead as well. The children, including Rose's baby, were blown to bits. If the mothers in the other part of the building survived the explosion and conflagration, they were probably put to death by the main camp authorities before the actual arrival of the Allies."

Muriel's shocking words returned Janet's mind to her nightmares of fire, explosion, and violence. Stunned, she realized that she had experienced everything Muriel had described in her nightmares: her dreams had actually been a psychic replay of those final, horrid moments in Dr. Renner's nursery.

254 / BEVERLY T. HAAF

Her mind grappled to find answers for the multitude of questions that poured in upon her. Had Dr. Renner's guilty memories so permeated the atmosphere that the past took on tangible form? But why had she been privy to it? Was it because it concerned children? Still raw from the tragic loss of her own child, perhaps she had been exceptionally sensitive to a message which spoke of children lost and hurting. The sound of the crying baby—no, *babies*—which had haunted her for so long... those sounds, along with the smell of smoke, had all been fragments re-created from a hideous incident in Europe that happened before her birth.

It seemed to fit together. But still, there remained unanswered questions. The gruesome history of The Beeches must play some part in what she had experienced. That too involved children. The ghost children—there must be some connection...

Her thoughts were interrupted as Muriel stood, her manner weary. "So, now, Miss Fairweather, you have been told of my husband's great knowledge of the dark aspects in this world. I think you no longer have things to ask him, am I right?" She did not await an answer. "It is time for you to take the little girl and go home." She bent to gently touch her sister's shoulder. "Rose, you are tired. Time for bed."

Rose looked up, then looked back at the sleeping child.

"Time for bed, come along." Muriel held out her hand.

Like an aged turtle tucking into its shell, Rose drew back. "I stay here. This my bed with my Lili. This, *thisss*," she hissed.

Still dazed from the revelation of Muriel's story, Janet shook her head, trying to clear her thoughts. The image of flames still scorched behind her eyes. Blinking, she looked at her watch. How long had it been since she left Kirby's house? It seemed a million years. Ben must have returned from his meeting. By now, he knew she had gone searching for Gina. Surely, he would know to look for her at the Renners' house. After all her concerns about the place, she had no doubt of that. He might show up at any moment.

Best to get Gina outside before he arrived and brought the risk of disturbing the doctor.

"My Lili," she heard Rose repeat to Muriel, her tone stubborn.

"Such a lovely name," murmured Muriel. "You can call the little girl Lili, I am sure, but I will call her Gina." She gave the child a shake. "Come little Gina, wake now." The child's eyes fluttered open. "Come, Gina."

Together, Muriel and Janet helped the groggy child to her feet. "You had a nice time with Rose," Muriel told her. "I know you will want to visit again."

"Visit," Rose echoed, seeming to like the sound of the word and accepting it. "We visit, we look at pictures." She pulled kitten and puppy cutouts from under a blanket. "See pictures?"

"How nice!" exclaimed Muriel, signaling Janet to leave. "May I look at them?"

With the old woman distracted, Janet moved Gina to the door, but then the child remembered Pagoda and turned back. Seeing what she wanted, Muriel reached for the animal as Janet went on to the door, opening it in readiness to leave.

As Muriel's hands touched the cat Rose grabbed at it also, pleading, "Soft—don't take!"

Startled awake, Pagoda, its eyes stretched wide in fright, uncoiled and sprang to the floor. Muriel reached for it, bumping against the stack of boxes, which toppled noisily. With a yowl, the creature darted across the room and out through the door to the hall. Gina, her booted feet clumping, followed before Janet could grab her.

Like a bolt of lightning, the cat shot across the open stair landing and was lost in the darkness of the doctor's corridor. Gina, in fast pursuit, came to a stop at the sound of a crash. The sound was followed by an outraged voice.

There was a long, frozen moment. Then, Muriel breathed, "Dr. Renner..."

A dim rectangle fell across the corridor as the doctor's light came on. There was a second crash. Pagoda streaked out and fled down the main staircase, gone by the time the doctor came into view.

His tall figure stood elongated in the pallid glow from his room, his robe dragging, hanging loose over his long nightshirt. Proud head looking too large for the frail support of his neck, he leaned forward, squinting without his glasses to better search the gloom, the dry, mummified flesh of his skeletal face making him a Ramses disturbed from an ancient sleep. He moved a rusty step, then came to a stop, focusing on Gina.

Janet saw the child silhouetted in the light from the doctor's doorway, the outlines of her corduroy jacket hanging comically over her nightgown and boots, but there was nothing comical in the grating accusation which emerged from the doctor's throat.

"You!"

Gina seemed to become smaller, shrinking in upon herself.

The hoarse, menacing voice carried clearly. "You, one of *them*?" The doctor advanced a threatening step. "Why are you here? What do you want of me?"

38

Janet dashed into the hall. Three frantic strides brought her almost to Gina, and there she abruptly stopped. A confusion of flickering lights were suddenly all around her. They floated above and about in the darkness, like phosphorescent creatures adrift in a midnight sea. She blinked as the lights assumed familiar forms. Rapidly, with breathtaking speed, the ghost children appeared: the little boy, his limbs now straight and sound, his thin chest filled out, plump and healthy; the toddler, her flesh restored to wholeness, smiling, her eyes glowing like dark and lovely stars. Marveling, Janet saw that all of the children, the babies, the older ones, all of them, were sound and whole and beautiful. Their lips moved and she felt the whispered chant weave through her—felt, not heard—subtly changed now, full and victorious, the rhythm transformed into a hymn of praise: *"Stronger, stronger, we have grown stronger. Stronger, stronger, we have been healed."*

The psychic message echoed in Janet's brain: *Healed.* Glowing insight burst upon her. The strength yearned for in the chant had been the strength of healing. A healing which blessedly had been accomplished.

Staring at the luminous figures, she finally realized the full impact of the story Muriel had told her. These ghost children—she now knew who they were. Kirby had been right. The house did not hold the souls of resident children. The forms before her were the phantoms of Dr. Renner's experiments, the victims of his nursery. They had loved him, Muriel had said. Because he had shown kindness when in their presence, these innocents had given him their trust. In the stricken violence of the explosion, their spirits had rushed to him, the one who had become central to their tortured lives, and throughout the years, they had continued to cling. The final, mutilated images of themselves in life had been impressed upon their psychic bodies by the shock of their awful deaths, yet now that the doctor had been drawn to the house Elizabeth Parke had dedicated to the care of the lost, they had been made whole again.

Janet knew she had been right in believing that the house had deliberately enticed certain families. But Kirby had been right as well. In one way or another, The Beeches bestowed not harm, but spiritual hope and healing upon its children. Under its shelter, their lives had been miraculously touched. And, in drawing the doctor and his invisible following, the house had extended its powers even beyond mortal life.

Dr. Renner's hoarse cry returned Janet's mind to the scene before her. Gina had turned to stare at the ghost children with wide-eyed wonder. The doctor's attention was also fixed upon them, but his expression was one of horror. "You're dead!" he screamed at the misty figures, shaking a trembling fist. "You've all been dead for a lifetime—what do you want?"

His cracking voice was drowned as the joyous chant began again: *"Stronger, stronger, we have grown stronger. Stronger, stronger, we have been healed."*

Breathlessly, Janet watched the apparitions advance upon the old man. She could only think they sought vengeance for their suffering, but instead, they wove gayly about him, extending their arms, twirling as if to display their newly perfect forms. Watching with stunned disbelief, Janet realized these innocents still saw the doctor as the loving center of their lives—they wanted him to share in their delight!

But he, without understanding, attempted to fend them off, frantically striking at the nearest figure, a three-year-old girl who held a baby which looked too big for her to carry. She moved before him, proudly presenting the infant for his inspection. Flailing, the doctor reached futilely through her vaporous form. The little girl turned, laughing, as if believing the doctor played a game. More children drifted toward him.

As if frozen, Janet watched as he snatched first for one, then another. It happened in a whirl, his wild-eyed panic increasing as the wraiths eluded him like smoke. Cursing, robe flying, he staggered drunkenly among them until one of his thrashing arms made contact with Gina. Feeling her solidness, he spun with a grating caw of victory to seize her throat.

"Janet!" came the child's frightened message. *"Mama—"*

Janet bolted forward. Peripherally, she felt there was yet another figure off in the direction of the stairs, yet as she rushed forward, there was no time to look. She fell upon the doctor, her fingernails stabbing into his flesh. He struggled, then a regathering of the spirits overwhelmed his attention. With a gasping screech he allowed Gina to slip free as he confronted the spectral figures anew. Clutching Gina's limp body to her breast, Janet sank to the floor as the phantoms swirled through and past them.

Sobbing, Janet crouched over the stricken child, seeing the welts which marred the whiteness of her slender throat. "Gina!" she cried in wild despair, and blessedly, the dark lashes fluttered. Gina's eyes, clear and lucid, opened to gaze up into her face.

A cry from the doctor caused Janet to look up as the ghost children descended upon him like a flock of eager starlings, hungrily seeking to embrace him, to hug his frantically kicking legs.

"But I was kind to you! I never really hurt you!" he babbled hysterically, twisting and jerking like a demented scarecrow. "I was your *friend*!" Their ethereal hands pawed his chest, grabbed at his arms, floated to cover his lined and horror-distorted face with countless, smothering caresses.

Raw, spasmodic shrieks, in German now, whistled with a terror that pierced Janet's ears. The doctor's strained, rattling breathing seemed to fill the room as the figures billowed thickly around him. Writhing, he clutched his chest, his face contorting into a mask of agony. He issued a final, tortured squall, and then, as if his bones and flesh had become as insubstantial as dried paper, his body slowly crumpled to the floor to sprawl in grotesque disarray, lifeless and still.

There was silence, then small murmurings of alarm from the ghostly children. In confusion, they drifted away from the corpse. Their whispers, as thin as the rustlings of wind through treetops, were bewildered and frightened. Hugging Gina protectively, Janet saw that Dr. Renner's death had broken his ties with the children, yet, with him gone, what fate was left to them now?

As if in reply, a soft illumination began to radiate gently upon the small, spectral forms. The frightened tones of their whisperings changed, becoming questioning, expectant. The light increased and Janet saw additional phantoms appear. More children? But no, for as the outlines became more distinct, she saw the figures of adults. A woman with a broad, sweetly smiling face reached toward the toddler. A hesitation, then the child eagerly accepted her hand. More adults appeared, welcoming children into their arms. *Their mothers*, thought Janet with a thrilling surge of emotion. *Their mothers, come at last to gather their lost little ones.*

"Lili," came a hoarse whisper as Rose stumbled from the storeroom. Janet thought she meant Gina, but the old woman, falling on her knees, scrabbled toward the three-year-old who held the baby. "Lili," Rose repeated, reaching with yearning toward the infant. As her trembling fingers traced the hazy outlines of the small face before her, the corners of the infant's rosebud mouth lifted as if in delighted recognition. Pathetically, Rose attempted to grasp the small, chubby form, but her shaking hands only moved through vapors.

A woman materialized to sit and take both the three-year-old and the baby onto her lap. She touched the infant's hand, then gestured first toward Rose, then to her own breast. Her expression was questioning. When Rose reached toward the baby again, the woman repeated her gestures.

Slowly, Rose sank back upon her heels. She nodded. "Lili," she said hoarsely. "Yes. Until I come."

The misty host of figures wavered before Janet's eyes. Like a morning fog before the coming of the dawn, the phantasma evaporated, mothers and reunited children, gone as swiftly as they had appeared, disappearing shades of the doctor's tortured memories, resolved at last, fleeing with his soul. Spectral light faded and became one with the shadows.

"Janet!" Just as she recognized Ben's voice, he bounded up the remainder of the stairs and was by her side. Stunned, she stared at him, realizing that the figure she had seen so briefly on the stairway had been his. Had it been only seconds ago that she had unknowingly glimpsed him as she rushed toward the doctor? It must be so, yet it seemed as if aeons had passed.

"Gina—is she okay?" As he touched the child's cheek, he was rewarded with her smile. "Thank God!" he exclaimed fervently, helping the little girl sit up although she still remained in the circle of Janet's arms. His voice shook. "Thank God, she's all right."

Getting himself in command, he directed his gaze to the doctor's limp form. "That's Dr. Renner? He's dead, isn't he? It must have been a heart attack." Voice still rough with emotion, he shook his head. "It all happened so fast! I could hardly figure it out, but I guess the doctor grabbed Gina to keep from falling, then went into convulsions. What a gruesome experience for the poor kid. The shock—that's what must have done it to her."

Janet couldn't understand. Did Ben think Gina had simply fainted? If he had been on the stairs when the doctor collapsed, he must have witnessed the ghosts. Why did he seem so ignorant of all that had happened?

"Didn't you see?" she demanded. "Didn't you see?"

"See Renner's death throes? Sure. Thank God you were there to snatch Gina out of his way. From what your sister told me, I figured you must be here. The door was unlocked and when I opened it, that Siamese cat zipped out and I heard a man shouting. It sounded like trouble, so I headed toward it." Excitement grew in his voice. "Then, on the stairs, that's when I heard Gina."

Janet stared. "Heard her? But no, unless—" Did he mean that the frightening experience of the doctor's attack had made Gina's psychic call reach out to him?

"Yes." He laughed. "*Heard* her. Don't tell me you missed it! She called, 'Janet,' and then, 'Mama.' " He smiled down at the little girl, tenderly stroking her dark hair. "Yes, she's your *mama*, all right, chicken."

Gina's small hand tugged Janet's wrist. When Janet looked down, the child, her eyes shining, hesitantly whispered, "*Janet.*" The sound was halting as she tasted the word upon her lips. She spoke again: "Mama." Her voice was husky. Then with a tremulous smile, she spoke more clearly: "Janet, my mama."

Hearing her, actually *hearing* her speak, Janet burst into tears. "Gina, you can talk! Oh, honey, you really can!"

Ben's tone was filled with wonder. "When the doctor lunged, she must have felt desperate for help—she *had* to call out. We knew she could do it, and this was the breakthrough."

Or the house, Janet thought, joy winging through her. *The healing shelter of The Beeches*.

From the corner where Muriel hovered over the doctor's body, Rose intoned, "My Lili was with him, but now she is free. Free. My Lili is free."

Dark head bowed, Muriel held the older woman close. "Now we are all free. Perhaps, even him."

As if from a distance, Janet heard Ben say, "We should call an ambulance for the doctor's body."

Muriel turned. The smooth oval of her face was now as peaceful and pure as alabaster, the tiger fires of conflict no longer blazing from her eyes. "I will make the necessary calls. Do not be concerned." Her soft voice was rich and firm with dignity. "There is no need for worry. Everything is all right now for my sister and for me."

Ben hesitated, then nodded, helping Janet to her feet. "We had better let Mrs. Ousler know that a certain little girl is safe and sound."

Shifting his gaze to Gina, he extended his hands. The child reached up, holding on as he swung her easily up into his arms. "We call that 'upsy-daisy,'" he told her, giving her a squeeze. Can you say that?"

"Upsy-daisy," she repeated parrotlike, her voice still husky. She gazed at him a moment, then rested her head on his broad shoulder. Her eyes were heavy lidded with the need for sleep. She reached for Janet's hand, and holding it, smiled contentedly.

Hugging the child close, Ben reached out his other arm to include Janet. His voice deepened. "I'm thinking of that new apartment, Gina's bedroom all ready and waiting. Let's say we have a few words with Mrs. Ousler and your sister, then take our Gina home."

Leaning against him, Janet looked around the gallery, so hushed, so silent. She knew what she had seen. She *knew*.

But in this life, none of it had the reality of Gina's hand so sweetly clasped in hers, nor the warm, earthly comfort of Ben's embrace.

"Yes," she told him softly. "Yes, let's go home."

HORRORS!

Mix chilling supernatural terror with relentless psychological suspense and you have what popular author Margaret Bingley is known for best: spine-tingling tales guaranteed to keep you up long past the midnight hour!

- ☐ **DEADTIME STORY**
  0-445-20722/$4.95

- ☐ **AFTER ALICE**
  0-445-20528-8/$3.95

- ☐ **CHILDREN OF THE NIGHT**
  0-445-20526-1/$3.95

POPULAR LIBRARY

Warner Books P.O. Box 690
New York, NY 10019

Please send me the books I have checked. I enclose a check or money order (not cash), plus 95¢ per order and 95¢ per copy to cover postage and handling,* or bill my ☐ American Express ☐ VISA ☐ MasterCard. (Allow 4-6 weeks for delivery.)

___Please send me your free mail order catalog. (If ordering only the catalog, include a large self-addressed, stamped envelope.)

Card # _____

Signature _____ Exp. Date _____

Name _____

Address _____

City _____ State _____ Zip _____

*New York and California residents add applicable sales tax.

438

THE

VAMPIRES ARE COMING!
BLOODSHIFT

by Garfield Reeves-Stevens
0-445-21012-5/$4.95

Lock the door, turn on the lights, and get ready for this true horror classic from "the Tom Clancy of horror" (Stephen King)—and best-selling author of *Nighteyes*.

"Garfield Reeves-Stevens produces a new genre: the vampire thriller." —*Quill & Quire*

POPULAR LIBRARY

**Warner Books P.O. Box 690
New York, NY 10019**

Please send me ___copy(ies) of the book. I enclose a check or money order (not cash), plus 95¢ per order and 95¢ per copy to cover postage and handling,* or bill my ☐ American Express ☐ VISA ☐ MasterCard. (Allow 4-6 weeks for delivery.)

___Please send me your free mail order catalog. (If ordering only the catalog, include a large self-addressed, stamped envelope.)

Card # _____

Signature _____ Exp. Date _____

Name _____

Address _____

City _____ State _____ Zip _____

*New York and California residents add applicable sales tax.

439